# TWENTY-SIX

BOOKS BY LEO McKAY JR.

*Like This* (1995)
*Twenty-Six* (2003)

# Twenty-Six

## LEO McKAY JR.

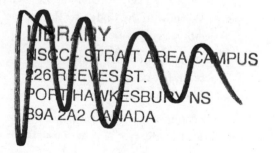

M&S

**National Library of Canada Cataloguing in Publication**

McKay, Leo, 1964-
Twenty-six / Leo McKay Jr.

ISBN 0-7710-5475-0

1. Fiction.  I. Title.

PS8575.K28747T84  2003      C813'.6      C2002-905714-0
PR9199.3.M42433T84  2003

We acknowledge the financial support of the Government of Canada
through the Book Publishing Industry Development Program and that of
the Government of Ontario through the Ontario Media Development
Corporation's Ontario Book Initiative. We further acknowledge the
support of the Canada Council for the Arts and the Ontario Arts Council
for our publishing program.

This is a work of fiction and all of the characters are fictitious.
However, this novel was inspired by the Westray mining disaster
and the tragic impact it had on families and a community.

The epigraph on page v is taken from an unpublished poem,
"Death Opens a Window in the Body," by Robert McCabe.
Used by permission of the author.

Designed by Terri Nimmo
Typeset in Janson by M&S, Toronto
Printed and bound in Canada

This book is printed on acid-free paper that is
100% ancient forest friendly (100% post-consumer recycled)

McClelland & Stewart Ltd.
*The Canadian Publishers*
481 University Avenue
Toronto, Ontario
M5G 2E9
www.mcclelland.com

1 2 3 4 5      07 06 05 04 03

*This book is dedicated to memory*

"Death opens a window in the body."

— ROBERT McCABE

# CONTENTS

**PART ONE**   1  Circling and Cursing / *3*
1988           2  An Inoperable Heart / *21*

               3  Packing / *38*

               4  Bakuhatsu / *47*

               5  Helmet with Lamp / *65*

**PART TWO**   6  A Handicap of Place / *93*
1982           7  A Sharp Eye for Fabric / *106*

               8  Scraps / *127*

               9  In a Quiet House / *156*

               10  Making Things Worse / *165*

               11  People Weeping / *175*

**PART THREE**   12  Close to Home / *181*
1988             13  Bodies / *210*

                 14  Memories / *229*

                 15  Culture / *235*

**PART FOUR**   16  Opportunity Knocks / *243*
1987           17  Heart Beating Fast / *272*

**PART FIVE**   18  An Intellectual Ruffian / *285*
1989            19  Telling the World / *307*

                20  Movement / *322*

                21  Canada Day, Years Ago / *332*

                22  A Moose / *337*

                23  The Rest House / *349*

                24  Under the Weight of Snow / *366*

*Acknowledgements / 387*

# TWENTY-SIX

# PART ONE

## 1988

# CIRCLING AND CURSING

Death hides its face in winter, when trees are impossible to distinguish. The bony hands of branches clutch at the sky, waiting for the sun to rise high enough to warm them back to life. With so many elms sick, and some of them dying now, the only thing was to wait for spring before you put your hope anywhere.

Spring was a far-off place to Ziv as he stood in his parents' driveway, his hot breath rising in clouds into the dark air above him. He looked up at the grey branches of the pair of elms that marked the boundary of his parents' property and could not recall whether they'd been dead last summer or merely sick.

He put a mittened hand on the rear fender of his father's car to steady himself as he stared at the translucent blind pulled down over the living-room window. "I hope the bastard's dead," he said out loud to no one. He was trying to detect movement inside the house, but he was good and drunk, and it was difficult to detect anything in his condition. He saw nothing but filtered light through the blind. All three bulbs in the pole lamp beside the couch were switched on; he could tell that. The TV was flicking the room light, then dark. But if there was any movement inside, he could not see it. The smell of furnace oil from the nearby tank hung in a thick layer over the more subdued smells of a cold winter night.

He took off his mitts, stuffed them into the pockets of his parka, and unzipped his fly in the biting February cold. "Shit," he said as he pissed onto the snow. When he was finished, he zipped himself up again, put the mitts back on, and went unsteadily back to the end of the driveway to continue his aimless walk. It was now one thirty in the morning and it had been more than an hour since his last drink. Still, he was too drunk to go inside. He hated being drunk now. He hated himself for having got so drunk that he could not show his face inside his house. It was his parents' house, actually, and he hated that, too. Five years ago he could have called it his house. But he was twenty-three years old now, he'd be twenty-four in a few months, and he could not bring himself to call it his house when he was paying room and board. He'd lived in this house his whole life. He'd been brought here directly from the Aberdeen Hospital in New Glasgow a few days after his birth, and except for a short time at university in the early eighties, he'd been here, a permanent resident of this address, ever since.

He walked to the corner of Hudson Street and looked down the channel the sidewalk plough had made. He'd passed through here several times already tonight, wandering around and around the neighbourhood, wishing for himself to sober up, or for the light to go off in the living room, the signal that his father had gone to bed, so he could go inside without setting off a row.

His legs felt wobbly and weak. He was drunk, he was tired, he was hungry.

The neighbourhood he was walking through was called the Red Row, a half-dozen or so blocks of duplexes built by the Acadia Coal Company in the first decades of the century. The Red Row had originally housed miners who worked in the many pits that had pocked the landscape of Pictou County, Nova Scotia. Although the original pits had long been closed, a few elderly retired miners and descendants of those deceased still lingered in the company houses at the north end of the little town called Albion Mines. This is what Ziv was: a descendant of coal miners. And he was acutely aware of it. Even drunk, when the list of what he was aware of dwindled to a dozen or so items, being the descendant of coal miners was on that small list. He only had to raise his eyes and look at the company houses all around him to understand how completely submersed he was in that murky history.

He walked drunk down Hudson Street, into the heart of the old neighbourhood. The steeply pitched roofs of the identical storey-and-a-half houses had all shed their snow. Snow lay clumped in even heaps below the eaves. Fifty, sixty years ago, a person could have walked down this street and known with certainty that someone in every house had worked in some capacity in one of the mines. But Ziv looked at the houses now and realized he did not know where all these people worked, though he could guess at the relative success of the occupants by the state of repair of the house itself. Some Red Row houses were dilapidated. They had not been painted in years, roofing shingles had not been replaced. Chimneys had crumbled, shedding bricks down the roof. Other houses, freshly painted or sided, featured newer windows. Some even had paved driveways.

Ziv himself worked at Zellers in the Aberdeen Mall, over in the nearby town of New Glasgow. His father, now on disability, had been one of the last few men employed in the Car Works, the shrinking railcar factory in Trenton. Once, he knew, in his father's lifetime, people had been defined by their work. "What do you do?" had been a question that opened conversations. But there was a growing class of people now, some of whom lived in the Red Row, who didn't do anything. They were not really unemployed, because they weren't looking for work. Long past their eligibility for unemployment insurance, many of these people lived on welfare, the generosity of relatives, and whatever odd jobs they could do for the neighbours in exchange for a few dollars.

His own job was barely even a real job. Zellers classified him as *extra*, a category that all but a handful of the people who worked at the store fit into. He received no benefits, contributed to no pension, had no reliable schedule. About all he got from Zellers was enough money to pay his keep and to get drunk a couple of times a week.

He'd been working earlier this evening, and had gone directly from his Zellers shift to the bar called Stumpy's.

He still wore the shirt and tie that were part of the Zellers dress code. When he'd started coming here, more than three years ago now, after he'd decided not to go back to university, he'd bothered to bring a change of clothes with him to work so he would not look so out-of-place. But now he didn't care what he looked like, and Stumpy's was so overcrowded that no one could step back far enough from you to notice what you were wearing anyway. The dance floor tonight had throbbed with writhing bodies. The music had pounded into Ziv's skull like nails. He had taken the letter from his pocket and unfolded it against the surface of the bar. Anyone who'd cared enough to notice might have thought him strange for that letter. He had it with him every time he came. Sometimes, when he was sober, he pictured what he must have looked like, night after night, unfolding that piece of paper against the surface of the bar. It was too dark to read, so he'd stare at the surface of the paper, where he could just see that there was writing on it.

He always put twenty dollars in his shirt pocket when he went into Stumpy's, and he'd stand at the bar, gagging on cigarette smoke, staring at a letter he was too drunk to read, going deaf to the music and to everything else, until he reached one final time into the shirt pocket and found it empty.

Halfway down Hudson Street he stopped and leaned over the sidewalk. He took a mitten off his right hand and jammed two fingers down his throat to try to get rid of the alcohol that was in him like a demon. Spasms pinched his guts and he dry-retched several times before ejecting a reddish-green jelly onto the brownish snow.

The snow chirped beneath his boots, a crisp high sound that meant it was minus fifteen or colder. The hard, frozen branches of trees clacked and rattled against each other in the breeze. Unnamed things around him went *snap* as something inside them froze and broke. Only the odd light in the odd window shone out onto the snow. The crystal air was so clear and empty that even up at this end of the neighbourhood, trucks on the Trans-Canada in Lourdes made a roar that echoed down the streets and between the houses.

As he walked through the Red Row, he saw his whole life twisted around itself like a dog staring at its own tail, running in circles, too stupid to know it was chasing itself. He walked because he was too drunk to face his father. How many times had he walked this same pathetic route for the same pathetic reason? How many times had he been in this same position: too drunk to show his face to anyone who was supposed to care? He was drunk and sick and useless. And tired. Tired into the marrow. This walking, this pointless circling of the neighbourhood, had gone on for years. If he had any brains, he'd be walking the loop through New Glasgow. It was 8 K and would take almost two hours. He'd be sober by the time he got back to his parents' place. But his hollow legs, aching from the ankles up, had already taken him from Stumpy's, a forty-minute walk. What if he started out around the New Glasgow loop, got as far as downtown New Glasgow, then passed out on Provost Street? He could picture himself face-down on the dirty snow of the sidewalk in front of Goodman Place, too exhausted to stand and too drunk to roll over. So he hovered around home, restlessly circling. He traced and retraced his steps, stopping in his parents' driveway, peeking in at the living room – watching the light from the television flicking against the curtains – then circling again. Cursing and spitting, hating his father for waiting up for him. Hating himself for doing the worst of what the old man expected. Hating his father for being drunker than he was, no doubt, but having the power not to have to answer to anyone for it. Would he have thought, at fifteen, the first time he got too drunk to go home, the first time he traced this useless trail, would he have guessed he'd be twenty-three and still doing it? Twenty-three and working at Zellers. Twenty-three and living at home. There were guys twenty-three years old making seven hundred and fifty thousand dollars a year playing hockey in the NHL.

In the side of a bank near the corner of Scott Avenue he kicked a ledge out of the snow and sat on it, pulling the bottom of his down-filled coat so the cold wouldn't soak in.

He took off his left mitt and searched with the bare hand under his parka. He retrieved the letter from his pants pocket and turned the envelope over in the light of the street lamp. He looked at the blue-and-silver foreign stamp: some sort of stylized bird with a long beak. A stork? The envelope was wrinkled and creased, soiled from being examined and re-examined in his big, clumsy hands.

*Dear Ziv:*

*This is the first letter I'm sending to you since I've been in Japan, but it's not the first letter I've written. I've got the others back in my desk drawer (I'm writing this in a coffee shop, drinking a coffee that cost me three dollars and fifty cents), all of them in envelopes. Some of them even have stamps on them. I don't know why I didn't send them.*

*I can remember each one. I can remember what I said in it, what I was thinking about, how I was feeling. It's funny how you do things. You just end up doing them and you don't know why. Sometimes you don't even know that you are doing them until later when you look back. I keep writing "you" but it's not you I'm talking about at all. It's me.*

*The first letter I wrote you started off like this:*

*Dear Ziv:*

*I don't know what I was expecting when I came here. I guess I was expecting things to be completely different from Canada. But what I'm surprised at is how similar things are. The sky is still blue, people here walk on two legs, and if you drop something, gravity brings it to the ground. I guess the world is the same wherever you go.*

*One reason I didn't send that letter is that it didn't take long for me to realize how wrong I'd been. This place is so deceptive. Things look so familiar on the surface, but the interior of the place and of the people is so completely alien to me. And the weird thing is, the longer I'm here, the less well I understand it.*

Without finishing the letter, he folded it up, put it back into its envelope, and slipped it into the front pocket of his parka. From the other big pocket on the coat's front, he pulled out a creased copy of *The Educated Imagination*. He'd bought it at the university bookstore while he'd still been a student. In the small hours of the morning on a night of drinking, the time he'd wasted on that particular night became a ragged patch of colour on the giant collage of his wasted life. At these times he always decided he had to read. He knew reading was something he did not do enough of, and he always carried some book or other in his parka pocket, intending to read it but never setting aside a specific time. He looked at the book and blinked at the glare reflecting up from the cover. He squeezed his eyes shut and tried a second look. He turned to the table of contents and looked at the letters that made up the words of the chapter names. "The Motive for Metaphor" was the first chapter. He'd read that one already, months ago. He blinked and looked away, up into the glare of the street light that blotted out the black-and-grey sky behind it. His breath rose above him, a white ghost disappearing. When he looked back at the book, he tried to read the title of the next chapter, but he was too tired to make sense of it. "The Singing School," the next chapter was called. He turned to page 12, where that chapter started. The bookmark that held the page was a laminated column of news-paper print, an obituary from several years ago. The edge of the lamination was serrated, cut with pinking shears to give a fancier appearance. The obituary, before it had been encased in clear plastic, had been backed by a yellowish length of ribbon with "A Prayer for the Living and the Dead" printed on it. Ziv read the name on the obituary: James Alexander Morrison, then quickly tucked the bookmark inside the back cover. On page 12 he read a paragraph that talked about being shipwrecked, about imagination and identity, and about associative language. All the words were familiar, but he could not decipher how they related to one another.

He put the book back into his pocket, slowly raised himself onto his feet, and continued his circuit through the neighbourhood.

The light was still on in the living room when he got back around to his parents' place. He crept up to the big new window in the west wall of the living room and tried to peek in again. Maybe the bastard had fallen asleep in front of the TV. There was a narrow space at the right where the blind did not completely cover the window. He could see the far edge of the TV set. It was turned on. The pole lamp was still on as well, and he could see an arm of the La-Z-Boy, but he was seeing it from behind. His old man could be in it and he would not be able to see.

He heard the light crunch of a footstep a split second before the voice: "Hey!" It jolted him. He straightened up so fast he lost his footing and landed on his back in the driveway. His drunkenness, the snow, and his heavy clothing cushioned him, but he lay on the ground for a moment, his limbs twitching with adrenaline.

"Jesus Christ! It's you, Arvel!" a vaguely familiar voice said, someone mistaking Ziv for his brother, who was two years older. Ziv had not managed to make it to his feet, but craned his neck around to see who was there. The short face, ruddy-brown hair that curled out from beneath a toque, and the heavy eyebrows were familiar.

"Jesus, Bundy, you scared me shitless." It was Bundy Burgess, who lived on Rutherford Street, and whom Ziv had not seen in years. Before they'd been old enough for school, Bundy and Ziv had played together, and they'd chummed around through elementary school. But Bundy had failed a few times in junior high, and Ziv had gone right through. When he reached an age when he was allowed to go by himself outside of the Red Row, Ziv had started hanging around with the boys in his grade. By the time he was in high school, there weren't many Red Rowers left in school, so Ziv had grown out-of-touch with most of his old friends from the neighbourhood. He looked at the thick, curly mutton chops on Bundy's face and realized that the last time he'd spoken to him, neither of them had even begun to shave.

"It's Ziv," Bundy said, having got a closer look at Ziv's face. "You two guys look so much alike now."

"I've heard that before," Ziv said. He made his way woozily to his feet, spreading his arms out at his sides to maintain balance.

Bundy was a tough, raw-boned, sinewy man. But even with Ziv stooped over drunk, Bundy only came up to Ziv's chin. In a heavy winter coat, Bundy's narrow shoulders and torso were a fraction the size of Ziv's.

"You're drunk as ten barls of shit," Bundy said.

"Two hours ago I was drunk as twelve," Ziv said. "Right now I'm down to about seven, I figure."

"I didn't think college boys got drunk," Bundy said.

"Then you've never been to college." As drunk as he was, Ziv knew that this was a mistake. Bundy hadn't finished high school, and even though Ziv had meant the remark as a swipe at university students, there was no way for Bundy to take it except as a swipe at him.

"Some of the biggest piss tanks I've ever seen are at university," Ziv continued, trying to erase what he'd just said with what he was saying. "I knew a guy stopped going to classes in January, never left the residence building in January or February. Put in a big order at the liquor store whenever somebody was going. Got people to smuggle him food from the cafeteria. Stayed drunk night and day for two and a half months. Every couple of weeks his roommate would do some laundry for him and force him to shower."

"What in Jesus' name are you doing snooping around your own house in the middle of the night?" Bundy said.

Ziv was starting to worry about someone inside hearing their conversation. He grabbed the sleeve of Bundy's coat and led him out to the end of the driveway. "Aw, I don't want the old man to see me this tanked up," he said.

"The old man! Jesus! How old are you?"

"Still the same age as you."

"It's freezing out here."

Ziv shrugged.

"Come away down to my place, if you want. You can sleep on the couch. It's better than your mother finding you stiff as a board on the back step in the morning."

Ziv sniffled in the cold. He knew his feet and hands needed warming. His face was beginning to become numb, and he'd either have to keep walking all night or go indoors at some time.

"Well, I don't need a place to sleep," Ziv said. "But if I could just warm up a bit. The old man is guaranteed to go to bed in the next half-hour or so."

Bundy's house was just on the far side of Ziv's backyard. In a couple of minutes, they had walked around the corner on Rutherford Street and into Bundy's driveway. The Burgess house had had no major upgrades, except for a reshingled roof, which Ziv could remember seeing Bundy pounding away at a few summers back, and a fresh coat of paint that had left the house, which had been a pale rusty red, a brooding shade of blue. The front step was crumbling and lopsided and the two-by-four pillars that elevated the roof over the rear porch showed signs of advancing rot.

For Ziv, entering Bundy's kitchen was like walking back into his childhood. The chrome kitchen set with cracked vinyl padding. The varnished plywood cupboards. Even the worn pattern of the linoleum on the floor, and the smell of boiled carrots, which Bundy's mother used to press through a strainer and serve mashed, like potatoes. Nothing had changed since he and Bundy had played together with Lego and Hot Wheels under the table.

"Should I make some coffee or tea or something?" Bundy said and moved to fill the kettle.

Ziv took off his boots and coat, piled them together just inside the door. There was a water glass beside the sink on the counter, and Ziv went over and filled it at the cold tap. "Just water is all I need," he said. He gulped down a glass, then another, then another.

He and Bundy sat at the kitchen table. Ziv looked through the doorway to the living room and saw the TV. It was the same one he'd seen in there the last time he'd been in this house, years ago. Bundy's family had the first colour TV in the neighbourhood. Ziv and Arvel used to love coming here to Bundy's place to see the blue faces of soap-opera stars, their bodies outlined in yellow.

"Last time I talked to you must have been in Grade 8," Ziv said.

"Grade 8 covers a lot of years for me," Bundy said. They both laughed. "What have you been up to since you finished college?"

Ziv fidgeted. "I never finished," he said. He stood up and looked out the window over the sink. He could see his parents' house from here, but he could not see the living-room window he'd been monitoring when he was outside. The street light over on Foster Avenue haloed the house in yellow.

"Well, you done a couple years there, didn't you?" Bundy asked.

"Ya, I lasted two years."

"That's more than a lot of people do."

Ziv had never thought of his two years of university as anything he'd accomplished. In his mind all they stood for was the two he hadn't completed. "I guess that's right," he said. "I had . . . troubles. Woman troubles. I don't know what the hell happened. I wasn't university material to begin with."

"You used to go out with Meta Nichols, didn't you?"

Ziv nodded.

"Hear she's in Japan now."

Ziv nodded again.

"Do you keep in touch?"

"Yeah, I guess," Ziv said. He shrugged. "The odd letter."

"Arvel's on at the new pit, I heard."

"He's there. We got on together."

"You were up there?"

"Arvel and I had a joint interview. A guy Arvel went to vocational with got us through the door. Some kind of favour deal."

"So you were underground, were you?" Bundy asked.

Ziv nodded. "Lasted one Jesus shift. Arvel was working on the surface. Using his trade, there. Electrical work. Then when I quit, they put him down on the job I was doing."

Bundy's father had been killed in the pit. When Ziv and Bundy had been children, the big coal boom of the industrial revolution had all but petered out. That coal boom had swollen Pictou County from a few farms and some trees into an industrial centre, a cluster of small, blue-collar towns. Before either of them had been born, the Red Row had been company housing for the workers at the bustling pits spread through Albion Mines and the next-door town of Westville. In those days, just about every adult male in the area, and many of the children, would have been employed at the pits in some capacity. But by the late sixties and early seventies, when Bundy and Ziv had been children, there were only one or two pits still running, and those at a capacity so small as to hardly compare with the glory days.

Bundy's father had been one of only two or three men from the Red Row to work underground when they were kids. And they had it easy, the old-timers said, compared to the pick-and-shovel days. Machines did the work for them. All the same, Bundy's father went below one shift and never made it home again. Ziv remembered the day it had happened, though he couldn't have been more than seven or eight years old. He remembered coming down the Catholic School Path at lunchtime, always at the head of the neighbourhood kids coming from the elementary school. He remembered stopping at the corner of Rutherford Street and seeing Bundy standing behind the screen of his back door. Bundy had always been slow and poky and had never gotten home this quickly. He stood absolutely still, a shadow with his head inclined on the screen.

"Doesn't matter how they ventilate the thing," Ziv went on. "You can't breathe down there. The whole fucking weight of the earth is pressing down on you. The tunnels aren't lit right and you got a light on your helmet that's like going out in a hurricane with a candle. People weren't meant to get that far away from the sun."

Bundy was looking at him. Ziv wondered if he was making any sense.

"All I could think of was how my grandfathers, both of them, did this for forty years. And my uncles. I kept thinking of the miners' monument over on Foord with more names on it than both sides of the war monument put together. I had this picture in my head, like a diagram, a cutaway of the earth, like that ant farm with the glass walls we had in Mrs. Sutherland's room in Grade 3. With me down there in one of the tunnels: a puny little ant."

"Arvel's down there right now working the back shift," he pressed an index finger hard into the tea-stained top of Bundy Burgess's kitchen table, as though he could hold his brother there under his finger.

"They're not organized, what I heard," Bundy said.

"They fucked up the certification or something. That's Arvel's thing. He's organizing. Doing the union stuff. Taking after his fucking old man." Ziv found himself pacing to the window where he could look up again and see the outline of his parents' house silhouetted against the yellow street light behind it. His legs felt weak and wobbly, even on this walk of only a few steps. He was glad now to be inside and warm instead of wandering the town drunk in the cold.

"I wouldn't go underground for a thousand bucks a day," Bundy said. "And without a union, I wouldn't go for a million a day. I'm going to make some tea." He opened a canister and took out two Red Rose tea bags, dropped them into a white teapot on the counter.

"So what are you up to these days?" Ziv asked.

"Unemployment enjoyment," Bundy said. "I do a lot of work in the woods, a lot of spacing, things like that. Silviculture, my crew foreman calls it. Tree farming. BYO chainsaw."

"That's the hard work," Ziv said. "Arvel used to do that. Before he got on at the pit. I used to see him with ice packs or hot-water bottles at night. Popping Aspirin like candy." He shook his head. He couldn't imagine going out into the woods, getting paid piecework, breaking his back at five in the morning. And when you took into consideration equipment maintenance, and layoff times, he was probably making almost as much at Zellers for stuffing Cabbage Patch dolls back into their boxes.

When the tea was ready, Ziv did not argue or refuse. He let Bundy pour him a cup with sugar and tinned milk. They each took their cup and went with it into the living room. Ziv sat on the couch. They sipped their tea.

"I'll get a blanket and you can sleep right there," Bundy said after a time.

Ziv waved the offer away, but Bundy poked his head into the cubbyhole and emerged with a grey-and-black wool blanket. "I don't need to stay the night," Ziv said. "Twenty minutes or so, when we finish this tea, the old man should be in bed."

"What's the big deal?" Bundy said. "You're twenty-three years old. What's he going to do, ground you?"

"All he ever does is harp on me. He spent his whole fucking life reforming the world and now he's got nothing to reform but me. I come home drunk it's just one more thing."

"It's not like he don't drink," Bundy said.

"Drink? He doesn't drink. He swims in it. One of these days I'm going to open that door and his big fat carcass is going to be lying on the floor dead. Keeled over with a heart attack or drowned in his own puke, and it's going to be the best day of my life, you can be sure of that."

The only light in the room came from a lamp on a table beside the couch. The wallpaper carried a faded blue paisley and floral design. The patterns cut into the wooden trim around the door frames were obscured by layer upon layer of poorly applied high-gloss paint. Bubbles and drips from old brush errors were preserved and compounded by new errors coated on top.

The tea and milk in Ziv's stomach had felt good at first. It had warmed him and stopped the aching he'd felt since shoving his fingers down his throat on Hudson Street. But now he felt queasy.

He put a hand to his mouth and ran to the closet under the stairs where there was a toilet and sink. He didn't have time to close the door behind him before he was vomiting the milky tea into the toilet water.

"You want to try to put something solid on that stomach, some dry bread or crackers," Bundy said.

Ziv washed and dried his face, then went back into the living room, lay again on the couch, resting his head on a frayed armrest. "No," he said. "What I need is just to get off my feet for a while. I'm more tired than anything." He closed his eyes and felt the earth open up and swallow him.

Ziv opened his eyes when the room began to move. It took him seconds to realize that he might still be drunk. He sat up on the couch, pushed the blanket aside, and placed his feet on the floor. It was a little late for the bed spins, which he'd only ever had when drifting off to sleep. In a second he remembered where he was: Bundy Burgess's house. He made for the toilet under the stairs, but when he clicked the light switch on the wall, the single bulb, hanging from its cord in the low ceiling, was swaying back and forth, casting moving shadows of itself against the walls. The boards of Bundy's house creaked against the nails that held them in place. Water in the toilet sloshed back and forth against the sides of the bowl.

# An Inoperable Heart

Cigarette smoke in the Tartan Tavern was as thick as Bay of Fundy fog. The floor was sticky with the residue of spilled beer. In the evening light, the ceiling was a washed-out grey, mostly invisible due to the glare of the recessed bulbs that lit the room inadequately, but in daylight, you could see that the dust-hung stipple had once been white. The smell of onions frying was so heavy that you could almost, by means of smell alone, hear them sizzling.

"They'll get it worked out," Ennis was saying. "It's my young fella doing the organizing. They'll be organized all right." Ennis was sitting at a table near the snooker floor. His big, meaty face was florid with anger and excitement, and he thumped his big fists into the table as he spoke. At the table were Leon Dudka, Dan McGraw, Elvin Carter, and Allie McInnis. This wasn't the first time any of them had seen Ennis excited. In the background came a clatter of snooker balls. "Bad Case of Lovin' You" started up on the jukebox, and the crowd around the snooker tables began to moan and complain at the sound of it. The server returned to the table and placed the beer pitcher in the centre of the men with their empty and half-empty glasses. "The United Mine Workers didn't get in because of its ties with the competition. I don't blame the miners for not signing on with that union. It's not really a conflict of interest when one union represents workers in competing operations, but it looks enough like a conflict to scare people off. The Auto Workers will get them signed up, you watch. It'll be my young fella that gets them signed up and voted in."

The mine where his son Arvel worked had only been in operation for about a year. So far, the miners had been unable to get a union certified, and Ennis talked endlessly of Arvel's involvement in the union drive. It was right and natural that the son of a labour leader would draw on his father's experience, this is what Ennis wanted people to believe. But the truth was that Ennis was not on the best of terms with his son. Arvel had not once asked Ennis for any union-related advice, and Ennis only knew of Arvel's involvement in the attempt to organize the Eastyard mine because he'd read it in the paper.

"They'll keep the union out. They will, all right," said Allie McInnis, goading Ennis as he liked to do. He was the only one at the table who approached Ennis in size, and the only one who came to the Tartan Tavern as a regular who wasn't intimidated by Ennis's self-taught vocabulary and knowledge.

"They'll put up a fight," Ennis said. "But they can't keep it out."

"Look at Michelin," McInnis said.

As though an ejector button had been pushed, Ennis rocketed out of his seat, the ridge over the top of his great stomach caught the edge of the table, sending the beer glass before him over the edge to the floor. Now stretched up to his full height, his leg-sized arms arching outwards from his shoulders, it would be impossible for almost anyone not to feel threatened merely by the presence of someone so big.

"My properties!" came the warning shout from behind the bar. It was Tommy, the owner of the Tartan Tavern, shouting his customary complaint when he felt something he'd paid good money for, in this case, Ennis's beer glass, was being threatened.

"Look at Michelin," Ennis repeated in an even tone. "All right, I'm looking at it."

McInnis had seen Ennis erupt many times before and had not flinched. He sat looking calmly into his draft glass, then glanced up at Ennis as though he had just noticed him there.

"Plenty of people who work there say there's no need of a union at Michelin," said McInnis.

Ennis had heard this all before. He sat back down, looked for his glass on the table. When he discovered it broken on the floor near his feet, he grasped the handle of the pitcher and took a big drink straight from it.

"Maybe they do," Ennis said, wiping his mouth with the back of his hand. "But it's *their* decision. It's not the government of Nova Scotia's business to make that decision for them. And it certainly isn't the Michelin management's decision. People deserve to have a say in how their lives are run. Unions are just an extension of democracy into the workplace." Ennis had been pointing a thick finger at McInnis which he now thumped end-first into the table to put a period at the end of his sentence.

"If it weren't for the Michelin bill, that company never would have come here in the first place," McInnis said. "They don't run union plants anywhere in the world."

"The plant was here before the bill," Ennis replied.

"They wouldn't have come if they didn't know they were going to get it."

For Ennis, this Michelin argument was like a sliver of shrapnel lodged in his flesh from a land mine that had exploded years before. The bill, long since passed into law, was a piece of anti-union legislation used specifically to lure the French tire manufacturer to the province and to encourage it to expand its operations once established. Ennis had watched incredulously as fifty years of advancement of workers' rights, his whole life's work, was set back in a single motion. He kept telling himself he'd given up caring about it.

"The government kept the unions out of Michelin and they'll keep them out of Eastyard," McInnis said.

"I'm telling you, it's not the government's decision," Ennis replied. "You don't know shit about labour law."

"The government can do whatever the hell they want. They're the government. They propped that mine up with taxpayers' money just to buy our votes. You talk about democracy, but Nova Scotia's not a democracy. If this was a democracy, our new Member of Parliament would not be the son of the old one. Your son is wasting his time if he's trying to organize that mine. The whole process is pointless."

Ennis reached across the table and clamped his big fingers around McInnis's neck. He pulled the man forward over the tabletop, sweeping pitchers, glasses, ashtrays, and lighters onto the floor.

"I'm going to do everyone a favour," Ennis said. He dropped McInnis onto the floor, put a foot on his chest to keep him there. He fumbled around on the floor until he found a draft glass.

"I'm going to plug that fucking mouth of yours." Ennis throttled McInnis until he opened his mouth.

"You fat fucking bully," McInnis managed to say before Ennis stuffed the butt end of the beer glass into his open mouth.

It was only a short walk through the Red Row from the Tartan Tavern to Ennis's house. In the old days, before the Breathalyzer, he'd driven it anyway. Even with the threat of the Breathalyzer, he would still occasionally drive home from the Tartan if he'd only had a few beer. But there were times in the past when he did not remember having driven home, times when the car was parked crossways in the driveway in the morning when he got up and he'd only been able to assume that he'd been the one who'd parked it that way.

Putting the Tartan Tavern behind him, Ennis walked south, under the Trans-Canada overpass, and listened to the cars whooshing past overhead. However many times he'd walk this route home, he was always surprised at how the Red Row had changed since he'd been a kid there more than fifty years ago. The single word that encompassed these changes was *prosperity*. The Trans-Canada highway itself was a huge marker of that prosperity. When he was young, if you wanted to go to Halifax, you had to wind your way through a crooked dirt road that would be rutted in spring and might be impassable with snow for a lot of the winter. The new highway's on- and off-ramps at Lourdes alone were a more massive construction project than the Red Row had been decades before.

Foord Street, the main street in Albion Mines, and the main road that cut through the Red Row, was now a wide, well-paved, properly drained thoroughfare. He remembered when it had been a lane and a half without ditches or stormdrains, knee-deep in water or eye-high with dust. The dwellings in the Red Row were as well-serviced as any modern suburb in a big city. When he had been young, there'd been an outhouse in every yard. Many kitchens had featured a hand-pump connected to a shallow well. Coal sheds and chicken coops, horse barns and ash piles, all stuffed into a yard less than half the size you could legally build a house on now. Houseflies spent half the day on what was deposited in the outhouse, the other half on the food in the kitchen.

He regretted what he'd done to Allie McInnis back in the Tartan. He'd left the man on his back in a pool of spilled beer, spitting out the butt end of a glass. But McInnis's cynicism had enraged him. That attitude of helplessness, of pointlessness, flew in the face of every worthwhile thing his life's work had accomplished.

He looked around the neighbourhood now and felt a sense of satisfaction. He knew that he had played a role in the transformation of the Red Row. His union work had put upward pressure on the wage market. The unions and the New Democratic Party had pressed for and won the grants that had fixed up those houses, and for the universal health care that had lengthened and improved the lives of the residents. People he knew, living in Red Row houses they'd grown up in, had gone from having no sewage or running water, to owning camper trailers to take their vacations in, and snowblowers to clear the driveway after winter storms. He knew people who'd been afflicted with the complications of malnutrition in childhood who now had plastic hip joints that the health-care system had paid for in full.

"Red Rowers of the world unite!" he yelled. His open mouth sent up a column of steam. He thumped his arms against his chest, and the sound echoed out around him. Just beyond the parking lot of the Heather Motor Hotel, the Quick Pick convenience store at the north end of the Red Row glowed icily in the black winter overcast. Ennis crossed the parking lot, went in, and stamped his feet on the grate inside the door.

"Too late for the lotto, Ennis," the girl behind the register called. It was a Sewell girl, one of Linda Sewell's daughters. Her name wouldn't be Sewell, though. Who was it her mother had married?

"It's never too late for that," Ennis said. "I can always buy for the next draw." The girl laughed and walked over to where the lottery machine was set up. She had her mother's square, honest smile and compact but shapely build. Ennis caught himself looking at her breasts, then turned quickly away before he could see if she'd noticed. He'd dated Linda Sewell several times in the late forties, right after the war. They'd been kids, really. Linda had probably been younger then than her daughter was now.

He walked to the pop cooler and stood swaying slightly before it. He put a hand to the door of the cooler to brace himself, then squeezed his eyes shut. He was trying to get rid of a picture that had arisen in his mind: Linda Sewell in the back seat of his '38 Ford. He shook his head vigorously, like a dog trying to kill the prey clenched in its teeth.

"You okay, Ennis?" the girl called from over his shoulder.

"Aw, I've been having a drink, is all. The heat hit me, coming in the door, there."

He went back to the counter with a 500 ml Pepsi. "Wet my whistle," he said. The girl was still poised over the lotto machine. She had a fresh, pepperminty smell that penetrated Ennis's drunkenness and had him breathing deeply through his nose.

"Just the Pepsi," Ennis said. He looked up and locked his gaze on the girl's eyes, afraid that if he let his gaze wander somewhere else, it would go where he didn't want it to.

"Down to the Tartan, were you?" the girl asked, moving in behind the register. With a different hairstyle, she could have been her mother. She had broad, flat cheekbones and a tiny, stone-chiselled nose whose nostrils scooped up and back in a way that suggested permanent arousal. Her eyes were . . . Ennis could no longer bear to look at her. He bowed his head over the counter and focused on the money he was handing over, and on the scratch tickets beneath the glassed-in case on the countertop.

"You're going home early," the girl remarked.

"There's some real arseholes down there tonight," Ennis said. He frowned at the memory of what had happened in the tavern, then looked up into the girl's eyes again. "You're Linda Sewell's girl, aren't you?" he said.

The girl looked surprised, then said. "I . . . guess so. Her name's MacKenzie now. Seems funny to hear that name . . . Linda Sewell."

"How's your mother these days?" Ennis asked.

The girl looked alarmed and began to stutter a reply.

Ennis stopped her. "I have no right to be talking to you this way," he said. "I've made a mistake. I told you, I've been having a drink." He plucked the Pepsi from the counter, pushed it down into a pocket of his coat, and rushed out through the door.

When he reached his own house, Ennis stood at the end of the driveway a moment and thought about how much the place had changed. He and Dunya, his wife, had moved in years before, just a few weeks before Arvel had been born. The house had barely been worked on since it had been built. So although the house was old, and no one would ever mistake its uneven floors and chipped and repainted door casings for new, almost everything in the house had been replaced since they'd lived here. Ennis had reroofed it the first summer. The next year he'd got together with Ab Arnold, who owned the other side of the coal company duplex, and covered the original clapboard with smart cedar shingles. The floors had been tiled, retiled, and carpeted. Pressboard ceiling tiles had covered up the original plaster ceilings. The walls were covered in the simulated wood panelling that had been so popular in the seventies. The windows downstairs had all been replaced, those upstairs had been sealed over with aluminum storm windows. When they'd moved in, they'd barely had a stick of furniture, but over the years they had accumulated so much stuff (couches, chairs, bookshelves, china cabinets, lamps, and magazine racks) that you had to turn sideways to enter every room, the doorways were all blocked by furniture.

Ennis entered the back porch silently, and silently slipped off his boots and parka. Arvel was sitting at the kitchen table. His wife had kicked him out again. He'd been back in his parents' house for several days, living out of the blue overnight bag that he always brought with him when his wife sent him packing. He was working the back shift, which started at midnight, so at eleven o'clock on Friday night he was chewing on toast and jam, washing it down with tea.

"You look like shit," Ennis said to his son.

"You're drunk, old man," Arvel said. He had both elbows on the table and stared blankly into his teacup.

"I'll old man you," Ennis said. "How would you like to be called old man?" He took the Pepsi from his pocket and set it on the counter by the sink.

"How would you like to be called *shit*?" Arvel said.

"Jesus Christ. You're the touchiest guy I know."

Arvel shook his head and stared back into his tea.

"What the hell's the matter, now?" Ennis said.

Arvel bit a corner off his toast and put the remainder of the slice back on the plate.

"For God's sake," Dunya called from the living room. "Leave the boy alone." The voices from her TV show rose up again behind her, and it was as though she'd never said a thing.

Ennis opened the Pepsi and half-filled a glass. He took a forty of black rum down from the cupboard, topped up the glass, and sat across the table from his son.

Arvel looked up at his father and shook his head. "You don't know how lucky you are," he said.

Ennis smiled and took a big drink of his rum. "What are you talking about?" he said.

"Your bad heart is saving you from getting your arse kicked."

Ennis stood up, arms out at his sides, at the ready.

"Sit down," Arvel said calmly.

Ennis knew the score. Arvel had inherited his size, his strength, and his temper. At twenty-six, the age Arvel was now, Ennis could have pounded him. Ennis had grown up in the old Red Row. The mean one. He had shovelled coal, picked peas, driven rivets, loaded wood. And he'd learned how to take a punch and give back two for every one he took. Arvel had grown up soft in comparison. All the same, Ennis's aging, overweight body was no match for his son's. He could not sit down on the command of this snot-nosed kid, so he grabbed his drink from the table and backed away to the counter, leaned against it, trying to look unaffected after such a loss of face.

Arvel showed no pleasure in the power he'd just exercised over his father. "Look at you," he said. "You lousy drunk."

"I'll kick you out of my damned house."

"Go ahead," Arvel said.

"I raised you, you . . ."

"Raised me? Raised me?" Arvel's voice was loud now. "You lowered me, old man. You lowered the bunch of us. You and your drinking and screaming and pushing us around. You spent your whole life looking after workers' rights. Those people were strangers to you. What about your own sons?"

"Again and again, you screw up your own life and every time you come crawling back to me to save you. Don't blame me if you can't convince your wife to let you live in your own house. You're not man enough to face yourself. Christ!" he said. He held the drink up to the light to examine its appearance.

"Did you poison this goddamned rum, woman!" he called into the living room. He sniffed at the glass and dumped the contents into the sink.

"Rum *is* poison," Arvel said, then in response to seeing his father dump out the rum: "It's like seeing the Pope dumping out holy water. You'd better cross yourself or you'll go straight to hell."

"Now I'm telling you, boy," Ennis said. "You get the fuck out of here if you're going to talk to me like that. Maybe I can't throw you out, but I got a thirty-thirty upstairs that'll get your arse moving, I bet. I'm nice enough to keep you here when your own wife won't have you. You'd get one hell of a shock if you woke up one night with a mouthful of the end of that goddamn rifle. Now

I'm telling you to get out of my sight, and I'm telling you to do it right now."

Arvel put the last piece of toast into his mouth and drank a warm drink of milky tea to soften the toast. "I gotta get up to that grave, anyway." He walked into the porch and put on his parka and heavy boots. He stopped at the door and turned to face his father, who stood backlit and grim-faced in the doorway to the kitchen.

"You ever point a gun at me, old man, it better be loaded and you'd better pull the trigger. That's just some advice."

Arvel left.

Ennis turned back to the kitchen. He swung up his leg to kick the side of the fridge. Twenty years ago, ten years ago, he could have knocked the fridge on its side with a single kick. This blow didn't even land. His sock slipped up the slick enamel of the appliance, and as his foot was coming down, the heel jammed onto the top of the handle of the fridge door. It felt like someone had driven a nail into his foot, and the next thing he felt was his tailbone smacking the floor.

Dunya was in the doorway: "Ennis! Ennis!" she cried. Ennis had his eyes closed in shame and anger.

After he'd got up from the floor, he'd taken two painkillers and a nitroglycerine and chased them down with a big drink of rum and Pepsi. He'd gone into the bathroom, taken off his shirt, and examined the scar down the middle of his chest. The wide pink line was like a pair of tightly pursed lips. It had been over a year since the operation, and the doctor said the incision was fully healed, but any time he suffered a bump or a shake, Ennis expected the place where he'd been ripped open to explode, his bloody heart to flop out onto the floor.

Bypass surgery was becoming routine, his doctor had told him before he'd gone to Halifax, but once they got him opened up on that table and had a look inside him, they'd pronounced his heart inoperable. They'd closed him up without having done the work and the surgeon signed the papers for him to draw on his long-term disability insurance.

"The heart is a queer machine," the surgeon had said afterwards. They sat in his oak-panelled office in New Glasgow. The leather padding of the chairs they sat in squeaked when they shifted their weight. Ennis looked at the framed degrees and certificates on the walls, and thought, *"A queer machine." Is that the best that all this education can come up with?*

"You've got some bad arteries in there," the surgeon said. "They may never cause you trouble. On the other hand, you might just go out one day like that," he snapped his fingers. "Like switching off a light."

His foot hurt when he paced, but the pain in his tailbone kept him from sitting for very long. He was thinking about Arvel, about how much he loved him, and how all that love had somehow got twisted around into hate. He knew that whatever had gone wrong in their relationship, it could only be his fault. The boy had only learned whatever he'd taught him. But how could the best intentions have got so far off track?

He'd meant to come home and ask Arvel how the organization drive was going since they'd switched to the Auto Workers. Everyone assumed that Ennis – who'd played a major role in the organization of the steel mill, the railcar plant, the pop plant, the Sobey's warehouse – was playing a major role in what his son was doing at Eastyard coal. When the first effort by the United Mine Workers failed, he'd read about it in the paper. Arvel hadn't mentioned a word to him. He hadn't even known his son was involved in the union drive. His heart had soared with pride when he'd read Arvel's name in the paper and saw that the reporter had asked Arvel to comment from the union's side.

He went into the front room and switched on the reading lamp. In the midst of his falling-apart life, the life in which his relationship to every member of his family was in shambles, evidence of another life abounded in this small room. It was propped in frames on top of the coffee table. It hung collecting dust against the knotty pine panelling on the walls. The life depicted here was one at which Ennis had excelled. Plaques of service and congratulations, certificates of appreciation and achievement, dating right back to the fifties. "Presented to Ennis Burrows in thanks upon the signing of our first collective agreement. Allied Food and Restaurant Workers local 324. January, 1958." "Ennis Burrows, in recognition of 10 years' service, United Steelworkers of America." "Ennis Burrows, in recognition of 20 years' service, United Steelworkers of America." "Ennis Burrows, in recognition of 30 years' service, United Steelworkers of America." "Organizer Award. National Day of Protest. October 14, 1973. The largest organized demonstration in Canadian history." Photographs showed Ennis shaking hands with provincial New Democratic Party leaders, handing out Labor Council Scholarships at high-school graduations. He'd run for the federal seat himself in 1968, and the most prized photo of all, the only one professionally mounted and framed in polished brass, showed Ennis with former Saskatchewan Premier Tommy Douglas, leader of the first democratic socialist government in North America.

Ennis had met Douglas briefly at a rally in Halifax during the campaign of 1968. New Democratic Party candidates from across the province were lined up backstage after Douglas's speech that afternoon. Ennis had just enough time with Douglas to snap a photo for inclusion in his campaign literature. The actual physical moment itself had been brief, but its memory had been immortalized with a permanent place on the wall here in the front room. The photo had come down twice before while they'd been re-papering that room, and once while he and Arvel had been tacking up the panelling from which it now hung, but each time it had come down, the photo had gone right back up to its original spot, directly above the only light source in the room, in the centre of the wall you faced as you entered.

Beside Ennis, the Prairie firebrand looked like a prematurely aging child. Ennis's big hand gripped Douglas at the upper arm, and standing so close to Ennis's side, Douglas's head barely came up to Ennis's shoulder. But Ennis was looking at Douglas in the photo, and the awe and admiration on Ennis's face, the pride in standing next to his hero, made it clear who was the bigger man.

He was waiting for Ziv to come home. He wanted to have a conversation with his son. He didn't care what they talked about, hockey, cars, work, it didn't matter. He just wanted to say something to one of his sons that would not get turned in the wrong direction. He wanted someone to speak to him without anger. He knew from experience that this was unlikely to happen, but he had an image in his mind of himself and the boy, sitting at the table in the kitchen, drinking tea with sugar until they both sobered up, until the light crept back into the sky, until Arvel came home from the pit and the three of them would sit there, two guys hungover, one exhausted from work. Dunya would come downstairs and they'd all eat a big breakfast together.

He paced back and forth, kitchen to living room, fridge to TV, table to chair to couch. Ziv would be drunk when he got home, Ennis knew that. He and the boy had fought before over this issue. Each fight with Ziv, it seemed, was an individual struggle over some specific issue. Their fights were about drinking or about something one or the other of them had said without thinking. With Arvel it was different. He and Arvel just had one long fight that got taken up anew whenever they saw each other.

When he awoke it was still dark. The TV was hissing, its grey eye dancing with random dots. Dunya was standing over him, shaking him awake.

"Ennis! Wake up, goddamn it. Did you feel it?"

"What's the time?" he said. He sat up, swung his feet to the floor.

"Something happened," Dunya said. He pressed the light on his watch. 5:29.

"What?" Ennis said. "*What?*" His hangover came in through his eyes, pushing backward toward his brain.

"The house shook. It woke me up."

"Forget it," he said. "It's nothing. Go back to sleep."

"Jesus, Ennis. Didn't you *feel* it? I'm telling you, Ennis. Something happened."

Ennis rose slowly from the couch. He went into the kitchen and stopped when he got to the side of the fridge. The fridge door was ajar and a plastic pitcher of orange juice had somehow shaken loose and ended up spilled on the floor.

"Did you do this?" Ennis said.

Dunya came up beside him. "I haven't been in here this morning. See? Whatever woke me up shook this juice right out of the fridge."

Ennis stepped around the pool of juice and filled a big glass with water. His heel ached, and now he remembered catching it on the door of the fridge. He put a hand back and pressed gently on his tailbone. It was bruised, but he wouldn't know how badly until later. He was drinking his second glass of water when he looked out the kitchen window and down to Rutherford Street. In the light of the street lamp, he saw Ziv coming out the back door of the Burgess house.

# PACKING

Jackie was leaving in the morning. Her friend Colleen was driving from Halifax to pick up her and the girls. They'd stay at Colleen's place until they could find an apartment of their own. After years of complaining about Arvel's drinking and his volatile temper, after years of throwing him out, taking him back, and throwing him out again, she was finally making a break.

So she could gather what she and the girls would need at least to get them through the next few weeks, she'd set up the girls in the living room with enough toys and games to keep them occupied. The packing had gone much more quickly than she'd expected, and she was finished early enough to have the girls in their beds at the regular time.

Yesterday morning she'd told them what was happening. The part about moving to Halifax, at least. The part about leaving their father behind she had not yet discussed with them.

The girls had not asked any questions. In her mind, she'd gone over possible answers numerous times since she'd asked Arvel to leave the house a few days ago and decided that this was it, this was the last time.

*Is Dada going to come with us?* she thought Kate might ask.

*No, dear, he can't come. He has to stay here and work and we all have to go to Halifax, to work and to go to school.*

*Why?*

*Well, Mama and Dada have problems they can't solve. They've tried to solve them for a long time, but they can't. Now we have to move on, move out of our problems.*

There were only a few suitcases and an old sports bag of Arvel's, full of clothing, some of the girls' toys and books. She'd packed what they'd need to get them through the next few weeks, at which point she would come back and organize the rest. She moved the packed bags from the living room and piled them next to the back door, made herself a cup of mint tea, and sat down at the kitchen table. Halifax. Her friend Colleen Chisolm had been trying to convince Jackie to move to Halifax for years, ever since she'd gone there herself.

Arvel would find a job there for sure. She said that it would be a lot easier for him there than in Albion Mines.

Colleen was working at Gregor's, an upscale women's clothing store in an area of the downtown called Historic Properties, and for years she'd been telling Jackie about the amount of money she was able to make, the clean, modern apartment she could afford, the almost-new car she was able to make payments on. Colleen had worked with Jackie for a brief time at Exception Elle in the new mall in New Glasgow, where Jackie still worked. She claimed all along that Jackie was much better at sales than she herself was and that any time she wanted to come to Halifax for a better job and a better life, Colleen would get her on at Gregor's.

She'd called Colleen a week ago, even before she'd kicked Arvel out of the house. Colleen had been as positive as ever.

"You've finally come to your senses!" Colleen had said.

"This is no joke, Colleen. I'm leaving . . . leaving Arvel," she'd felt herself choke up just uttering the words, the words she'd formed in her mind already but had yet to speak. Arvel was at work, the kids were asleep, but she found herself crouching over the phone in a secretive manner and looking over her shoulder to see who might be there looking at her.

"The way Arvel drinks. The way the two of us fight. This is not the kind of life I want for myself or for the girls. I told him I wanted to move to Halifax, but he's on at the mine now and he thinks that's the only thing he's ever going to have to do. He refuses to see what this family really needs to better ourselves."

"So is Arvel just letting you go like that – Goodbye?"

"Not on your life. He doesn't know."

"You're sneaking out?"

"You don't have to put it like that. I feel bad enough as it is. But this is the only way it will work."

"I'm sorry," Colleen said. "If this is what you're going to do, just come. You and the kids can stay with me until you get set up. Is this it? Is this the end, do you think?"

Jackie paused. She looked around the tiny kitchen, lit only by the light from street lamps on Pleasant Street. "I don't know. It feels like the end. I feel as though my whole life needs to be turned in a new direction."

She took the last drink of mint tea and looked at the kitchen. She wondered what she was headed for. It suddenly seemed unimaginable to her now, after more than six years of marriage: a life without Arvel, a life outside of Pictou County.

Arvel had grown up in Albion Mines. Jackie had grown up in New Glasgow, a nearby town. She had no siblings, no aunts, uncles, or cousins. In the seven years since her parents passed away, her husband's family had become her only link to a sense of rootedness or permanence. Her mother had a cousin in New Glasgow with whom Jackie was not on good terms. There were a few old friends from school, but most of the people she'd known then had gone off to university and either not come back, or come back changed and disconnected from her somehow. Colleen Chisolm had been her closest confidante after high-school graduation, and they had stayed in touch, but it had been years now since Colleen herself had moved to Halifax, and it was hard to stay close over that distance. Tomorrow she'd be living with Colleen and it would be Arvel who was a hundred miles distant.

By looking around her, by examining the possessions they'd collected, she could trace a history of her life with Arvel. There was a pattern, as easily identifiable as the rings in the stump of a cut tree. Their bed, a ragged double mattress with no box spring and no frame, was from the meagre early period of their marriage. For a short time, a week, perhaps, it had been the only piece of furniture in their old apartment, a tiny one-bedroom on Bridge Avenue, bordering the Red Row. They had not conceived a child for the first time on this mattress. That had taken place before they were married, on a blanket at Melmerby Beach. But the first signs of the miscarriage which ended that pregnancy had started while she'd been lying on this mattress: the few days of heavier and heavier spotting, followed by the intense, painful cramping.

The kitchen table was too small for a family of four and was surrounded by chairs that did not match each other or the table.

She still thought of the table as new. Six years was such a short time. But the varnished surface of the tabletop was scratched and pitted, the result of countless turbulent meals.

The living-room furniture, two matching couches and a wing-back chair, were on the outer edge of the concentric rings. They were Scotchgarded, nylon-wool, button-tufted furniture, made by Sklar, and paid for in two payments less than a year ago, when Arvel's mining cheques had started coming in.

She wandered from room to room, taking a final look at what she'd be leaving behind in a few hours. She felt removed from the house already, as though in deciding to leave, in knowing she'd be gone in the morning, part of her had already left. As she looked at clothing and furniture, it struck her that all those things would have to be sorted through and divided. Final decisions would have to be made.

From the floor of the closet in the hallway she dragged a grey plastic storage bin to the centre of the living-room floor. This was the box of memorabilia. All the loose ends of memory in her history with Arvel and before. When they had moved out of the old apartment on Bridge Avenue, all of the things this container held had been scattered about, some in smaller, disintegrating boxes, some loose at the bottom of drawers. Jackie had gone out and bought this box. She'd taped a label to the lid that said "Memories" and thrown things in in no particular order. She'd planned to sort through it all at a later date, but had never done so.

She snapped the lid from the box and sat on the carpeted floor to examine the contents. The smell of yellowing paper and closed up dust rose into her nostrils. On top there was a scroll of paper tied with pink ribbon, a religious certificate. It was her first confession or confirmation document. The next thing that caught her eye was a square of yellowed newspaper. She picked it up and looked at the photo from the *New Glasgow Evening News*. This was a photo she'd seen several times before. It was Arvel at age two or three, sitting on Santa's knee. Arvel's big, square face was recognizable even as a toddler. The caption below the photo read: "Checking it twice. Santa stopped by the Steelworkers' Hall last Thursday to double-check on his list of children who were being naughty or nice. Little Arvel Burrows, from Albion Mines, claims he's been a good boy all year."

Jackie felt her throat thickening with emotion and snapped the lid quickly back on the box. She found a pencil on the shelf above the bar in the closet, and added a note to the label: "Arvel: half of these things are mine and half are yours. We'll have to go through it some time soon." She placed the box back inside the closet and closed the closet door, and considering what she'd just written on the box, realized that she had been putting off writing a note to Arvel.

She dug in a drawer full of cookbooks in the kitchen and found a spiral notebook that looked as though it had never been used. Opening to the first page, she wrote *Dear Arvel* at the top. It was such a strange thing to be doing: writing a note for the husband she was leaving. It was an act from a soap opera. The page she was writing on was smaller than letter-size, but it seemed enormous and empty, white as a blank mind. What did she want to say?

*I'm sorry*, she wrote. She paused a moment and considered keeping the note to these two words. *I have moved to Halifax with the girls.*

*The girls will miss you and in lots of ways I will too, but you know as well as I do that we just could not go on with things as they've been for a long time. There's been so much strife, so much turbulence between us and it makes us both lesser people every time we go through it. But it's been the effect on the girls that I've really been worried about. It's just not right and we both want better than that for them.*

*I'll call next week and give you a number where you can reach us.*

She almost wrote "Love" before her name at the bottom of the note, but realized how strange that would look to him.

The girls had migrated to her bed and were both asleep, curled beneath the ragged quilts when she entered the room. Not wanting to disturb them by turning on the overhead light, she crawled into the corner where the desk lamp stood on the floor. She switched on the lamp, aiming the broad end of its cone-shaped shade at the nearby wall, and changed into her flannel nightgown in the subdued light. She moved Melanie to the edge of the mattress and rolled Kate gently beside her to make room for herself. She set the alarm on the clock radio for seven, switched off the light, and crawled wearily between the sheets. She lay a short time awake, her eyes open in the total darkness.

She remembered what this house had looked like the day they'd moved in, how big it had seemed compared to the apartment they were moving out of, how hopeful she'd been of her future here, how her life had seemed to be taking a shape she'd felt positively about.

She thought back to when she and Arvel had first started dating. There had been a dance for which they'd gotten dressed

up: she in a gown of some sort, he in a dark suit with a white bou-
tonniere in the lapel. It must have been a wedding party, what
else would he have dressed up for? They had only been seeing
each other a short time, and she could remember the remarkable
sight of him in that suit: so large and powerful a man somehow
tamed or gentled by his attire. She remembered dancing close
with him that night and the soft way he spoke in her ear as he
held her. That tender, beautiful side of her husband was real. It
was a part of him she'd always tried to nurture.

She'd been optimistic when he'd started working in the mine.
Their financial troubles ended overnight. She saw Arvel's self-
confidence surfacing, especially since his recent work on the
organization drive for the union.

But they always found themselves shouting at each other.
Drinking had been such a large part of his life for so long that he
never managed to step away from it completely. Always some
irresponsible action managed to further erode her faith in him.

She closed her eyes and concentrated on breathing slowly
through her nose, and before long she drifted into an uneasy sleep.

It was almost five thirty when she opened her eyes. Something
seemed to have happened. A motion or a noise. She sat up in bed
and listened, then put her head back to the pillow and drifted
off again.

It was the phone that woke her next, what seemed like a
very short time later. She staggered to the kitchen and picked up
the receiver.

"Hello," she said.

"Is Arvel at home?" a woman asked. She offered no explanation of who she was.

"No, he's not," Jackie said. "Who's calling?"

"Is he at work, today?" the voice said.

"I'm not . . ." Jackie hesitated. "I'm not exactly sure, but I think he's twelve to eight this morning. Who is this?"

There was a click, and the line went dead.

# BAKUHATSU

Meta had drunk her fill of Tokyo again. She took the secret key from its hook inside the cupboard, climbed into the elevator, and pressed the button for the twelfth floor. As the ancient lift creaked its way to the top, she prayed no one else would get on. She wanted a Japanese-free zone for herself, a small space around her with only her and her own cultural expectations in it. She had to be secretive on her way to the roof anyway, as she did not want anyone to see that she had a key. She was one of the only residents of the building to have one. Yuka, her neighbour from across the hall, was the building's unofficial superintendent, and had surreptitiously copied her one from the storage box mounted on her kitchen wall.

When the door opened at the twelfth floor, she rushed down the hallway, through the door at the end, and up the two flights of stairs to the steel door that led to the roof. Once through the door, she instantly felt her insides loosen, relax a little. It was the perspective that did it. This was the only place she knew in

Tokyo where you could stand back and look at something from a distance. The building was only twelve storeys tall, but it stood close to the crest of a hill in Shinjuku Ward. As she leaned on the chest-high concrete ledge, she could see in one direction all the way to the skyscrapers at Shinjuku Station, the few tops of blue-and-red neon signs that rose up in the foreground only a hint of the glitter of Kabuki-cho. In the other direction she could see clear to the Sunshine Plaza tower in Ikebukuro. Slightly north of the centre-point between the two gleamed the white roof of the Big Egg, Tokyo Dome, where the Yomiyuri Giants played their home games.

The air was crisp and, for Tokyo, wintry. The lower temperatures made the air, usually laden with pollen, cooking smells, auto exhaust, sewage, and industrial effluent, seem relatively brisk, odour-free, and refreshing. She sniffed some in and held it in her lungs a moment before exhaling. The NHK forecast she'd listened to on the radio had said *kumori, tokidoki, yuki desu.* Cloudy with the possibility of snow.

It would be good and cold at that moment in Nova Scotia, and Meta closed her eyes very briefly, pictured the big fields below the Red Row covered with snow all the way to the river.

There was no cure for culture shock, she knew. After a year and a half in this foreign environment, she'd learned that culture shock came and went in surges. Only time would make the fed-up feeling, the sadness, the mental fatigue, go away. And they would eventually return. But coming to the roof helped her clear her mind. Moving above and away from so many of the things that physically boxed her in was always a relief. Getting a broad view of the sky was a reminder that she still inhabited the same planet on which she'd been born.

This fresh wave of culture shock had come on in mid-afternoon Friday, two days ago now. Classes had been doing "how to" speeches, something most Japanese students were very good at. The culture was built around the kata, the series of programmed moves carried out in the martial arts. There was a prescribed and accepted way of doing almost everything, from greeting someone a certain number of years older, to arranging flowers in a vase, to wrapping a gift. For most of the morning and past the lunch hour, she'd sat through speech after boring speech. From "How to Smoke a Cigarette" to "How to Sharp a Pencil" to "How to Make a Maki Roll."

Then, completely unexpectedly, a bright but usually silent and reserved student, in a class of students with mid-level English abilities, walked to the front of the room with an easel under her arm. The full attention of the class had transformed her from a shy and contained young woman to a broadly smiling, highly animated performer. She set up the easel, established eye contact with everyone in the room (the first item on Meta's evaluation form), and peeled back the cover sheet of the easel to reveal the topic of her speech: "How to Curse Someone with Straw Doll."

She had all the transitional words perfectly positioned. From "First, you must select your victim," accompanied by a drawing on the easel that showed a large disembodied hand pointing an index finger at a frightened-looking asexual cartoon figure, to "*Next*, you obtain some hair or clothing" all the way through to the conclusion: "Please follow these steps carefully, and your victim will become sick," here she bent over and mimed vomiting. "Or will surely die." She lay her head gently on the podium and closed her eyes calmly in mock acceptance of her inevitable fate. The procedure described was a traditional Japanese form of voodoo called *nenokoku mairi*, practised at night, in secret, on the grounds of a shrine. Meta had read a reference to it a few months before in an article in the *Tokyo Journal*.

The students in the class were obviously familiar with the practice, too, for they were in stitches from beginning to end of the speech. Or was it the young woman's changed demeanour they found comical? Meta knew that the closest she'd ever get to the meaning of any gesture on the part of Japanese people was a guess. Though she laughed through the speech along with the students, there was something vaguely disconcerting about it. The procedure described was something all the students knew how to do, how to put a death hex on someone. After that class had left her room, the memory of her own laughter began to make her feel queasy.

Meta had learned a way of coping with the kind of cultural alienation she was feeling at the moment. The best thing to do in this case was to share the voodoo story with a fellow foreigner and chuckle and shake your head at how nothing made sense away from home. But Meta did not dare make any remarks about Japan in her office that could even remotely be construed as negative. The man at the desk next to hers was practically psychotic with hatred for Japan and the Japanese. Greg Ulesso was an East-European Londoner, the son of Estonian parents who had emigrated to Britain. He'd come to Tokyo via Burma, where he'd taught English at Burmese National University for a small salary and a huge allowance of unearned respect. In Tokyo, he must have known he was facing a huge salary and no respect. Still, when he balanced Tokyo with Burma, he found Tokyo wanting. When Meta had first met Ulesso, he spent most of his time comparing

Tokyo unfavourably to Burma. "These surly fucking Japanese gobshites! You walk down the street in Burma and everyone has a smile for you."

Meta felt more sorrow than anger for Greg; she knew he was deeply unhappy and that he had probably had as many bad things to say about Burma when he lived there. But she cursed her bad luck at having been assigned a desk right beside his. Every other teacher on staff could leave, turn their back, or slink away when he entered the room.

So Meta stayed quiet and, instead, she started a letter to Ziv back in Canada. She wrote him instinctively at times like this, times of alienation and despair. She rarely sent him one of the letters she wrote. They were usually attempts at explaining the inexplicable, and he was the only person she felt would understand. Even when she did send a letter, he did not always reply. She kept the partially completed attempts in a plastic case file in a desk drawer in her bedroom. Together, the notes she made this way composed a half-formed journal of her experiences in Japan. Still, all the entries began as letters to Ziv. She was incapable of starting them any other way.

*Dear Ziv*, she began.

*Today in class we had speeches.* She stared at the sentence for several minutes. Without crossing this out, she started again. *How to Curse Someone with Straw Doll*, she wrote. *First, . . .* Her thoughts were still too jumbled and unformed. The task of describing what she'd just been through seemed enormous. She turned the sheet she'd been writing on face down and placed it in the top drawer of her desk, then silently began making notes for Monday's lessons. At three thirty, the earliest she was allowed to leave the office, she hurried out the door to the bus stop.

She'd spent the weekend trying to avoid the feeling of detachment and succeeded only, she now realized, in making herself feel even more detached. She'd drifted alone on foot through the Shinjuku district, stopping in coffee shops, drinking coffee by herself. She'd spent more than five hours on Saturday on the English-language floor of Kinokuniya Books. At the end of that day, her eyes had ached from reading the titles of thousands of books sideways off the spines. She'd drifted through every section of the shop, luxuriating in the profusion of printed English. From Maps and Travel, to Science, to Sociology, to Philosophy, to Fiction, and back around again to the big rack full of magazines and newspapers from the U.S., Britain, Australia. Sunday she'd gone alone to mass at St. Ignatius Church on the campus of Sophia University, then walked down Shinjuku-dori to the Mr. Donut, where she'd spent hours at a table by the window, hunched over the copy of *The Handmaid's Tale* she'd bought at Kinokuniya the day before.

It was now just after four thirty on Sunday afternoon. She had an English lesson at five with Yuka, the woman who lived across the hall. But at the end of such an empty weekend, facing a full day of teaching at the college the next day, she was not looking forward to the lesson. She stood on the roof of the building and looked out in the direction of Ikebukuro, out to where she knew the countryside was the closest. Tokyo was a tax on the imagination, a real place that had to be dreamt of to be believed. Everything about it was difficult to hold in the mind. It was difficult to look at the Chinese symbols for the names of the neighbourhoods and imagine that the crowded urban sprawl of Nakano had once been a central well. Who would draw water from that source today and drink it? The name of the area next to her own, Haramachi, meant *field town.* How could there once have been a field there, where there was not a square metre of earth to be found? But as difficult as it was to imagine Tokyo before it was Tokyo, it was equally difficult to imagine it as it now existed. She wondered if part of the reason she came to the rooftop so frequently was to confirm that there was actually such a place.

As she looked out over the city, she tried to go back in her mind and find her thirteen-year-old self, the person she'd been ten years before. She closed her eyes, mentally trying to shed the last ten years of experience, then opened her eyes, hoping to get an idea of what she would have thought of this place if she'd seen it back in 1978. Take that girl she'd been. That girl from Nova Scotia, from Pictou County, from Albion Mines, that girl who'd never seen Halifax, let alone any place bigger or more cosmopolitan, drop that girl here on this rooftop in Tokyo, show her this view, this jam-packed landscape: How would she react? What would she think? What words would she use to express what she was thinking? Most important, how would she be different afterward? This was a mental exercise Meta often put herself through. Why couldn't I have known this before? she would think. My life may have turned out differently.

Above her, thick clouds rolled past beneath the overcast, oblivious to the city that strained and strove beneath them. Across the narrow street at the back of the building, the tiny family-run print shop hummed and buzzed and clicked. The sound carried up to the rooftop and blended with the *smack . . . smack* of two preteen boys playing catch with baseball and gloves on the street in front of the shop.

She couldn't handle the English lesson with Yuka today. She would go downstairs now and cancel. She wanted to retreat into her apartment, lock the door. Maybe rent a video and pretend she couldn't see the subtitles, make believe she was in a theatre in Canada. She walked the two flights, descended in the elevator, and noticed, after months of looking at the same marks with incomprehension, that she could now understand the single word of graffiti scratched into the grey paint on the back of the door. *Kuso*, it said. *Shit*.

The hallway outside Yuka's and her own apartment was dark and silent and smelled of the mouldy red carpet on the floor and the miso soup that at various times in the day would be cooking in every apartment in the building. After pressing the buzzer several times, Meta turned her back on Yuka's door. She had a hand on the knob of her own door when the one behind her opened.

It was Kazuhiro, Yuka's seventeen-year-old son. Kazu looked much more relaxed and confident than he usually did. He was taking some time off school. This was his final year to prepare for university entrance. A solid A student for most of high school, he had brought back his report card in January with the news that he'd failed everything.

Yuka had called the school for an explanation, and discovered that Kazuhiro had done well all term, handed in assignments, listened attentively to lectures, and taken notes. He'd shown up for every exam at the end of the term and left every exam paper blank. He had not even put his name on the papers. Teachers had guessed which had been his through a process of elimination.

Kazuhiro's father, Yuka's late husband, had been a highly placed salaryman in a Japanese pharmaceutical company. He'd barely been in their apartment while the boy was awake, his own life had been so subsumed in the company, but he'd died several years ago from what the doctors at the time had called a heart

54

attack, but everyone at his workplace had recognized as *karoshi*, death from overwork. The father had been a graduate of Todai, Tokyo University, perhaps the most distinguished, highly ranked university in the country. Kazuhiro idolized the memory of his father, and he so wanted to pass the Todai entrance exams himself that he had paralyzed himself with anxiety over his studies.

He was home now on the advice of the family doctor, who'd prescribed two weeks of rest for him, completely away from school. No books, no studies allowed.

Kazuhiro stood in the doorway, his eyes dark. His mother was having an affair with a gaijin, a Caucasian British man who, in his late twenties according to Yuka, must have been ten years younger than she. Meta had never met him, and Yuka had taken great care to keep the affair a secret from her son, who had been terribly affected by the death of his father. But people find things out that they're not supposed to know, and in Kazuhiro's blank gaze, Meta always felt accused, somehow partially responsible in a racial or genetic way for the frustration of all that remained unspoken in the apartment across the hall.

"Mama-san wa?" she said simply.

"Imasen." No offer of explanation. No apology.

"Imasen desu ka?" a stupid repetition of what the boy had just said.

"Eh," the boy replied. He closed the door.

It was too late now. She couldn't cancel right at five o'clock when Yuka showed up on time. In her kitchen, she ran water into a kettle and sparked a gas burner to life beneath it. She sat at the table and looked out the window to the narrow street below. Behind the translucent glass of the little print shop across the way, she could see the computerized equipment flipping, waving, and jerking. The people who worked there flashed between and around the machines, adding paper, making adjustments, replacing small components. Seven days a week, sixteen or eighteen hours a day, they went at it back there.

The boys who'd been playing catch a short while ago had vacated the street, leaving it looking empty and cold.

At a little past five, the kettle whistled. It wasn't like Yuka to be late. On the street below, the son of the old couple who owned the noodle shop at the corner went past on his motor scooter, a spring-mounted tray loaded with big bowls of soup swinging to and fro from a gooseneck hook at the back of the bike. Meta's mouth watered. She should have eaten.

The electronic doorbell buzzed angrily. Meta looked at her watch. Twelve minutes after. When she opened the door, Yuka began apologizing from the corner of a swollen mouth.

"Oh, Yuka," Meta said. She put a hand on Yuka's shoulder. Yuka winced away from her touch.

"Sorry to be late," she said.

Meta looked over Yuka's shoulder to her apartment door. "You'd better come in here quickly," she said. She moved out of the way, and Yuka slipped into her kitchen.

Yuka kept the materials for their weekly lesson in a heavy folder fastened with an elastic band. She sat at the kitchen table and began unpacking the folder in preparation for the lesson. Meta sat across from her and examined Yuka's face to more closely assess her injury. Her left cheek was only slightly discoloured, but it had ballooned to two or three times its regular size, pushing the straight hair back away from the side of her face. There was a trace of blood visible in the left corner of her mouth. Though she'd just applied fresh lipstick, little creases in her lips held unmistakable traces of both fresh and dried blood.

"I'm not sure my pronunciation," Yuka said. She put a textbook called *Side by Side* on the table and ran her fingers over the swollen flesh of her face.

Meta shook her head. "We're not having a lesson," she said.

Yuka looked at her with astonishment. Meta thought she could see a tracing of broken blood vessels between Yuka's left eye and her temple. "I'm sorry to be late," Yuka said.

"It's not because you're late."

"Why, then?"

"Don't be ridiculous," Meta said. "You think I want to teach a lesson to someone who's pronouncing through a swollen mouth?"

"I'm sorry," Yuka said.

Meta bit her own lip.

"I put ice on it at the hospital. And the . . . nandaro . . ." she pointed at her distended cheek.

"Swelling," Meta said.

"Swelling got smaller," Yuka said.

"You went to the hospital," Meta said.

"Of course," Yuka said. Meta's breathing quickened.

"What did he do to you?" she said. "Tell me what he did to you. What did the doctor say?"

Yuka pushed her chair back from the table and stood up. She flattened her hands and pushed them under the elasticized waist of her skirt. She grasped the hem of her blouse and lifted it to reveal the bandages: They began just above her waist. As she moved her blouse higher, Meta saw that the bandages went so high Yuka had not been able to put her bra back on. Yuka pulled the blouse over her head to reveal two dark nipples, breasts so small they were almost non-existent. On the left side, the bandages half-covered one breast, squeezing it up at an odd angle.

Around the torso, the bandages covered the bruises. But her left shoulder and upper arm were a dark violet-red, and on the strip of flesh between the bottom of the bandages and the top of her skirt there were signs of bruises to come, only now beginning to form beneath the skin.

Meta felt her insides wrench. She jerked Yuka's blouse from her and threw it back in her face. "Put that back on!" she shouted. "Put it on, now!" Yuka struggled painfully to get the blouse back on. Her arms were stiff and it hurt her to put them above her head. Meta held the hem of the blouse for her, and together they tucked it back into the skirt. Meta put a hand on Yuka's right shoulder, where she knew there was no bruise. "Sit down, Yuka," she said. "I'm sorry I yelled at you."

They'd been through this several times before, but the violence had never been so extreme. And this time it had happened in public. Yuka and her boyfriend had been having coffee in a Kohikan near Ginza Station when he'd flown into a blind rage, pounding and kicking her repeatedly. More than once the owner of the shop had been in the midst of phoning the police, when she'd begged him herself not to. She'd blacked out several times and did not know how she'd got to the hospital. Meta asked about the other people in the coffee shop. What had they done? Hadn't they tried to intervene? But Yuka had no recollection of anyone else in the shop.

Meta listened to the story with tears in her eyes. She nodded and held out a hand to touch Yuka's. But when Yuka had finished,

Meta felt a terrible contradiction in herself. What her friend was going through was sad and enraging. But what was her role in it? What could Meta do? She didn't have enough Japanese to make a report to the police. The only person who could help her do such a thing was Yuka, who would not. Meta felt such a course of action would be useless anyway, since the man who was beating her was a foreigner, and the Japanese police, like the rest of the society, were unsure about how to treat foreigners. The likelihood was slim that a single report of violence would result in his arrest.

"Yuka," Meta began. She stopped. She'd said it all before. *This man has no right to hit you. It's not anger, it wasn't a fight, he's sick. The only thing that's going to stop the violence, realistically, is an end to the relationship.* "I've said it all before," she said. The image of Yuka with her blouse off flashed in Meta's mind. Her bandaged, bruised body like a broken twig. Something new occurred to her.

"He's going to kill you," she said. "Take a look at yourself in the mirror. He's going to kill you. He almost did this time."

"No," Yuka said, her high voice becoming shrill. "I kill him!"

Meta shook her head. "That's stupid," she said. She pointed a finger at Yuka for effect. "He . . ." she paused. ". . . is going to kill . . ." another pause. ". . . you."

They sat at the kitchen table most of the evening. Meta made green tea and they drank it. Yuka called the noodle shop on the corner and the son of the owners came on his scooter with noodles and broth in two big china bowls that they rinsed and left outside the door when they were finished. The conversation went in circles a number of times: Yuka talking about the violence she'd endured, talking about the most recent attack as though she were surprised it had happened. Meta did not want to seem unsympathetic, but she was tired of talking with Yuka about the same problem they'd been discussing for over a year.

According to what Yuka had already told her, the first hint that the British boyfriend was violent had come when they'd been playing a board game. Yuka had been winning, and after protesting jokingly several times, he'd taken a lit cigarette from an ashtray and stubbed it out on the back of her hand. Meta had noticed the burn, and at first Yuka had claimed she'd burnt her hand in the kitchen. But when Meta learned the truth, she decided she did not want to meet the boyfriend. She did not even want to know his name. She told Yuka immediately what she thought: This was not normal behaviour. Unless he'd burnt her by accident, he had a serious problem. And since then, the outbursts and attacks had followed a predictable escalation: pushes and pinches turned to punches and kicks. Bruises became commonplace. Hidden injuries caused Yuka to wince in pain when standing up or sitting down.

Meta feared that she was growing hard-hearted about Yuka's situation: she'd begun to worry primarily about its effects not on Yuka, but on herself. She'd done everything she could think of for her friend and neighbour: she'd recommended sending the boyfriend to counselling. (He admitted he had a problem and was going to a British-educated analyst, but this did nothing to slow the frequency or to stem the severity of the attacks.) She'd recommended Yuka seek counselling herself, secretly hoping it might give her the strength to end the relationship. (The counsellor had actually told her she must be doing something to provoke the man's behaviour.) Meta had even gone as far as to tell Yuka she did not want to see her again until she ended her relationship with the abuser altogether. This resulted in a two-week lie in which Meta believed Yuka had broken off the relationship. Then one day Yuka had come into Meta's apartment trying to disguise a limp.

By now, Meta and Yuka's relationship revolved primarily around Yuka's violent affair, and they'd gone through the same cycle several times: advice, decisions, lies, broken promises, broken blood vessels.

Meta was beginning to think she'd done what she could to help her friend and that she should start thinking about herself. Though her own family was peaceful and loving, she'd seen violence and mistreatment as she was growing up. She'd pursued an education for herself to make sure she could lift herself out of the hemmed-in world of poverty, ignorance, and violence she'd been forced to look at up-close. Now, despite her best efforts, here she was: mired in the same muck she'd moved away from in Canada. She wasn't sleeping well at night. She'd have nightmares when she did sleep. She was distracted in the daytime, wondering how many of the strangers she saw were enduring a home life that was making them less than fully human. This was the last way she'd expected to be living when she'd come to Tokyo.

She had promised herself before now that the next time Yuka came to the door with a bruise or a swelling, she was going to close the door in her face. But she'd been unable to go through with it. She'd resigned herself to resolving nothing with Yuka, but she felt a responsibility to listen with even a pretended sympathy. She was the only support Yuka had.

It was past ten when Yuka left Meta's apartment. They stood inside the door and embraced carefully, so as not to cause Yuka further pain. Yuka smelled of hospital disinfectant and the tobacco of the last cigarette she'd smoked, hours before. The next day was a workday, but Meta felt she'd sleep better if she went up on the roof one more time. She might be able to unwind a little. She put on her heavy jacket and boots and watched out the peephole in the door as Yuka went back to her own place. When she thought Yuka could not hear, she left her apartment and rode the elevator to the top floor again, for one more look from the roof before she went to bed. The sky was still clouded, and in the darkness the reflected light of Tokyo turned the clouds a sickly yellow-brown. Shinjuku was in full bloom. A few tops of the highest neon signs were visible to her, and a red-and-blue haze enveloped the entire western sector of the horizon. The city roared and blinked in the darkness, creating its own kind of daylight. She lay on her back on the sand-and-asphalt roof, looking up at the hazy yellow clouds. The chill from the cold roof seeped up into her through her clothes. An imperceptible breeze moved the sky to the east, and now and again, when the clouds thinned and the sky got dark in a particular spot, she caught a hint of the stars that lay beyond.

She jolted awake and pressed the light button on her watch. It was almost one thirty a.m. She stood unsteadily, pounded her feet into the roof to warm up, and walked the two flights to the elevator. As she waited for the elevator to arrive, she had the sensation she often got while waiting for an elevator in Tokyo, the sensation of the building moving slightly in a lateral direction, and for a moment she wondered if this would be another earthquake. And as always when an earthquake would begin, she wondered if this would be the Big Earthquake, the one everyone knew was coming, the one that would flatten the city again, as had happened in 1923. When the elevator doors opened, she understood that what she'd felt was the motion set up in the building by the moving elevator. She got in and rode it to her floor.

The radio alarm came on at six and she quickly hit the snooze bar to give herself a few more minutes. It took several seconds for her to realize what she'd heard, and by the time she'd switched the radio back on, the AP network news was over. She lay in bed pondering. Could she have heard the words *Albion Mines*? It was rare to hear the name *Canada* on the American Armed Forces Radio broadcasts, and for a few moments she thought she must have been mistaken.

But when she switched on the television in the living room/ kitchen, the 6:00 a.m. newscast showed a picture of the giant twin silos of Eastyard Coal's pit at the south end of Albion Mines. Her heart began to pound. She'd seen them in photos and news clippings her parents had sent. The mouth of the pit had been damaged in some way. White panels from the enclosure that led into the ground lay scattered like shed teeth. The scene switched to show the Albion Mines Volunteer Fire Department's two trucks parked below the blue-and-grey coal silos. She could not recognize the faces of the firemen moving purposefully about the trucks; their heads were covered with oxygen masks. The voice of the Japanese reporter was serious and matter-of-fact, but Meta understood less than 10 per cent of what he was saying. She could hear times being talked about. Five twenty-nine a.m. was one. She checked her watch, although she knew what time it was. She struggled in her confusion and disorientation to calculate the time difference between Tokyo and Nova Scotia. What was the date the newscaster gave in Japanese? Was it yesterday's? She listened hard for anything she could understand. A word came through clearly. One she understood: *bakuhatsu*: explosion. And *niju-roku nin*: twenty-six people.

## HELMET WITH LAMP

Arvel put the last piece of toast into his mouth and drank warm, milky tea to soften the toast. "I gotta get up to that grave, anyway," he said. He walked into the porch and put on his parka and heavy boots. He stopped at the door and turned to face his father, who stood backlit and grim-faced in the doorway to the kitchen.

"You ever point a gun at me, old man, it better be loaded and you'd better pull the trigger. That's just some advice." Arvel turned his back on his father and walked to the end of the driveway. Even the rich black of the sky was different, was better. You could look up there and you'd know something about life. On a clear night you had the delicate patterns of stars. In overcast you got the town's reflection of itself. The black overhead in the pit was meaningless, and it went on forever through the rock. His brother, Ziv, said lighting the pit with a cap lamp was like trying to get through a hurricane with a candle.

Ziv hadn't lasted in the pit. One shift and he was out. His brother thought of himself as a coward for not staying, but sometimes it took as much courage not to do things as it did to do them, and that's what Arvel admired about Ziv: he did only what he wanted to do. He wanted to go to university, so he went. He wanted to quit university, so he did. He wanted to work in the pit, then he wanted to stop working in the pit. If everyone hired at the Eastyard mine had quit after a single shift, things could have been different underground.

Unlike his brother, Arvel didn't feel he knew how to get out of anything. His life now existed beyond his ability to control it. The problems he and Jackie were having seemed unsolvable; his job was murdering his spirit. If he had any guts, he'd get out of all of it. He'd move to Halifax, which is where Jackie wanted to go. He'd get a job out west, working in a hard-rock mine that wasn't seething with methane. He'd get an electrician's job, something he was actually trained for. He'd start all over out there, where nobody knew anything about him.

All he had in his life that he took any enjoyment from was this short walk outside in the fresh air, and this ended in his arrival at the pit. There was nothing in any way scenic or beautiful about the walk, but it was a stroll outside under the sky and in the air. Since he'd been working in the pit, where the feeling of being enclosed was extreme, any time outside had become precious to him.

But recently the walk to the pit had become haunted. Every step reminded him of a dream he'd had. It was a dream about walking to a pit, and since he'd had the dream, his walk to the Eastyard site had been charged with flashes of dream pictures.

His alarm goes off just before six. He wakes up, pulls on a pair of work pants and a shirt, picks up a lunch can, and walks out into the streets of the Red Row. The backyards are dotted with outhouses and coal sheds. A plume of black smoke rises from every chimney. The unpaved streets are full of men dressed like him, each carrying a lunch pail under his arm. The year is 1928, thirty-four years before Arvel will be born.

At the bottom of Hudson Street, Arvel meets his grandfather, his mother's father. He is the same age as Arvel, and even though he died at seventy, when Arvel was only ten, Arvel recognizes him immediately by the thick glasses that blur his eyes huge, and by the big forehead, a trait Arvel has inherited, that rises above his glasses.

"Good morning, Didu," Arvel says.

"Good morning, boy," says the grandfather. His accent is so heavy that Arvel can hardly understand. He has lived in Canada for less than ten years, Arvel realizes, and he came without a word of English.

"It's a beautiful morning," Arvel says. From the street, he looks in through the window of his grandfather's kitchen and sees his grandmother, six months pregnant with his mother. In less than twenty-five years this woman will be dead from tuberculosis, but this morning she appears as vigorous as any woman her age. She is washing apples under the water pump at the sink, working the handle up and down.

"All begin beautiful, boy," Arvel's grandfather says.

As they walk together to the pit, their leather boots crunch the gravel of the unpaved streets. In the clear air of morning, they can hear the wheels and gears of the elevator working in the shaft.

When they pass through the gates and into the mine yard, Arvel's heart jumps. He has only seen this place in pictures. By the time he is born, the coal boom will have passed and most of the operations will be shut down. But these buildings before him, this smokestack, the wheels

67

*that turn on the big lift: these have been written on his mind by some-*
*thing stronger than memory.*

*"You're frightened, boy," his grandfather says. "I won't tell you not*
*to be."*

*In the change house they don what they'll need for work. The boots,*
*the coveralls, the gloves. They check out their equipment from the tool*
*room. The hard hats, the lamps, the shovels, the axes. They gather with*
*the rest of the day-shift men at the mouth of the shaft, smoke final cig-*
*arettes. The sun splits down on them in rays between the beams and*
*cables and pipes that run in all directions above their heads.*

*The wheels on the giant elevator turn. A dozen men before them*
*walk onto the platform and drop from sight. Arvel and his grandfather*
*move ahead, and twelve more descend. Cables quiver. A platform*
*swings into view. "I wish this could be different," the grandfather says.*
*Two men remain. They step forward and disappear from the surface of*
*the earth.*


His grandfather Staciw had been a survivor of the mines. He'd
worked his whole life in the pit and lived to see his retirement.
The work had killed him nonetheless: he'd suffered chronic
debilitating health problems in the time he'd survived after
retirement, each year spending at least a month in the hospital,
and suffering almost monthly from what Arvel's mother called
"turns," violent convulsions that led to unconsciousness.

His grandfather had probably counted himself lucky nonetheless. He'd been born into debt to a peasant family in southern
Ukraine and had come to Canada before the Bolshevik Revolution
to get a job and buy his family out of economic servitude. So
however miserable his life in Canada, however dangerous the
work, however meagre the pay, he'd always known he was

better-off than he would have been if he'd stayed in Ukraine. After the revolution, he'd lost contact with his family, only getting letters through again during and just after the Khrushchev era. One of Arvel's earliest memories was of a photo his grandfather had received of his village in the Ukraine. It had come in a paper-wrapped package that most of the extended family had gathered in Didu Staciw's kitchen to see opened. It had been one of the first warm days in late spring. The windows and doors were open, letting in the earth smells from the damp garden at the front of the house. Didu was sitting at the kitchen table with a crowd of people standing expectantly around him. He cut the twine from the bundle and folded back the heavy paper wrapping. Inside were some pieces of cloth that Arvel was too young to understand the significance of. The women in the kitchen raised a fuss over these. In a yellow envelope inside the package was a photo of Didu's village. Several stern-looking, bony-faced men and women stood, stuffed into ill-fitting clothing, in front of a small group of farm buildings.

Arvel's father began laughing. "Look at what they're living in," he exclaimed. "Thatched roofs! Holy shit! Welcome to the twentieth century!" Didu pulled the photo from Arvel's father's hand, shouted something at Arvel's father, and stormed into the living room. He sat in the swivel chair and spun his back to the kitchen. Arvel, three, maybe four years old, followed his grandfather into the living room and approached the swivel-based armchair from behind. When he got to the front of the chair, he looked up at his grandfather. The old man was holding the photo close to his face, a few centimetres from his glasses. Behind the thick lenses, his grandfather's eyes were blinking rapidly, tears were pouring freely down the sides of his nose.

The air was dry and cold now and smelled of the frozen earth that had been ploughed up with the snow. Banks of old snow were pushed up on either side of the sidewalk as he made his way up Foord Street. Near the corner of Bridge Avenue, naked trees thrust their frost-whitened branches against the sky. A few ragged wreaths, weather-beaten, face-down, and half-covered with ice and snow, remained on the steps that led up to the war monument, leftovers from Remembrance Day. It could have been last winter that the wind had blown massive drifts over the ridge at the edge of the Anglican graveyard, up behind the monument. He and Ziv and Bundy Burgess and other kids from this end of the Red Row had taken running leaps into the snow, diving headlong into the powder, going so deep that a semi-darkness set in amid the translucent white of the drift. It could have been last winter, but it wasn't. It was more than ten years ago, that day he remembered so well. No, it was more than fifteen years ago. Why did he remember this so clearly, when yesterday and the day before had already gone shapeless in his imagination?

Travelling south from the Red Row, it was only a short distance to the centre of town. Once across Bridge Avenue, a block of tall, square Victorian houses with big front porches and paved driveways quickly gave way to what was once, before the advent of one-stop shopping, the commercial district of Albion Mines. The century-plus-old buildings maintained their commercial appearance: front doors that opened directly onto the sidewalk, large display windows that had once housed samples of merchandise. But commerce had largely left the area. There were still a few banks, a couple of convenience stores. The original cut-stone post-office building still stood, still housed the post office. But many of the buildings, which had once held candy shops, tinsmiths, clothing outlets, hardware stores, now were used as residences.

The Tim Horton's on Foord Street stood out like an alien. With its plate-glass windows, brick and steel construction, paved parking lot, and iridescent plastic and aluminum sign, it was an envoy from another time. This was the unmistakable stamp of the present on the main street of Albion Mines.

Arvel crossed Foord Street and turned up the sidewalk. As he reached the doughnut shop, he crossed the salt-tinged pavement of the parking lot and looked through the front windows. From the back he recognized the square, shaggy head of Gavin Fraser, who'd worked Arvel's shift at the pit until a short time ago. Gavin had been the most vocal member of the shift to try to get some safety improvements at Eastyard. He had connections in the United Mine Workers and, during their certification drive, had put his name down as interim local president. Gavin and not Arvel's father, a man who had worked his whole life for the union movement, was the one who had convinced Arvel to get involved in the drive to certify the United Mine Workers union. As it had turned out, the UMW was a poor choice to organize Eastyard. The UMW represented Devco miners in Cape Breton, and Devco miners had fought the opening of the Eastyard operation, because the mine, once fully operational, would rob Devco of one of its markets: the Pictou County power station.

Despite Arvel's months of work, despite Gavin's assurances to workers, the UMW had lost the vote at Eastyard, and organization was back to square one. Gavin had always been more positive and direct in his approach to certification than Arvel had. Gavin did not have a father who'd spent his life battling anti-union companies and governments. He'd worked in unionized mine operations in central and western Canada and had seen harmonious labour/management relations. He did not assume, as Arvel did, that management would fight tooth and claw against any idea that was not their own. So after the certification vote, Gavin went directly to the Eastyard management with safety concerns. He complained to the shift boss, the supervisor, the underground manager, and had a face-to-face meeting with the vice president and general manager of Eastyard Coal. Gavin had worked in mining operations in Alberta, British Columbia, and Ontario, and was the most knowledgeable of anyone on the shift about how to run a safe mine. He'd drawn up a list of improvements that should have been made to the underground operations, but at his meeting with the general manager the man had not even glanced at the list. He was puffed up with confidence after the failure of the certification vote, and what he told Gavin, after Gavin had spent weeks agitating his way into the office, was simple, and the same thing Gavin had been told by others all the way along: if he didn't like the way the mine was run, he should quit. The man pointed at a filing cabinet in the corner of his office and said, "We've got applications from thousands of guys ready to replace you." Gavin left the general manager's office, walked down the hall to personnel, and put in his notice.

Gavin's experience of trying to solve problems directly after the failure of the union certification vote only convinced Arvel that his own response to the failure, complete despair, had been appropriate.

But after Gavin quit, Arvel had called a contact at the Auto Workers in Halifax and had got the ball rolling to start a new certification drive with a union that was not carrying baggage.

One day, not long after Gavin had left, they arrived at the mouth of a new drift and listened to the roof dripping. Bits and pieces of the chocked rock were clattering down like rain. They'd been working in this drift for a couple of weeks, and there had been two close calls already. The roof was not properly supported, and two good-sized rock falls had just missed men on their crew. They stopped outside the shaft, seven or eight of them from the A-shift, discussing what they should do, when Fred Brennan, the underground manager, had come along.

"What the hell are you doing standing here? Where are you supposed to be working?"

They pointed into the new drift.

"Well get your arses down there."

There was a brief silence. Then Arvel said. "We don't think it's safe. The ground is working. Listen."

Brennan took off his hard hat and smacked it into the floor at his feet. His lamp sprayed light in a crazy beam across the ceiling, then blinked out. Spit came flying from his mouth when he spoke. "Get the Jesus down there and get producing coal or you're all Jesus fired."

At that exact instant, with Brennan pointing right at it, the entire drift collapsed into itself. The noise was deafening and the ground shook. Dust billowed out to the main shaft where they'd been standing, and all the men there began to choke on it, coughing violently.

When the dust began to settle, Brennan's eyes narrowed. He looked at the men before him as though they were guilty of some conspiracy.

"Get a fucking scoop down here and clean this mess up," he said.

When Brennan had gone back up the shaft, they stood without speaking a moment, shaky with fear from the tons of rock they'd just missed being crushed beneath. Arvel looked down at the black-and-grey dust that had gathered on the tops of his boots. "Well, what the hell should we do?" someone said. Arvel realized everyone was looking at him, waiting for him to answer.

"I told you guys what you should have done," Arvel said. He shook his head. "You should have voted to certify the union. If you had, we wouldn't be standing here scared shitless right now. We'd have a safety officer in a meeting with management."

"I *voted* for the union," Steve Jenkins said. Steve was the only man on Arvel's shift who'd been born in Albion Mines. And Steve was Arvel's age, exactly. They'd gone right through school together. Steve's father had worked at the Pepsi plant that Arvel's father had organized, against great opposition and threats of violence from management, in the fifties. Steve had trusted the union drive because of Arvel's involvement in it. But he'd beaten Arvel up once, in Grade 7, before Arvel had reached his present size. So he wasn't beyond standing up to Arvel when he saw the reason and the opportunity. "You're fucking right I voted for the union," Steve went on. "So don't look at me." He was the only one to speak. Everyone else shifted uneasily.

"We have to have a meeting," Steve said.

"A meeting!" said Arvel. "What the Jesus for? A meeting's going to get us sweet fucking nowhere. What we need is to certify a union. You guys need to sign cards and vote for the Auto Workers."

"Sure, maybe in a hundred years that'll do us some good, but what about today? That's going to do piss all *today*."

"You're fucking right it is."

74

"What we need is a safety meeting. And we need one with Gavin."

Arvel shook his head in disbelief. "Jesus, I can save you the trouble. You know what Gavin's going to tell you about safety? Do what he did: quit."

"How many think we need a meeting," Steve said. Everyone's hand went up but Arvel's.

"I'll *come* to a meeting," Arvel said, "Fine, I'll come to the goddamn meeting. But I'm telling you it'll do no good. Gavin's going to tell us to quit. Either that or sign cards with the Auto Workers and *hope* we get to have a certification vote before . . . In the meantime . . ." he mimed throwing his pit cap on the floor and screamed in imitation of Brennan: "*Get a fucking scoop down here and clean this mess up!*"

The next day was a day off, and they gathered at the Tartan at just after noon. It was a Thursday, the place was quiet. Seventeen of the twenty-six men turned up, pulling their cars separately into spaces in the parking lot. All of the single guys had brand-new vehicles: four-by-fours, Toyota pickups with roll bars behind the cabs. The men who were married and who had children made do with whatever vehicle they'd had before getting on at Eastyard. Arvel was the only one who lived close enough to walk, and the vehicles of almost all the other men were already in the parking lot by the time he came striding in from Foord Street.

Entering the Tartan Tavern was like diving into a dirty aquarium: the beverage room was little more than four glass walls and a roof. Light inside came from all four directions, but was dimmed from having filtered through the grime-coated windows. At the far end of the room, the bluish screen of a television set blinked behind its chain-link bottle-deflector. As always, there was the smell of onions frying in cheap fat, though none of the items on the menu ever seemed to contain onions. The men had pushed tables together, end-to-end, and they sat as though at a banquet. Arvel shook his head in exasperation when he saw that, consciously or not, they left the seat at the head of the table empty for Gavin.

"What the fuck Gavin is going to tell us that we don't already know is beyond me," Arvel muttered as he approached the table, but if anyone heard him, they did not answer.

Tommy, the owner of the tavern, and its only employee at this time of day, sat behind the bar with his feet up, watching whatever was on the screen. The only other people in the room were a pair of underage boys, obviously on hook from school, who sat guiltily crouched over their beer glasses at the far side of the snooker tables.

It seemed the others had not been here long, and when Arvel sat down, Tommy came to the table without a word and distributed draft glasses from two trays he held stacked in one hand. Then he went back behind the bar and started filling pitchers from the tap.

Arvel sat back with his glass of draft. He picked up the salt shaker from the centre of the table and dusted the top of his beer. Foam rushed up through the beer as the salt fell through it. Arvel took a drink and looked out the window at the north end of Foord Street. The field across the way was encircled by an off-ramp from the Trans-Canada highway, the grass there tall and brown.

When Gavin entered the room, there was a light around him that Arvel saw shining. It was the light of someone who has exempted himself. He sat at the head of the table, and his erect, fluidly moving body made the men who flanked him appear twisted, self-conscious, and jerky. He was the only one to order food: a beef sandwich. When it arrived, he saw that Tommy hadn't cut it, but instead of sending it back, Gavin pulled it apart with his fingers and ate it. For a while, the men waited for Gavin to speak. They'd been used to letting him lead, to his explaining issues and strategies to them. But of course he had nothing to say. The meeting had not been his idea.

The men had not agreed on anything particular to say, so when they did start speaking, it was each man to his own grievance, from being pressured to work longer hours than the mining act allowed and the dangerous levels of explosive dust in the drifts, to the methane gauges on machinery that had been tampered with and rendered useless.

These were all things that Gavin himself had once educated them about, but if he was growing impatient, he didn't show it. He sat benevolently at the head of the table and nodded at each speaker in turn.

Finally, in frustration, Arvel spoke: "Jesus, Gavin. These guys want to hear you say something."

Gavin laid both palms flat on the table. "I can tell you what you have to do, but every one of you guys already knows. Arvel, you know. You either do what I did and get out, or you wait to die."

There was the secret word: death. All of them could talk freely of accidents and explosions, but no one ever broached the truth. Now that the word had been spoken, it was as if the roof had been lifted off the Tartan Tavern and a gust of air had entered.

"You've got to get a union in, is one thing," Gavin said. He seemed unaffected by the emotion around him in the room. "But you fucked that up by not voting yes the *last* time." Some of the men squirmed in their seats. "That process is going to take months now," Gavin continued. He looked at Arvel. "Arvel has started up with the Auto Workers. You guys are fucking lucky he didn't quit, too. You're lucky he's got the guts to put his neck on the line. And he's willing to do the work that has to be done. But he has to start all over. In the meantime, you got to look at your day-to-day options, and there are two: quit or die."

Steve Jenkins looked at Arvel and shook his head. Arvel wondered what he was thinking. Death again, probably. The thought of death.

"There are two ways to quit," Gavin continued. He picked up his beer and placed it forcefully and as far to the left as his right hand could reach. "You can quit one by one," he said. "In which case management either replaces you one by one, or rearranges the shift each time to do with one or two less men." He picked up the beer glass and transferred it dramatically to the right to mark the other pole of his idea. "Or you can all quit together, in which case management has to act. They've got to clean up or shut down."

"They could replace all twenty-six of us at once, just about overnight," Arvel said. "You know what this economy is like."

Gavin shook his head. "The federal and provincial governments are into this mine for a hundred million dollars. If a whole shift quit together, you'd have the media doing handsprings in a second."

"But what would happen to us?" Someone asked. Arvel looked around at all the grim faces, but could not determine who'd spoken.

"Well, you'd be out of a job, for one thing," Gavin said.

Men were nodding into their beer glasses. At some point, the two underage boys across the room had got up unnoticed and left. At their table now sat two trim middle-aged men in white shirts and blue ties. One man had his tie flipped back over one shoulder to keep it out of his fish and chips. The other man had his shirtsleeves rolled to halfway up his biceps.

Arvel stood up and moved in the direction of the bathroom. The few beer he'd had on an empty stomach had left him feeling woozy and oppressed, as though the air were being squeezed in around him.

When he returned, the atmosphere at the tables had changed. Men were arguing heatedly about what they should do. Gavin's face looked strained. He'd quit his job to get away from the endless, fruitless arguments and worries. "Listen boys," Gavin was saying, though only a few were listening to him, "Listen boys . . ." Arvel knew the next thing Gavin said was going to be goodbye. Arvel stepped up to the edge of a table. "Listen up, now . . ." Arvel said more loudly. The bickering continued. He reached across the table, picked up an almost empty beer pitcher, and emptied it into his glass. "Listen here, now," he shouted. Nothing. He raised the pitcher over the table and brought it down in a swift motion, its thick flat bottom smacking the tabletop, the sound shooting through the room and bouncing off the plate-glass windows.

"My properties!" Tommy shouted from behind the bar.

"Aw cripes!" came a voice from across the room. One of the two men in white shirts had jumped at the noise and knocked his plate of fish and chips onto the floor. Dabs of ketchup were spattered over his white shirt.

"For God's sake will you stop and listen," Arvel said. "Gavin's about to go and I want to say something." Everyone was looking at him. Tommy had come out from behind the bar and was approaching the table where Arvel stood. When he got there he picked up his beer pitcher and inspected it in the light. He ran his hand over the tabletop where the pitcher had hit. He scowled at Arvel and returned to the bar with the pitcher cradled against him like a baby.

"I hope to Jesus," Arvel said, "we can decide what to do. Gavin, you said we could quit one at a time or we could quit all at once. You're right. That's our choice, and every day we don't make that choice is a day closer to the other option. Only with that one, we'll have no choice. If we die, we'll all die together. No one will be left."

Death again. Arvel picked up his beer. Took a drink. "That leaves you, Gavin."

"That leaves me what?" He looked steadily into Arvel's eyes, as though he knew exactly what Arvel was suggesting, but wanted to make him say it.

"You're one of us," Arvel said. He felt himself puffing up, almost patriotically. "But when we go, you'll be the only one left."

"*When* we go," someone piped up. "We went from *if* to *when*. Jesus!"

"Shut up!" someone else said loudly. "Let him finish."

Arvel looked seriously at Gavin. Gavin looked at him and at every other man in the room.

"Just tell people," Arvel said. "Just tell them what it was like. Just tell them what happened."

Gavin nodded.

Arvel remembered that nod as he stood outside the doughnut shop, his breath rising from his mouth in clouds. Through the broad windows, he watched Gavin inside, sitting serenely, nodding his head in the same thoughtful manner. He was like a vision of an otherworldly creature. Since he'd quit at Eastyard, no more than two months ago, his face looked younger than it had in years. His gestures and movements were smooth and relaxed. He sat and listened to the conversation going on around him, his head inclined slightly forward. He narrowed his eyes. He threw his head back and laughed at something someone said. Through its streaked windows, the Tim Horton's emitted cold light into the dark winter night.

I'm quitting, Arvel thought. I'm not going to turn up tonight. To hell with it. He stepped around to the entrance and walked through the first set of doors. He stood in the semi-warmth of the storm entrance and watched the little crusts of snow fall from the sides of his boots into the grating, then turned back and continued up the street toward the mine.

Something had changed in the atmosphere among the men on their shift. They barely spoke to one another, and when they did speak, it was only about things not related to the mine: curling or hockey or hunting. When a sparking engine or a miner whose methane detectors had been disconnected flared blue momentarily in a pocket of gas, or when several men were trudging through fuel-soaked explosive dust that was halfway up their shins, or when a foreman or manager ordered them to continue using damaged equipment, the men no longer spoke about these things. They clamped their jaws and shook their heads.

The change room was full as Arvel got into his working clothes: coveralls, boots, hard hat. He remembered a film he'd seen in junior high called *The Productive Classroom*. According to the film, the productive classroom was a silent one. Each student was hunched over an open notebook. The sound of pencils scratching paper, and occasionally the sound of a pencil being sharpened: these were the only sounds in the productive classroom. In the productive change room, there was the ripping sound of laces being pulled tight in stiff leather boots. Zippers were being zipped, snaps snapped. Buckles and cinches and Velcro closures were being pulled at and folded over.

Arvel held his hard hat in one hand and looked at it strangely before he put it on.

His hard hat, the one he held at arm's length every day and examined before putting on, the simplest piece of safety equipment he owned, and one he could have used every day without thought, was an emblem for him. It was like a fossil retrieved from the prehistoric, black-and-white world of his grandparents. But it wasn't like a fossil at all, because fossils were impressions of bygone worlds, and as though having slipped through a hatch in a sci-fi movie, Arvel's pre-past, the world of his grandparents, had been transported forward through time. The helmet with lamp connected him to his own childhood, in which he used to dream of having such a piece of headgear to play with. It connected him to a past he'd been told was over. When he'd started school, it was the late sixties. He was the tail end of the baby-boom generation. His teachers were the front end of the same boom, and they taught the kids to expect everything. The teachers said Arvel and his friends were the luckiest generation ever. They'd never known economic hardship, they'd never known war. They were the children of industrial workers whose twenty years of pay raises had lifted them from impoverished childhoods into the lower reaches of the middle class. By the time he graduated, the teachers were feeling sorry for the students they were sending off into the world. They were the least-fortunate generation of the century. Industries were shrinking, the job market was disappearing. They would be the first North American generation to fare worse than their parents.

*Miner's helmet with lamp*. These words had been typed in black on a white file card under a glass display case at the old Albion Mines Miner's Museum up the hill from the Albion Field ballpark. He and his friend Billy Michaels from the Heights spent two or three weeks' worth of afternoons one spring going into the museum after school. The main purpose of each visit was to sign a false name in the guest book. Name: Jesus Christ. Date of Visit: 24 A.D. Remarks: I am the way, the truth, and the life. Name: Bobby Orr. Date of visit: May 1, 1971. Remarks: I wish I could play for the Albion Mines Royals. Ha! Ha! The last time they'd gone, Billy had just written Adolf Hitler under *Name*, when the museum's caretaker clamped the two boys around the neck with his bony hands. They both wiggled free and bolted out the door. The old man was George Hannah, a retired miner, a survivor of the Allan Shaft explosion of 1935, a decorated veteran of two wars, a man who wore his Royal Canadian Legion uniform daily, beret clamped over his white, bald head, medals and ribbons pinned stiffly to the breast of the jacket. He chased them halfway down Park Street, shouting: "No respect for the dead! No respect for the dead!"

In the time before the caretaker caught on to their silly forgeries, they'd seen a lot of the museum. There were dusty frames full of black-and-white photos. White men, their faces blackened with dust, black men, skin coloured darker, staring steel-eyed at the camera. Some men, unable to stand still for the seconds-long exposures, were smears of black and grey, identified in the accompanying lists of names with a question mark. The pictures of the town of Albion Mines showed streets very different from the ones Arvel knew. Many of the buildings were the same, but time had changed the names of the businesses decorating their fronts, had turned the dirt sidewalks to concrete. When Arvel was a boy, when he was visiting the miner's museum, the coal pits of Pictou County were all but closed. The McBean mine in Thorburn closed when he was nine or ten. There was a working pit in Westville, but the mining days depicted in the photos at the museum, when trolleys ran through the busy streets and thousands of men were employed underground, those days were gone.

The equipment on display at the museum was of special interest. The pieces were like the relics of a lost civilization. There were instruments that had been designed for procedures no longer carried out. Lamps and picks and shovels and buckets, and hundreds of nameless items for which Arvel could not have imagined a use. But the black pit caps with lamps affixed, these held a special fascination, because a ten-year-old boy could think of immediate uses. He imagined himself with the helmet on his head, lamp alight, running through the dark backyards of the Red Row, lighting the ground before him like a locomotive.

He tucked the pit cap under his arm and headed across the change room for the door. Halfway there he ran into Gerry Taylor, who was just coming up from the night shift. Gerry's face, his hands, and the front of his coveralls were smeared black with coal dust. Sweat had plastered it especially thick just above his eyes. There were streaks sideways across his forehead where he'd tried to wipe the dust away. He shook his head at Arvel going past.

"What?" Arvel said.

"You don't want to know," Gerry said. He started taking off his coveralls.

"You better tell me," Arvel said.

"They got the fucking methanometer at the miner disconnected."

"Why?"

"Why do you think? The methane levels are so high, the fucking thing keeps gassing out."

"What's Brennan say about it?"

"Brennan! What's that guy ever say: 'Get the fuck back to work.'" Taylor turned his furious face away from Arvel and headed toward the showers.

When Arvel stepped outside, there was a tractor parked at the portal to the number-one deep that already had six men on it waiting to go down. Arvel paused for a moment and looked at the machine. He exhaled sharply, shook his head, then jumped onto the platform at the back of the tractor as it took off down the decline. So much ice had built up on the floor of the twenty-five degree decline that, even on the way down, the tires were having trouble getting a footing.

The tractor bounced and hopped on the uneven floor. It slid sideways into an arch and a couple of sparks flew off the fender.

"Get ready for the fourth of July," said Steve Jenkins, who was right beside Arvel and had seen the sparks too. Arvel rolled his eyes, and neither of them smiled.

There was debris piled up on either side of the number-one deep, but once they passed the number-three crosscut, it got worse. Roof bolts, oily rags, sheets of plastic, empty hydraulic fluid containers, all things that according to the Coal Mines Regulation Act should not have been there. Once in a while there was a little brown splat that was recognizable as human shit.

There was an accumulation of explosive coal dust on the floor of the deep the whole way down, but once they got into the east section, where most of the mining was taking place, the dust was drifted up like black snow. The tractor stopped when they turned onto the number-twelve road. With the tractor engine shut off, the corridor was relatively quiet. There was the background hum of the ventilation system and a faint rumble of machinery from somewhere. Their mouths picked up the grit of the stirred dust from the floor and it mixed with the fading taste of diesel exhaust from the tractor.

As they began piling off the machine, they saw a light coming toward them from down the number-twelve. It was Albert Moss, the supervisor. He always chewed Juicy Fruit gum, and started every statement with *All right, boys*.

"All right, boys," he said, when he got to the front of their tractor. His dentures clacked as he chewed his gum. He gave them their job assignments. "Fuck," Arvel said when he got his. He'd been promoted to second operator of the miner. Months ago, when he'd just started, this would have seemed like an exciting chance. The miner was where the real production was taking place, where coal was being torn away from the face and conveyored back to a shuttle car. As second operator he would be a step away from the operator's compartment itself. And running that big, important machine was a challenge he had once looked forward to.

But with the methanometer disconnected, the miner would be a hazard. And in this particular drift, they had been instructed to save some time by not bolting the roof over the miner. This unsafe practice had become so commonplace at Eastyard that hardly anyone seemed to give it a second thought. They'd cut six feet off the face, put in a set of arches, and cut six more feet off the face. The bolter would come in behind them, drilling holes into the roof, inserting resin tubes in the holes, and bolting in place the big mesh screens that would catch a lot of the ground that fell. He'd been working back at the bolter for a few days now, and though using that machine was no picnic either, at the bolter you were at least working under a supported roof.

John MacDonald was the miner operator for the shift. Arvel stood back by the trailing cable and waited for MacDonald, who'd come down on a different tractor.

"Methanometer's been fucked with," Arvel said when he saw MacDonald come round the bend in the number-twelve. MacDonald spat tobacco juice onto his own boot and kicked absently at the trailing cable. The plug in his jaw stood out like an abscess.

"What do you mean, *fucked with*?"

"Disconnected."

MacDonald glanced at the idle miner. "Gassing out?"

"I met Gerry Taylor up on the surface. They used it that way all last shift."

MacDonald shook his head. They both looked back up the drift to where the bolter crew was getting ready to start.

"What about this thing?" MacDonald gave the vent tube a boot.

"Working, I guess," Arvel said.

"And she's still gassing out?"

"According to Gerry."

MacDonald reached two fingers into his mouth and pulled out the plug of tobacco he'd been sucking on. It oozed red-black juice into his palm a moment before he threw it angrily against the wall.

"Aw, fuck!" he said. He wiped his hand against his overalls. "This is typical. Do we operate this fuse while we're in this cannon barrel, or do we get screamed at and maybe fired?"

Arvel looked at him, shook his head, and shrugged.

"I say we get screamed at," MacDonald said after a long pause.

"It's all the same to me," Arvel said. "We can start now on our own, or we can start later with Brennan screaming at us like a big fat baboon."

MacDonald had already tucked his gloves into the side pocket of his coveralls and headed back up the drift. He got back on the tractor he'd ridden to the face, and set off up the drift to look for Albert Moss. Arvel sat on the idle bolter with the bolter crew and waited for him to come back.

"You know exactly what's gonna happen," said Steve Jenkins. The rest of the crew sat reclined as well as they were able in their respective places and did not respond. Around them the hum of the ventilation system and the roar of machines being operated a short distance up the ramp vibrated against the walls.

"He won't come back here with Moss," Jenkins continued. "He'll find Moss, Moss will tell him to find Brennan, Brennan will come down here and have a seizure, and the absolute most he'll do will be to reconnect the methanometer and block the vent tube at the bolter. Which'll make *us* first to fry instead of *you*," Jenkins indicated Arvel.

It was an hour and ten minutes before the tractor reappeared. Brennan was behind the wheel. John MacDonald stood behind him, holding onto the back of the seat. The tractor lurched to a halt and Brennan's fat body came flying off of it, arms flailing in rage.

"I can't . . . I can't . . ." Brennan said, choking on his anger. "I cannot fucking believe what I'm seeing. You fucking bunch of worthless pieces of shit punched in over an hour and a half ago and you've been sitting on your arses ever since!" Brennan's face was scarlet. Saliva dripped out the corners of his mouth. "Why don't you just sign on for pogey, like you've done all your worthless lives, and sit in your fucking living rooms doing nothing."

Arvel stood up. Brennan instinctively backed up a step in the face of this mass of muscle and bone. "Why don't *you* operate that fucking miner without a methanometer," Arvel said.

Brennan clenched and unclenched his fists. He went back to the tractor and took a handheld methanometer from a bag. Arvel stood near him as he took a reading: 3.75 per cent. Close to the explosive range. Without looking up at any of the men, Brennan said, his voice strangely calm, "Reconnect the meter." He walked over to the end of the vent tube near the bolter. Arvel saw Steve Jenkins roll his eyes. "We'll need extra suction at the face, so block this tube and get the fuck to work."

"So we're not going to vent the bolter," Arvel said.

"No need to vent both machines," Brennan replied. He was already halfway to the tractor, his back to the crew.

"The gas'll build up back here," Arvel said.

"The tube at the face will draw it forward," Brennan said. He was not looking anyone in the eye.

"The bolter's got no methanometer on it."

Brennan started up the tractor. It sparked to life and immediately began making a soft knocking and a sort of muffled pinging-buzzing sound, the little complaints that an oxygen-starved diesel engine made in a methane-contaminated atmosphere.

Arvel ran ahead to the tractor and jumped up beside Brennan. Brennan's face went white and he flinched backwards, as though he expected Arvel to hit him.

Arvel placed one hand in the centre of Brennan's back. The other he placed over the top of both of Brennan's hands where they gripped each other at the crest of the steering wheel. Arvel looked down to where his big left hand was almost as massive as both of Brennan's hands together. Then he looked into Brennan's eyes. "If we get killed down here," Arvel said. The tip of his nose was almost touching the tip of Brennan's. He had the man's full attention for the first time ever. "Don't expect me back next shift." Arvel hopped down from the tractor and began to laugh. Brennan gave him a startled look, put the tractor in gear, and sped away.

# PART TWO

1982

# A HANDICAP OF PLACE

Ziv looked at the stack of textbooks on the shelf above the desk in his residence room. At the beginning of the term, his first at university, he'd been overwhelmed by the amount of work he was expected to do. The reading list for one term of a single course was more than he'd had to do in all of high school. It had seemed impossible. Now, with two of his exams written already and only a week to go before his first term was over, he had a great feeling of accomplishment. He'd tackled that impossible mound of work, and for the most part, had conquered it.

The smell in the residence was of disinfectant and barely masked carpet mould. In late afternoon, he sat at the desk before a pile of class notes and texts whose pages were stained yellow with Hi-Liter pen and looked out the window at the last glint of light from a short December day. He'd only ever lived in one house before, only ever had one bedroom window, so he was struck with the difference a simple change of scenery made. What he noticed was light. He'd never noticed that before: that you could tell what time of year it was just by the quality of the light. In September the air began thinning out. Everything leaned northward. Some colours got more noticeable, more brilliant. By now the leaves had turned and fallen, there had already been several sprinklings of snow, and the span of light in a day was almost as short as it would get. Colours had slowly drained from the scene outside his residence-room window. Everything had lapsed into brown or dull grey.

Elsewhere on campus, there were craggy trees that covered the lawns with deep shade in the early fall. But on this newly developed corner of the university's real estate, the trees were all under ten years old, and in winter stuck out of the ground like spindly broom handles, barely taller than most students.

Someone knocked. He looked at his watch. Could it be six thirty already? He opened the door on Meta and was surprised by her appearance. In high school she had always seemed a bit dull or frowzy, dishevelled, stooped at an odd angle. It had been this awkwardness or uncertainty that had first attracted Ziv. But here she stood in the hallway of his residence smiling confidently, her frame erect, her hair brushed back, silken and glowing from her forehead. She wore a purple-and-black knit coat with brass buttons she'd bought as a joke at Frenchy's, but had later decided to wear.

"Oh God," Ziv said. "Look at you." He threw himself face-down on his bed.

"What?" said Meta. She closed the door and folded her coat over the back of a chair. She sat where Ziv had been sitting.

"You look like you belong in an Ivory commercial."

Meta laughed. "Healthy-looking! Are you calling me healthy-looking?" she said.

"You won't even take a proper insult," Ziv said. "Nothing sticks!"

"Can I help it if university agrees with me?" She stood up and did a mock soft-shoe routine. "Tappety-ta. Tappety-ta. Tappety-tappety-tappety-ta."

Ziv pulled the pillow over his head, tucked it in at his ears.

"That's right, close your eyes and cover your ears. Happiness is contagious. If you're not careful, you might get infected." She threw herself on top of him and tried to wrestle the pillow away. "I'm going to ruin you," she said. "I'm bent on construction and positivism."

Ziv turned over and embraced her. He lay still and let her weight push him down into the bed. Everything about her excited him: her warmth, her glowing skin, the smell of her hair. He moved a hand under her shirt and let it rest on the smooth skin at the small of her back.

"Wait a minute," she said.

"I love the way you feel," he said. "I love everything about you." He slid his hand higher until it rested at the clasp of her bra.

"Wait a minute!" she said. She sat up. "We're going to the library to study Sociology, remember?"

"There are some other studies I'd like to do here first," he said. He sat up, put both arms around her, and kissed her on the mouth.

"Look," she said, drawing back from him. "There are things we have to do. It's the middle of exams. There's work to be done. I can't let myself get distracted."

Ziv laughed and lowered his head to the pillow. He brought his hands up and put them underneath his head. "Sex is a distraction from work?" he said. "You've got it backwards." She was kneeling beside him on the bed. Hair that was not pinned back at the sides fell forward over her ears and down either cheek. Her breasts made soft mounds beneath her sweatshirt.

"There are things I want to get done at the library tonight." She settled back to explain, placing a hand on his lower thigh, just above the knee.

"I've got to finish studying that Soc." He put his hand on the back of hers and pulled it halfway up his thigh. "There's a History article on reserve I was supposed to read in October." He brushed her cheek with the backs of his fingers, then scooped the fingers around to the back of her neck and gently massaged the muscles there. She moved her head sideways and closed her eyes to enjoy the massage.

"And I want to get at least a start on the research for that Psychology paper I have to have done for next term." She placed her palm firmly on the swelling in his jeans. With her free hand she undid the buckle of his belt and unhooked the button of his pants.

She stood up at the side of the bed and slid her jeans and panties to the floor. She looked at her watch as she stepped matter-of-factly from the discarded clothing. "It's twenty to seven now," she said. "By seven thirty I'm going to be sitting in a cubicle on the second floor of the library, reading."

———————

Most of the other young women in her residence complained about the noise in the building, but it was the relative quiet that Meta was having a difficult time getting used to. She had grown up in one end of a Red Row miner's duplex, a house built by the

Acadia Coal Company in the early part of the century. In their own half of the house, Meta and her family did their best to live quietly and peaceably. But they shared the place with the Donat family, one of the largest, poorest, and rowdiest families in the neighbourhood. Meta's parents had painted the clapboard on their side of the house three times, in Meta's memory, but in all the years they'd lived there the Donats had never painted theirs. According to Meta's grandmother, that side of the house had been coated with whitewash in the year it was built, but never saw a lick of paint again. The clapboard on the Donat side of the house was so bare and weather-beaten that it was hard to believe there had once even been that one white-washing. The Donats had let the grass grow wild so many summers running that there was now very little grass left in their yard at all. Big thistle shrubs, burdocks, and giant dande-lions flourished in patches and clumps. Amongst these, there was the odd patch of grass, gone to seed by mid-season. But most of the yard was bare, hard-packed earth that after years of being heedlessly trampled underfoot had long given up on nourishing life.

There had always been small incidents with the Donat kids, beginning when Meta was a toddler and a couple of the bigger kids turned the garden hose on her as she sat outdoors in her playpen. There were the toys broken, the toys that disappeared, the toys stolen and sold to someone at the other end of the neighbourhood. She'd been punched in the teeth, kicked in the shin, she'd been shot at with elastic guns, homemade zip shooters, and pellet guns. At thirteen, she'd been held down by two of the older Donat boys while the third grabbed and pinched her newly developing breasts.

The Donat parents fought like animals. Her whole life Meta grew up listening to them through the walls. One morning at breakfast a particularly violent shouting match between the parents had started over money. The father had been out of work long enough that his unemployment insurance had run out.

"Who gets the welfare cheque every month and then spends it like it was piss!" His voice came pulsing into the Nicholses' kitchen so that Meta and her mother and her father all stopped chewing in mid-bite to wait for the answer.

"You!" came the reply in chorus, the whole family joining in, ganging up on the father.

One winter morning before school Meta had gone next door to call on Tammy Donat, who was one year younger than she was. The Donat kids were slouched silently over their toast and tea. Mrs. Donat was at the stove, scraping scrambled eggs off the frying pan. Mr. Donat was out-of-sight in the pantry, but his enraged voice careened off the walls in the kitchen. Meta felt a rush of fear enter her chest.

"I bought the fucking thing, and I put it in this fucking pantry, and if it's not here now, woman, you'll fucking well find it."

Mrs. Donat's calm but forceful reply: "You were drunk when you bought it and you were drunk when you put it away. I'll not take responsibility for where it is. Why don't you ask Captain Morgan to find it for you?"

At this, a burst of encouraging laughter from the kids.

Meta stood with her back to the door that led directly from the kitchen to the backyard. She drew herself back farther, away from the terrible words being spoken in the room, until her heels and shoulders pressed against the wooden door itself. Her breath caught in her throat at the sight of Mr. Donat rushing from the pantry. His jaw and neck were covered with thick black stubble. He was naked to the waist, the bones and sinews showing on his thin, alcohol-ravaged body. Without a word, he rounded the corner into the kitchen, stepped up to Mrs. Donat at the stove, and drove a solid punch to the side of her head, just below the ear. She went down to the floor without making a sound, and he stormed back into the pantry.

Reggie, the oldest boy, who must have been sixteen or seventeen at the time, stood up at the table and made a move for the pantry. From her position on the floor, Mrs. Donat held up a hand to stop him. She shook her head briefly and Reggie sat back down. Mrs. Donat pushed herself to her feet and opened the drawer under the oven. After clanging through several items, she selected a large cast-iron frying pan.

Meta heard one of the kids, perhaps Reggie, say, "Watch out, old man." But it was barely audible in the kitchen, and the man raving in the pantry never would have heard it.

Mrs. Donat weighed the cast-iron pan at the end of her arm for a moment, then thought better of it. She replaced the cast-iron pan in the drawer and withdrew a large stainless-steel saucepan. She held the handle of the saucepan in both hands, went to the doorcasing at the entrance to the pantry, and raised the pan to her shoulder like a baseball bat.

"Hey, shit-for-brains!" she yelled. The noise and cursing from the pantry ceased. Kids at the breakfast table snickered and fidgeted. "Get your skinny arse out here." Meta put a hand on the doorknob. It clicked at her touch, but she was so stricken with fear that she could bring herself to move no farther.

Like all skilled batters, Mrs. Donat knew how to wait. She did not swing at the first glimpse of the hollow-cheeked face coming through the doorway. She held back until he was a half-step into the kitchen, and then she cut loose.

The sound of the pan hitting Mr. Donat's face was like a home run with a metal bat. When the high metallic *ping* ceased ringing through the kitchen, Mr. Donat was unconscious on the floor. His nose had once hooked slightly left, but now it was flattened, smeared up the right cheek halfway to his eye. Beside his face, a dark pool of blood was beginning to collect. In and near the pool of blood there were whitish fragments: teeth and pieces of teeth.

Mrs. Donat trembled only slightly. She walked to the sink, washed the blood off the bottom of the pan, examined the size of the dent in the stainless steel, and replaced the pan in the drawer beneath the oven.

A profound silence came over the kitchen, a silence in which the faces of the Donat children took on a beatific aspect. Mrs. Donat took her place at the head of the table and took a few sips from a cup of milky tea.

A sound arose from somewhere in the room. Meta looked at the kids at the table, at Mrs. Donat. She took a quick look at Mr. Donat on the floor and wondered whether he was dead. At this thought the sound in the room grew louder, and Meta realized she was crying.

It didn't take much of an imagination, especially once she got into school and met kids from all the different neighbourhoods of Albion Mines, for Meta to realize that being from the Red Row, she suffered from a strange sort of handicap. There was poverty and desperation and violence just about anywhere, but it was concentrated in the Red Row. It was so thick there, it formed its own horizon, one that at times was impossible to see beyond.

Meta understood how lucky she was. The fact that she was discontented with the neighbourhood meant that somehow she had been offered a glimpse beyond that impossible horizon. She did not have a clear notion of the world beyond the Red Row, so it was not a pull from a softer, more welcoming world that propelled her. It was everything in the Red Row that she'd learned to fear and hate that pushed her out.

The final boost had come just the summer before. She'd graduated from high school and been accepted at university for the fall. The Donat house had gradually quieted over the years as the parents were slowed down by physical wounds and the mellowing of internal pains that comes with age. In the late winter, Willy Donat, one of three children still living at home, had been caught shoplifting at the new mall in New Glasgow, violating the probation he was on from an earlier offence. He had eluded the custody of the store detective in Woolco before the police had arrived, and a judge, a man reputed to dislike probation in the first place, ordered Willy *in absentia* to serve the remaining four months of his sentence in prison.

Willy was classified by the police as "at large," although the police and everyone else knew he was living at home, escaping through a window any time the police showed up to arrest him.

Meta's bedroom window looked out over the roof of the ell that contained the kitchens of both families. The room on the other side of the wall, in the Donat house, was a bathroom. Several times that spring, she'd lain in bed and heard Willy scrambling out his bathroom window and across the kitchen roof when the police had shown up at the front door. But once, in mid-summer, when for several nights in a row Meta's family had left all the windows open to cool the house off overnight, she heard the police pounding at the Donat front door. She woke up and looked at the LED display of her alarm clock. It was two thirty in the morning. The police must have finally grown tired of chasing him and decided to actually catch him. The pounding came again, and this time, from the other side of the building, she heard a deep voice giving some sort of command. The only word she heard plainly was "police." Through the wall she heard a great crash. Someone had run into something, knocked something over.

There was a scraping sound as Willy Donat climbed through his bathroom window. Meta sat up in bed and clutched a blanket around her. The sudden clamour stirred her senses and set her heart pounding. A street light out on Foord Street lit the curtains in her room faintly. She heard Willy run to the lower edge of his own kitchen roof.

"Fuck," he said. His feet pounded the roof again. She saw a shadow pass before her window as he ran across to her family's side.

"Hands in the air," someone said, and suddenly a floodlight lit up the window, brighter than daytime.

"Fuck you," Meta heard Willy say, and the next thing was the sound of the screen on her storm window tearing and Willy's dark torso protruding into her bedroom.

Meta opened her mouth to scream, but her throat had dried up and all that came out was a dull croak. Willy heard the croak and called to her. "Meta!" he said. The floodlights had switched on his day vision and now he was blind in the dark. She heard him stumbling into things.

"Meta!" For some reason he was whispering, as though his whereabouts were still unknown to someone. "Meta! For Christ's sake, turn on a light!"

"Willy Donat, you arsehole," she said. "Get the hell out of my house." She wrapped the bedsheet around her, tucking it in at the front.

"If you turn on a light, I'll be able to find the goddamned door."

Meta knelt on the bed and began fumbling around on the shelf above the headboard.

"I will, like hell," she said. She found the handle of her tennis racquet and swung it at Willy's silhouette.

The nylon mesh boinged off the crown of his head. "What the hell was that?" Willy said. She could see him more clearly now. He was stooped over at the foot of the bed, both hands on the edge of the mattress for balance while he waited for his eyes to adjust. She turned the racquet sideways in her palm so that the wooden frame would be what made contact this time, and let go with a forehand where she thought the top of his neck would be.

A deep sound came out of him and there was a thump as he landed on the floor. Footsteps pounded up the stairs and the bedroom door burst open. Two Albion Mines police officers burst in, guns drawn. In the light from the lamp in the hallway, Meta saw Willy Donat sitting on the floor at the foot of her bed. He held both hands to his head. Blood trickled from his left ear.

"Put your hands up," one of the police officers said.

"For Christ's sake," Willy said. "I'm unarmed. This crazy bitch just whacked me."

The second officer looked at the racquet in Meta's hand, then back to the bleeding man on the floor. "Fifteen-love," he said, and both officers began to laugh.

It seemed odd to Meta when she heard young women in her university residence complaining about noise, or about how the building lacked security, even when the main entrance was locked at midnight. People could turn up the stereos and drink beer until 2:00 a.m. three nights a week and blast the TV in the lounge. For Meta, not having people inflicting hospitalizing injuries on each other on the other side of the wall, not having a pursued criminal fumbling through her bedroom in the dark, these were signs that her life had reached a sort of tranquility she'd never known, but always suspected was possible.

Her roommate was a Celtic Studies major from Ottawa, a thin-faced girl with pale skin and legs that seemed to reach up to her armpits. She'd grown up in the Glebe, an old Ottawa neighbourhood. Her parents had moved there from Cape Breton to work for the government.

Julia had dark, soft hair that she brushed one hundred strokes every night before she went to bed. She'd spent years doing competitive Highland dancing and kept her kilts and blouses and dancing shoes hanging at one end of the closet as though she might need them in an emergency. When they'd be drinking on the weekends, she'd sometimes rush back to their room from whatever part of the building they were in, put on her kilt and her dancing shoes, and go dancing about the building, throwing her long arms over her head in graceful arcs, leaping and kicking higher than seemed possible.

Julia said she was a virgin, and she was fascinated by Meta's relationship with Ziv. Meta told her everything. What did she care? The most surprising thing about sex, she said, was how messy it was. Sperm got all over everything, and a vagina secreted a shocking amount of liquid. These were things you didn't get an inkling of from books or movies. If you wanted to have sex, Meta told her roommate, you had to have access to soap, running water, and some good absorbent towels.

One night after a lot of drinks at the campus bar, Meta had had to help Julia walk back to their residence room. The two had stumbled across the campus with their arms around each other, singing and yelling and hooting.

When they got inside the room, Meta had dropped Julia onto her bed, where she landed with a thump. Meta tripped over the leg of the bed in the dark, and found herself lying on top of Julia. Before Meta had a chance to move, Julia's hand came up and pulled Meta's face down to hers. She kissed Meta solidly on the lips, a deep, passionate kiss. Meta was surprised at the kiss, but even more surprised that her own mouth opened in response. She lowered herself to Julia's mouth and they kissed slowly and deeply for a few moments. When they paused for a breath, Meta said, "I've got to get to sleep." She fell onto her own bed and passed out instantly. Afterward, neither of them spoke about what had happened.

# A Sharp Eye for Fabric

The baby was asleep. Thank God for that. Arvel sat on the couch in front of the TV and finished the third cup of his second pot of tea for the day. By the time he'd drunk this much tea, he was not enjoying it any more. He only tasted the bitterness now, no matter how much milk he diluted it with. But tea was all he dared drink, and he gulped it compulsively, as though he were trying to get drunk quickly from it. Last week Jackie had come home early from her shift at the store to find him drinking beer in the middle of the afternoon. She'd threatened him then. The threat had not been of anything specific, but Jackie had a way of making herself clear. In high school she'd got high marks in English.

"Don't threaten me," Arvel had said.

"I'm not threatening you."

"What the hell are you doing, then?"

"I was stating a fact: I will not be married to a drunk."

"What do you mean, 'You won't be married . . .' You're married to me, and whatever the hell I am, that's what you're married to."

"A drunk is not the only thing I won't be married to. But don't worry. I'll always let you know what you're turning into."

He emptied the teapot into the cup and went to the window. The apartment was on the second floor, and because the building was positioned at the top of a hill, he could see out over the weed-ridden field, and could take in almost the whole Red Row at a glance. The sky was overcast, tingeing everything with a chill greyness. Grey branches of leafless elms and poplars and maples stuck up from between houses in a tangled mesh that hung in the lifeless air like a haze. Smoke rose in columns from the chimneys of the houses that used wood heat. For a moment, he could not bear to turn around and look at the shabby, half-furnished apartment he was living in. When he was younger, he never dreamed he'd look at a Red Row house and envy the people who lived in it. He'd always assumed he was headed right out of there and into something better.

The building they lived in was a converted school. When he had been growing up, it had been empty for several years, since the first phase of the new elementary school had been built. People his age had called the building the Catholic School, and the wide pathway, actually an old street that had never been paved and had been closed off to traffic, they called the Catholic School Path. Both school and path hearkened back to the days of parochial education in Nova Scotia. His parents, for some reason, had gone to the Catholic schools in Lourdes, at the other end of the Red Row, and people of their generation called this building St. Bridget's.

There was a sense in which living in St. Bridget's was an improvement over living in a Red Row house. Since the building had been completely renovated less than ten years ago, the walls were of convenient drywall, instead of the brittle, old crack-prone plaster of the Red Row houses. Walls and floors and corners were all square and true, making wallpaper easy and hanging pictures a snap.

Hasty workmanship to begin with and years of settling onto stone foundations had left the floors of the old houses wowed and bent, the walls all out of plumb. To make a picture look straight on a wall, you had to hang it exactly as crooked as the nearest adjacent corner, a tricky procedure that might take the better part of an afternoon to get right.

The house Arvel had grown up in was small and stuffed with a clutter of accumulated furniture and objects. There were moments when he looked upon the scarcity in his new apartment as something desirable. But mostly he saw it as another sign of squalor in his squalid life.

The previous spring, more than a year and a half ago, Arvel had graduated from Pictou Regional Vocational School with a certificate in electrical construction. He'd done well in the course, both in the theoretical and practical assignments. His teachers had praised his flair for understanding and designing circuitry, and had written him glowing reference letters. But 1981 had been a bad year. And 1982 had turned out to be worse. Everyone was saying it. You could see it in the headlines, you could hear people talking about it every night on the news. Unemployment was at its highest level since the thirties. Just last night Arvel had watched an hour-long TV special comparing the eighties to the thirties. The conclusion the show reached was that people in the eighties were materially better-off. Clothing was cheaper than it had been in the thirties, food was more readily available, the social safety net kept people from crashing as hard as they once had. But morally and psychologically, the thirties had been an easier time to get by. Families had not yet disintegrated, human relationships had been closer in a society that was still largely based on agriculture. Part of the show featured a panel discussion on youth unemployment in which a group of young unemployed people discussed the difficulties they were facing. When it came time to field questions from the audience, one of the first to speak was a short, white-haired man with little deep-set eyes and a white moustache. His face turned red as he spoke. His voice trembled with emotion.

"If you ask me, you're all just a bunch of crybabies," he said. "Why I remember the hungry thirties. My mother had to make do once with a loaf of bread and a few home-grown radishes. For a whole week, that's what she fed five hungry kids. You people know nothing of real hardship! Just look at your shoes!" The camera panned down and across the well-shod feet of the panellists. "When we were kids, we had to go to the junkyard and cut the treads off of old rubber tires to make our own shoes!"

Arvel's fingers clutched the arms of the chair he was sitting in. His breath choked with pent-up rage at what the man was saying. He got so upset that he had to turn his back on the television for a few moments, go into the kitchen, and drink a glass of cold water.

A person certified in electrical construction was directly qualified for a range of jobs, including wiring new building sites, upgrading existing systems, and troubleshooting in small and large appliances and electrical equipment. Arvel had tried everything since his graduation. He'd filled out applications for work from Canso to Halifax. He'd gone through the North Eastern and Halifax phone books, both Yellow and White Pages, and called the number of any company with a name that sounded like it might have something to do with wiring or running electrical equipment. In his English course at the vocational school, he'd had to write his resumé and cover letters and practise job-interviewing skills, but in the year and a half since he'd graduated, he had not been called in for an interview, or even heard back with any acknowledgment that his applications had been received.

Arvel turned away from the window and faced into the apartment. There was a whole list of things he should be doing today, none of which he'd even started yet. There was a stack of dirty dishes piled on the counter by the sink. A corner of the bedroom was heaped with dirty laundry. The carpets needed hoovering, and he wanted to look through the classifieds in the *Chronicle-Herald*.

The baby had been silent for a long time, so he went into the bedroom to check on her.

The apartment faced north, and with the curtains drawn on the tiny window in the bedroom, it was like night in there. Arvel drew back one side of the curtain. The white rails of the crib glowed in the room like a religious relic. It was the only new piece of furniture in the apartment, the only piece of furniture he would not have tossed directly into the garbage without giving it a second thought. Inside the crib, curled up on her side in a tangle of receiving blankets, lay Kate, his three-month-old daughter. She'd been born with a full head of dark hair, but it had gradually thinned out so that now she was all but bald. And what little hair she had was a reddish-blond fuzz above her ears and at the top of her neck.

He looked at her now and hoped she would not awaken. He hated the innocence of her wide-open eyes upon him.

The toxic buzz of the building intercom shot through the apartment. The baby stirred at the sound of it. Arvel tightened up and cringed. He knew who it would be. He considered the possibility of not answering it, but Alec Morrison would not take no answer for an answer. He knew Arvel would be in here – where else would he be? – and repeated ringing of the buzzer would wake the baby for sure.

Arvel closed the bedroom door and rushed to the intercom before Morrison rang it again.

"Hello?"

"It's me," Morrison said. Arvel pressed the button to unlock the door. In the minute or so it would take Morrison to climb the stairs and come down the hall to the apartment, Arvel frantically looked about the room, as though he'd be able to hide when Morrison got there.

The first thing Arvel saw when he opened the door was a red, white, and blue Pepsi Jeux Canada Games knapsack that Alec had over one shoulder. He shook his head at Alec in disbelief. "What is it this time?" Arvel said.

The pack meant Alec had run away from home. He had done the same thing before, several times. He'd stayed at Arvel's house for a few days once when Arvel was in Grade 9. He'd taken off by train to an aunt's house in Cape Breton before, and he'd even camped out for three days, with no food and only a wool blanket to keep him warm at night, in the woods on the banks of the East River.

Alec was really Ziv's friend, but since Ziv had gone off to university more than three months ago, Alec had been showing up at Arvel's door almost daily. Alec was seventeen, younger even than Ziv, but getting a little old to be running away from home. He'd repeated twice in junior high and now found himself, in what should have been his graduating year, entering Grade 10.

Just about everyone Arvel knew had a father who drank too much. There were binge drinkers and problem drinkers, weekend alcoholics and just plain drunks. But Alec's father was different. He was what most people called a *bad alcoholic*. A bad alcoholic was one who had entered the advanced stages of the disease. Many weekend beer drinkers, like Arvel's father, had big beer guts. But bad alcoholics were almost always skinny. Alec's old man was bone-thin, and because he'd clogged a couple of major organs with booze, his complexion had a waxy yellow look to it, like a boiled garden bean.

He was a heavy-duty mechanic by trade, and he made good money at it. He and his wife had been born and raised in the Red Row, but had migrated as far south as one of the less desirable streets of Valley Woods. Their split-entrance bungalow, with spanking new furniture and two new cars in the drive every two years, was the envy of every kid from the Red Row who ever visited the place. But the economic rise of the Morrisons masked a physical and spiritual decline. Ziv had been in their house plenty of times over the years, and he'd told Arvel he'd never heard anyone talking in there. Never. The father stayed in the kitchen or the TV room. The two kids were both holed up in their separate rooms. They did not eat meals together or even watch TV together.

There wasn't much to like about Alec Morrison. He was so starved for attention that from the time he'd been in elementary school he was loud, pushy, and obnoxious. Ziv had started hanging around with him in junior high, mostly out of sympathy, Arvel had always suspected. By the time Alec was in Grade 7, almost no one would have anything to do with him. Alec had a diamond-sharp wit and a great deal of surface charm and energy that attracted people initially, but when he sensed people getting close, he did his best to drive them away with annoying pranks. The only exception seemed to be how he treated Ziv. Maybe Ziv just had thicker skin than most people, but Arvel noticed that Alec was not as bent on pissing Ziv off.

Arvel hadn't realized how desperate Alec must be for friends until Alec had started seeking out Arvel's company after Ziv left. Arvel had never expressed any interest or particular liking for Alec Morrison in the better than ten years they'd known each other. In fact, he could recall several incidents when Alec had so enraged him that he'd lashed out.

Once, two days after Arvel's birthday, Arvel had come home from school to find Alec in the kitchen. There was only one piece of the birthday cake left, and everyone in the family understood that it was Arvel's. Alec was sitting at the kitchen table, with the opened serving tray in front of him like a plate. He had a half-drunk glass of milk beside the tray and had already forked down a couple of good-sized pieces of cake.

"Where's Ziv?" Arvel said, ready to blame his brother for what his guest had done.

"Not home from school yet," Alec gave a big smirk and began breaking off another morsel of cake with the edge of his fork.

"Who gave you that cake?"

Alec continued smirking. He shrugged. "It was sitting there," he said. "I took it."

"That was my birthday cake," Arvel said, his voice rising.

"Oh," said Alec. "Is it your birthday? Happy birthday!"

Arvel picked the remainder of the piece of cake from the tray and squeezed it in both hands. The icing oozed out from between his fingers as he compressed the whole thing into a golf-ball-sized pellet. Alec remained seated with a blank expression. When Arvel clamped him hard in a headlock, Alec opened his mouth to protest. The cake ball fit perfectly into the open jaws, muffling any words Alec might have said.

"How's that taste?" Arvel asked after he'd released Alec. Alec did not seem put out in the least. He chewed the lump of cake slowly, savouring the rage he'd sparked in Arvel as much as the cake. When he had part of the cake pellet swallowed, he said: "Tastes pretty good. Does your mother put coffee in the frosting?"

Still standing in the doorway of Arvel's apartment, Alec shifted from one foot to the other. "Are you going to let me in, or what?" he said. Arvel moved out of the way and Alec entered the living room. He sat down on the couch, his navy parka rising around his ears like a shell. He zipped open his knapsack and dug around inside for a moment.

"Here," he said, more to himself than to Arvel. He pulled out a quart bottle of Captain Morgan rum.

"Put that away!" Arvel said without hesitation.

"Just relax, man," Alec said. "It's only a bottle."

"I said put that away, and I meant it. You either put that back in that bag or I'll dump the whole fucking thing down the toilet."

"Jesus Christ! That'd be a good one. Arvel Burrows is going to throw away booze!"

"You've got a lot of nerve coming into a guy's house and talking to him like that. Most people would kick you right the fuck out on your arse."

"Most people wouldn't have let me in in the first place. It ain't my fault you haven't wised up enough to figure that one out on your own."

"You're some fucking piece of work, Morrison. Why don't you just sit there and see if you can keep your mouth shut for half an hour. I've got a lot of stuff on my mind, I don't want to have to deal with your foolishness. And put that bottle away."

Morrison hesitated with his hand on the neck of the bottle for a moment, then put it back into the bag. He did not zip the bag closed, and the neck of the bottle protruded from the sack near his ankle.

"You've got stuff on your mind, all right," he said. "What do you do, get your secretary to hold your calls while you change a shitty diaper?"

"Last warning," Arvel said. He pointed directly in Alec's face, his finger inches from Alec's nose. Alec opened his mouth. Arvel's index finger was as thick as two of Alec's fingers. Arvel's arm was bigger at the biceps than the thickest part of Alec's legs. Arvel towered over him, a big hill of bone and flesh and muscle.

Alec closed his mouth. "I don't know what you're doing here," Arvel said, turning his back. "I don't know what happened. I don't want to see you or talk to you right now." He opened the bedroom door, stepped in, and closed it. The crib lit up briefly, then disappeared in the black. He crawled into his bed and pulled the covers over his head. The caffeine from all the tea he'd drunk was burning through his limbs. He felt like walking out to the living room and pounding on Morrison until his tongue fell out. He gritted his teeth, clenched his fists against the sheets, and stared open-eyed into the mattress.

———

The Highland Square Mall in New Glasgow had been open for less than two years and the early signs of decline were already setting in. When it had opened, the chrome, the retro-neon lights, the mirror-covered walls, had transported Pictou County shoppers. "It's just like Halifax," people said when they were describing it to a friend who hadn't been there yet. "Just like something you'd see in Halifax." By now, in 1982, everyone had been there, yet everyone had not been enough people to keep some of the expensive specialty shops open. There were empty shop stalls, their windows papered over with For Lease signs or the Coming Soon signs belonging to the next, lower-end business that would set up shop. A couple of the trendier, higher-priced women's clothing stores had gone under almost right away. There was a Dollar Deals store in the mall now, an ultra-low-end department store dealing only in items that cost exactly a dollar.

Jackie worked at Exception Elle, an expensive clothing shop that had opened with the mall and prospered. Part of the reason Exception Elle did so well was Jackie herself. She had a flair for communication; she could tell women exactly how they looked when they tried something on. She had a sharp eye for fabric and colours, and how well they suited a particular woman's hair and skin and eyes. She was attuned to different body shapes, and knew what fashions suited women with small or large busts, women with thick waists, what cut of dress hung most flatteringly over thick thighs.

She got paid a commission on top of an hourly minimum, and the longer she worked there, the more money she was able to make. Women trusted her and came back. Middle-aged women with lots of money seemed pleased when she was talking about how they looked, and they sent their friends. Jackie's boss had known very early on that she was drawing customers into the store, and Jackie had already managed to negotiate an increase in her commission.

Jackie's old high-school friend, Colleen Chisolm, had moved to Halifax a few months earlier and was working at Gregor's, a fancy clothing store in a downtown area called Historic Properties.

The day Colleen had got her first paycheque, she'd called Jackie and started listing the virtues of Halifax, trying to convince Jackie to bring Arvel and the kids to live there.

"If *I* can make this much here, just imagine what *you* could make," Colleen said on the phone. Jackie could tell that in celebration of her first paycheque, Colleen had already had a few drinks. "Things would be easier here for Arvel, jobwise."

"I'm doing pretty well here," Jackie said. "We're doing fine."

"I've already mentioned you to my manager."

"You what! I did not say you could do that!"

"I just told her about my friend in Pictou County who's the best salesperson in women's fashions I've ever come across."

Moving to Halifax was out of the question. Even without discussing it, Jackie knew Arvel would never agree to it. But the phone call from Colleen had been encouraging. The knowledge that she might have an option open to her gave her a little charge, seemed to set her free.

Jackie was closing by herself tonight. She'd already tied up the garbage and put it in the Dumpster out back. She barred the fire door and padlocked it. She'd straightened all the racks and shelves and run the carpet sweeper through outerwear. At ten fifteen she sat down in fatigue and disgust. There was a woman trying on dresses from the reduced-to-clear rack who simply would not leave. This was the one thing Jackie disliked about selling to the wealthy: they knew that rules were not made for them. Jackie had told the woman at nine thirty that they would close at ten sharp. But this woman was Carmen Denelda, the wife of James Denelda Jr., one of the wealthiest men in the province. Mrs. Denelda spent two-to-three hundred dollars a month in this store alone. The retail conglomerate of which her husband was CEO owned a controlling interest in the mall. She understood that whoever else the mall closed at ten for, it did not close at ten for her. Of course, her demeanour had never been anything but gracious, but if she wanted to try on dresses until ten thirty, trying to find the right one, that is what she would do.

At 10:21, according to Jackie's watch, the woman apologized for keeping her late and left without buying a thing. Jackie did a cash-out on the till, filled out the deposit slip for the bank, and locked the money into a night-deposit bag. She took her purse out from behind the register and shut the machine down. With the folding partition that walled off the shop from the rest of the mall closed and locked behind her, she walked the short distance down the hall to the night-deposit slot. There was something spooky and awe-inspiring about a big empty building. Part of what she felt now was the contrast between the cavernous spaces of the mall and the tiny, dingy apartment she was returning home to.

Even in the dim overhead lighting of the parking lot, her little two-door Datsun showed poorly. You could see from the imbalanced way the car sat on its wheels that the suspension was going. And as she drew nearer, the uneven way the paint was fading gave it a homemade body-filler look, even though this was the original finish.

She wound the window down a crack and took a spin through the loop in New Glasgow before going home. Maybe she could convince Arvel to take a day trip to Halifax a week from Saturday. She still had not told him about Colleen and the possibility of a job, and if she could convince him she only wanted to do some Christmas bargain-hunting, maybe she could quietly visit Gregor's in Historic Properties, just to see what it might be like to work there.

As she was putting the key into the lock, she heard the baby crying. As soon as the door was open a crack, she could tell that it was not a cry at all, but a desperate scream. The stink of booze was in the air. An empty bottle of Captain Morgan lay on its side on the coffee table. Arvel was asleep in the armchair in front of the TV, which was on, but had the volume turned so low she could not hear it over the raging blood in her head. Passed out on the couch, with one dirty sneaker scuffed across the end table beside the couch's arm, was Alec Morrison.

Jackie did not stop to take a second look at the drunks in the living room. She rushed into the bedroom and lifted the screaming baby from her crib. She was wet and dirty and hungry. Jackie switched on the light overhead and quickly set about changing the diaper, putting on a new undershirt and sleeper, then wrapping the child in a clean receiving blanket. "There, baby, there," she said in a soothing tone. Normally she would have fed the child first, but the smell in the room, and the degree to which the wetness and dirt had soaked the clothing and bedclothes, made cleaning the child first priority.

She put the soiled clothing in a pile beside the covered bucket of clothing disinfectant. She'd rinse it later and add it to what was already in the bucket. She wiped the baby from head to foot with a succession of moist towelettes, rubbed her with a clean receiving blanket, and put on a new diaper and sleeper.

"Poor baby," she said soothingly. "Poor baby." She sat in the rocker and hoisted the edge of her blouse from the waistband of her slacks and quickly touched each breast to judge which held more milk. The baby was crying more quietly since being changed, but she was gasping now, she was so hungry. In the absence of nourishment, she'd begun gulping down air. Jackie unclasped the front closure of her bra and brought the child to her left nipple. It took a minute or two before she would settle in to nurse, but when she began to suck, the apartment went silent.

Kate nursed for twenty-five minutes on the left side without pausing. To make sure she was still getting milk, Jackie switched her to the right breast, where she nursed a short while longer before falling asleep. Jackie laid Kate momentarily on the bed while she changed the bedding on the crib. With fresh sheets and a blanket in the crib, she curled up and moaned softly in her sleep. Jackie bundled the most heavily soiled items into her arms and brought them to the bathroom sink for rinsing. When all had been rinsed and wrung out, she went back into the bedroom and submerged everything in the disinfectant solution she kept in a covered bucket by the crib.

She sat on the edge of the bed for a moment and blew out a breath. Then she got up and went into the living room.

The two drunks were sound asleep and snoring; neither of them had moved since she'd first come in. What she had to say was brief, but she paused a moment and reminded herself to say it calmly.

She leaned over and thumped Arvel solidly in the chest with the end of her closed fist before stepping back beyond his reach. His eyes snapped open and lolled stupidly in their sockets. When they closed again, Jackie took a step in his direction, thumped him in the same place again, and again stepped back. Arvel began speaking unintelligibly. He shook his head as though trying to get his eyes to focus.

When he was looking at her and nothing else, Jackie held up her arm and pointed with her index finger at the door.

"What?" he said, his fogged up brain becoming a little clearer. "What the Jesus are you doing?"

"I'm not doing anything," she said. "You're leaving." Then, so he wouldn't have to ask her to repeat it, "You are leaving."

Arvel looked at her and then searched the room for a clue as to what was happening. His gaze rested momentarily on the form of Alec Morrison, still unconscious on the couch. He looked at the empty rum bottle on the coffee table. Then he looked back at his wife. "I can . . . I can . . . I just . . ." he said. His brain would not work.

"There's nothing to talk about," Jackie said. Already she was saying more than she'd planned, more than was needed, more than he deserved. "Just get up out of that chair and get out the door. And take this . . ." She nodded at Morrison, who in his sleep was beginning to drool down the side of his chin, ". . . with you, too."

"You're kicking me out of my own apartment."

"This will be your apartment when you start acting responsibly. What am I talking for? I'm not going to talk. You're leaving. There's nothing to discuss."

"Where am I supposed to go?"

"That's not my concern."

<hr/>

Ennis opened his eyes. The room was black. The illuminated face of the clock radio said 12:05 a.m. He wondered what had awakened him. He usually slept like a rock. He closed his eyes and as he began to drift back to sleep, the pounding started up. It was the back door, directly below his bedroom. The knocking shook the panes in the window by the bed.

Dunya stirred on the bed beside him. She mumbled something he couldn't make out. He raised himself onto his elbows and swung his feet over the edge of the bed to the floor. A knifing pain shot through his hip and throbbed in one direction all the way up to the middle of his back, in the other direction down to the top of his right knee.

Tomorrow was a working day. He'd soaked his sore muscles in hot water before going to bed and he'd have to do the same thing in the morning to get himself going again. He suffered angina pain, and carried nitroglycerine tablets to help with that. Physical labour was for young men, and in better economic times, he would have graduated right out of the toughest jobs by now. But the workforce at the Car Works had slowly shrunk from a high of well over two thousand, shortly after he hired on, down to a few dozen at present.

The first-in, last-out policy for layoffs was one he himself had helped negotiate, and he knew it was the only fair way to operate. But it had hard consequences when all the young lads had been let go, leaving men in their fifties, men who had already toiled at the tough jobs for twenty, thirty years, to do the heaviest of the heavy work.

He had started out driving rivets in the days when welding was considered untrustworthy for the sort of heavy work they did at the Trenton Works. The rivets, about the size of a large man's thumb, were heated white hot in a stationary forge. A man with tongs worked the forge, picking up the glowing steel and tossing it to the riveter who was working the railcar they were assembling, and who caught the rivets in a dipper and drove them home while they were still white- or red-hot.

Riveting like that was a lost process now. Welding was fast and cheap and strong enough to replace the finicky old rivets almost completely. Ennis ran a spot welder most days now, a hulking, awkward, dangerous machine that almost tore his shoulder out every time he had to manoeuvre it.

He put a hand up and tested his aching right shoulder as he limped down the upstairs hallway. The pounding set up again.

"Hold your Jesus horses!" he yelled. From the bedroom behind him, Dunya shouted some gibberish in response, still asleep. He gripped the railing heavily on the way down the stairs. "This better be good," he said to himself.

He'd forgot to turn the outside light on, and when he opened the door all he saw were two young men, stooped over drunk, standing with their hands in their pockets.

"What the hell is going on?" Ennis said angrily.

"Dad!" one of the figures said.

"Arvel. It's after midnight. People with jobs have to work in the morning."

"Jackie kicked us out," Arvel said without explaining who was with him. "We've been wandering all over town, but we're getting too fucking cold."

"Jesus! She's got two husbands! No wonder she's giving ye's the boot in the middle of the night. She's got to get some rest."

Arvel did not ask to come in. He brushed past his father, through the porch, and sat at the kitchen table. Alec followed him.

In contrast to the well-lit, modern, neatly appointed kitchen in his apartment, his parents' kitchen was a mixture of colours, patterns, and styles. They'd never been able to afford to redo the whole room at once, so they'd worked an item at a time. The oil stove had been in the house when they'd bought it. The cupboards had been painted one year, the new counter had been added the next, the chrome table and chairs had been added a couple of years later. By the time the wainscoting had been painted, the paint company had changed its palette and they were unable to find a colour that looked right with the cupboards.

On the kitchen table sat several newspapers, the *Globe and Mail*, the *Chronicle-Herald*. Each had holes in the front pages where articles had been scissored out.

"Hey, Mr. Dressup," Arvel said to his father. He held up the remains of a sheet that had been clipped. "What are you doing, making a paper tree?"

"Come right in. Make yourself at home. Start shooting off your big fucking mouth," Ennis said. He scooped up the papers from the table and took them out to the porch.

"Ah, fuck it, I'm drunk," Arvel said. He put his face down in his hands, then raised his gaze to Morrison. "I knew I should have kicked you the hell out of my house when you turned up this afternoon."

"Nobody had to pry your lips open to pour it in you, that's my guess," Ennis said.

Arvel looked at his father and held his tongue. He wanted to leave off getting thrown out of houses at the count of one.

"Listen to your father," Alec said.

"You little thief," said Ennis. He levelled a finger at Morrison. "I had two beer go missing from a box in the porch the last time you were in here. With Ziv. Don't think I forgot."

Alec grinned idiotically. "It couldn't have been me," he said. "I'm not old enough to drink."

Arvel plonked his forehead against the kitchen table. "What the hell am I doing with this guy?" he said.

"Birds of a feather," said Ennis.

"By my count there are three of us flocked in this fucking kitchen," said Arvel. "The only reason you aren't drunk is that you've got work tomorrow."

"Only reason, nothing," said Ennis. "I've got thirty-fucking-eight years' seniority down there. You don't have shit. You don't have thirty minutes."

Morrison chose this minute to stand up and open the fridge. "You got any cold drinks in here?" he said. "Any orange juice? Any pop?"

Ennis pushed him away from the fridge. "Jesus Christ!" he said. "The nerve! You want something to drink, the tap's right there." He pointed at the sink.

Arvel shook his head and looked at Alec. "This guy! This guy is ruining my life! He got me kicked out of one house already."

"He never got you kicked out of nothing," Ennis said.

"What do you know?"

"I'm fifty-four years old. *That's* what I know. If you want to know why your wife kicked you out, it's because you don't have a job. You think she kicked you out for getting drunk? If you were pulling in twenty-five grand a year she'd be up there right now mixing the rum and Pepsis for you!"

"That makes a fuck of a lot of sense."

"You're goddamned right it does. If your mother was going to put me out for drinking, I would have been out on my arse in 1955. Women *want* men to drink. It keeps them out of trouble."

Arvel clamped his teeth together and shook his head. He walked into the living room and lay down on the couch. The room tilted slightly, but when he was sure he would not throw up, he closed his eyes. He could still hear his father, his mouth shooting off about something, but he wasn't listening. It was bad enough he had no choice but to humiliate himself by showing up on the old man's doorstep in the middle of the night. He did not wish to punish himself further by actually listening to what his father was saying. He rolled over, buried his face in the back of the couch, and drifted off to sleep.

# SCRAPS

The bus turned off the highway, descended the ramp, and began the uphill climb that would bring it eventually to downtown New Glasgow. A thick, steel-grey overcast suffused everything with a fading, subdued light. Steam swirled around automobile exhaust pipes, and although no snow appeared to be falling from the sky, powdery wisps puffed up in the slipstreams of cars, tracing a shifting, lacy pattern of white across the dark-grey pavement.

The towns of Pictou County were all larger than the university town, and had probably grown just as much since the Second World War. But whereas growth in the university town had taken place along with the campus, growth in the towns of Pictou County had come in the waves of the boom-and-bust cycle of capitalism, and each bust had left its scars on the landscape. There were abandoned industrial rail lines here and there, their railbeds gone over to weeds. There were old sheds and warehouses, small factories that had been sitting empty since before Ziv was born. There were factories large enough to house a workforce of thousands, in which mere dozens were now employed.

As the bus pulled off of Provost Street and into the loading zone next to the rear door of the Acadian Lines terminal in New Glasgow, Ziv caught a glimpse of his father standing uneasily against the sandstone wall, waiting for him. When Ziv stepped off the bus, Ennis rolled onto the balls of his feet. His shoulders moved up and forward. The heavy canvas of his coat crinkled in the cold.

"Is this your only bag?" he said. He'd been suppressing a smile up to now, but one sneaked out, and once it had appeared, he was unable to wipe it off. He leaned forward and took the knapsack away from Ziv. Neither of them spoke as they made their way across the quiet parking lot. As his father drove from New Glasgow to Albion Mines, a feeling grew in Ziv of having been disconnected, unplugged from the place of his birth. He'd spent his whole life in Pictou County up to four months ago. Before he'd left at the beginning of September, the landscape of Albion Mines and the other towns, these had etched themselves on his mind as something permanent. The whole world, before September, had sloped slowly to the East River. The university town had its own topography that had begun eroding the permanence of the shape of Pictou County in his mind. But the most remarkable changes since September were completely internal. In four months, he'd been exposed to Freud, Pavlov, Marx, Weber, Socrates, Plato, Aristotle, Milton, and Chaucer. He'd never had an inkling before of how deeply and completely the world had been examined for and shaped by ideas.

After an intensive two-week period of exams, he emerged from the Acadian Lines bus, his head aswim with notions. The whole universe seemed to have been pried loose from itself.

His father was talking to him as they drove, had been talking to him since they'd got into the car. But Ziv had not been hearing or listening. Ziv had written his philosophy exam that morning: three hours of rehashing the Sophists to Scholasticism. He had a hand on the dashboard before him and he kept drawing it back and replacing it on the padded surface, each time surprised that his hand did not pass through the plastic, rubber, and metal.

He knew he was sitting forward in his seat, and that his head was tilted forward on his neck. He knew that the top of his back and shoulders were not touching the seat behind him, and that there was a forward twist in his neck. But his equilibrium was out-of-order. He felt as though he were lying back, far back on a flat surface, his feet elevated above his head, the world pouring through his forehead and directly into his brain.

〰〰〰〰〰

Ennis had left school at the end of Grade 8, back in the mid-forties. So the notion of university and what Ziv was doing there was vague and alien to him. All the same, he had an idea that Ziv was reading. He'd always been an avid reader himself: non-fiction books, pocket novels, magazines, and newspapers. He was so familiar with the literature of the labour movement that the younger people in the movement referred to him as a walking encyclopedia of labour history and law.

Secretly, all fall, for the first time in his life, Ennis began to keep a scrapbook. He'd bought a cheap one at Stedman's on

Foord Street with a picture of a covered bridge on the front that looked like a photo for a jigsaw puzzle. He'd filled that with newspaper and magazine clippings.

He read the *New Glasgow Evening News*, the *Chronicle-Herald*, and the *Globe and Mail* almost every day. On the weekends, he picked up the *Cape Breton Post*. He read *Canadian Forum* magazine, *This Magazine*, *Atlantic Insight*, *Maclean's*, and *New Maritimes*.

Anything he thought might have held interest and deserved a second look, he clipped. He bought a Swiss Army knife, one with a little pair of scissors, at the House of Knives in the Highland Square Mall, and hooked this to his key ring. When he read something he thought was of particular interest, he snipped out the whole article and Scotch-taped it into the scrapbook. After he'd filled the first, cheap scrapbook, he went back to reread the articles so he could brush up on the issues in them. He quickly realized that the thin newsprint paper and glue binding of the scrapbook was not very durable, so for his next book he went to the art-supply section of Hobby World and got an artist's sketch-book with a spiral binding. Using a glue stick, he discovered, was faster, cheaper, better-looking, and gave a more reliable bond than Scotch Tape. By mid-October, he had the first scrapbook and two sketchbooks stuffed and bulging with clipped articles. Every individual piece he read at least twice, and soon he'd started a special scrapbook in which he put all the material he'd deemed worthy of a third look.

At first he thought he was collecting random bits of unrelated information, so the first few books had no organizing principle. But on rereading the material he collected, he noticed that there were certain ideas he was drawn to collect over and over again. Eventually he began to notice that almost everything he clipped fit under one of four headings: Labour Issues, Nuclear Issues, Nova Scotia Heritage, and Futurism. There were also articles on the Tylenol murders that had shaken up the U.S. that fall. These did not belong neatly in any particular category.

Under the heading of Labour Issues, there were articles on unemployment, workplace automation, two-tier contracts, and the massive wave of layoffs washing over every industry.

He hadn't shown anyone the books of clippings. And though Dunya knew he was doing something that he wasn't telling anyone about, she never asked what it could be. Wasn't that typical of her?

He took the longer way to Albion Mines from the bus station: up Provost Street, East River Road, and through Blue Acres, the whole time his tongue and brain working furiously. Ziv sat silently beside him and did not say a word. Why did the U.S. refuse to ratify SALT II? Where was the Canadian government going to store the long-term waste from the Point Lepreaux reactor, set to start production soon? Why was the Canadian government kowtowing to the American military by allowing cruise-missile tests in Canadian airspace? Management was squeezing union members hard, pressuring members with seniority to sell out those at the bottom of the scale. The media and politicians were such hypocrites that they could cry real tears over union leader Lech Wałęsa when the economic establishment he was up against was a communist one, while at the same time being so obviously biased against the union movement here at home. Researchers in artificial intelligence were creating new life, silicon-based life as opposed to the carbon-based life that evolved on Earth by itself. Soon the silicon-based life would be in direct competition with humans for control of the planet. All of these advances were put in perspective by the failing health of Barney Clark, recipient of the first artificial heart.

By the time Ennis had pulled the car into the yard, he'd worked himself into a lather.

"I've got something I want to show you, Ziv," Ennis said once they were inside the unheated porch. He was huffing and puffing. His blood pressure was up.

"Don't get yourself so worked up," Ziv said. "You're red as a beet."

"Come on upstairs, I've got something I want to show you."

"Geez, Dad. Can't it wait? I'm tired and hungry."

"Ziv!" his mother said when he entered the kitchen. "Look at you! Son, you look terrible. What's wrong?"

"I'm exhausted. I just finished my exams this morning. I was up half the night. My head is swimming."

Ennis grabbed Ziv by the elbow and pulled him in the direction of the stairs. "He don't have time for this right now. I got something upstairs I want him to see."

Ziv was blinking away his bewilderment as his father almost dragged him through the two rooms and up the stairs at the front of the house.

"I've been using your desk," Ennis said. "I knew you wouldn't mind." They entered Ziv's bedroom. Ziv plunked down on the bed and sprawled back onto the mattress. "Ah," he said. He closed his eyes and looked to be drifting off to sleep.

"Look at this," Ennis said, slapping Ziv's leg lightly with the back of his hand. "Jesus, don't sleep. It's the middle of the day. Look at this."

Ennis had placed a cardboard box on a shelf of the brown cabinet that had been in this room when he had bought the house. He unfolded the flaps of the box now as though he were expecting the package to explode. He took scrapbooks one at a time from the box and set them on the desktop nearby.

Astonishment was the only thing Ziv felt as he looked through the scrapbooks his father had put together. The books had been thumbed through so many times that they looked aged. The covers were crinkled, the corners dog-eared. After the weeks of writing exams and four months of stuffing his head full of information that, just last August, he had not even been aware existed, Ziv had no room in his brain for any of this. His eyes passed over the headlines and photographs. Labour relations, he thought. Nuclear waste. Some of the articles were labelled as to their sources: the *Chronicle-Herald*, the *Globe and Mail*, the *Cape Breton Post*, and the *New Glasgow Evening News*. *Time* was represented in the pages his father had collected. *Maclean's*. There were several magazines he was unfamiliar with.

"I don't have time to read this stuff now, Dad," he tried to sound apologetic. His father was waiting for him to do something; Ziv was trying to imagine what.

"I don't want you to *read* it," Ennis said. His voice was tender; the unfamiliar tone of it frightened Ziv. Ziv's tongue was dry. He could taste the metallic flavour of the roof of his mouth. He set the book he was holding to one side and picked up one he had not yet seen.

"I . . . I don't really understand," he said. He looked out his bedroom window at the lamp out on Hudson Street and the circle of dun earth it illuminated. It had grown dark in the short time since the bus had arrived. A tremor set up in his chest. A hollow feeling. An awareness of the importance of whatever words he'd be able to summon.

"It's a scrapbook," Ennis said, his face slowly darkening. "I collected this stuff."

"Why? I don't get it." It was all Ziv could think to say.

"I knew it," Ennis said. "I knew I shouldn't have shown these things to you." He began angrily repacking the cardboard box, throwing scrapbook upon scrapbook, then folding the flaps back over the top.

"Dad, Dad, look," Ziv said. He got up and followed his father into the hallway and down the stairs.

"It's my mistake," said Ennis. "Everything's my goddamn mistake. I never should have tried to show you nothing."

"Dad, I'm tired. You don't know what I've just been through."

"No, I don't know. Of course I don't. I don't know nothing."

"Let's look at this stuff tomorrow. You can tell me what you've been thinking about."

"Like hell," Ennis said. "I won't make that mistake again."

"What are you two fighting over already?" Dunya said when she caught sight of her husband and son.

Ennis set the box down on the floor of the porch and put on his coat and boots.

"Dad, for God's sake," Ziv said. "Let's look at that stuff. We'll look at it now. For God's *sake*."

When Ennis left the house he took the box of scrapbooks with him. Ziv went to the living-room window and watched his father putting the box into the trunk. Anyone watching from another house, or from the sidewalk on the way past, would have thought merely: *there is a man putting a box into the trunk of his car*. Ziv had been part of the scene leading up to this, but he understood little more. He knew what was inside the box, and he knew that wherever the man was going, when he returned, the trunk of the car would be empty.

⨳

The Christmas holiday was almost a month long, and Ziv decided he was going to spend most of it reading for pleasure. He'd done as much reading in the first term of university as he'd done in all the years of high school combined. One of the first things he'd learned at university was what a poor reader he was. He'd spent three hours in the first week of classes, reading and rereading the first two paragraphs of his Sociology textbook, unable to grasp a single concept or understand fully a single sentence. So to help build his reading skills and in order to reduce the length of the list of important books he'd never read, he'd stacked a pile of novels beside his bed when he got home. Some were his father's. Ziv had culled them from the backs of bookshelves where no one had looked for years. Some were his own, bought at Back Pages, a used bookshop in Halifax. Two or three were ones he'd borrowed from the university library.

At university, some people seemed able to balance watching TV with studying. But Ziv found that the moment classes had begun early in September he'd completely lost interest in TV. He never went near it. The early supper crowd, those who went to the meal-hall at four thirty, were almost all doing so in order to finish the meal and get back to their residences to watch *General Hospital* at five. He heard people discussing *The Thornbirds*, a miniseries that, from what he'd heard in discussions, seemed like little more than a soap opera. Even *The Waltons*, which came on in syndicated reruns nightly at eleven o'clock, had a cult following. If he was awake at midnight on a weekday he could hear the sardonic calls of "Goodnight John-boy" echoing down the halls as people responded to what was being said on the screen.

Nothing about TV could attract Ziv. He had his nose in textbooks. He explored the library. He got involved with the student newspaper. Early on Saturday mornings, he assisted Mike Davidovic, who lived down the hall from him, with his jazz show on the student radio station.

But in the first few days of his holiday, the television was a narcotic. After four months of overtaxing his brain, Ziv found the TV was a welcome release from thought and meaning.

He sat half-reclined in a La-Z-boy, his mother across from him on the couch. Barely a word passed between them during the day. His father was not speaking to him since the terrible incident with the scrapbooks, but in the evenings after he got off work, he would come into the room, flip through the channels two or three times, mumbling responses to what was being said or criticisms of what was being done. Then he'd get up and go into the front room, sit in the big plush armchair beneath the photo of himself with his arm around Tommy Douglas. Once settled in, he'd stay there for hours, wrestling the newspaper back on itself and swearing into the pages of the National section.

On the Friday before Christmas, the phone rang at three thirty in the afternoon. It was Alec Morrison. Ziv had not heard from Alec since the end of the summer, but his mother had told him that Alec and Arvel had been hanging around together and that in the fall, the two of them had got drunk while Jackie was at work, and Jackie had kicked the both of them out of the apartment.

"Ziv," Alec said. "What's going on, Buddy?"

"Not too much. Hanging around. Resting up."

"How's university going?"

"It's . . . it's hard to describe. I feel like I've been through so much since summer. Like I've lived a whole lifetime in four months."

"You getting any smarter from what they're teaching you there?"

"I don't know if I'm getting any smarter or not, but I understand one thing clearly that I did not understand in September."

"Four months seems like a long time to learn one thing."

"It seems like a lifetime."

"So what have you learned?"

"I've learned that I don't know anything. Nothing. I'm ignorant. I learned that I've got a fuck of a lot to learn."

"Shit. That's heavy."

"Well, it feels heavy. But it's also a good feeling. There's something positive about realizing your own ignorance. It's like . . . finding a starting place."

"Oh man, I just called to see if you wanted to go to a party in the Heights tonight. I didn't know I'd be getting into an egghead conversation. Maybe you're too educated to get drunk."

"Ha, ha. Fuck that. Who's having a party?"

The Heights at one time had been the name of a few rows of postwar bungalows built on the side of a hill at the south end of Albion Mines. Now it was less a neighbourhood than a collection of two or three areas that included the original bungalows, plus the several blocks of sixties and seventies bungalows to the south of them. The Heights even included Valley Woods, the subdivision of new, modern, upscale homes on large, landscaped lots that occupied the extreme southern section of town. If it were not for the public-education system that brought the kids from Valley Woods downhill to the same elementary school, junior high, and high school that kids from the Red Row went uphill to, the north and south sections of Albion Mines would never meet. They were divided by a downtown that either side had to get to, but neither had to cross, and the histories of the ends of town, and the status and backgrounds of the people who lived there, could not have been more different. In a city, a person from the Red Row would never meet or get to know someone from the Heights, or especially Valley Woods. But they were all stuffed into this little town of six thousand. They went to the same schools, played on the same sports teams, shopped in the same grocery stores, and bought double-double Tim Horton's coffee from the same doughnut shop.

The party was in a big square two-and-a-half-storey house on Weir Avenue, right at the edge of Valley Woods. Ziv wouldn't drink rum, so he and Alec bought a quart of vodka and a two-litre bottle of Sussex orange pop for a chaser. Neither of them was old enough to be legally served at the liquor commission, but Alec was wearing a cheesy-looking moustache that he kept smoothing with this thumb and calling his ID. Ziv waited outside on Foord Street and Alec came out with the vodka several minutes later.

By the time they got to the party, the place was already packed. The young woman whose parents owned the house was several years older than Ziv. She'd just got her B.A. degree and was one term into law school. Her parents were in the States somewhere for the holidays, visiting relatives.

Weir Avenue was a steep incline, and cars belonging to people who'd gone into the party lined both sides of the street. A flood-light over the driveway lit up five or six more cars parked on the asphalt there. Ziv and Alec entered through the back door and took a tour through the downstairs: four big rooms plus a kitchen, stuffed with people whose age ranged from twenty-five down to sixteen. Every room was wall-to-wall. Conversations were going on, people were passing cigarettes and joints. In the doorways and the two halls, party-goers shouldered past each other in a tight squeeze on the way to the bathroom or the front porch or the fridge. First-year university students wore grey sweatshirts with PROPERTY OF and the name of their school. You could see circles gathered around those who'd gone out of province, especially to Ontario: everyone dying to know what things were like there.

Ziv recognized several people he hadn't seen in a while, but there was so much going on that he didn't know who to begin speaking to. Having come full circle through the downstairs, Ziv and Alec stopped in the kitchen and set their bottles on an empty corner at the end of the enormous bottle-lined counter.

They didn't bother with ice or glasses or with trying to chill anything. They had warm vodka and warm pop. They took a drink of one straight from the bottle and followed that up with a drink of the other, taken the same way.

As midnight approached, the house got fuller. Someone had rigged up the stereo so that there was a speaker blaring in every room downstairs. The volume kept edging louder, and along with it the voices of drunk people shouting at each other over the din of music.

Ziv and Alec stood side by side at the counter, passing their two bottles back and forth. Ziv could tell by the way he was guzzling the vodka that there was something eating Alec, but there almost always was. Alec tapped his foot impatiently between drinks.

Someone Ziv recognized as having played hockey against Arvel – was he from New Glasgow? – staggered up to him.

"You're Arvel . . . Arvel fucking something," the guy said. He was drunk enough and his tone was mild enough to be innocuous. He had a stain down the sleeve of his sweatshirt that might have shown where he'd washed away some vomit.

"That's my brother," Ziv said.

"You bruised my fucking pelvis at that tournament in Thorburn, you bastard."

"I've got a brother that looks something like me," Ziv said.

"Put me in the fucking hospital." The young man's eyes were rolling around in their sockets.

"Ya, sure, buddy," Ziv said. "Get some fucking padding next time."

The young man paused for a woozy instant, looking from Ziv to Alec, then opened the cupboard door between them. The door brushed a few inches from Alec's nose, and Alec shoved the man with both hands, sending him and the empty glass he'd had half a grip on to the floor. His head smacked a table leg, but he was too drunk to feel a thing. He had a dopey grin on his face and probably had no idea what had sent him to the floor. The glass bounced once on its butt end before smashing against the wall. All noise but the pounding of the stereo stopped. One side of *Get the Knack* was on its fourth or fifth straight playthrough. The bass line of "My Sharona" pounded against the walls.

The young woman whose house it was was standing in the doorway to her dining room. Ziv went to her swiftly.

"Look," he said, consciously straightening the face he knew was twisted with drunkenness. "It was my friend's fault. I'd like to take him right out of here without any trouble. Could you sweep up that glass? I'd do it, but that would only slow down getting my friend out of here." He could tell she appreciated his eagerness to avoid more trouble.

"I'll get the glass," she said. "You get him the hell out of here."

Outside it was mild for late December, though their breath billowed out before them in thick clouds. The floodlights on the side of the house and on the two-car garage nearby lit up a large area around the driveway.

Someone had thrown up on the landing of the step directly outside the door. Ziv saw it in time and instructed Alec to step over it. Several people stood around outside, smoking and taking drinks from beer bottles. It was a little cold for party overflow to be spilling onto the lawn, but bundled up and a bit drunk, it was possible to hold a conversation outdoors. Now and again people beat themselves on the chest with their arms, to get the blood going. They stamped their feet into the paved driveway.

There was nowhere else to go, so Ziv and Alec settled in at the far corner of the pavement on the driveway, near the front bumper of a yellow Volkswagen Beetle. With the racket of the party and the music gone, for the first time they were able to talk.

"What's going on in Albion Mines?" Ziv said. "I heard you got Arvel kicked out of his house."

"That fucking guy! Blames everything on me. She took him back, anyway. If you ask me, she'll fucking regret it."

141

"What were you doing leaving home in the first place? You've got nowhere else to go. You don't have a job, and with things looking the way they do right now, you're not going to get a job. Don't you think further ahead than one day?"

"No."

They passed the vodka and chaser back and forth, though they were drunk enough now that they didn't need chaser. They drank the orange pop absent-mindedly, sometimes taking a sip minutes after a drink of vodka.

They heard a car passing slowly out on the dark street. It was the one cruiser of the Albion Mines Police Department.

"Go back into the house with the liquor," the metallic voice of the police PA system said. "Go back into the house with the liquor." A spotlight suddenly glared from the passenger seat. It passed over the people standing in the driveway. No one moved.

"Go back into the house with the liquor," the voice said once more. The spotlight dimmed and the police cruiser drove away.

A cold wind set up, and along with it came a light spray of ice-cold rain.

"Shit," Ziv said. "Let's see if one of these cars is open." He tried the driver's door on the VW Beetle and it was unlocked. He climbed into the driver's side and leaned over to pull the latch handle on the passenger's door, which was not locked either. Alex sat down in the passenger seat and shut the door behind him.

Rain drizzled onto the car. The tiny droplets on the windshield caught the light of the floodlights on the house and shimmered in a way that made them look like they were breathing.

Ziv rested his forehead on the cold steering wheel. The interior of the Beetle was not designed for someone of Ziv's size. His knees and the tops of his legs were cramped by the steering wheel.

The back of the seat was barely wide enough for his torso. Little spits of rain ticked against the roof. When the wind picked up, it whooshed over the car and rocked the vehicle on its suspension.

"I thought I'd drink myself to death," Alec said out of nowhere. Ziv wondered if he'd missed something Alec had said previously. "But that's too slow. The old man is proving that. And who'd want to end up like him, anyway? A fucking scarecrow with liver damage. And his brain don't work any more either. I think it took over for his liver when that quit."

"Your old man will get himself straightened around," Ziv said weakly.

"Fucking MacQuarrie's Funeral Home are the only ones going to straighten him out."

"My old man's going to need two more caskets than he can get. They'll have to cut him up. Put him into three different boxes," Ziv said.

Neither of them laughed.

"I'm going to kill myself," Alec said.

"Fuck off," Ziv replied. His heart began to pound.

"I've had enough," Alec said. "There's nothing here for me. Everything just fucks up."

"Fuck off, man. Don't talk like that. Things'll pick up. Things'll change. It's attitude. You've got to change your attitude. Look, there's this thing I learned about in Psychology class. It's called learned helplessness. It's a depression. It's what happens when you think that no matter what you do, it doesn't make any difference."

"That's not psychology, that's my fucking life."

"That's what I mean. You've got to make something work for yourself. Do something positive. Start small. When you get up in the morning, say, *Today my goal is to not miss a single class in school.*

Never mind anything else. Never mind what you do or don't do there. Just get yourself to all of your classes. And at the end of the day when you've made it to those classes, you've accomplished everything you set out to do that day. You've had a one-hundred-per-cent successful day. You've got to see that whatever occurs in your life, it was your actions that caused it."

"Getting to every class in a day! What are the chances of that?"

"That's the point! You *make* it happen."

A commotion started up in the house behind them. Through the walls of the house and the closed windows of the Beetle the only sound that made it to them was a big wooden knock. They turned around to look. There was an unusual amount of movement inside, but from the small squares of light they could see through the windows, they couldn't tell what was going on.

"Somebody scrapping," Alec said.

Ziv shrugged and they both turned back around.

Alec and Ziv sat in the Beetle until the vodka was gone. And when it was gone, they decided to walk. They circled Valley Woods, went up and down Cambey and Belmont avenues. They walked through the shortcut and down Acadia Avenue to Foord Street, where they turned south back up to Weir and passed again in front of the house where the party had been, looked in at the driveway, empty except for the yellow VW they'd sat it.

Anyone who'd been of legal drinking age had taken taxis over to Stumpy's bar in New Glasgow once they'd got drunk for cheap at the party. Some of those who were underage, the ones who were able to get past the bouncer without getting IDed, would be in Stumpy's, too. The rest had wandered somewhere into the night: to another party, a friend's house, home.

At one point they found themselves on the part of Foord Street that formed the downtown area of Albion Mines, what people in the Red Row called upstreet. They were sitting on the steps of Peerless Paints, across the street from the movie theatre. When the second show let out, a group of preppy-looking younger teenagers had walked past. One of them was Ken Morrison, Alec's brother. Ken stopped momentarily on the sidewalk in front of Peerless Paints and looked up at his drunken brother slouched against the sandblasted bricks of the building. The pack of his friends continued up the street and only got a short distance ahead of him when he shook his head disdainfully at the sight of Alec and caught up quickly with his friends. The brothers had not exchanged a word.

Ziv looked at Alec for a response to what had just happened, but if Alec had even noticed Ken, he did not let on.

A few hours later, Ziv and Alec split up on the sidewalk in front of the town hall and went in opposite directions. A few stars managed to beam their pinprick lights past the yellowish glare of the street lamps. The leafless maples along Foord Street etched ragged patterns against the black beyond them. By the time Ziv got home, he was weary-drunk and his legs felt hollowed-out and shaky from drinking and walking. He looked through the window of his living room. The light was on, and he was peering through an almost non-existent crack between the curtains, trying to see if his father was still sitting up on the La-Z-Boy.

His father would know he was drunk, and Ziv did not want the humiliation of having his father see him that way. One staggered step in front of the old man, one word slurred when he spoke, would be enough ammunition for his father to berate and harass him for what would seem like forever. Even when he went back to university in a few weeks, his father would save up the abuse until summer.

From the driveway, Ziv looked at the light-suffused curtain in the living-room window and felt the full weight of his exhaustion. The evening had started out mild, but the temperature had dropped steadily all night, and now the cold started to bite into him. It came in through the soles of his feet and travelled up the bones in his legs. It crept into his neck and pecked away at his wrists where the winter coat stopped protecting him. He couldn't wait here for the light to go out, he'd freeze. He walked to the end of the driveway and turned left onto Foster Avenue. He began walking, walking nowhere in particular as he waited for that light in the living room to go out, cursing his father and the scrapbooks he'd made. Cursing himself for not having learned by now how to deal with his father, how to at least understand him. Cursing himself, too, for being drunk and for acting exactly as though he'd never been away to university, as though he had not learned a thing.

The next morning, Ziv was pressed into his bed like a footprint in mud, a hangover clanging like a fire alarm in his head.

Arvel entered Ziv's room and opened the curtains, raised the blind. "Man, this room stinks," he said.

"Well, get out of it! Nobody asked you to come in here," Ziv's throat tightened around each word as it left his mouth. His stomach convulsed once, but nothing came up.

"What the hell's the matter with you, man?"

"I'm hung the fuck over. Leave me alone."

"You've been home a week and I've barely seen you. What have I got, the plague?"

"I don't know what you've got, Arvel. But I'll tell you one thing, you're about to get a foot stuck halfway up your arse if you don't get out of here right now."

Arvel sat in the chair by the desk and swivelled it around to face the bed. He looked at the stack of books on the floor near where Ziv's head was. He began to read some titles. "*Surfacing. The Metamorphosis. Man Descending*. You have to read all this stuff over Christmas?"

Ziv lifted his head to see what his brother was talking about. When he saw the pile of books, he said, "That pile of books is called a symbol," he put his head back on the pillow and closed his eyes. "Those books represent how I thought I was going to spend my Christmas holidays. This hangover is how I'm really spending it."

"There was this thing on TV about hangovers. Apparently, it's best just not to get them."

"Really now. Isn't that cutting-edge advice."

"But there's three things you can do to help once you've got one. You drink as much water as you can. You keep drinking water until you're just about ready to puke."

"That shouldn't take long."

"You've got to get a bath or a shower. There's something about alcohol that clogs up your skin."

"Maybe it's the poison in it."

"But if you take a bath first thing, you unclog the pores and your skin can breathe. The last thing is vitamin B. You have to have it. Alcohol washes it out of you. You take pills, vitamin pills, or you eat foods rich in vitamin B. Don't ask me what."

"Did this show say anything about smoking two packs of unfiltered cigarettes and scarfing up a big, greasy plate of Polish sausage?"

147

"No."

"So much for common sense, then, eh?" Ziv rolled onto his stomach and pulled the pillow over the top of his head. He turned his head sideways so his brother could hear. "Well, it's thanks to people like you, who have dedicated their lives to science, that people like me, who have dedicated their lives to debauchery, can get up in the morning and get the garbage to the curb on time."

Later, Arvel and Ziv made their way to the Tim Horton's on the west side of New Glasgow. The front of the doughnut shop looked out at the strip of road that had been a main highway before the Trans-Canada had gone through. Twenty years ago, some local businessmen had taken risks, opening Chinese and pizza takeouts along here just as the takeout craze was beginning to build. There were a few of these old business left, but they were being pushed out by big convenience stores, the food chains, the coffee-and-doughnut places, and a few car dealerships that had begun to cluster here.

Ziv and Arvel sat in a steel-framed solarium with a glass roof and looked out over the lip of a steep hill, down to the woodsy backyards of a neighbourhood of older two-storey houses. Ziv had taken Arvel's advice on water and a bath, but the only vitamins he could find had been a ten-year-old bottle of Flintstones chewables with two orange Barneys and a purple Dino, faded and chalky, in the bottom. So in lieu of pills, he'd carefully chewed and swallowed two pieces of dry white bread, and when he felt them settle on his stomach, he took a jar of Guest raspberry jam from his parents' fridge and ate a spoonful of it straight from the jar.

He told Arvel to order him a black coffee, since he was afraid cream might set his stomach off. He sat under the glass of the solarium and felt the strange way his sick feeling quieted him. Another grey day outside. He leaned back and looked up through the glass ceiling at the high overcast. A light powder of snow began to fall, so fine it was barely visible.

A balding man at the next table finished the last of his coffee and brought the cup down hard on the tabletop. The sound echoed off the insides of Ziv's skull, and he closed his eyes as though that would keep unwanted noises out of his head. The coffee smell in the restaurant was thick as mustard gas. And beneath the coffee was a trace of the cleaner they'd used on the floor.

"I want to talk about the old man," Arvel said when he sat down. He placed Ziv's coffee within reach of his hand. Beside Ziv's coffee, he put a glazed chocolate doughnut. He'd bought tea for himself and he swished the bag about in the hot water, watched the liquid darken.

"What you really want to talk about is yourself," Ziv said matter-of-factly.

"What are you talking about?"

"It's a theory I have," Ziv said. "Anything anyone says is about themselves. It's related to Jung's ideas about dreams."

"You can have all the theories you want, smart-arse," Arvel said, his face becoming redder with every word. "If I tell you I'm talking about the old man, I'm talking about the old man."

"That may be your intention," Ziv said.

"Will you just shut your over-educated mouth for about one minute? I want to talk to you. Since you came home, the old man has gone on one of his sulks."

As Arvel spoke, Ziv brought the coffee cup slowly to his lips and sipped a first sip. He held it in both hands, like a chalice. *Let your spirit come upon this caffeine.*

"The only thing worse than that guy shooting off his mouth is when he keeps it shut and makes everyone else suffer," Arvel went on. "I came down yesterday. You were already gone. But the old man wouldn't talk to me. He wasn't talking to Mum, either, apparently."

"Ya," Ziv said. "I don't know what happened, exactly. He got his nose out of joint over some crazy scrapbook."

"Scrapbook?"

"Well, ya. There was more than one. There were several, a few. I don't know. There were clippings in them. News clippings. Something about labour laws and nuclear disarmament."

Arvel squinted and shook his head.

"He tried to get me to read them all at once. I mean, there was enough reading there for a week. He shoved it on me right after I got off the bus. I'd just written my last exam. I told him, *Look, can this wait till tomorrow?*"

"You think this is what set him off?"

"I don't know. It could be an ingrown toenail. Who are we talking about here? You know as well as I do. It could have been anything."

Snow had started up for real outside. People in the coffee shop were commenting on it.

"I heard Jackie booted you out a while back," Ziv said.

For an instant, Ziv saw fear and sorrow cross his brother's face. Arvel sat up straight and folded his hands protectively across his chest and Ziv watched as he squeezed all of his emotions into anger.

"Booted me out?" he said. "Do you think it's funny, what happened to me?"

"Funny? Jesus, no."

"Well, don't talk about it like it's some fucking joke." Arvel clenched and unclenched his fists. "It was *your* friend that caused that whole mess, anyway."

"Alec."

"The bastard brings a bottle of rum to my house in the middle of the afternoon."

"I was out with him last night. Did you hear about that party on Weir Avenue? That's where I picked up this attractive hangover," he pressed his fists into his temples silently for a moment. "So Alec came over with rum and you just had to drink it."

"What am I telling you about making jokes? Getting asked to leave my own apartment just doesn't feel that funny to me."

"All right. Sorry. Okay. I'm honestly trying to show some concern here. It's just all coming out wrong. How are things going now? With Jackie, I mean."

"No good. Now she wants to move to Halifax. She thinks I don't know about it, but she's got a job waiting for her up there."

"She's started applying for jobs in Halifax?"

"Her friend Colleen can get her on where *she* works. Same kind of store she's at now, but even more money. Nothing guaranteed, I don't think. It's mostly commission in that business."

"Well, good for her. In this economy, to have another job if she wants it."

"She's good at what she does there. The sales. The ladies' wear. Fashions, or some goddamned thing. You wouldn't catch her calling it ladies' wear."

"So why don't you guys move?"

"I don't know what the hell I'd do in Halifax."

"More jobs in Halifax than there are in Pictou County. You'd have a much better chance of finding work there."

"There's a big difference between a job and a chance at a job."

"But you need that chance at a job before you can find one."

"Jackie had a job come and find her."

"Jackie married you without a job. You think she'd dump you for not having one?"

"Jackie married me because she was pregnant."

Ziv's coffee cup froze before his lips. He looked straight into his brother's eyes. Much of the anger that had been there moments ago had softened back into something else. Sadness. Bewilderment. "Wait a minute," he said.

"She had a miscarriage right after the wedding," Arvel said. "Remember when she went into the hospital that time?"

Ziv could not think of what to say.

"You don't remember. You never pay attention to anything that goes on in my life."

Ziv wanted to argue about that statement, but decided to let his brother talk. He clamped his lips tightly together and forced himself to be quiet.

"The thing that pisses me off is that I've got a trade. I finished high school, I did a two-year trade. The old man. Look at him. He didn't have shit when he started. What's he got? Grade eight? Did he even finish Grade eight? He starts on at the Car Works at sixteen. He's still there! He's harping on me for not doing stuff right. But I did right. I followed all the steps, but nothing happened. Him: he fucked up, dropped out, and the world put a forty-year job right in his lap."

"He was laid off plenty."

"Boo hoo hoo. They always took him back. Nowadays, when people get laid off, their job is gone. Laid off used to mean laid off. Now it means fired."

"You're right. He was pretty lucky. He worked hard, but there's plenty of people worked just as hard who have shit. People willing to work as hard who never get the chance."

"Fucking right," Arvel said.

"I heard these two old guys talking one day," Ziv went on. "I can't remember where, standing in line some place. Maybe here." He looked around the room for a detail that would bring the memory back to him. "They were talking about making people work for welfare. One guy says, 'They should have to work for it. Give them a job cleaning up the streets or the beaches. Just until something better comes along.' I felt like saying 'This is the eighties, you shitheads, not the forties. Something better is *not* coming along. Something *worse* is coming along.'" His voice had gotten steadily louder as he spoke. People in the coffee shop were turning their heads to look at him.

"Keep your voice down, man," Arvel said.

Suddenly Meta appeared, walking toward them from where she'd been ordering coffee to go, at the counter. "I might have known if someone is going to be screaming his head off at Tim Horton's who it would be." She wore her purple-and-black knit coat. Ziv had been with her when she'd bought it for two dollars at Frenchy's. The big brass buttons were from an old coat of her great-grandfather's. She'd sewn them on herself.

"You wore that coat because you knew I was hungover, didn't you," Ziv said. He was smiling and pretending to cover his eyes from the glare of the coat. Both brothers calmed in Meta's presence. There was something about her. She wasn't pretty in any conventional sense. Her cheekbones were prominent to the point of almost erasing the rest of her face. There were marks on her forehead and at the outer edges of her cheeks where she'd fought off acne in her early teenage years. But there was an aura about her of calmness and power, which made her beautiful.

"Have a seat, will you," Ziv said. "That coat is distracting people. It's causing a disturbance."

"The guy who is yelling and swearing in Tim Horton's is telling me I'm causing a disturbance." Meta sat at the table. Both brothers flushed in her presence.

"You two horny gorillas," Meta said. "If you could see the looks on your faces. Can't you even talk to a woman without getting a boner?"

Arvel went pale. He was shocked that she'd understood exactly what was going on. He was about to deny that's what was happening when Ziv said, "It's that coat. Some men get horny just seeing it. That's the direct hornification factor. The indirect hornification factor is when a man sees it and hates it so much all he can think of is taking it off you, then he gets horny at the thought of undressing you."

Arvel stood up. "You and your fucking jokes," he said. "Some people have serious shit going on in their lives, you know. Some people have families and responsibilities and don't appreciate arseholes who do nothing but fucking laugh at everything."

Meta squirmed back in her seat, lengthening the distance between herself and both brothers. "What did I get myself into," she said. The whole restaurant had gone silent, everyone looking at them.

Once Arvel was on his feet, Ziv knew it was pointless to argue or try to make amends. Arvel had made the decision to leave, and the less that got in his way, the better.

"I'm sorry," was all Ziv said. He raised his open hands in a gesture showing he meant to pose no threat, then lowered his head in disgust at himself and his brother.

When he looked up again, the rage had gone out of Arvel, who was standing now, awkward and self-conscious beside the table, as though wishing he could sit back down, but knowing that once he'd had an outburst like the one he'd just had, the only thing left for him to do was leave.

"Arvel," Meta said, but he did not answer. He walked to the door, slumped like a crestfallen child. When he was gone, Meta said, "What the hell happened?"

"I don't know," Ziv said. He felt suddenly exhausted, the last spark of life gone from his body. It had been Arvel who'd wanted to talk. There'd been something he was trying to say about their father. And Ziv had driven him away. "Just another example of my incredible sensitivity," he said.

Meta put a hand on the back of his head and let it rest there softly, without movement.

# In a Quiet House

Alec was a good enough goalie to play for the county AAA midget team. He'd tried out for the team his first year of eligibility and made the final cut, but had quit after only a couple of regular-season games. The coach had tried to coax him back, offered to pay for new pads, get sponsors to keep him supplied in sticks. Alec wouldn't bite. During any given game, he'd get excited about the level of play in the AAA league. He could feel himself rising to the challenge, quickening to the increased pace compared with the B-leagues he was used to playing in. It was not the hockey itself he disliked about the league. It was all the other things that went along with AAA: the pressure some players were under to get scouted for university and major junior teams, the vain hopes so many players held out for the NHL.

At almost eighteen, he would be too old for midget play soon, anyway, and if anything, the competition at the junior level would only be worse. He played a game a week in a pickup league which mainly comprised people too old for junior and not ambitious enough for senior play. They all put money toward ice time, and whatever was left over from that went into the after-game beer budget.

Late Saturday afternoon, the day after the party on Weir Avenue, Alec slung his gear bag over his shoulder and trudged the whole way to the Albion Mines Memorial Rink. Though he'd spent his whole life in the south end of town, walking in this direction to the rink felt wrong to him. He felt like an impostor living in Valley Woods. Who were his parents trying to kid? They were Red Rowers. They had never fit in in Valley Woods, and Alec had never felt like he belonged at this end of town, either. He always felt stiff and awkward in Valley Woods, as if he were being watched. Behind the gauze curtains of blank windows that gazed without expression at the street, he imagined critical stares. He could almost hear the emotionless voices of adults in well-appointed breakfast nooks, questioning his right to be in his own neighbourhood. *Who is that kid? Does he belong here?*

It had snowed that afternoon, and in some places, where he'd cut across backyards or clearings, he was the first person to make tracks in the snow. Outside the house where the party had been the night before, the vw Beetle that he and Ziv had sat in was blanketed in white. In places, clumps had stuck together and rolled off the roof, leaving trails where yellow showed through.

By the time he entered the dressing room he was late, especially for a goalie, who had more and bulkier gear to put on. Some guys were already fully dressed and waiting at the gate to the ice surface for the rink manager to give them the signal to go on.

Alec dropped his bag in a corner of the room and silently went about putting on the gear.

He was quieter than usual, not so full of wisecracks, comments, and complaints. Some of his teammates remarked on this.

"What did you do, leave your tongue at home?" someone said during the warm-up.

His team only had three defencemen, so after the first period of play they were tired, and a lot of shots from the point were being deflected by forwards the defence did not have the energy to shove out of the slot.

When the game was over, he stayed and drank one beer with the guys in the dressing room before strapping his gear over his shoulders and marching all the way back to Valley Woods. Everyone was home at his house, but the place was silent. His mother, his father, his brother, all were in separate places in the house, all doing whatever they did there on their own. He carried his gear into the basement and unzipped the bag in the furnace room. A smell of sweaty canvas and mould rose up into his nostrils. He carefully laid out each piece on the concrete floor to dry. The chest protector he hung on a line that went across the room at eye level. Beside this he hung his jersey and socks, and the underwear he always wore beneath the gear. The oil burner hummed to life, and in a moment, the circulation fan started up.

He left the furnace room and went into the basement TV room. He lay down on the worn couch that had been moved down here from the living room, and turned on the TV. He flipped through several channels before stopping at a James Bond movie. It was one of the ones featuring the gigantic villain with steel teeth. Just past ten thirty, he called Alice's Pizza and ordered a small combo. When it came at eleven, he was waiting for it at the front door so the delivery man would not ring the bell and disturb the others in the house.

"Hey, Alec," the delivery guy said as he rummaged in the front pocket of his jeans for the change.

"Hey," Alec said. The guy's name had slipped his mind. When he got his change, he handed back a dollar tip and went back downstairs to the TV room, the smell of pepperoni and yeast twingeing in his nostrils, his palm warming under the heat from the corrugated paper box.

When he'd eaten the last of the pizza, he folded the box and stuffed it into the wastebasket in the basement bathroom. He washed his hands and face and dried them on the towel over the sink. He sat on an arm of the couch and picked up the basement extension of the phone. He held it against his ear a moment and dialled Ziv's number. The line went clear a moment, then clicked through to the number he'd dialled. Before it rang on the other end, he hung up and headed for the stairs.

He crept up the stairs quietly, and at the top step opened the door to the garage. Behind him, he heard the hockey game playing on the TV in the kitchen. He flipped on the garage light and quietly closed the door behind him. He began to shake a little in the cold of the uninsulated garage. His father's sky-blue '72 Chevy Nova dominated the room. The rear end was jacked up and blocked. One of the mags was off, lying on its side by the jack.

Amanda Morrison sat at the dressing table in her bedroom. She was forty-two years old, but had been told by men who knew that her husband was a drunk and probably did not pay enough attention to her that she could pass for thirty. Amanda looked at the face in the mirror. Behind her the fifteen-inch TV, which sat atop one of the night tables at the side of the bed, silently flashed pictures from the news. She knew that no one would mistake this haggard face for thirty, and she knew what the men who told her otherwise were hoping for. Yet at least she was desirable enough to be lied to, and this held a sickly sort of pleasure.

She came to this table to practise her faces. With the makeup laid out before her as carefully as surgical instruments, she would dab and smear and trace, sending her cheeks receding into her skull, bringing the ridges of the cheek bones out to shadow over them. When she invented a face that pleased her, something that usually happened once by the end of an evening spent this way, she'd take a long look at her new self, then walk to the ensuite bathroom and scrub off all the makeup.

She had plucked out all the hairs of her eyebrows, one by one, and she sent the metal ends of the tweezers probing along the bare skin where the brows had been, searching for the first signs of a new hair coming through. She'd bought two new eyebrow pencils, in two shades of brown, and she applied them now, one over each eye. The light brown she applied in an arc of arousal or intrigue over the left eye. The darker brown she pressed into a stern straight line over her right. With a hand mirror, she studied the effect of each in its profile.

She had a new Revlon lipstick in a shade of dark red called Black Cherry. Her bottom lip was half-covered when a flash at the bedroom window distracted her. She pulled back the sheer and looked to the street. The little yellow-green station wagon that was parked at the end of the driveway was familiar to her: Alice's Pizza delivery.

She went back to the table and continued applying the lipstick.

In the garage, Alec rooted in a wooden box in the corner opposite the door to the house, moving aside end-cut sticks of wood, lidless pickling jars, and greasy rags until he found a blue coil of vinyl-sheathed clothesline wire. He set up the stepladder so he could easily reach the crossbeams of the rafter trusses, and climbed up. He wrapped the end of the wire three times around the two-by-six crossbeam, and twisted the short end into a tight knot around the part of the wire that hung down. He got down from the ladder, reached up the wire on his tiptoes as high as he could, and twisted a loop of wire back onto itself. He put a slip knot at the end of the loop, and inserting his wrist into the noose, jerked it downward to make sure the wire tightened around his flesh. He opened the top drawer of his father's toolbox and took out a pair of wire snips. He cut the extra wire from where it dangled on the slip knot and replaced the wire cutters in the drawer.

In Ken's room, there was a TV that took up half of the top of the dresser, but he kept it shut off until the two hours he'd set aside for homework were over. It was the Christmas holiday, and there was no homework to be done, but he'd disciplined himself all of first term to set this time aside, and he wanted to keep himself used to the pattern. He'd taken his history and biology texts home and decided to read ahead in them.

Scheduling Saturday night as a homework night was a compromise. He'd prefer to do it on Friday, so that it would not hang over his head for the whole weekend. But Friday was the night that people went to movies or had parties in their basements or went cruising through the countryside with the first of their friends to have a license. Doing homework on Saturday meant that he could go out and do something with his friends on Friday and not have homework looming when he got out of bed on Sunday.

He was more conscious of doing homework this year, his Grade 10 year, as a way of distancing himself from his brother. Ken had been in the same grade as Alec last year, so he was used to the idea that his idiot brother, who was supposed to be two years ahead of him, was in the same grade. But this year they'd got put in the same homeroom, so Ken had to face the embarrassment every day, the constant association with a fool. Every time Alec shot off his big mouth to a teacher, Ken had to endure the uncontrollable impulse of the teacher to look at *him* for an explanation of his brother's behaviour. Every time Alec skipped class, which happened almost every day, Ken had to endure a pause before his own name was called, as the teacher waited in vain for him to explain his brother's absence.

Doing well was his only defence, his only way of separating himself, of making sure that there was no mistaking him for his brother. And sacrificing a couple of Saturday nights over the Christmas break was a small price to pay to keep his self-respect.

He was reading a shaded insert from the history text in the section on the fall of Rome when he heard a noise from the basement. His brother was down in the furnace room, setting his hockey gear out to dry. He heard the buzz of the oil burner coming to life, then the sound of the furnace room door swinging shut with a bang. He went back to the insert, about Flavius Maximus, "The Delayer," and how he put off potential invaders by paying them not to attack the city.

There was a James Bond movie on TV tonight. The theme music seeped up through the floor as his brother settled in downstairs. Ken turned to look at the dark screen of the set on his dresser, then went back again to Flavius Maximus.

In the garage, Alec gripped the wire above the noose and yanked it hard, testing the knot that held it to the cross-beam. He moved the ladder directly beneath the wire and climbed up to the fourth rung. He noticed a drop of red paint stuck to the stamped aluminum of the top rung and scratched at it with his thumbnail. There was nothing painted red in the house, and he wondered momentarily where that paint had come from.

When the noose was snug around his neck he lowered his gaze to the concrete floor of the garage. After undoing the noose, he stepped off the ladder and stood back from where the wire hung. He looked up at the knot on the rafter, down at the concrete floor. Now directly below the wire, he reached over his head to where the noose hung. At the top of the ladder again, he twisted the whole apparatus twice more around the two-by-six, so that it swung a foot higher than it had before.

He stood on the fifth rung of the ladder, wrapped the noose about his neck. He grabbed hold of the rafter over his head and let his weight off of the ladder, so he swung by his hands from the two-by-six. He hooked his toes under a rung of the ladder and kicked the ladder so far away that it clattered into the wall before striking the floor. He chinned himself, making his eyes level with the two-by-six. His arms were tired from the game he'd played earlier, and the taxed muscles set his arms trembling. The end of the wire, where it was twisted around the rafter, dug into his cheek. He let go.

Ron Morrison sat at his kitchen table, a bottle of Captain Morgan rum, cap screwed off and nowhere in sight, planted on the table before him. Beside it, a large bottle of Pepsi. In a tall glass near his elbow was a mixture from the two bottles. The twelve-inch TV on the counter was tuned to *Hockey Night in Canada*. They were announcing their lineup of interviews and commentaries for the second-period intermission.

Ron looked down at his hands where they were curled around his drink. They were already the hands of a much older man. The hairs that protruded from the backs of the fingers were thick and coarse and black. The fingernails were yellow and thick, like the skin over a rancid pudding.

On the TV screen, hockey players skated and swerved and shot. The excited announcers described it all. But Ron was too drunk now to follow it. He knew which teams were playing. Now and then the score would register with him. But the mad panning and switching of cameras on the hulking players in their uniforms was blending into mere swirls and flourishes of colour.

He heard a clatter, and in a moment he realized it had come from the garage. He stood up, both hands on the tabletop to steady himself. He put one foot in the direction of the doorway that led down the few steps to the garage, but he forgot why he'd stood up. He paused a moment, swaying unsteadily with only one hand on the table to hold himself upright, then sat back down.

## MAKING THINGS WORSE

Sunday morning Ennis rose just after five thirty. Since the incident with Ziv over the scrapbooks, he had been furious with himself for having thrown away months of work. The memory of his failure to understand and communicate with his son humiliated him and made him angry at himself, his failure. He wanted to be long gone from the house before anyone else was up.

It was just after six when he walked into the Tim Horton's in Albion Mines for a cup of coffee and to catch up on the latest gossip. The place was unusually empty, even for so early in the morning. In the far corner, deep in the smoking section, sat Ivor Thompson and the rest of the early-morning crowd, half a dozen men and one woman, most of them middle-aged, all of them puffing on cigarettes as though their lives depended on it. They were huddled close together in a single booth, so intent on whatever they were discussing that they hadn't even noticed Ennis coming in.

Ennis ordered his coffee with milk and headed in their direction. As he approached the booth, Ivor Thompson looked up and caught Ennis's eye. Immediately Thompson shook his head at Ennis and frowned.

"What carcass are you people chewing on over here," Ennis said. "I could hear your teeth grinding as soon as I came through the door."

"Bad news," Ivor said. Everyone else at the table looked up now, their faces all marked by the simultaneous sadness and self-importance of people who've been first to discover tragedy.

"Jesus, you's all look some grim," Ennis said.

The only woman at the table, Mary Cameron from up in the prefabs in the Heights, said, "Ronnie Morrison's son."

Ennis knew Alec was dead before she said another word. It was the darkness in her voice as she said the father's name.

"The older boy. He's gone, I guess," Mary continued. "I guess he hung himself is what they're saying."

"You guess! Jesus! Who's saying?"

"I been here since three," Ivor Thompson said. He took a deep drag of his Export A and tapped the ash into one of the empty coffee cups on the table. "I been trying to quit smoking if you can believe it. I been three days without a smoke and three blessed days without sleep. Round two thirty this morning I give up tossing and turning, keeping the wife awake, she was cursing at me there. Anyway, must have been before three I came in here.

"Cochrane White was sitting with a newspaper and a large double-double right over there." He pointed at the booth by the door. "Come about twenty-five after three or so, a call comes across his police radio. He had the damn thing up so loud I heard it plain as day. 'Go to such and such address in Valley Woods,' it

166

said. Some teenager's voice. Isn't it White's own boy that works dispatch on the weekends? Anyway, plain as day it says, 'We got a call from Amanda Morrison says her son Alec hung himself.'"

Ennis went straight to the garbage can, and without realizing what he was doing, he threw his coffee, china cup and all, right into the trash.

"Ennis!" Mary Cameron called after him, almost laughing with the shock of what Ennis had done. "What the hell are you doing?"

Ennis did not reply, but walked as though in a trance to his car. He drove directly to the Morrison house in Valley Woods. The Albion Mines police cruiser was parked on the street in front of the house. Every light in the house was on and the door to the garage was criss-crossed with yellow police tape.

Ennis sat in shock for a long time on the street in front of the Morrison house. Without pulling to the side, he put the car in park and shut off the engine. In a moment an ambulance pulled in behind him and he had to start up the car and make way for it. He pulled ahead and to the side of the street as the ambulance, without siren or flashing lights, pulled quietly into the Morrison driveway. The garage door lifted up, releasing a breath of steam into the cold and breaking through the police tape. Inside the door stood Cochrane White, a stout man dressed in a blue uniform. On the floor of the garage behind him was a sheet-covered body. The only other person visible appeared to be Amanda Morrison, who stood slumped in the doorway that led from the garage into the house.

Ennis put the car in gear and drove out of Valley Woods and back into town. There were a few more people in Tim Horton's when he drove by. The people he'd spoken with were still huddled in the corner of the smoking section. He pulled into the driveway of his own yard and looked at the building. No one was up yet. It was still well before seven in the morning. Both of his sons, one in this house, the other in an apartment just up the hill, would still be asleep. And their friend was on his way to the morgue by now.

Ennis felt himself begin to panic. His limbs jumped involuntarily into action as he slipped the car into reverse and pulled out onto the road. He headed straight for the Highland Square Mall, to the service road at the back. The big garbage Dumpster behind Woolco was where he'd thrown the box of scrapbooks the day Ziv had come home from university. A little more than a week ago, he'd driven off in a huff with the box in the trunk of the car. He'd had no clear plan of action. He had not been able to see that his son was tired. He was angry at Ziv for not understanding that he was only trying to reach out to him. He'd pulled away from the house without a plan, but as soon as he found himself within sight of the mall he drove with a purpose directly to the nearest bin. He'd hoisted to his shoulder the box that contained hours of painstaking work, and heaved it onto the bulging pile of boxboard and Styrofoam already there. In the time since, he had not once thought about the scrapbooks, what he'd done with them or where they might be. But now all his anger and hurt seemed pointless, something he had done to himself.

He found himself pulling in behind Woolco, parking perpendicular to the Dumpster. The light of morning was just starting to colour the cloud cover above, but big square security lights illuminated the whole service area behind the mall, a long row of nondescript fire doors, each with its own trash receptacle. Some of yesterday's snow still clung to the ground, most of it up close to the building where the sun did not reach during the day.

As soon as Ennis flipped back the hatch on the top of the Dumpster, he knew he was too late. The box had been stuffed full when he'd tossed his scrapbooks in here. He could tell that it had been emptied already. Nonetheless, he put a foot up on the big iron hook where the garbage truck took purchase, hoisted himself up to the container's lip, balanced a moment, took a quick look before himself, then jumped down inside. He knew the box was not here, but he felt desperate now to find it, as though he had no choice but to look. He dug his hands down into the corrugated paper and began turning the trash back onto itself. A foul odour that could only have come from rotting food rose into his nostrils. As he worked away, he grew warm in the confined space, unzipped his winter coat and tossed it up out of the bin toward his car. On the backswing from the throw, his shirt sleeve caught on a bolt and he heard the ripping sound of a seam letting go.

〰〰〰

Just before waking up, Dunya had dreamed a vivid and powerful dream. The images in the dream were unclear and nonsensical, but when she thought about them in the morning, she thought of the dream sensation as moving forward and backward at the same time. She stood on an unpaved street of her childhood, outside her family's house at the north end of the Red Row. She felt or maybe saw her future, somewhere over the western horizon, luminous as the sun and almost hidden. There were flowers and the fragrances of flowers. There was the smell of tomato plants pungent on her fingers after she had pinched off suckers and unwanted runners and cascades of hard green fruit with no time left in summer to develop. She was a little girl, not even school-age. She turned to look at her house and felt it throbbing with life. Her father was there, her mother, mysterious relatives from the old country. Her future family was there, too: never-spoken-of Ennis, her children, unborn and as yet unthought-of. She entered the house through the back door, and all the people she loved and ever would love were glowing spirits, floating, almost unformed but identifiable in the air. She raised a hand to touch them and they spiralled together in a great human/spirit knot. The knot formed itself into a globe of light, bright as a hot white star, and when she put out a hand to touch it, the globe became flesh, coalesced into a pulsing, blood-filled fist of bone and muscle and living energy. She held the ball in her two upturned palms and looked at it, half-entranced, half-repulsed by its carnality. She brought it to her lips and bit into it, felt the juice of blood run down her chin. There were deafening screams, coming from a place unknown to her, reverberating through her chest. Bones crunched and snapped, some of her teeth gave way and cracked, she swallowed them with the flesh she was eating until it was all inside of her. She walked out the front door of her house, pregnant with the burden of her life, the past and future gurgling inside her like a plugged drain. She leaned down into the turned earth in the front garden and vomited onto the soil. When she stood straight, what she had thrown up had become the countless thick stalks of giant sunflowers, reaching up to touch the low overcast sky. She dug her fingers into the fibrous stem of the closest one and began to climb.

She awoke, raw and disturbed, convinced that the dream had revealed something terrible to her, something she could not quite understand. When she got down to the kitchen, Ziv was already there, waiting for the coffee to drip through.

"Are you all right?" he said. He must have been able to see how disturbed she was. "You don't look well."

"Yes," she said unsteadily, and sat at the kitchen table across from him. She rubbed her cheeks with her open hands in an attempt to wake herself up. "I had a really disturbing dream," she said.

The phone rang. It seemed Ziv had picked up the phone, listened a moment, then put the phone back down without having spoken himself, although she realized he must have said something, however brief. Some of the brewed coffee had drooled down onto the hot plate beneath the pot, and the bitter smell of it frying penetrated the room.

Ziv looked at her, his face gone an expressionless blank. "Alec's dead. He hung himself." He appeared to melt down into the chair nearest the phone. Dunya never did find out who'd called. Someone who lived near Alec, probably. There would have been police, an ambulance.

She stood in stunned silence a moment, then went over beside her son and put a hand on his shoulder.

"He told me he was going to kill himself. Just the other night. He told me!" Ziv's hands began to tremble. Dunya felt herself weakening and pulled over a chair to sit on while she remained by her son's side. They couldn't have been there for more than a few moments when Arvel came in through the back door. The short burst of cold air he'd let in chilled the kitchen slightly.

Without a coat or hat on, he'd come down the hill from the apartment he was renting on Bridge Avenue. His leather boots had been pulled on hastily and were loose and untied.

"Is it true, what I just heard?" he said. He had a scared look on his face that Dunya had not seen since he was a child.

Ziv nodded. "He's dead," he said. He looked up at his brother. "I believe it. He told me the other night at the party we were at. He said he was going to kill himself. Jesus, I didn't do anything about it."

"How were you supposed to know?" Arvel said. "All the crazy talk that guy was prone to. How was anyone supposed to sort out what was real and what was bullshit?"

"Don't speak ill of him, Arvel," Dunya said. "That poor boy. What must have he been going through?"

The back door banged again and Dunya heard Ennis mumbling in the porch. She set the three steaming coffee cups on the table and went out to the porch to tell Ennis the news about Alec.

She started at the sight of her husband. For a sliver of an instant she thought she was looking at a stranger. Ennis was bent over, wrestling with the laces of a boot. His clothes were covered with dark stains, his hair was spotted with what looked like fragments of dirty paper and Styrofoam. From the doorway, with her back to the kitchen, she smelled a terrible sour odour from him, like a sink full of dirty dishes that had been left to moulder for a week.

He glanced up when both boots were off his feet, but his eyes did not exactly meet hers. His expression was desperate. He looked right through her.

"You're drunk," she said. "Aren't you." She did not know what else to say. She'd never seen him drunk in the morning and she'd certainly never seen drink do anything like this to him. When he took off his coat she saw that his shirt was in tatters, stained much worse than the coat had been.

His eyes focused on her. "Drunk!" He was outraged. "Nobody ever saw Ennis Burrows drunk at eight thirty in the morning. You must be drunk to suggest it."

Dunya remembered her sons in the kitchen and lowered her voice. "Ennis," she said. "Something terrible has happened."

"Something terrible *has* happened," he repeated her words and moved to push past her into the kitchen.

She set herself solidly in the doorway in front of him. "No, listen, Ennis. There's something I have to tell you."

"I already know," he said.

He placed a hand on her shoulder and moved her easily out of his way.

Dunya followed him into the kitchen to shield her sons from their father in their time of grief, but stopped when she realized the kitchen was empty.

She called after them. She ran through the house to the bottom of the stairs and called again, then noticed that the front door had been opened and not closed the whole way. She opened it and the cold bite of early winter entered. In what was left of yesterday's snow on the front steps, she saw footprints where her two sons left the house in order to avoid their father.

She closed the door and turned back into the house. There was a crack of light beneath the bathroom door. She walked down the hall and tried the handle. Locked. She felt a light-headedness strangely akin to elation.

She curled her hands into fists and began pounding at the door. She banged some more. "Those boys have troubles today and look what you did. You made a bad situation worse. As always,

Ennis, as always. Don't you ever think of anyone other than yourself?" She continued to pound on the door. "Your own sons can't bear to be around you." She listened for any sort of response from inside the bathroom. She waited a long time, finally sitting down on the floor of the empty hallway.

## People Weeping

Ziv and Meta entered the church together, hand in hand. They made their way to the closest empty seats available, genuflected, then knelt for a moment of prayer. The smell in the air was of expiring candles and the stale incense that clung to the walls and furniture.

Mr. Morrison was so drunk that two of his friends had to carry him into the church, one under each arm, walking slowly enough that Alec's father had time to alternately place his left and right foot beneath himself to simulate walking. He had made a brief appearance at the funeral home the night before, in a similar condition. Instead of having him wait and go to the front of the church with the procession, where he'd only make a bigger spectacle, his friends helped him to the reserved pew at the front of the church and set him up between them, where he could not fall over.

The priest had asked friends and family members to do the scripture readings but everyone refused. No one thought they would be able to hold up.

Alec's mother stood motionless in a black knee-length dress, her face overpowered by two thick, stern lines of eyebrow pencil. At the corner of her mouth, her lipstick was smeared halfway to her chinline, giving her face a deformed aspect. Beside her, a handsome middle-aged man had an arm draped consolingly around her shoulders. He was the next-door neighbour, a CPA whose wife had left him for an old boyfriend not quite a year before.

Alec's brother Ken stood at the far end of the waiting procession. He was turned at an odd angle, as though he did not belong to any of these proceedings and was about to walk out at any moment.

The church was decorated with greenery and seasonal banners in preparation for Christmas. At the foot of the altar was a nativity scene with a manger empty and waiting for the arrival of the infant Saviour.

The whole town seemed to have come. There was standing room only downstairs and every seat was full in both balconies. All the teachers from the high school were in attendance.

Ziv held tightly to Meta's hand. As the organ music started up, he looked back toward the main entrance where the men from the funeral home were putting the casket on a trolley, ready to wheel it forward. The priest was at the back of the church, stoking the censer. A seven- or eight-year-old boy held a big brass crucifix overhead and was positioning himself to move forward at the front of the procession. Two rows back, Arvel stood by himself, squeezed into the suit he'd worn at his high school prom, shoulder to shoulder with people Ziv knew were strangers to his brother. Ziv scanned the room in disbelief, looking at all the people, their forms crowding and darkening the church.

"They all hated Alec," he said to Meta. "The adults, the kids. They all despised him. They dumped on him every chance they got. What are they doing here, crowding around him now that he's dead? When he was alive, they were tripping over themselves to stay away from him."

Meta put her free hand on his forearm. "They feel badly," she said. "They know now that he needed help. They knew it all along, but they didn't do anything."

Ziv looked at the faces, the downcast eyes, the stooped shoulders, the stricken expressions. He became aware of how many people were weeping. Their muffled sobs echoed up into the vaulted ceiling. Meta was right. Everyone was here because they wished they'd done something to help Alec.

When Father Boudreau reached the head of the church, he circled the casket, waving the censer, filling the air with acrid smoke. When the censer had been placed next to the boat of incense, the priest stretched out his arms in an attitude of prayer.

# PART THREE

## 1988

# CLOSE TO HOME

Ziv's first thought had been the same one he always had when some unidentified disturbance awoke him in the middle of the night: nuclear war. He'd waited in Bundy Burgess's bathroom for the light to blink off. He knew that just before the heat blast vaporized you, radio communication and electrical service would black out. The shadows in the tiny space beneath the stairs danced and skidded about as the bulb that cast its light onto the walls rocked at the end of its wire. Water in the toilet made waves against the sides of the bowl. He put a hand to the bulb to stop its swinging and awaited the loss of electricity. He wondered whether he'd have time to feel any heat before he was turned into steam and smoke and ash.

The house had stopped moving, and a profound silence had set in. He stood looking at the worn pattern in the linoleum and felt the pressure of a headache pushing in at his temples. Whatever had awoken him had not disturbed anyone else. He stepped out of the little bathroom and looked at the walls. To his groggy eyes, they looked fairly straight and sound. Subsidence, a fall of earth from the cave-in of an abandoned mine shaft, sometimes swallowed up a house. But it had not happened in the Red Row in his lifetime. Not yet, anyway. Several homes had given way in Westville, and there was an area near Bridge Avenue that had sunk by several metres when he was a kid.

He flipped on the kitchen light and filled a glass from the tap. He gulped the water, refilled the glass, and downed the contents again. Then he put on his boots and coat at the door and made for his parents' house. The brisk air of early morning caught in his lungs and in his nostrils, and his head began to clear a little. The light in his parents' kitchen burned white against the black row of spruce trees at the edge of the graveyard beyond. There were days when the old man might already be up this early, but not on a Saturday morning, not hungover. There were a few other lights on at this end of the Red Row, more than there should have been at this time. He became aware of his breathing and watched the ghost of his breath rise up into the dark air.

"What the hell else was it?" his father was bellowing. Ziv was in the porch taking off his coat and boots. Even through the closed door to the kitchen he smelled coffee brewing.

"It could have been anything," his mother was saying. "It could have been anything."

Ziv opened the door to the kitchen. "I was down at Burgess's," he said when he came in. He heard the fear in his own voice. "The house shook."

"Your mother felt it," his father said. He stood in the dead centre of the kitchen, his arms held out at an awkward, unfamiliar angle. "We came out to the kitchen here and saw it had knocked the juice pitcher right out of the fridge. Must have banged the door open first. I don't know how the hell it could have done that without waking me up."

The floor in front of the fridge was wet, freshly mopped. The empty juice pitcher sat on the sink.

"Your father thinks it was the mine," Dunya said. Her face was white.

"It wasn't anything else," Ennis said. He had a confused look on his face, as though only part of him understood what he was saying. He looked down at the back of his leg, where a purple bruise carried from his heel to his lower calf.

"Do you think it could have been anything else?" Dunya said, looking desperately to Ziv. Ziv sat at the table. His stomach felt lighter than air. It rose slowly into his chest and squeezed against his heart, which began to pound with the struggle to beat.

The coffeemaker gurgled and sputtered.

"Arvel . . ." Ziv said.

"There would have been an alarm," Dunya said. She went to Ziv and grabbed his shoulders in both hands. She dug in her fingers until Ziv pulled away in pain.

A high-pitched whining, muffled by the closed-up house, entered the kitchen from outside. It was the big siren at the town hall.

Ennis looked up.

The ringing of the telephone woke Jackie up, and she instinctively reached for the clock radio. She'd pressed the snooze bar several times with no effect on the ringing before she realized that it was too early for the seven o'clock alarm. The ringing was coming from the phone in the kitchen. She almost went over on an ankle on the way out of the bedroom.

She stood over the ringing phone an instant before picking it up. If it was Arvel, she would prefer not to answer. She did not want to take the chance that talking to him would change her mind, but a call this early in the morning could be something important.

"Hello," she said when she finally picked up.

"Is Arvel at home?" It was a woman's voice.

"No he's not," Jackie said, looking at her watch to make sure it really was before six in the morning. "Who's calling?"

"Is he at work today?" the voice said.

Jackie hesitated, wondering who she was talking to. "I'm not . . . I'm not exactly sure, but I think he was twelve to eight last night. Who is this?"

The woman hung up.

The call bewildered her. Who calls before 6:00 a.m.? She sat at the kitchen table and put her head down into her hands. In a few hours Colleen would be here and they'd be off to Halifax. She hoped that an incident with Arvel was not going to interfere with that.

She was up now and thought she might as well make some coffee. She took the carafe from the Proctor-Silex, filled it with cold water from the tap, and poured the contents into the back of the machine. She took the coffee can from the freezer and set it on the counter beside the stove.

A noise rose up outside the house, a high wailing sound. Jackie went to the back door and opened it, put her head out into the cold air. It was a siren, but it was too loud and persistent to be a siren from an emergency vehicle. It must have been the big siren perched on the tower in the parking lot at the back of the town hall. They'd used it years ago, a single blast to sound the nine o'clock curfew for kids under sixteen, but she'd never heard it wailing like this, rising and falling, sending a cold shiver through the town.

⚬⚬⚬⚬⚬⚬

First thing on Monday morning, the city hummed and throbbed. The clack and whir of the machines in the print shop across the alley came in through the open window. Meta slid aside the pane and stuck her head out the window into the cool Tokyo winter. When she came back inside, she left the window open a few centimetres and sparked the gas heater to life, positioning it so that it faced away from the vinyl tubing that connected it to the wall. She sat at the table, consciously holding off grief. She had to call home, but she wanted some time to herself first. She wasn't awake yet, and knowing earlier was not going to save anybody's life. She wished she could close her eyes and stop time: She'd sit in this crummy little apartment in Tokyo forever, never knowing, never having anything to know.

There was a thirteen-hour time difference between Tokyo and Nova Scotia. The news reports had said the explosion had taken place at five thirty in the morning, but that must have been on Sunday morning, Nova Scotia time. It would now be after five in the afternoon on Sunday in Nova Scotia.

With a cup of hot tea in her hand, she went into the hallway, taking care to close the door noiselessly behind her. She rode the elevator to the twelfth floor without meeting anyone. Once on the rooftop, she put her cup down on the ledge and stared out over the buildings that cluttered the landscape. How early in the morning was it? She couldn't remember. She always got up long before she had to go to work, so she wasn't thinking about that yet. Even with a lined windbreaker she began to feel chilly. But it was not cold enough to see even a hint of steam on her breath. She looked down at the little side street that twisted up behind the building and saw that it was alive already. A paperboy, the basket of his bicycle now empty, limped along beside the bike, drinking something from a can. Old women were out, sweeping the spotless pavement in front of their little shops and apartments. The old man who lived in the storefront of a defunct small-engine repair shop stepped into the street wearing only his grey one-piece long johns.

She was sure that Ziv was dead. She had learned from her parents that Ziv had hired on at Eastyard and was working underground.

A strange new emotion began to affect Meta, and though she had never experienced the feeling before, she felt as though she had. The pit had exploded, the alarms had gone off. The alarm she'd heard had sounded halfway round the world. Now she was waiting for news of a loved one. She felt she was living in the wrong decade, the wrong century. She felt like her own grandmother, who had done this same waiting first for a father, then a brother, and then a husband.

There were two messages on the machine when she got back inside her apartment. The first must have been there, unnoticed, since last night. It was in garbled Japanese, half-spoken, half-sputtered. Meta guessed that in recent months a phone-sex line had opened with a number that must resemble hers. Men had been calling, leaving messages that had turned Yuka red when Meta asked her to translate. Some even switched languages when they heard her speak English on the tape, repeating the single related word they knew: sex, sex, sex, sex.

The next message was from her parents, telling her there was some news.

She went to the teapot and poured herself half a cup, sat at the table and drank it slowly, then went back to the phone and, after several attempts, was able to get through.

Meta told her mother she'd heard about the explosion. Her mother exhaled heavily into the telephone, making a dull percussive sound.

"Everything is just . . . it's so unclear," her mother said. "I don't know what you know there. The company doesn't know exactly who all is down there, yet. They didn't have a list of the shift."

"They don't know who's underground in their own mine!"

"Only immediate family has seen the list of names at this point, the people they know for sure are underground. They've got it posted in the fire hall in Plymouth. They're only letting family members see it."

"Is it Ziv, Ma? For God's sake, is it Ziv?"

"Someone at Tim Horton's told your father that his neighbour's boy was on the shift before and no one had been in touch with him since, so they let the neighbour see the list. And . . . well . . . the fellow your father spoke to . . . he thought the other fellow saw Arvel's name there. I tried to call Arvel's mother, but the phone's been busy there all day. Likely off the hook."

Meta looked about her tiny apartment and felt all connection with Japan dissolve.

"Oh my God," Meta said. "Arvel. You're sure it's not Ziv?"

"Your father said Ziv doesn't work at Eastyard any more. He hired on and then quit not long after."

"Why didn't you tell me," Meta said quietly, more a statement than a question.

"The company is talking about rescue operations. The draegermen have started down the main shaft already, but it's slow going. They're measuring for gas. The ventilation system is knocked out. But honey . . ." Her mother's voice became dark, disappeared briefly in the staticky vapour of thousands of kilometres. "The explosion," she continued. "It shook the house, here. It cracked a pane of glass in one of the old windows upstairs. The roof over the main shaft where it comes to the surface . . . the blast blew it all to pieces, bent the steel frame and everything. The old-timers here . . . the ones who remember other blasts. They say . . . well . . . they're not very hopeful."

"I'm going to hang up now. I've got to sit down and process some of this. If there's any news, call me right away, will you?"

"I will. Are you going to be all right?"

"I'm okay. I'm okay. Just let me go now."

Meta put the receiver down. She thought about Ziv and his family, pictured them huddled together in the living room, watching the TV, waiting for some news from underground. The sound of her own blood rushed through her head. Ziv had died and come back to life.

For the first day after the explosion, the AP Radio Network news featured stories about Eastyard on its hourly news broadcasts carried by American Forces Radio. In the ten-minute break between each class, Meta had rushed back to her office to listen. The draegermen were still underground, no survivors had been located or returned to the surface. No bodies had been discovered. So with no immediate drama to report, the network dropped coverage back to once or twice a day.

She had made several attempts to call Ziv at his family's number, but got busy signals each time, just as her mother had. It had been so long since they'd spoken, she was half-relieved not to have got through. She feared the awkwardness between them in spite of the circumstances.

Outside, cold rain had been pouring down. Meta stopped inside the door of the staff room, twisted her brown umbrella so it would fit in the rack, and stuffed it into a square in the wire mesh. Greg Ulesso's desk was empty. She felt relieved.

She noted that her hands were steady as she poured herself a cup of coffee and walked with it to her desk, where she sat and looked at the planbook and the texts she was supposed to use to organize her day. This office was officially called the Foreign Languages Department by the college. But some of the more jaded long-term foreign teachers had dubbed it "The Gulag," since it housed the desks and working space of almost exclusively foreign teachers, and, except for a few administrators who had private offices adjacent, it was almost two city blocks removed from any of the other faculty rooms. It got a decent amount of natural light from a bank of windows at the end of the room opposite to Meta's desk, and the decor was bland office beige and grey and white. Most teachers were in the room at the moment, but it was close enough to class time that conversations were at a minimum, as last-minute preparations were being made.

"Good morning," called a voice from behind a filing cabinet. She stiffened. "Good morning," she said.

"How was your weekend?"

"This is Tuesday," Meta said. "The weekend's long gone."

"But I don't think I saw you yesterday."

Should she tell him? She had no desire to be on personal terms with Ulesso, but found herself saying, "There was a disaster in my hometown. Did you see it on the news?"

Ulesso reached into his rear pocket and pulled out a rolled up copy of the *Daily Yomiyuri*. "It's right here on the front page . . . Nova Scotia . . . Isn't that where you're from?"

"Yes."

"I guess this hits pretty close to home."

"It *is* home. It's not pretty close. The explosion cracked a window in my parents' house."

Ulesso stopped for a moment, his face working to find an expression. "Coal mining is a dangerous business. When I was in Wales . . ."

"This isn't Wales. It's Nova Scotia. Can't you see I'm upset?" She was starting to shake.

"Come on," Ulesso said skeptically. "What are the chances you actually know someone underground?"

"Jesus, Greg! The chances are one hundred per cent!"

She turned away from him, scooped the books for her first class from the desk, and made for the door. Ulesso had turned his attention to another teacher who was at the photocopier, frantically doing some last-minute copying.

"Isn't this smashing weather? This rain? All it does in this bloody country is rain. I've never seen a country with such appalling . . ."

Meta had had enough. She walked over to the photocopier and turned Ulesso around so he would listen to her. Not until she began speaking did she realize that she'd been unconsciously preparing for this moment for months. She'd been writing a speech, a tirade, in her head, storing it away for the moment she would confront Greg Ulesso and tell him what she thought.

"Listen, Greg," she said. At the sound of her voice the whole office hushed. She took a breath and continued. "If it didn't rain so much here, the Kanto Plain would not be a good place to grow rice. If the Kanto Plain were not such a good place to grow rice, Ancient Japanese culture would never have developed. If Ancient Japanese culture had never developed, there would never have been a Shogunate. If there had never been a Shogunate, there would never have been a Meiji restoration or a Commodore Perry. Without them, there would not have been an economic boom and military buildup before the war, there would have been no Pearl Harbor, the Japanese would never have been defeated, there would never have been the postwar Economic Miracle, and you wouldn't have your cushy job." She was speaking very loudly now. People had come in from adjoining rooms to hear. "So every time it rains in this town, you'd better get down on your knees and thank God for the rain that's making you rich and keeping you from having to do honest work!"

She turned around and stormed out the door. Behind her the room erupted in applause.

Meta left school at three thirty and arrived back at her apartment after four. There was a white envelope taped to her door. She removed the envelope and looked around the hallway for a clue as to who might have left it. On the address side of the envelope was carefully printed *Mrs. Meta*. The writing did not look like Yuka's. The writer had to have been Kazuhiro, her son. The envelope was thin and flimsy; it obviously did not contain much.

She ran a thumbnail under the fold of the flap and extracted a single half-sheet of cream paper.

*Dear Mrs. Meta:*

*Mrs. Yuka is hospital. Please call to her.*

This brief message was followed by a telephone number and a room number. She knocked on Yuka's door to see whether Kazuhiro could give her any further information, but there was no answer.

The note made the decision for her, the one she'd been avoiding making all day. The first call she made was to Korean Airlines, to use the second half of her L.A.-Tokyo return ticket, and to make the arrangement with Delta and Air Canada to get her to Halifax. She'd tell her principal in the morning that she was taking a couple of weeks off. Family emergency. She could explain it without straying too far from the truth. There was an article a day on Eastyard in the *Daily Yomiyuri*; it wouldn't be hard.

The door of Yuka's room was ajar and Meta paused in the gleaming hospital hallway outside it, closed her eyes briefly to compose herself before entering. She was relieved to see Yuka no more obviously injured than she'd been the last time she'd seen her. On her way to the hospital she had been steeling herself for lacerations, burns, traction, anything just short of death. All she could see poking out of the sheets was Yuka's face, which had healed considerably since the last time she'd seen her. The swelling had gone down and some of the bruised flesh had already gone through its darkest phase, was lightening to a yellowish brown.

Meta knew from experience that the only way to get information from Yuka was to grill her with questions. Otherwise, she could skirt a problem or issue indefinitely. She approached the bedside and sat in the chair there. Carefully she sought out Yuka's hand, coaxed it from beneath the sheets, and held it.

"Yuka, what happened? Did he hit you again?"

Yuka smiled, an action that, in its context, sickened Meta's stomach. "No," she said. "It's same. Same as other day. You saw."

"He hasn't hit you since the other day?"

She shook her head, no. "Something happens. I don't know before."

"You went to the doctor the other day. There was something wrong that he didn't know about then."

Yuka nodded. "Inside. I am broken inside." She patted her stomach gently with her free palm. Meta held the other hand more tightly, careful not to squeeze too hard. "A thing inside me is broken."

For a moment Meta could not understand. Her struggle to comprehend the words had momentarily blurred the meaning of the gestures to her.

"Is it a bone?" she asked. "Do you have a broken bone you didn't know about?"

Yuka shook her head. "I wake up," she began miming the actions of her discovery. Her mouth fell open and she pointed into it. "Blood is coming out."

"Jesus Christ," Meta said. "Internal hemorrhaging. Are you going to be okay? What have the doctors said?"

"They think okay," Yuka said. "They will make a operation soon."

Meta searched her brain for a way of saying *exploratory surgery* in simple vocabulary. "Is the operation for the doctors to find the problem?"

Yuka answered *yes*, but Meta was not convinced the meaning of her question was clear enough.

"Do the doctors know exactly what the problem is?"

Yuka was smiling and answered with another *yes*. Meta realized that with the combination of anxiety, pain, fear, language limitations, and the pain-killing drugs that Yuka had probably been given, she would not find out exactly what was wrong.

"Does your son know what happened?" Meta asked. Yuka shook her head, still smiling. "Does he know what your injuries are?" Yuka nodded. "Did he ask how you got them?" She shook her head.

Meta considered asking Yuka if her son needed to know why she was in the hospital. He obviously knew his mother had been assaulted. No one could have been in the same room with her and not come to this realization. Did it not occur to him to ask by whom? Did Yuka not think it important to tell him?

Meta had been wondering whether or not to tell Yuka about what was going on back in Canada, but that seemed impossible now.

Yuka's energy seemed drained from the visit. Meta watched as she drifted off to sleep.

It was only a few blocks from the south end of the Red Row to the little bungalow that Jackie and Arvel rented, but Ziv noticed a change in the usual sparse traffic on the streets. Already, outsiders were flocking to Albion Mines in the wake of the explosion. He saw three four-door rental sedans go past with what looked like plainclothes Mounties in them. Up in the parking lot of the elementary school, two television news vans were parked side-by-side and facing opposite directions as the drivers conversed.

When Jackie opened the door and saw Ziv, she pulled him in through the doorway and hugged him, pushing her face into his chest. As he held her, he noticed there was luggage piled near the back door.

"We want to know how you and the kids are," Ziv said. "My mother wants you to come to the house." He could hear the children somewhere out of sight, one of the bedrooms probably, playing with a toy that made a rattling sound.

"I can't go down there," Jackie said. She was holding him so tightly that her words got muffled by his shirt and were difficult to understand.

"Jackie, don't be so proud. It's a time to be with family now."

"I kicked him out," Jackie said. "A lot of times. Look at this," she pointed at the luggage. "I was going to Halifax today. Stealing away. Leaving. Without even telling him."

"That doesn't matter," Ziv said. "Not now."

Jackie stepped back from him. An angry look spread over her face. "How can it not matter?" she said.

"You're family, Jackie," Ziv said. "You're married to my brother."

"I can't face anyone right now," Jackie said. "I was sneaking out of here like some kind of criminal. I can't face your parents. The kids . . . the kids are all mixed-up. I told them we'd be in Halifax today."

"Jackie," Ziv said. He hugged her against him again. "I won't tell anyone about the luggage. Just come on down home. Bring the kids. Don't do this to yourself."

"I said no, Ziv."

Ziv got home from Jackie's and sat silently in the living room with his parents. It was as if the fear and panic that had enveloped them had dissipated, replaced now by a lifeless shock and numbness. The only sound in the room came from the television. They'd taken the phone off the hook to avoid the reporters who had been calling incessantly to ask them for a statement. They were uneasy about missing some important news, but the company had promised to update them in person about the status of rescue operations.

They sat silently before the television, waiting to see something happen, waiting for news of rescue to break.

Aside from speculation about what had caused the explosion, and whether it had been localized or had gone ripping through all the shafts, one of the first things the media reported was that the mining company did not know who had been working and who hadn't at the time of the explosion. Within an hour of the mishap, many employees and their families received anonymous phone calls they later realized were from the company. Someone – in most cases it was a young woman on the other end of the phone – asked if the employee in the family had been working the back shift. Ziv looked at his father, but except for a very slight shaking of his head, as though in disbelief, Ennis did not appear to respond to anything that was being said.

By late afternoon, the TV news had turned George Hannah into a prophet. When the Eastyard mine had still been in its planning stages, a news crew had gone to the Albion Mines Miner's Museum, where the old man worked as the caretaker, and asked him what he thought of opening a new mine on the volatile seams that had been worked in Pictou County for over a hundred years. "You'd might as well build the memorial to the dead right now," the old man had said, the crest on his Royal Canadian Legion beret glinting in the sun. The camera zoomed in on his face so that its shadows showed every crag and scar. "Just leave plenty of room on it to carve the names in later." Even the American networks had picked up on the year-old footage, and it was impossible to watch any channel for very long without seeing it.

At the surface, the TV showed the draegermen reappearing from the twisted portal, black with soot and dust. Shaking. A supply of fresh air had been restored to parts of the number-one deep, but in the areas without ventilation, the air temperature soared to a swelter that made the full draegerman's gear almost unbearable. With the shaft so badly burnt, the metal supports so twisted and melted, the primary fear of the draegermen was rock fall from overhead. Even a minor collapse under these conditions could prove fatal, since access to machinery and personnel was limited.

Media were being held at bay some distance from the portal, when it was announced that the relief draeger crew was put together. A reporter from an American network caught up to someone who must have been part of the original crew as he was driving away in his pickup. The man was reluctant to talk, but just before he closed the door of his truck, the reporter shouted: "What's it like down there?"

The draegerman rubbed a hand over his face, looked down a moment, then faced the camera. "Hell," he said. "Except . . . If you were in Hell, you'd have the peace of mind of knowing you were dead."

By the third time this clip was shown, it was already after midnight. Dunya stood up and shut off the TV. "This is telling us nothing," she said, and neither Ziv nor Ennis stood to turn the thing back on.

The morning of the second day, after very little sleep, they sat together in the kitchen. Ennis got up and made himself a ragged-looking fried egg, put it in a bowl, and poked at it with a fork, moving it back and forth across its own trail of grease. The three of them sat silently, sipping at black coffee because they were afraid they could not hold down milk. This was the first time in years that the three of them had sat at table together without fighting.

They did not discuss going to the fire hall. When the coffee pot was empty, they got up from the table, put on their coats and boots, and got into the car together.

Snow fell lightly as Ennis drove south on Foord Street. The early-morning winter light was dim, and diminished further by the curtain of falling snow that seemed draped over the car.

"You had a hand in this, Ennis," said Dunya, her voice quiet, but menacing.

"For the love of God, woman," Ennis said.

"You encouraged that boy to go into the mine."

"It was my shift," Ziv said. "Arvel got moved onto it the day I quit."

"Nobody blames *you*," Dunya said.

"Who are you blaming, then?" Ennis said.

"I can't see the town clock through the snow," Dunya said as they drove past the town hall. She pulled back the sleeve of her coat and looked at her watch.

"I asked you a question," Ennis said.

The Plymouth Fire Hall was just across the river at the south end of Albion Mines, only a few hundred metres from the gates of Eastyard Coal. It was still snowing as they approached. Through the heavy gauze of flakes, Ennis could see the crowd of media, cameras, microphones, vans with satellite dishes bolted to the roof. This group was being held back, within sight of the fire hall, but beyond a distance at which anyone on the outside of the makeshift fence of yellow traffic barricades could communicate with anyone in or around the fire hall. Police patrolled barricades vigorously and pushed back newspeople to make way for the approach of the car of a family member.

Ennis sat bolt upright. He felt like a scab, driving through the throng of cameras and reporters, where a Mountie unhooked a chain and pushed aside two yellow barricades to let the car pass through. He instinctively held a hand at the side of his face so no one could take his picture.

In the room usually used for wedding dances and community meetings, families hugged each other and wept. There were only two small windows, which let in hardly any natural light. Bare bulbs in round fixtures poured out a glare that was almost audible.

A big woman in a grey sweatshirt met them when they arrived. Ennis forgot her name as soon as she said it. Sheets of newsprint, painted in a childish way with the names of all twenty-six men, hung on the walls around the room. A small woman with broad shoulders, whom people called Audrey, was taping the last of these to the scuffed gyproc wall, as though in preparation for a homecoming. When he saw Arvel's name, painted in big letters, a flower where the "e" should have been, Ennis had a vision.

Blackness turned to glinting half-light in the still atmosphere of the mine below. Overhead, melted steel arches curled toward the floor. Face-down and scorched blacker than coal, Arvel's body lay in a powdery bath of ashes.

"I'll not stay here," Ennis said, his eyes racing about for something he could rest them on that made sense. Dunya was halfway across the room, a woman from the Catholic Women's League had an arm around her shoulders and was leading her toward a tray of sandwiches. Ennis made his way to her. "I'll not stay here," he said.

Ziv had driven him home, and as they pulled into the driveway, he tried to change Ennis's mind.

"You'll be alone down here," he said. "Come back up to the fire hall."

Ennis would have none of it. He shook his head and stepped out into the ankle-deep powdery snow on the driveway. He bent over and looked at Ziv in the driver's seat, shook his head again, and slammed the passenger door.

When he got inside, he sat at the kitchen table and listened to his silent house. His heel and his tailbone still throbbed from his kick at the fridge two nights ago. He looked at the familiar kitchen. Arvel had lived so much of his life within these walls that he must in some way still be here. Arvel's voice had vibrated through this air and had been absorbed by these walls. In the future, Ennis thought, there will be a machine that you can plug into a room which will replay every conversation that ever took place there.

He'd like to believe now that if there had been no explosion on Arvel's shift, he would have apologized when Arvel had gotten home that morning. But even in his grief, he could not fool himself into thinking he would have done so. He'd never apologized to anyone in his life. For anything. He'd gone to confession in the days when he'd been a practising Catholic, but he'd done it by rote. His trips to the confessional had been little games of scorekeeping, where he'd rattle off a list of sins, prattle his way through the act of contrition, and go home feeling no freer of sin than he'd ever been.

He rose from the table and took the forty of rum from the cupboard. The furnace came on downstairs, setting up motion in the curtains. In the half-dark of the north window, a few dust motes rose up to the light. He poured Pepsi into a tall glass, then topped that with Captain Morgan. He stared hard at the doorway and tried to will Arvel to appear again in it. He recalled what they spoke of, the last words he would ever say to his son: a threat. He watched Arvel leave again, heard his own voice bellow.

Ennis was certain Arvel was dead, and thinking of Arvel's body now, smothered with coal dust far below the surface of the earth, he remembered once having saved his son's life. The boy could not have been more than five or six years old and the whole family was swimming in the river at Iona Park, south of Albion Mines.

Both boys had been knee-deep in the water when Ennis had turned away to get a beer from the cooler. When he looked back, Ziv was standing alone, pointing soundlessly downriver to where Arvel was rolling over and over like a log down some light rapids.

He recalled running through the shallows and scooping his spluttering son from just beneath the surface. He remembered the exact way he'd held the boy to his chest, and how warm he'd felt against him even after his plunge into the cold water.

The phone rang. Ennis took a moment to bring himself back to the world, then brought his rum and Pepsi to the table, sat, and picked up the receiver.

"Hello? Hello?" It was a young man's voice, formal and rehearsed. The connection was slightly staticky.

"Hello," Ennis said.

"Could I speak to Ennis Burrows, please?"

"This is Ennis Burrows."

"Mr. Burrows, it's Randolf Meyers calling from NBC television news."

"I've talked with enough reporters already," Ennis said. "I'm sorry." He hung up abruptly. The instant he put the phone on the hook, it rang again, startling him.

"Hello," he said warily, ready to hang up if it was another reporter.

"Ennis, it's Allie."

At the sound of Allie McInnis's voice, Ennis remembered the argument they'd had at the Tartan. In a flash, he saw himself pushing a beer glass into McInnis's open mouth. Had that been only two nights ago?

"I'm sorry," the two men said in unison.

Ennis picked up his tumbler of black, syrupy rum and Pepsi and looked at the acid bubbles that rose through it to the top, where they burst into the air. He raised the glass to his lips and drank.

"I heard your boy is down there," McInnis said.

"He's found a place to stay," Ennis said. McInnis was silent. How could he know what Ennis was talking about? "His wife kicked him out of one house, then I threw him out of another. He found a place now that he can't get kicked out of." Ennis picked up the rum and took another big drink.

"Don't talk like that, Ennis," McInnis said. "You have to stay hopeful."

"Kaboom, and the whole fucking world changes. Listen to you. After what I did the other night, you should be waiting outside my back door with a baseball bat."

"Forget about the other night. We were drunk, the two of us. I deserved to have my mouth shut for me."

"And I deserved to be blown to fucking bits. Only it was my son that got that treatment."

"I don't want to tie up your line, Ennis. I'm sorry about this. I don't know what the hell I can do, but if you think of something, just call me."

"I never should have done it," Ennis said.

"Will you forget that? I got you worked up. I knew what I was doing."

"Anyway . . . I'm sorry." Ennis hung up the phone and lowered his face toward the table, resting his forehead on the back of his arm.

The phone started up again, and he listened to it ring four or five times, certain it was another reporter. It rang again and the thought that it might be Dunya with some news made him pick up.

"Hello."

"Mr. Burrows?"

"Yes."

"John Wexler, ABC news."

Ennis put the phone back on the hook, waited a few seconds, then picked it up again. When he heard a dial tone, he left the receiver off the hook and put his head back down onto his arm.

They'd bought this house just before Arvel was born, moved out of the one down near Kirk Avenue they'd been renting from Stan Kravchuk, a friend of Dunya's father. He'd spent years in this house, a young man's entire lifetime, years at this table in this kitchen, years of ranting and storming. The room had soaked up all that anger. It had absorbed all that had taken place in it. He turned his head so his ear rested on the table. All those years, all that pain, could never be forgotten or erased. So he listened. He closed his eyes, silenced his own thoughts, and listened.

⊰⊱

Jackie arrived at the fire hall with Colleen and the girls. Someone at the door told them there were toys set up for the kids in a room downstairs. It was a chilly room with a concrete floor that sloped in all directions toward a big steel drum in the centre. It looked like a place where equipment cleaning and maintenance might take place, though there was no sign of any gear in the room. Against one wall, three big fan-driven electric heaters created a warm blast at eye level, but did not dispel the chill that crept up from the icy floor.

As soon as they'd entered the room, the two girls ran to a big pile of yellow and black construction toys without even glancing back at their mother. Jackie checked to see that the children were supervised and she and Colleen climbed back up the stairs.

In the far corner of the big room upstairs, a group of haggard women consoled each other. As the day wore on, the group swelled and shrank and swelled again. At times there were men sprinkled in amongst the women. Almost always there were children. Sometimes the group formed a large, almost perfect circle, at times it broke up into smaller huddles. Among this odd collection of people who were on intimate terms with each other, despite the fact that most were strangers, Jackie was able to come face-to-face with her shock and grief. So many of the other wives of the twenty-six underground seemed to be holding out hope, believing, mustering the strength within themselves to believe that their husbands were still alive. These women were boisterous and demonstrative, giving encouraging hugs when someone showed signs of despair. Jackie was one of the others, one of the quiet, sullen women who strained through a tired smile when someone else tried to cheer her up.

She was sure it was too late for hope. She was sure Arvel was dead. And this realization shocked and grieved her in spite of everything.

As Jackie sat at one of the folding tables that had been set up with little triangular sandwiches on it, she took some comfort from Colleen's hand on her shoulder or placed gently on her forearm. But any time Jackie looked Colleen in the eye, Colleen would tear up and turn away, unable to say anything.

Across the room she saw Dunya. She had been in the room for some time, but did not seem to have noticed her. For a while

Ziv had been with her, but he seemed to have disappeared somewhere. Dunya sat alone now at a table, dressed up as though for church and looking stiff and uncomfortable. Yesterday, Jackie had refused Ziv's request to go down to their house. The invitation had been from Dunya, she knew, and she could not imagine Dunya really wanted to see her. She had kicked the woman's son out of his own house innumerable times, and now that son was . . . she could not bring herself to think it.

She remained seated, Colleen at her side, half-hoping her mother-in-law would never see her, half-hoping she'd come seeking her out and find her.

"Go over and talk to her," Colleen said, nudging her gently with an elbow.

"I know I should," Jackie said. "But I just don't have the heart."

"It doesn't take heart. It takes feet. Stand up and walk over. I'll go with you if that'll make it easier. Or else I'll stay here. You decide."

"Jackie," a voice exclaimed. She scanned the room and saw Ziv coming toward her, looking so much like Arvel as he lumbered in her direction, towering above everyone around him.

The sight of him brought tears to her eyes. She blinked them back and choked on the sobs that wanted to bubble up into her throat.

They sat for some time without saying anything. Their hands covered each other's, and the warmth that built up there might have been a little fire they were sheltering.

When she noticed Ziv looking at Colleen, Jackie said, "You've met Colleen Chisolm before, haven't you?"

Ziv nodded. "At the wedding, I think," he said.

Colleen said nothing but nodded back at Ziv.

After a while Jackie said, "I guess you know now who was right."

Ziv raised his eyes and gazed into her face. "I don't know what you're talking about," he said.

"When you quit the pit," Jackie said. "You always saw that as a weakness. Arvel talked about how brave you were to quit, how that took more guts." She used the past tense without thinking about what it meant.

"I don't have a family to support, for one thing," Ziv said.

"Look . . . now . . ." Jackie said. She knew exactly what she wanted to say, but this was the wrong time to say it.

Ziv brought Jackie over to the table where Dunya was sitting on her own. Dunya stood up and the two embraced. Dunya asked how Jackie and the kids were doing. Before any of them had a chance to sit back down, Ziv suggested that they go home. It was early evening by now and he had been feeling uneasy and on display there all afternoon.

Jackie agreed to go back to their house and Ziv thought she actually looked grateful and relieved to be going. Colleen offered to bring the kids back to Jackie and Arvel's house with her, but Jackie said that as tired as the girls might be at this time of day, she wanted them with her.

"I'll leave you with your family," Colleen had said. She drove her car back to the house on Pleasant Street. Jackie and the kids got into Ennis's car, along with Ziv and Dunya. Though it was only a few minutes from the fire hall, both kids were already sound asleep by the time Ziv pulled his father's car up to the house in the Red Row.

As soon as he saw it, Ziv didn't like the look of the house. Although it was dark now, the curtains were not closed. A light was on somewhere in the downstairs, so he could see the surfaces of some interior walls and the dark outline of a doorway.

Jackie picked up Melanie from the back seat and Ziv took Kate. The snow from earlier had continued on for several hours before it stopped. There was now a light sprinkle on the ground. The temperature had gone down, and in the few places where a centimetre or more of snow had collected, their feet squeaked down into it, packed it down into what had already accumulated.

Dunya was first to open the door and step into the porch. "Oh my God!" she said. Ziv readied himself for anything, for the body of the old man even, strung up from the ceiling.

But as soon as he entered the porch he saw why his mother had exclaimed, and why she was now having a difficult time making her way into the kitchen. The porch was in complete disarray. Coats had been taken from the coat rack and lay strewn around the room. Ennis's two tool boxes, which usually sat on a small table by the door, had been overturned, the tools thrown every which way. There was a small electric range in the porch. It had been upended and hurled across the room, where it knocked out a big triangle of plaster when it had hit the wall.

In the kitchen, the curtains from the window had been ripped off their rods and stuffed into the sink. The refrigerator was on its side, half-blocking the door from the porch. The contents of the fridge – meat, eggs, milk, vegetables, opened cans of fruit, bottles of pickles and jam and olives – had been thrown against the walls, up into the ceiling, where the tiles were full of dents and stains. The kitchen table had been knocked over.

In the living room, the two chairs and the couch were over-turned. The magazine rack was gutted. The china cabinet had been pulled forward onto its face. Broken glass and china shards lay before it, thick as spilled paint. The big ornamental cast-iron kettle from the cabinet top had put a large ding in a metal serving tray it had landed on.

Ziv and Jackie and Dunya stood frozen in the midst of the disaster, as though, by standing still, they could stop this scene from progressing. "Let's put the kids back out in the car," Ziv said to Jackie. She nodded, but neither of them moved for a moment.

Ziv shifted the weight of the sleeping child over one shoulder, and with his free hand guided Jackie out the door. They laid Melanie in the front seat, Kate in the back, and took off their own coats to cover them. They heard screaming when they re-entered the house, and followed it, stepping over and around the obstacles in the trashed rooms. At the foot of the stairs lay Ennis, his head on the floor of the lower landing, his feet up five or six steps. An empty forty of rum lay in the corner by the front door, just beyond his reach.

Dunya was astraddle Ennis's torso, as though she were doing CPR. In both hands she was holding the single handle of a big black cast-iron kettle. The one that had come from the top of the china cabinet. Then, as if everything in her life had been leading to this moment, as if all the years of rage had arrived at his breaking point, as if the reason her son had been taken from her lay drunk and unconscious at her feet, she brought the kettle up over her head and slammed it down on Ennis's face. The kettle made a deep metallic *kong* on impact. She drew it back and brought it down again, and then again. "You bastard!" she said. "You bastard! You always make everything worse."

# 13

## BODIES

Ennis Burrows with his jaw wired shut had been like a bucking bronco sealed up to its knees in a block of concrete. Agitated, angry, he lay grunting, mumbling, and struggling against the restraints that had shut his mouth for him. He had been told he'd been unconscious for more than two days, and that he was lucky more internal damage hadn't been done. He'd asked the doctors what the hell had happened to him, but aside from outlining the details of the fractures in his skull and how they'd been put back together, the doctors were mum about his injuries. Ennis himself had no memory of what had happened, but he guessed, from the uncomfortable silence of the doctors, that someone had clubbed him good and the medical system was trying to stay out of it. Still, Ennis spent little time thinking about what had happened to him. All his mind seemed capable of thinking of was the mine, about the financial support that the federal and provincial governments had lent the Eastyard company: a hundred million dollars, and

Ennis was determined that someone had to get to the bottom of what happened. Those responsible had to be held accountable.

On the second day after he'd awakened, Ziv had come, and he stood beside the hospital bed, looking awkward and uncomfortable, and was silent while Ennis ranted. The combination of painkillers and the immobility of his jaw reduced everything he said to a series of guttural exclamations. When he stopped, his energy expended, Ziv asked him how he was feeling. Ennis shook his head, then pointed at the swelling. "Did you do this?" he managed to say.

Ziv looked away a moment, and immediately Ennis knew it was Dunya. His own wife had done this to him. "Dunya!" he said through his teeth. An emotion forced a sound out of him, but he could not tell what the emotion was.

"Dad," Ziv said. "They've given up the search."

Ennis had looked at his son intently, trying to read his face. He was aware of his own breathing, and how the sound of it through his clenched mouth must have made his every expression seem angry.

"Arvel's dead, they –" Ziv was unable to go on. His eyes blinked rapidly.

Ennis tried to speak through his wired mouth, but he was saying too much too fast, and Ziv could not understand. Ziv had brought his ear closer to Ennis's mouth, and Ennis was able to pull his lips back enough to say, "Your mother. How is she holding up?"

Ziv lowered his gaze and Ennis said, "Is she feeling up to coming?"

"I don't know, Dad," Ziv said.

But by now, two weeks later, Ennis had given up on speech completely. His only form of communication was to smile at the nurses who came into the room to check on him or to nod or shake his head at one of their simple questions. When Ziv came in, they usually sat in silence. Occasionally Ziv would ask him a question and he'd write a short response on a notepad he kept at his bedside.

He was allowed up to use the bathroom now, and every time he did so he became mesmerized by the sight of himself in the mirror. Barely an external scar or blemish showed on his face, yet the bone structure beneath his skin had been broken and then reassembled. The flesh over the bones was so swollen and blood-engorged that his face was unrecognizable to him. He looked to himself not so much like a monster or hideous freak as he did a total stranger, someone whose eyes were a bit familiar but whose features sparked no recognition.

He'd been in plenty of fights in his life, had suffered innumerable injuries on the job. He'd had his nose broken, his eyes swollen shut. He'd suffered burns from red-hot rivets, he'd had flashes from arc welders. He'd been punched in the side of the head hard enough to break an eardrum. But he'd never before been rendered unrecognizable to himself. And this at the hand of his own wife.

Whatever had forced him and Dunya apart over the years, they both loved the boys. Ennis knew that whatever he could be accused of, neglect, mistreatment, pigheadedness, stupidity, he could not be accused of not loving his boys. What hurt more than the bludgeoning itself was that Dunya was staying away now, consigning herself to mourning her son alone.

Ziv had told him that there was going to be a memorial service. But now in his drug-hazy memory the details, time, and place had escaped Ennis's mind. He had a little television beside his bed, and it was only by accident that he stumbled upon live coverage of the memorial to honour his son and the other men who were lost. They were carrying it on the national television, pre-empting regular programming.

He recognized the building immediately as the United Church in Albion Mines. The cameras panned through the crowded church, then switched to the auditorium in the hall next door, then to the overflowing crowds on the street outside the church that spilled across Acadia Avenue and onto the Albion ball field, already softening into mud with the first inklings of spring. The perspective of the cameras was from such a wide angle that it was difficult to pick out individuals as, one at a time, priests and ministers led the crowds in prayer. Dunya and Ziv would be there somewhere, Ennis knew, but when he scanned the crowd for their faces, more closely when the cameras went inside the church, he was unable to find them.

Then someone began reading a poem. Ennis started when he realized it was Ben MacGillivary, a representative of the United Mine Workers at the podium. What the hell was he doing there? The UMW lost the first certification vote at Eastyard. He should know better than to get involved in an Eastyard memorial. Inviting him there was only an attempt on the part of the company to blur public perception, to create the impression that the labour movement had somehow been involved in the operation when it had not. Ennis could remember when MacGillivary first got involved in unions. He'd seemed such a young man, a smart, well-educated idealist. It was a shock now to see how old MacGillivary had gotten, old enough to be thinking seriously about his own retirement. Ben had always been a reader, and it was just like him to bring a poem to such an occasion. He would have the best of intentions, Ennis knew, but it was still a mistake for a union official to speak at a memorial service for non-unionized workers. It was playing into the hands of the company, giving the public the impression that the union was somehow involved or associated with the mine.

The poem MacGillivary read seemed to be about toughness, strength, endurance, about how people cannot be defeated. At the line "Split all ends up, they shan't crack," when he heard the emotion break MacGillivary's voice, tears blurred Ennis's vision.

From the podium, the camera switched to a close-up of the prime minister.

Ennis's eyes had been wet from the emotion of the poem, but they immediately dried, and pain like a nerve with a spike in it shot through his jaw as he strained to open his mouth to scream at the image of the nation's leader. This was the bastard who'd tried to buy votes by setting up the mine in the first place. Arvel's death was as much this man's fault as it was anyone's. An *ack*ing sound, muffled through his clamped mouth, began to rise from Ennis's throat. Even so, it must have been loud enough for the nurse at the station to hear from down the hall.

"Mr. Burrows, Mr. Burrows," she was saying as she came through the door. She looked at the television, which had switched to an exterior shot of the church. "Well, if this is upsetting you so much, I'm going to switch it off," she said. The screen went grey when she twisted the knob and Ennis settled his head back on his pillow. His anger subsided and all at once a stronger emotion overtook him. He began to weep. The tears rolled down his face and he could feel the moisture moving back past his ears and soaking into his hair.

The nurse moved to his side and took his hand gently in hers. "It's an awful thing," she said. "What happened to your son."

<hr/>

All media coverage of the Eastyard explosion had ended in Japan. But as soon as Meta landed in Vancouver, on the other side of the country from Albion Mines, she realized what an impact the event had had in Canada. She was still thousands of miles from home, but it was as if she had stepped into the middle of events, as if news of the tragedy had just been heard. The sound was turned down on the big television in the corner of the passenger lounge she'd parked herself in until they announced her connecting flight to Halifax, but from time to time, an image of the mine site would appear on screen. Once, she looked up and recognized the face of George Hannah, the old man she remembered as caretaker at the Miner's Museum in Albion Mines. The waiting was over now. In a copy of *Maclean's* magazine she'd bought at a newsstand, she read a one-page timeline of events. On the fifth day of rescue operations, draegermen recovered eleven bodies. All the men were found about where they'd been working, which meant they didn't have time to run from the fireball that must have ripped through the shafts. The men had died instantly, the ignited gas and dust robbing them of air. They would not have known what had happened. With no chance that anyone else survived, authorities decided that risking the lives of draegermen could no longer be justified.

Her mother had told her on the phone that Arvel's body was not among the eleven recovered.

This was only Meta's second visit home in the almost two years she'd been living in Japan. Last year's visit, in the summer, had been brief, and she had not been away long enough to see things differently on her return. But immediately upon getting onto the highway from the airport, the surroundings looked alien to her. She was shocked, as they drove, by the unbroken stretches of green.

When her mother drove into the Red Row she realized that the Red Row in her imaginings was out-of-date. Her memory was of the Red Row of her childhood, with the neighbourhood's run down houses, heaved and bumpy concrete block streets. Now she saw a respectable-looking working-class neighbourhood. As the car pulled into her parents' yard, she noticed that the Donats, on the other side of the duplex, had actually painted their house, and it was the same colour now as her parents' side.

Her father greeted her at the door with a hug. He did not say anything about the explosion or Arvel's death. He merely held both of her shoulders in his hands and looked her in the eye for a moment, as though to assess her emotional state.

"It's nice to see you, Dad."

"How are you, Meta?" She shrugged and looked away.

Meta had eaten on the plane, so she sat quietly at the table and drank tea as her parents ate. She looked out the kitchen window to the backyard, which was small even by Red Row standards, but which, by contrast with what she was used to in Tokyo, looked substantial to her. There had obviously been some snow this winter, since the thawed and refrozen pile at the end of the driveway remained, and the low spot in the backyard, where the outhouse had stood long before Meta's time, contained a flat layer of refrozen white. But the ground showed through, brown and grey and black, just about everywhere.

Meta looked at the Donat backyard. There was evidence of a lawn there.

"How are things next door?" she asked.

"They've been pretty quiet recently," her father said between bites of spinach quiche. "Willy is in Dorchester. I can't remember what for, offhand. Some of the other boys have gone out west for work. Leanne, I think she was a few years behind you in school, she's got a baby and she's moved in with the father in New Glasgow. Things are quieter there than they've been in years."

"I wonder how things are at Ziv's house." She could sense her parents' awkwardness as they both paused to consider before replying.

"Well," her mother began. "I think it's safe to say that things are not well in that house. Keep in mind that what I know I've got from the rumour mill only. But most of it is pretty reliable, I think." She went on to explain how Ziv's father had trashed the house after the explosion. He'd gotten drunk and thrown most of the family's furniture and belongings about the house. In response, Ziv's mother had somehow beaten him up badly, broken his skull, in fact. And afterwards, when the search for the missing miners was called off, she had thrown away most of her belongings.

Meta wished she'd been unable to believe the details of what her mother had told her. She worried terribly about Ziv. How would he be holding up in all of this?

After supper when she went out and stood in the backyard, breathing the icy air. She looked around her parents' backyard and tried to let the stillness comfort her. Her parents had planted shrubs here at the back, with raised beds of chipped bark encircling their bases. Against the boundary with the old alleyway there was a row of spruce saplings that might some day form a hedge. Late winter would soon turn to early spring, and she could almost catch a scent of earth when she breathed in through her nose.

She turned back into the house and came in to the clanking of dishes in the sink and the smell of warm suds.

Her father had one arm around her mother's waist, and they were leaning into each other. When her father nuzzled his face into her mother's neck, and she leaned her head back, it struck Meta that since she left home, her parents had rekindled their sex life. Meta lowered her head, suddenly embarrassed, then cleared her throat.

"Wow!" she said. "It's wilderness out there!"

***

It was already getting to be late on a busy day when the customers at Zellers started to seem especially rude to Ziv. First, a woman got angry with him because he was unable to copy a key for her. When Ziv had tried to explain that the rack behind the hardware counter just did not have a blank that matched the one she'd given him, she'd snatched her key from his hand and stormed off in a huff.

A sick-looking bald man with an untrimmed beard got Ziv to get a ladder and pass him a Shop-Vac from a top shelf at the far end of the hardware department. The man's two kids stood and looked on like mannequins, stiff and silent with blank expressions on their faces. When Ziv set the box with the vacuum on the floor, the man dug into it as though it were Christmas morning. He peeled back the top flaps, snapping the factory sealing tape that held them down. "Sir, there's one with the box already opened." Ziv pointed at a box on the bottom shelf.

"I don't want one that's been opened," the man said. He spilled the contents of the box onto the tiled floor and rummaged through what had come out, poking disdainfully with the toe of his leather work boot at pieces encased in cardboard and wrapped in plastic.

One of the kids picked up the brush attachment. "Hoi!" his father barked. The kid dropped the brush and hid behind his brother.

"How many gallons does this hold?" the man asked.

Ziv moved around to the front of the box the man had just gutted. "Eight-gallon wet/dry vacuum," he read.

"And this model is good for both wet and dry spills?"

"Apparently," said Ziv.

"Now, what's the difference between this model and the five-gallon one?"

"Three gallons," Ziv said with a straight face.

The man nodded gravely. "I'll take this one, I guess," the man said. He carelessly picked up what he'd spilled onto the floor and stuffed it back into the packing box. Nothing was in the right place, and hoses and attachments stuck up from the box's mouth, making folding down the flaps impossible. He left the box on the floor and silently stepped up Ziv's ladder, took an unopened box from the top shelf, and started down the aisle with it.

"Sir!" Ziv called after him. "Don't you want the one you looked at?"

"I don't want one that's been opened," the man said without turning around. His kids filed in behind him and they marched off toward the mall checkouts.

"What is this place? Self-service?" a gruff woman's voice called from the next aisle. Ziv was partway through repacking the vacuum, but he wasn't going to jump when someone yelled at him that way. He had to take everything, including the body of the vacuum itself, from the box, reposition it so it all fit, then reseal the box with a roll of clear packing tape.

"Can I get some service here!" came the voice again from the next aisle. He put the box back on the top shelf, replaced the ladder, and casually sauntered into the next aisle as though he hadn't heard the voice bellowing for him. Leaning against the glass power-tool cabinet was Meta. They hadn't seen each other in a long time, but it came back to him instantly, how good it felt to hold her.

Ziv was working until nine thirty, so they agreed to meet at nine forty-five at the Tim Horton's behind the mall where he worked.

Meta had not arrived yet when Ziv got there. He ordered himself a coffee and sat in a booth as far away from the smoking section as he could get, his every move monitored by the clutch of nosy people who were responsible for the blue haze in the restaurant.

Neither one of them had a clear idea of how or why they'd split up. At the time, Ziv said Meta had broken up with him after he got into a fight with another student. Meta claimed she did not break up with him, instead that he had given up on them.

It had been the end of their second year, and Ziv had done something he would find difficult to explain. For two years he had hardly drunk at all, then he had gone out with a group from his residence to celebrate the end of exams, and he'd gotten into a terrible punch-up. Meta had seemed upset when he told her the next day. She had even seemed a little sorry for him. He had a cut over one eye. Then they'd gone to dinner at the cafeteria and they saw the man he'd been fighting with. His nose was broken and taped up, his lips and the lower part of his face swollen grotesquely.

A conflict with Meta had started with this fight, a conflict that had dragged on for the four months of the university summer. There were details of this dispute that Ziv could not remember clearly, but he recalled several heated arguments he and Meta had had, always sparked somehow by that night.

They'd seen each other less and less as the summer went on, but their interactions had become strained. She seemed to sense that there was something seriously amiss with him, but each time she tried to get him to talk about it, he refused. She had shaken him up with her response to the fight he'd been in. She'd noticed something in him, a part of him she did not like. And in response, partly as a way of protecting himself from her disapproval, he'd hardened himself to her.

At some point, he'd made the decision not to go back to university. Meta had gone back and completed her degree. In his memory, his reasons for not returning were tangled up with his own disappointment in himself for his violent outburst, and his shame and anger in the face of Meta's obvious disappointment in him. He began to wonder what he ever thought he was doing, going to university in the first place. He didn't belong there. Now, four years later, the whole incident and its aftermath seemed immature and pointless.

They'd exchanged a few letters and seen each other infrequently since then.

Although they'd been separated for years and had only been in contact intermittently in the meantime, their former closeness had survived, and it was as natural as breathing now to settle in across from her, to feel himself relax, his whole body loosen again, in Meta's presence.

Ziv had been through so much, he wished he could tell Meta all about it all at once, send it to her telepathically so she'd immediately understand how he felt. His eyes began to fill up, and seeing this Meta said, "Oh, Ziv!"

He felt himself recoiling from his own emotion. He collected himself and sat up straighter in his seat.

"How's the land of the rising yen?" he laughed.

They chatted for a while about Meta's life in Japan. She told him she was banking between a thousand and fifteen hundred dollars a month.

"Wait a minute," Ziv said. "You're *making* a thousand to fifteen hundred a month?"

She shook her head. "I'd hate to tell you what I'm making. What do you make at Zellers?"

When he told her, she said, "Doesn't it bother anyone in that company that a full-time employee can't even afford to live?"

"Full time? I'm not even part-time. You know what they call my job? 'Extra'! Almost everyone who works there is *extra*. The biggest mistake I ever made was not going back to school. Now I feel as though I'm stuck."

"It's not too late. You can go back."

They stopped speaking for a few moments and the noise of the coffee shop rose up around them. There was the taste of lukewarm coffee in Ziv's mouth and the smell of cigarette smoke. He noticed Meta's hands. He'd forgotten how beautiful her hands were, how he'd used to admire the slender elegance of each finger and the incongruously homely nails, which she habitually bit to the quick.

He looked up to her face and could sense the seriousness, the tender concern of her gaze.

"Ziv," she said. "Tell me how you're doing." She reached out in his direction as though she wanted to take his hand. "I've been thinking about you and your family. It was hard for me to be so far away." Suddenly there was anger in her eyes, "How the hell could such a thing have happened?"

"That's what we're all wondering. It seems like such a shock. But at the same time, looking back, it seems obvious that something like this was going to happen." He looked down into the small space between them, as though that were the place the whole world had fallen. He reached across the table, held out his hands for Meta to take. When she held them, he felt relieved, as though some of the pain lodged in him had found its release.

---

Meta drove her parents' car from Tim Horton's to the parking lot behind the Heather Motor Hotel. Her ability to pay for the room, cash, without flinching, without even thinking about flinching, gave her a sense of freedom and power. She flipped on the light and walked into the room as though it were a new house she'd just bought.

In the middle of the hotel-room floor, they undressed each other. She unbuttoned his shirt and slipped the white T-shirt beneath it over his head. He seemed so large and hairy. His shoulder muscles were round, his chest hair crept up in a V from beneath the waistband of his pants. Motion became liquid as he unclasped her bra. She felt the cool air of the room on her breasts. They warmed again as he cupped them in his hands, brought his mouth to her nipples. Gently she tried pushing him to the bed, but his pants were halfway down, at his knees, and he toppled over, bounced, laughed. After pausing a moment to take her own pants off, she began rubbing the palms of her hands over all of him. She wanted to feel all of him at once. She pulled up on his knees until he was curled into a ball on his side and draped herself over him like a blanket, spread her arms to touch all of him. This feeling, the feeling of covering him, possessing him, was what she'd been thinking about, somewhere hidden at the back of her thoughts, since leaving Tokyo. The relief she felt was momentary. When it had gone it was followed by an empty feeling deep inside her, a hunger. She pushed back on the thigh of his upper leg, slid a hand over his hip to touch the penis that revealed itself as he moved.

Beginning at the bottom of his ribs, she moved her lips slowly along the skin of his belly until she felt his warm erection at her cheek. She turned her head and took it into her mouth.

"Oh," he said, and exhaled.

She held his penis in her mouth and tasted the salty heat of it. She moved on it, up and down. Felt it sliding on her tongue.

He began to speak her name. Softly. So softly. She could hardly hear. "Meta. Meta. Meta. Meta."

When it was over, Ziv began to cry quietly. She pressed herself into his back and felt the sobs shaking him. Soon she was crying too, and when they'd both stopped crying, they were asleep.

<hr />

On the day of the explosion, Gavin Fraser had called the mine office without even thinking about it and told them to put him on the list of draegermen. While he'd been employed there he'd been the best-trained mine rescue worker Eastyard had, so he felt obligated to be a part of the rescue by his bond to the men he'd worked with. It had not been very long since he'd quit, and Roscanne, the member of the office staff who answered when he finally got through, was obviously not aware he didn't work there any more. "It's funny we didn't call you already, Gavin," she said. He could hear her shuffling through papers, looking for his name on some list.

He'd been placed with a crew who had come, within hours of the explosion, from New Brunswick, and since none of them was familiar with the operation at Eastyard, his main job with the team was as guide. The captain of the team was one of the New Brunswickers.

They sat in their full gear in the change room, and after they'd all been introduced they had nothing left to do until they got the word to go down. Gavin was sick to his stomach, and the little wooden benches in the change room, with lockers around them full of the clothing of the men who were underground, seemed like they were made of broken glass. None of the men from the rescue crew could get comfortable on them. Though they all knew they should be sitting down, conserving their strength for what they'd have to do underground, they each spent more than half the forty-five minutes they were kept waiting on their feet and pacing. The men from New Brunswick knew Gavin had worked with the crew that was underground at the time of the explosion, otherwise they might have made a few jokes to cut the tension.

Someone from outside the room opened the door a crack and told them to proceed to the portals, the entrances of the main deeps. They all breathed a sigh of relief to be on their way finally, but at the portals, they had to wait again in a little camper trailer.

At last somebody came with the go-ahead from the rescue co-ordinator for them to proceed down the main decline. In the hour or so they'd spent together waiting for the signal to go down, the men had been mostly quiet, but the moment they entered the portal they fell completely silent. The place smelled charred, a sickening mixture of every burnt thing from the shafts below. Everything, every pipe, every arch, every piece of steel and concrete debris, was covered with a hard, black coating, the burnt remnants of the explosion. Gavin felt himself start to gag, but he knew that if he threw up now, it would slow down the progress of the whole team, so he fought his nausea and kept going.

They took the first five hundred feet slowly, careful of every piece of debris underfoot, watching the roof overhead for any signs of weakness. Thick concrete bulkheads had been thrown far back up the shaft and smashed into little pieces. Big pieces of steel, once part of doors that towered to the ceiling, were strewn about, twisted almost out of recognition. The men came across two tractors slammed together with such force that at first Gavin thought the debris heap was one smashed vehicle, until he counted eight tires underneath it.

Looking at this mass of compressed metal, Gavin stopped in sudden shock. He looked down for a moment, at his own feet and legs, at how the dust and soot had gathered on him already. He turned his back to the rest of the draeger team and felt himself well up. His vision blurred dangerously in the already poor visibility and he shuffled carefully until he could steady himself with a hand against a stone wall. A sob welled up in him, followed quickly by another. He closed his eyes and spoke aloud to himself briefly. "Okay, get hold of yourself. Get hold of yourself." He took a few deep breaths of processed air.

When he pulled himself back together, he took the team captain aside. Without anger, he confronted the man. "I think I've figured out what this rescue is really about." The man had dark features and a bushy black moustache that made his face even harder to read beneath his breathing apparatus. "Is someone on this team carrying body bags?" Gavin asked. The captain looked down at the floor a moment, at the charred and strewn debris, then nodded without speaking.

In an old scrapbook, something put together by a relative he never knew, Gavin had a clipping about the Moose River mine rescue of 1936. The clipping did not mention his great-grandfather, Leander Fraser, who had been a draegerman at Moose River, but Gavin knew about his family's involvement. He knew that the reporters of the time referred to all the rescuers as draegermen, although most of them were not. Leander Fraser was the real thing, trained in the use of all the equipment and techniques. His brother's name was William Barkhouse Fraser.

He was a member of the Acadia Rescue Corps in the twenties. William's picture appears in James M. Cameron's book, *The Pictonian Colliers*, dressed with his team members in the full rescue gear of the time. Gavin took that book off the shelf in his bedroom from time to time and looked at the picture of his distant uncle, searching for something of himself in a man he never met.

At Moose River, the Pictou County miners, unpaid volunteers all, had worked for eleven days, at times with pickaxes and bare hands, to save three company officials after the main shaft in a gold mine collapsed. Two of the three men were brought out alive, both with a Pictou County man on each arm to guide him. Descriptions from the time used the word *elated* to describe the rescuers, who were lauded as heroes on radio and in newspapers around the world.

Gavin had first read the article as a kid, and he'd had to look up *elated* in a dictionary. It was such an exhilarating word. He used to say it aloud to himself when he'd flip through the scrap-book, and it somehow became connected with how proud he felt to be descended from such a skilled and brave man as Leander Fraser. Elated.

## 14

### MEMORIES

After Arvel's funeral, a funeral held without a body present to consecrate or bury, she and Colleen had packed most of the furniture and belongings in the house into a rental truck and put them into storage in Halifax. And now, three weeks later, she was back, pulling again into the driveway of the house on Pleasant Street in Albion Mines for the final time. The new renters would move in the next day. There were still a few belongings for her to collect, and if she wanted to get back the damage deposit, she'd have to do a little cleaning. Kate had started school in Halifax, but this was March break, so Jackie had taken both kids to daycare and left them for the day. If she was going to be a little late getting back, Colleen was working the eight-to-four shift and had said she'd pick the kids up and get them supper. They were still at Colleen's apartment, but Jackie was hoping a unit would come open in the same building within the next month or so.

She eased the parking brake into place and looked at the back door of the house. There was a fist-sized hole in the mesh of the storm door where Arvel had put his hand through last summer to let himself in after she'd mistakenly left the door latched. On the passenger's seat beside her was a package from a convenience store that held garbage bags, Lysol, and J-Cloths. She picked this up, took her as-yet-untouched large Tim Horton's coffee from the drink tray, and stepped out onto the driveway.

The amount of salt on the roads at this time of year was apocalyptic. She wiped a finger through the white residue on her rusted vw Rabbit and looked at the tiny patch of black paint where the finish could almost have passed for new. When she got to the top of the steps at the back door, she looked back at the car. The gas station attendant in Halifax had squeegeed the front and rear windshields, and the cleaning solution had run down through the salt on the car, leaving the vehicle looking like a complete disgrace.

Once through the back door, she was surprised that the house was so empty. She set the convenience-store bag on the counter and looked at the kitchen, bathed in the light that came through the windows. There was a smell in the air of closed-up rooms, of carpets holding odours from even before she'd lived there.

She remembered how positive they'd all been, she, Arvel, and the kids, the day they'd moved in here. They'd come here straight from the old apartment on Bridge Avenue and the place had looked huge and pristinely clean.

"Things are going to work out for us here," Arvel had said. He'd bought a bottle of Windex and was going through the house, cleaning every pane of every window until it was spotless. Even when he'd expressed such optimism, as much as she'd wanted to believe in the same dream, as much as she'd wished she could face the new house with bright-eyed optimism, part of her had already lost faith that she and Arvel could work out their differences.

But how could she have predicted this state of affairs? Arvel was dead. She was a widow. The girls only had one parent. She shook her head in sad amazement.

In the kitchen, all that remained of her and her family were stains. A ring of grime encircled the handle of the refrigerator. The linoleum floor was scuffed with dark heel marks and the prints of dirty shoes. She opened the cupboard below the sink and took out an aerosol can of Easy-Off. She read the directions on the can, removed the racks from the oven, and sprayed a thick layer of foam over each surface inside the oven. The fumes burned her eyes and nostrils. She closed the oven door and switched on the vent fan over the stove. The fumes were still strong, so she rinsed her hands under the tap and took her coffee into the living room. She sat on the floor with her back against the front door. The carpet still held impressions of furniture that had been removed. Couch, couch, wingback chair, coffee table. She could make out clearly where each piece had been. On the bare wall opposite where she sat, there were outlines of the pictures that had hung there.

Beyond the living room was the hallway leading to the bedrooms. The closet door was open, and Jackie caught sight of something in the darkness beyond the door.

She stood up to investigate, then drew in a little breath as she realized what it was. She'd put it there herself on the night before Arvel's death. She remembered now making a conscious decision to leave it where it was on the day she'd finally moved. She hadn't wanted to face it then, and she had not had a thought about it since.

There were handgrips moulded into the plastic at either end of the box. She grasped the closer grip and dragged the grey box out into the light. The paper taped to the lid said "Memories" in black ink, then below that, scrawled in pencil: "Arvel: half of these things are mine and half are yours. We'll have to go through it some time soon."

She lifted the box from the floor with both hands and was surprised at how heavy it was. It made no noise when she shook it slightly as she carried it to the spot by the front door where she'd been sitting. She set the box on the carpet beside her coffee and sat again with her back against the door. Resting the side of one leg against the box, she picked her coffee from the floor and took a sip. The cardboard cup had already pressed a little circular outline on the carpet.

She got up onto her knees, pushed both thumbs down on the lid of the box, and lifted the locking tabs that held the lid in place. At the top of the box was a photo of Arvel, age two or three, sitting on Santa's knee. Below the photo, the caption read: "Checking it twice: Santa stopped by the Steelworkers' Hall last Thursday to double-check on his list of children who were being naughty or nice. Little Arvel Burrows, from Albion Mines, claims he's been a good boy all year." This photo had made its way into this container via an old shoebox full of childhood things that Arvel had toted around with him for years. When they were moving into this house on Pleasant Street, Jackie had seen Arvel taping the shoebox, which had disintegrated several times already, back together with Scotch tape. She'd urged him to go through the contents of the box, pick out what he wanted to keep, and toss the box itself away. Without thought or hesitation, he'd handed her the news clipping.

The child in the photo was in the foreground, and since that child had grown up to be her husband, that's all she'd ever taken notice of before. But there was something striking or off-putting about the picture.

Santa was not merely large in comparison to the child, but almost gigantic. His big, meaty hand supported Arvel's backside, the fingers nearly as large as arms. She suddenly recognized, behind the cheap cotton-batting beard, Santa's dark lips and broad face. It was Ennis, though thinner than he was now. Behind the corny beard, he was smiling in a joyful way that seemed completely at odds with the man she knew. Was it just for the photo that he'd mustered this grin? Or had Ennis been a different person all those years ago?

Arvel had never known it was his father in this photo: Jackie was sure of it. Over the years they'd looked at the picture several times together and he'd never mentioned anything about the identity of Santa. Would he have thrown the picture away if he had known? Would he have cherished it all the more?

Jackie put the photo back inside the box marked "Memories" and snapped the lid down on top. She looked up at the living room, at the barren house, at the meaningless impressions her time there had left on the walls and the carpet. She walked into the kitchen and placed the box just inside the back door, where she would not forget it on the way out. The smell of Easy-Off in the kitchen was less corrosive than it had been. She took a heavy rubber glove from the cupboard beneath the sink, pulled a fresh J-Cloth from the box, and opened the oven door. The white foam of the oven cleaner had gone brown as it melted crusted grease inside the oven. Gobs of thick, toxic ooze dripped down from the top surface of the oven and drooled down its sides. She got down on her knees and began to wipe the oven walls clean.

## CULTURE

In a frozen moment in Dunya's mind, she stood over her drunken husband with an iron kettle in her hand. His face was fairly flattened by her pounding. He was still breathing. She could see the bubbles coming up through the pond of blood below his eyes. She knew a few more swift, hard blows could have finished him. In a split second, she decided not to do it, not to kill her husband. Then Ziv grabbed her, stopped her hand, and it was all over. So it had not been Ziv who stopped her, though she could not have continued the beating once he'd had hold of her. This recollection, this knowledge that she'd stopped herself before killing him, was perhaps the only thing that spared her from complete condemnation of herself, the only thing that enabled her to go on.

Sometimes this bloody image sprang itself upon her by surprise. She would be sitting in the front room drinking tea, when her imagination took over and she'd be right back at the foot of the stairs, blood splashed on the cuffs of her pantlegs. Other times, she sought out the memory and replayed it deliberately, trying to refind the moment, the spark of goodness and forgiveness that must still be inside her.

With Ennis in the hospital and the house wrecked, she remembered she'd tried to clean up in the kitchen, where so many things had been broken and spread about. Bottled spices and boxes of cereal had been tossed from the cupboards, the walls dented where heavy cans – tomatoes, soup, kidney beans – struck. She'd started by picking the larger items from the floor and stacking them on the counter, but she could not move without stepping ankle-deep in some mess that needed sweeping: cornflakes that had spilled from their box; rice grains from an exploded five-kilogram bag; dried baking beans. Some things were pasted together with milk or pickle brine or mustard that had been thrown from the fridge. She'd got Ziv to help her locate and straighten up all the expensive items: electronic goods, appliances. She took a breather from her work, stood with her hands on her hips, and looked around the downstairs of the house. Then she got the phone book and looked up Danny Dykens's number. He had a covered half-ton and did light trucking for a living.

When she and Ennis had married, they hadn't had a thing. They'd nailed three planks to a couple of orange crates, and called that their kitchen table for more than five years. Nowadays, everyone had to have a house full of furniture right away, and they went eye-deep in debt to get it. She'd done without things before, and when Danny came with his truck, she decided there were things she could do without again. Beds were expensive and you had to have them. The big-ticket appliances were also pricey and useful. She didn't want to be stupid, and she didn't want to have regrets. She walked through each room in the house, looked at everything, broken and unbroken, spread out before her on the floor, and decided what would be on the small list of things to keep. The rest, she told Danny, she wanted done with as quick as he could carry it.

The blue overnight bag, from the room where Arvel had slept the few nights before the explosion, hung on a hook in the porch.

One thing that would not budge was the brown cabinet with glass doors in Ziv's bedroom. It had been there when they'd bought the house. They'd tried at the time to move it downstairs and use it for dishes, but they could not get it through the door. She told Danny Dykens to take it out the window if he had to, but he got out his tape measure and said it would not go through the window frame either.

"It must have been built in this room," Danny said. He opened a drawer and looked at the wood. "Pretty solidly put together," he said. "Look at this," he ran his hand along the inside of the drawer. "This says 'explosive.'"

"It was made with old powder boxes from the pit," Dunya said.

"Somebody put a lot of work into this," Danny said.

"I guess it stays," said Dunya.

Anything that remained on the walls, photos, paintings, calendars, she'd ripped down and piled on the floor, too, to take away. Ennis's plaques and photos she saved in a cardboard box for him to decide about when he got out of the hospital. Once Danny had gone with the contents of the house, she realized how cluttered the house had been for years.

On the day the rescue was called off, she came back from the fire hall and took Arvel's overnight bag down from its hook in the porch. It felt so light in her hand, somehow lighter even than it was on the day she'd put it there. She brought it into the front room of the house and sat beside it on the floor. It had been years since she'd sat this low in the room, if she ever had. She noticed a faint dusty smell from the carpet. Arvel's overnight bag was closed. She'd zippered it herself after the explosion. She looked at the tab a moment, watched the way it reflected light that came into the front room through the curtainless windows. She put a hand on the zipper, thinking to open it. But she knew what was inside. Some underwear, some socks, a couple of clean work shirts. Maybe a pocket novel that Arvel had thrown in without thought as he left his house. There was no need to open the bag. It was full of meaningless objects. She hugged the bag to her chest and slowly lowered it to the floor, rested her head against it as though it were a pillow.

She remembered when Arvel was smaller than the bag. Her first baby. Her first son.

He had been big from birth. Almost eleven pounds, which in those days had been a lot. His size was his father in him. Dunya's people were all small. But she never let his size fool her. Perhaps it was because she was older when he had her first. Older for those days. She and Ennis had been married almost ten years before she got pregnant. They had already given up on having kids. They'd forgotten, even, that it was a possibility.

There were only cloth diapers, and the only thing to hold them were deadly big pins. She was scared of diaper pins. Her heart would skip a beat every time she had to open one to fasten a clean diaper on him. She'd look at his stubby body, see him wiggling around like a frisky puppy.

She'd put him down for his nap and be unable to rest her mind. She was always sure she'd walk back in after an hour and he'd be dead, stuck through the heart with a safety pin. It seemed she'd always known how close he was to death.

She'd lain for a time on the floor, her head resting on the overnight bag, drifting in and out of a light sleep. Later, she stood stiffly and looked around the empty room. She went into the kitchen and put the overnight bag into the garbage. When the lid dropped onto the can, she had an idea. She got out her Sears card and the catalogue and ordered three gallons of flat white paint. A few days later, Ziv rolled over everything; wood panelling, wall-paper, broken old plaster, bare wood, all of it. She covered it all in white, drawing up a sheet over the inside of the house.

And this was more or less the way the house remained. Ziv told her about futons, big pads of covered cotton you could buy for cheap. One of these was folded in half, part of it on the floor, part of it against the wall in the front room. She was getting old to be raising and lowering herself to such a level, but she noticed that it got easier, week by week, as she kept doing it.

She made a clean, white space for herself to thrive in. She thought of it as culturing herself, the way they cultured bacteria when they did a test on you in the hospital. She needed an environment where she could breathe and live. She came down the stairs every day, made herself some tea, and sat in the curtain-less, colourless, furnitureless front room, and waited as the sun moved around, reflected off the snow outside, and filled the room with light.

People came to visit her. People from the neighbourhood, Arvel's widow, people who had worked at Eastyard. They wanted to know how she was doing. "I don't know yet," was the answer she always gave. Many more people crossed in front of the house on the sidewalk, shamelessly curious to look in at her. They'd heard all sorts of stories. They'd heard she slept on the floor some nights with no blankets, in front of the window in her clothes, which was true. They'd heard she took her clothes off sometimes and sat in the middle of the room where everyone passing by could see her naked, which was not. They'd heard she chopped the furniture up herself with an axe and was in the middle of chopping up her husband when her son stopped her.

Ennis occasionally entered as she sat in silence in the front room. He came in with the aspect of a non-family member, stood awkwardly in the doorway and said a few words that she might respond to. She'd say yes or no. She'd speak briefly about bills that had to be paid. She'd answer his questions when he was searching for something, questions about what she had and had not thrown away. But they hadn't really spoken since he got out of hospital, not said anything of substance or consequence. He looked at her as though he was waiting for something. An explanation, an apology, forgiveness, another attack. She did not know. She did not know if she could forgive Ennis. She did not know if she could forgive him for what she'd done. They listened to each other's breathing, as though the simple fact that they were both alive was all they had left to share.

# PART FOUR

## 1987

## Opportunity Knocks

When the ad appeared in the *Evening News*, Arvel had gone five and a half years without work that was steady or reliable. He'd worked more than half of the time, earning stamps for unemployment insurance to hold him through the periods when he wasn't working. He never waited for the UI cheques to run out before looking for work, which is what a lot of people did, and the longest consecutive period he drew full UI was nine weeks. But a lot of businesses were only set up to employ people for the minimum it took to earn a new set of pogey cheques, and the longest consecutive period he'd drawn a paycheque from the same place was sixteen weeks. Just about everyone he knew was in similar circumstances.

He'd done a lot of work in the woods, which was the hardest physical labour, and, since it was all piecework, was stressful from morning to night. He planted trees, he harvested trees for pulp, he helped people with hardwood lots cut and split cords for firewood.

He did spacing for the silviculture industry. He handled small jobs that private contractors did not have time to get to, some of which actually involved his trade. He rewired people's houses to upgrade their service, he crack filled drywall with a team that did the finish work on factory-built homes. He got hired in the falls by Nick Lowen, a man from the Red Row who ran his own burner service, checking and cleaning oil furnaces before the peak heating season. "Jobbing around" was what people called what he was doing, and although jobbing around kept him busy, and he sometimes earned a half-decent amount of money from it, it was no way to live for the long term. He looked at Jackie, who was the top salesperson at the store where she worked and was earning good money in commissions. She also had her friend Colleen in Halifax, who could get her an even better-paying job there.

Seeing how valued she was made him realize how unvalued he himself was. Arvel knew that the sort of work that had been sustaining him was economic table scraps, and when you are being thrown table scraps, you are no better than a dog whose owner doesn't care enough to buy it its own food.

And as if it was his Jesus fault for not having steady work, Arvel had his father's constant disappointment and lack of sympathy to contend with. His father had quit school in junior high and gotten on at the Car Works immediately. With the exception of occasional time he was laid off due to a reduction in demand for railcars, he'd been employed at the Car Works since. In his father's mind, anyone without a full-time job for longer than a few months was lazy and shiftless, not trying hard enough to find steady work. He would see Arvel at the end of an especially hard day's work, covered in dirt and sawdust, or elbows deep in soot from mucking about in people's chimneys. He'd take a look at him and say, "Don't you have a job yet?"

EASTYARD COAL COMPANY, A DIVISION OF COUGHLIN RESOURCE MANAGEMENT. The lettering was huge. The ad took up a whole page in the *New Glasgow Evening News*. The company was getting a big dose of taxpayers' money, and there would probably be an election within a year. Everyone in Pictou County knew that the federal government wanted the operation up and running at full capacity by the time the campaign started.

The ad said nothing about mining experience, which everyone knew meant old-timers need not apply. Most of the experienced miners in the county were over the hill by the standards of an industry driven by demanding physical labour. There was a list of trades given that included electricians. Arvel knew that he had to apply for work at Eastyard, that he'd be one of thousands from across the region, across the country, applying for a few dozen jobs, and he held out no hope of being hired. Any workplace with that much government money tied up in it would be clogged up with political bumlickers, people who'd made a point their whole lives of getting themselves seen at all the Tory hot-dog roasts, and whose families for six generations had been doing the same low-grade schmoozing. The Eastyard offices were "under construction," according to the ad. According to the construction site, where the buildings were set to go up, the ground had yet to be broken, except for the beginnings of the main shaft.

Selection wasn't going to be first-come, first-served, so Arvel waited until the applications had been available at the employment office for five days before dropping in one afternoon right at four thirty as the office was closing, hoping he would not run into anyone who knew him. He knew he would not get one of Eastyard jobs, and that many people would be in the same boat: qualified for something, good for nothing. But all the same, he did not want anyone's sympathy when the first shift of Tory Youth went marching up to the chain-link gates on the first day of work.

That night on the supper-hour news from Halifax, there was an interview with George Hannah, a war veteran and retired miner from Albion Mines. Arvel recognized him instantly because he was wearing his Royal Canadian Legion uniform, as he always did. He'd been the caretaker of the Miner's Museum when Arvel had been a kid. There was a newly built museum now. Hannah might still be caretaker, for all Arvel knew.

The TV lights glinted off the ribbons and medals on his chest as the old man warned about the hazards of the Pictou County coalfield.

"Nobody's going to listen to an old fella like me," Hannah said. "But it's insanity to mine that coal. The politicians love the idea of this mine because they want to get elected. But if you start in on that gassy old seam again, you'd might as well build the memorial to the dead right now. Just leave plenty of room on it to carve the names in later." Arvel had already filled out the application, and after the interview with Hannah, he gave some thought to what the old man had said. Coal mining had always been a dangerous occupation, especially in Pictou County, where he'd heard there was something about how the coal was formed that made it especially prone to producing explosive gases. But this was the only real job application he'd filled out in years where there was even a remote possibility at getting a steady job.

He dropped the application off at the employment office first thing the next morning, when the employees there were just opening the doors.

There was a special box for Eastyard applications, and he added his manila envelope to the stack in the box. At the door on the way out, he stopped and looked back at his application and thought for a moment about retrieving the envelope, withdrawing the application before it was ever submitted. He turned and walked outside.

At ten thirty that morning, he was sitting at the kitchen table with a cup of tea in his hand. Both kids were in front of the TV in the other room, Kate sitting on the couch, Melanie in the playpen, and he was hunched over a sheet of paper with phone numbers on it, scratching little *x*s by names as he dialled them up and asked whether they had been happy with the painting or roofing or electrical work he had done for them last time, and asking if they had any more work they needed doing around the home. He'd even split firewood, if they needed that done: no, no, he'd use an axe.

The receiver was under his left hand as he was about to make another call, so when it rang he picked it up before it had even finished the first ring.

"Jesus," the voice on the other end said, not even giving Arvel time to answer. "You had that phone off the hook all morning."

Arvel gave some silence to the person on the other end, then said: "I've been making calls all morning. And to whom do I have the pleasure of speaking?"

"Ya, right," the voice said. There was a pause and a sucking sound as the person took a drag on a cigarette. "You got your electrician's papers that time, didn't you?"

Now the voice was starting to come back to him. Someone he'd known at the vocational school. "I spent two years studying electrical construction, if that's what you're talking about."

"And what have you been doing since then? Somebody told me you can't find steady work."

It was Sam Kowalski, a man at least ten years older than Arvel, who'd lasted until Christmas of the first year in electrical construction. Everyone called him Roly-Poly because he was so fat that he waddled. Roly was such an abrasive person that no one in the program had liked him. Arvel wondered what he could possibly be calling about. He probably wanted something.

"What the hell do you want, Roly?" Arvel said.

"I got a job for you, that's what I want."

"Sure! You're giving out jobs. How does a guy with no job himself end up giving them out?"

"I'm assistant manager of Atlantic Video Supply."

"And I'm CEO of the Toilet Bowl Sanitation Corporation."

"You're lucky I'm not the kind of guy who hangs up on mouthy arseholes, because today I am opportunity, and the sound of my voice is opportunity knocking."

"Hey. I'd be the last guy to knock opportunity."

"Well shut up for two minutes and I'll tell you what I'm calling about."

Arvel did not believe in hanging up on people, but for a moment, fed up with Kowalski's rudeness, he considered putting down the phone.

Roly said, "How'd you like one of those Eastyard jobs?"

Arvel began to laugh. "What are you? Personnel manager? Ha, ha, ha, ha, ha!"

"Just shut your smart mouth and listen. Did you see those guys with the shovels in the paper last week? Breaking sod or whatever?"

"Breaking wind is more like it. The premier and some other idiots."

"Well, one of those idiots owes me a big favour, and I'm about to cash it in. Lucky for you I need someone who actually has some training to come into an interview with me. Don't you have some college-boy brother? I seen him over at Zellers in the toy department. He looks just like you, the poor unfortunate bastard. Tell him he can have one of them jobs, too, if he can get his lazy arse outta bed for an interview."

Someone at Eastyard Coal must have been mixed up with the wrong people in the past. How else did he owe the likes of Sam Kowalski a favour? Arvel never found out what the favour was about, but Kowalski did explain that he was using Arvel and Ziv to make himself look better. He had worked out a scam with someone on the inside where his own interview would be a joint interview with one or two other applicants whose education or qualifications were supposed to be real. He'd embellish his own resumé to make it look like he'd actually done some worthwhile work before, and his contact would make sure he only had to answer the easy questions in an interview. The technical stuff could be directed to someone else who actually knew something.

Whatever his feelings about Sam Kowalski, the mining jobs at Eastyard would be major, solid employment, and Arvel could not afford to turn his back on this sort of opportunity. He called Ziv as soon as he got off the phone. Ziv was reluctant.

"Coal mining? In 1987? That's like deciding to be a caveman. Do you have any idea how many people have been killed mining coal in this county?"

"Come on, man," Arvel said. "Do you want to work at Zellers for the rest of your life? Kowalski wants two people for this interview. Just come along for my sake. Nobody can force you to go underground if you don't want to. And what are the odds we'll get jobs there, anyway? This is a chance I just can't pass up."

Within a week, Arvel and Ziv were standing outside the new Miner's Museum in Albion Mines. Even though Arvel had already filled out an application, Kowalski got both of them to fill out fresh forms, which he had given to his contact in the company. Coughlin Resources was holding interviews in one of the conference rooms upstairs. The two brothers were stuffed into suits whose legs rode up their shins when they bent their knees.

A maroon taxi pulled off Foord Street and parked in the no-parking zone in front of the main entrance to the museum. Kowalski squeezed his huge waist through the driver's door and walked straight to the entrance without looking at or speaking to either of the Burrows brothers. When Kowalski was inside, Arvel and Ziv looked at each other, shrugged, and followed him.

As it turned out, at the interview, no one was expected to know anything technical at all. The interviewers first wanted to know whether Arvel and Ziv were twins, even though their birth-dates were on their application forms and the forms were on the table in front of them. They talked about Blue Jays baseball for a while. They sat in padded swivel chairs in a room just big enough for the few people and pieces of furniture that were in it. The room smelled of crack filler, primer, and industrial adhesive, as though construction of the place had just been completed in time for this interview. The company president drank coffee from a cup so large it made his small hands look frail and childish. One of the two other management types, a man with a bald head and a big, square face, was from Alberta, and Ziv talked to him for twenty minutes about the scenic Cabot Trail in Cape Breton, about how beautiful it was and how, while the man was in the province, it would be a big mistake to leave without seeing it. When Arvel and Ziv stood up at the end of the interview, they towered over their interviewers as they shook hands. The other men stood back a little, as though intimidated.

Roly drove them to the Tartan Tavern in the maroon taxi he had come in, and bought them a pitcher to share. "How the fuck do you know so much about Cape Breton?" he asked Ziv.

"I've never been to the other end of the causeway," Ziv replied. He laughed loudly. "My first roommate at university was from Mabou. I guess I must have soaked something up."

Arvel picked up the salt shaker and tossed a light dusting of white over the head of his beer. Bubbles came rushing up through the amber liquid. He tapped the bottom of the salt shaker on the lip of the glass, causing another surge of foam. "Well," he said. "We're not getting anything out of that."

"What do you mean?" Roly said.

"They'll not give us jobs based on that foolish interview." Arvel turned a grim eye on Ziv, who was still laughing.

"Boys," Roly said. "You've got jobs. You can start spending the money right now. These guys owe me big time. The interview was just a hoop."

"We'll see," said Arvel.

"No great loss, anyway," Ziv said.

"Are you out of your fucking tree?" Roly said. "You're working at fucking Zellers."

"At least I'm qualified to work at Zellers," Ziv said. "And Zellers has never blown up."

"This mine ain't gonna blow up. This is the 1980s, not the 1890s."

"I'll worry about that mine blowing up *after* I've got a job in it," said Arvel.

"Wait and see, boys, wait and see," Kowalski said.

Ziv flattened the letter from Eastyard against the surface of the kitchen table and reread the words that told him he had gotten the first real job of his life. He thought about calling Arvel to see whether he'd heard anything, but decided against it. He was already beginning to feel some fear and regret at the prospect of working in a coal mine, in a job he'd heard spoken of his whole life as the rough equivalent of being a soldier in a war. He did not want to call Arvel and find out Arvel had not gotten an Eastyard job. He did not want to feel Arvel's envy for a job he only half-wanted himself.

The letter said he would be working underground, and as he looked at the word now, he felt a tightening in his chest, as though the weight of the earth were upon him, pushing him down.

He walked into the living room, where his mother was watching *Card Sharks* on TV.

"Look at that dishwasher!" she said. He looked at it. It was an Amana. Fully automatic, energy-saving and water-saving settings. Available in a range of colours to match any decor.

"These people don't know how lucky they are," his mother said. She sat with a blank glare at the tube.

"How long did Didu work at the pit?" Ziv asked.

"What?" his mother said. She shook her head and peeled her eyes from the TV.

"How long did your father work in the pit? I know he retired from there. But did he work there his whole life?"

"All of it that I remember," she said. She was looking at him suspiciously. "He lived in Winnipeg when he first came over."

"Winnipeg! I didn't know that!"

"That was where most of the Bohunks were going. He did something for the city there. There's an old picture of him in front of a fountain. That is from Winnipeg. Then he moved to Halifax and worked as a streetcar conductor. Why are you asking me about all this now?"

"Why in the name of God would a streetcar conductor go into the mines? Especially in the old days, when there wasn't very much money in it?"

"He fell in love with my mother. I guess there weren't many Bohunks in Nova Scotia at the time. My uncle Stan, my mother's uncle. He was born in the old country. He ran into Daddy up in Halifax and invited him down for the weekend. He met Mumma and that was that. They got married. She didn't want to move to Halifax, so . . ."

"Mum . . ." She had drifted back to the TV. "Mum . . ." She turned to face him again.

"I've been offered a job at Eastyard. Eastyard. You know, the new mine."

He considered mentioning that Arvel had applied, too, that they'd both been interviewed and there was a good chance they'd both be hired. But he did not want to bring up that possibility now. And it was Arvel's job, anyway, to tell her what he was and was not going to do.

His mother hit the remote, shutting off the TV. She sat back in her chair and eyed him up and down.

"They want me for underground. I applied. I didn't think I had a chance. Because I've got two years of university on my application, I thought that if I did get hired, they'd put me in an office job. Shuffling paper or adding up columns. I don't know a thing about underground work. Maybe it's because of my size."

"Well, Ziv," she was silent for a long time. "This is a complete shock to me."

"The money is good there."

"The people who worked the mines in the old days didn't have the choices that you do. I can't believe the politicians who are pushing to get this mine started. Do they have rocks in their heads? They're offering you a free ticket on the *Titanic*, and you're taking it." She had a desperate look on her face, somewhere between fear and anger.

"I'm going to have to think about this. Anyway, don't tell Dad about this. Whatever I decide, I want to be the one to tell him."

His mother gave him a stern look. "A young person today would be crazy to go down there," she said.


The old neighbourhood looked much better than it used to, even in his own childhood. Federal grants in the seventies had reroofed most of the places, provided energy-efficient windows, and covered the buildings with vinyl siding that was almost a visual duplicate of the clapboard that had been on many of them originally.

Ziv went for a walk. It was moving into late fall now. Many trees had shed their leaves completely. Those with leaves remaining held a ghostly yellow halo of light. Most Red Row backyards looked well-kept. The odd sundeck had sprouted at a back door. There was wooden lawn furniture scattered about, here and there. Piles of leaves had been raked up, orange garbage bags held more.

He passed the house his father had grown up in, stopped and tried to imagine it in 1928, the year his father was born. He sketched in a picket fence, an outhouse. He shrank the cherry tree to a sapling. He looked at the side yard and the area around the back door, and tried to imagine his father out there as a child, playing in the dirt.

At the north end of the Red Row, just before the Heather Motel and the Trans-Canada overpass, he came to the house where his mother had grown up.

The people who lived there now had done some upgrading since he could remember visiting his grandfather there. The original shed and outhouse had been replaced by a prefab plywood garden shed. The big black spruce tree his mother had told him she'd planted as a little girl was gone, the branches had been close enough to the roof of the house to cause a moss problem. The white picket fence that encircled the little front yard was the same one he remembered from his childhood. But his grandfather's garden, once the pride of the family, if not the neighbourhood, had grown over with grass. He stopped at the fence for a moment and looked at the ground there, the plot that was in fact tiny, but that had seemed enormous when he'd been a boy. He remembered walking through it, between the rows, flowers towering over him, the fragrance of fresh-grown lettuce, the excitement of pulling a carrot right from the ground, wiping it on his pants, and eating it, the flavour bursting in his mouth, the dirt and grit scratching his teeth.

Across the street stood the big cut-stone remains of the Cornish Pumphouse, a hundred-year-old relic of the mining heydays.

Ziv climbed up to the top of the highway overpass on Foord Street and leaned against the guardrail as cars whizzed past. Before him he could see the whole Red Row. Though the peak of his own family's roof was obscured by houses and trees, he could see the steeple of Christ Church right across the street.

He looked at the river, the railroad tracks, the Cornish Pumphouse, the wash plant that had operated until recently for the tiny strip mine out on Foster Avenue, the single-storey row-houses and duplexes at the north of the Red Row, leading to the storey-and-a-half duplexes farther south. This neighbourhood was built almost a hundred years ago, and it hadn't been meant to last. It was supposed to just crumble and disappear when the big seams had been depleted, or to be razed and replaced with something bigger and better as industrialization expanded. The supply of coal in Pictou County was far from exhausted. Having heard about the size of the original coal seam beneath the ground at Albion Mines, he'd once asked Fred Moore, an old Red Rower who'd been an underground foreman, about how much of the coal had been mined. "We haven't had the half of it," he said. "In a hundred and fifty years we haven't had the half of it." A hundred years ago, the possibilities for this area mushrooming into a city to rival Halifax must have seemed pretty strong. The steel industry had a strong foothold, the first hold it had in North America. North American railroading had started here.

The harbour in Pictou was excellent, the shipyard there as good as any.

When you stood back from this place you could see the marks, like looking at the rings of a stump: the growth, the stunted growth, the decay, the resuscitation. Albion Mines was not so much a ghost as an exhumed corpse, a half-charred body pulled prematurely from the crematorium.

That night, at the desk in his bedroom, he took out a sheet of loose-leaf and wrote the date at the top. He was going to write a letter to Meta in Japan. Her mother had been into Zellers last week and had given him her new address. He couldn't believe that she'd really gone through with it. She'd moved to Japan. He remembered the first poster she'd ever seen advertising teaching opportunities overseas. It had been in a stairwell of the Student's Union building, years ago, when Ziv had still been a student and he and Meta had still been going out together. She'd said then that that was what she'd do when she got out of school, but it had seemed so remote a possibility at the time.

He couldn't help but admire Meta's ambition and determination for making such a big decision for herself and following through with it. And he wished he could feel so certain about what to do next. But he felt like hell. His relationship with Meta had officially ended years before, and they'd only seen each other occasionally since, but he thought of her at times like this. Times when he needed consolation.

*Dear Meta:*

*I hate it here.*

He wrote these words, then sat back. He read the sentence again and realized several things. It was true. He did hate it here. What seemed odd was that, when he began the letter, he had thought he was going to continue writing about Albion Mines and how smart she'd been to get out of it. *Here*, he had supposed to mean just that: this town and every miserable aspect of the fact he was stuck in it. Especially the fact that he felt he had no other option than to choose between a shitty job and a deadly one.

But he realized that, though the sentence he'd written was true and felt true when he reread it, *here* did not mean Albion Mines at all, for when he tried to think about what it was that he didn't like about the place, everything seemed several times removed from him, as if on the other side of a glass wall. *I hate it here* had very little to do with what was on the opposite side of the glass. Little to do with Albion Mines, and nothing to do with his parents' house, though he resented living in it, resented having to live in it, and resented each of the people who lived there, most of all himself.

He straightened up in the chair, put the pen back to the paper, scratched out the original sentence, and restarted the letter.

*Dear Meta,*

*I hate myself.*

He looked at this sentence and knew that there was something important in it. He knew that if Meta were here instead of on the other side of the world, he'd be able to talk to her. But how could he write a letter that began with that sentence? And how could he continue a train of thought in that direction that had any bearing on what he was feeling? How could he expect her to understand what was inside of him with just a few black squiggles on a page to represent it all?

He picked up the page, folded it neatly several times, then tore the paper into many tiny pieces.

***

It was the following morning when Arvel called to tell him that he had been hired.

"I got my letter yesterday," Ziv said. "I'm not sure what the hell to do. I do not want that job, but I feel like I can't pass it up."

"Just think it over for a few days. You'll come around. This is going to be the best job you've ever had."

"I wonder if Roly got on."

"He called me this morning already. They gave him some kind of custodian's job. Sounds like one step up from janitor, if you ask me."

At Arvel's request, Ziv agreed that they'd tell their father about the job offers together, that night after supper.

Ennis was late getting home from work that evening. They had already eaten. Arvel had come down from the apartment on Bridge Street, and he and Ziv waited in Ziv's bedroom for their father to get home. As soon as they heard Ennis's voice, they made their way to the kitchen, where Ennis had already settled himself at the table.

The brothers stood in the doorway between the kitchen and the living room, Ziv looking at Arvel with a slight frown, Arvel smiling, barely able to contain how pleased he was.

Ennis was bent over a plate of baloney and molasses and had not turned to speak to them.

"Dad," Arvel said.

Ennis turned around long enough to take in the two of them, then went back to his baloney.

"We've been hired at the new mine."

Ennis sat up straight in his chair. For a moment he remained facing away from them, then he turned again.

"You're shitting me!" he said. He looked at Arvel and Ziv, then turned to Dunya. The two sons shook their heads. They both looked at their father now. Arvel was grinning, but Ziv stood silently with a blank look on his face.

"I still haven't decided . . ." Ziv began to say, but he did not know how to continue.

"Ziv told me yesterday he'd been hired on," Dunya said. "I didn't know I'd have two sons working there." She was not smiling.

"Well, now. Don't be so down-in-the-mouth about it. This will be good, steady work," Arvel said.

"I only have two sons. That's all I have," she said. "I'll be left with no one, you wait and see." Her face was dark with anger and concern.

"Boys," Ennis said. "I'm proud of ye's. The two of ye's." He stood up from the table and approached them both, and they instinctively backed away from him. "Come here till I slug the two of ye's." He slammed the thumb-ends of his fists into their shoulders, then took the car keys from his pants pocket. "We're going to the Tartan, boys. I'm buying the pitchers."

"Don't do this, Ennis," Dunya said. Ennis looked at her and waited. His big, childish grin melted her hot stare.

"You should know better," Dunya said. "You of all people should not be encouraging your sons to go into that mine. You can't let this happen. Put a stop to it."

"Jesus, Dunya, neither of these boys has had a decent job between them. Now they've both got good jobs."

She shook her head in disgust. "This is what you call a good job?"

He looked at her blankly.

"So now you're going to take your sons out drinking?"

Ennis grinned at the boys. "You bet your arse I am."

"And what about the operation? Does that mean nothing to you, either? You know what the cardiologist told you about alcohol."

"Drinking never killed me yet," Ennis said. "The operation isn't for two weeks."

Ziv shook his head in disbelief. "You're a textbook case of something," he said. "I wish I'd stayed in university long enough to find out what."

"I wash my hands of the bunch of you," Dunya said. "Ennis, go ahead. Give your sons a lesson in foolhardiness and lack of responsibility. Boys, pay careful attention tonight. You're learning from a pro." Dunya turned her back on the three of them and walked through the living room toward the stairs that led to the second floor.

"Don't worry," Ennis said. "She'll come around. You boys'll get your first paycheques and she'll realize you did the right thing." He had his coat on and was heading for the door with the car keys in his hand.

Ziv stayed back in the kitchen, not wanting to spoil the moment of celebration Arvel was probably looking forward to. All the same, he did not feel like going to the Tartan tonight to rejoice and then have to tell his father tomorrow that he wasn't going to take the Eastyard job.

"I'll walk," Arvel said.

"What!" Ennis said. "I'm driving. Get in the car."

"If we're going to be drinking, I don't want to take the car," Arvel said.

"It's my goddamned car. I'll drive it if I want."

"I don't have to get into it, do I?"

"I'm treating you to the goddamn beer, and if I say we go in the car, we go in the goddamn car," Ennis said.

Ziv stepped off the back doorstep and moved away from the house. He wanted to stay out of the argument.

They ended up at a standstill in the driveway, Ennis in the driver's seat, the door open so he could bicker with Arvel. Ziv stood back and stayed out of the way.

"We're not even drinking," Ennis kept saying. "We're just going to have a few *drinks*."

Without making any suggestions or getting involved in the argument, Ziv called Jim's Taxi. Arvel and Ennis bickered pointlessly back and forth until the car came. When the headlights of the cab were shining on all of them in the driveway, Ziv said, "Let's just get in the fucking taxi."

Ennis looked at him, then back at Arvel, who was already moving back from the car to give his father room to come out.

"To hell with it," Ennis said at last. He put his own car keys in his pocket and followed his sons into the taxi.

Finally, his sons had begun lives he could understand. So what if they were in their middle twenties, and he had started his working life at sixteen? They were finally going to do real work.

For the first time ever, the three of them were going to do something together: get drunk.

"Two more pitchers!" he shouted towards the bar. It was a quiet night at the Tartan Tavern, a few people were scattered here and there throughout the room. Most of the action was taking place in the snooker area, where every table was full and the players leaned seriously and quietly over their cues, as though some money might be at stake.

"Christ, boys," Ennis said when the pitchers he'd ordered arrived. He threw back his head in reverie. "I remember when I was starting at the Car Works." He shook his head and laughed. A clatter of snooker balls punctuated his speech. "Those were crazy times. We were kids back then. Just kids, a lot of us. Quit school in Grade seven, eight, nine. Start earning your keep young. That's something young people today don't understand." He hadn't meant this as a dig at his sons, but Arvel began to bristle in response.

"Another thing we don't understand," Arvel said. "Is how anyone could quit school in junior high and get any job, let alone a good one. Let alone keep it."

Ziv shook some salt into the palm of his left hand. He prodded the salt with his right index finger as though counting the grains. Ennis put his beer glass down in front of him. He hunched over it and peered quickly back and forth at his two sons. "Those jobs were good jobs because we made them good jobs. We organized and we fought for what we wanted. You think the company was tripping over itself to give us a seniority system, a decent wage, holidays? We got that stuff because we were smart enough to demand it. If young people today aren't happy, it's up to them to fix it."

"You can only make demands if you have an employer," Arvel said. "Who are today's young people going to threaten with a strike? The unemployment office? Their social worker? The parents they're living off?"

Ziv spilled the salt from his palm over his draft. Foam began rising vigorously to the top.

"Take this guy," Ennis said, indicating Ziv with his thumb. "He's been working at Zellers for years, now. If he's not happy, why doesn't he organize? Get a bargaining committee instead of that Employees Relations Council he's got."

Ziv seemed in no mood for a fight and did not reply to his father's dig.

"Have you had your head up your arse for thirty years?" Arvel continued. "Unemployment for people our age is through the fucking roof."

"Quit your crying. You're crying about unemployment when you're not even unemployed."

Ziv spoke up. "Look," he found himself saying. "We've both got jobs now. Good jobs. Why can't we just sit here, drink a few beer, and act like normal people. Why do we always have to jump around each other screeching like a pack of gorillas?"

Arvel and Ennis backed off, each of them with a face his own shade of red. "I'm going to put on some music," Ziv said. He stood up and jangled the change in his pocket.

"The boys won't like it," Ennis said.

Ziv ignored his father and walked past the pool tables, where the regulars were playing snooker.

As he approached the jukebox, the snooker players began yelling, "Don't! Don't!"

Ziv made a face in their direction and put three quarters into the slot. He pressed off some songs.

"No!" the snooker players shouted in unison. Ziv shook his head at them. As he was sitting back down at the table with Arvel and Ennis, the introduction to "Bad Case of Lovin' You," by Robert Palmer, started up.

"That's not the song I pressed," Ziv said.

"No matter what you press, that's what it plays," Ennis said. "That song got played so many times that some kind of groove must have got worn in the machine. That's all it knows how to play now."

The men at the snooker tables were covering their ears.

"I guess these guys are pretty sick of this song," Ziv said. The three of them looked at the pool players, who were shouting at Ziv, giving him the finger.

"Well, they're about to hear it six more times," Ziv said. Ennis started to laugh, and his sons joined in.

Winter was still weeks away, but the fall feeling had already gone out of the air. There were no more earth-smells, no more scent of decaying leaves. As Ziv walked he could feel a fear building up inside him, as though he were making a big mistake. He'd grown up with the myth and the lore of the Pictou County coalfield, and that lore was about nothing if it was not about injury, perilous danger, and violent death. He'd learned about the Hundred Years War in Grade 11 history, but all that remained with him now was the name. The queasy, sick sensation that was starting to grow in his stomach might be something felt by a soldier going off to fight in a war like that, a conflict that had claimed or maimed or changed generations of your own family. The town was as grey as an old photo as he walked through it. Things moved, people, cars, but these belied the uneasy stillness that seemed to blanket everything.

As he turned off Foord Street and followed the twisty road through the little cluster of houses before the Plymouth Bridge, the silos at the mine site came into view. Constructed of ugly concrete and steel, there was nothing remarkable about the look of them at all. This was the same sort of unsightly industrial complex that scarred the landscape in other places in the county, except that this was new. Some parts of the above-ground operation were still under construction. In contrast to other operations Ziv had seen – ones with rusted machinery strewn about, or with buildings whose roofs had collapsed – the Eastyard site gleamed like a new Buick on the lot, the latest model, fully loaded with options.

The height of the silos, and their newness on the landscape, made them look large from a distance. But as he crossed the bridge and got to the straight stretch that lead right to Eastyard's gates, the mine seemed to shrink. The whole industrial site itself, silos, shaft portals, buildings, stacks of materials and equipment, was a little larger than the Zellers store he'd worked at. But compared to the whole mall, with its huge parking lot and adjacent stores and complexes, the mine was small.

The work site was just being set up for production, no coal was coming out of it yet, so there were only a half-dozen or so cars in the parking lot, and aside from some low electrical humming, the place was eerily devoid of noise. He heard a voice and looked between two small shed-like buildings where two men in coveralls and hard hats were stacking metal rods onto a forklift by hand.

Once in the parking lot, Ziv walked immediately to the building with the most cars parked near it. As he got closer, he saw the word *office* stencilled on the plate-glass and aluminum door.

Inside, there was a small carpeted reception area and a secretary behind a desk. The woman was about forty, narrow-faced with straight black hair.

"You must be Mr. Burrows," she said without looking up.

"That's right," said Ziv.

"Are you a friend of . . . that Kowalski . . . gentleman?" She looked him in the eye now with an expression that almost seemed suspicious.

Ziv cringed. "Well, I know him," he began.

She turned her eyes up to the ceiling in a way that suggested she was somehow already fed-up with Roly.

"I'm *Ziv* Burrows," Ziv said, trying to deflect the blame for whatever Roly had done to offend her. "Kowalski knows my brother. Arvel. He also hired on here, but he hasn't gotten a call to come in yet."

The secretary double-checked a list on her desk and shrugged. "He'll get one before too much longer," she said. "You're the only one on the list for training this morning."

She seemed to have said all she was going to about Roly, and led Ziv to a small conference room with plush leather chairs and beautiful wood-grained tables. At the far end of the room was a sleek, new-looking television on a cart, a VCR on the shelf below it. On a shelf beneath the VCR was a stack of video tapes.

"As you know, your first day is training and orientation," the woman said. "So these are the tapes they want you to watch."

"Begin with this one, then the rest you can watch in whatever order you like. This afternoon Mr. Brennan will come by to take you on a tour underground." She smiled momentarily, as though she'd suddenly remembered something. "Bathroom is out this door and down the hall." She closed the door behind her.

Ziv looked after her quizzically. Was this it? No one else with him? No other instructions? A stack of video tapes and that was all? He shrugged and put the first one into the machine. It was a forty-five minute PR video for Eastyard Coal, obviously designed to impress potential investors. Considering the lengthy, gushingly positive section on what life in Pictou County was like, it must also have been intended to lure skilled workers, most likely from Alberta.

The rest of the tapes were obviously video supplements to manuals that had come with various pieces of equipment and machinery. Most of them assumed that you either were already an expert in hydraulics, diesel mechanics, welding, industrial robotics, or some other discipline. One after the other, Ziv dutifully popped the videotapes into the machine and watched them, trusting at first that eventually this Mr. Brennan was going to come and make clear the connections between all the scattered information he was getting from the tapes.

At noon, after a brief bathroom break, he unrolled the brown bag he'd brought and ate a baloney sandwich, washing it down with partly skimmed milk that he drank from an orange juice bottle.

The last videocassette clicked to a halt at about 1:20 in the afternoon, after which Ziv sat, idle and disoriented, for more than half an hour before Fred Brennan showed up.

Brennan was a fat, hard-looking man with woolly, decades-out-of-fashion mutton chops and a purple-red complexion.

"You Burrows?" Brennan asked without introducing himself.

"That's me," said Ziv. He snapped to his feet in a show of vigour that was hard to pull off after such a day of lethargy.

"Christ, look at the size of you," Brennan exclaimed. "There two of you or something?"

Ziv pondered this a moment, then said, "Oh, yes, my brother. He's an electrician."

Brennan nodded, a puzzled, almost cross-eyed look on his face. "He's above-ground. We'll have him in next week. We're bringing people on in ones and twos as we need them right now. You watch this stuff?" Brennan pointed a thumb at the video machine.

Ziv nodded. He braced himself for a quiz on what he'd spent the day watching.

"Better show you the mine," Brennan said. He walked out the door and Ziv followed him out of the office building to another building, sheathed with blue sheet metal, containing showers, locker rooms, and equipment.

From a table in a locker room, Brennan picked a hard hat with a lamp affixed. "Put this on," he said. He smacked Ziv in the chest with the helmet and glanced at Ziv's boots. "Those safety boots?" he said, and without waiting for an answer, he walked out a door that led to the outside. A few metres from the door sat an idling tractor. Brennan retrieved his own hard hat from the seat of the tractor and hopped up onto the seat himself. The tractor was a modified John Deere farm machine. There was a platform on the back for hauling people and machinery, but Ziv could tell by looking at the engine casing of the machine that something had been changed to make this tractor suitable to go underground. There had been no instructional video about this machine.

Brennan waved a thumb at him to get on the platform at the back. Ziv did so, and no sooner had Brennan thrown the thing into gear than Ziv's heart began to race. He was not comfortable entering a mine shaft on a vehicle powered by an internal combustion engine. He remembered a story his mother had told him, part of the lore of mining in Pictou County, about the dangers of bringing flammable materials into the mine. Her father had discovered one day that he'd accidentally brought two wooden matches into the pit with him. They'd been in the deepest part of a pocket since the day before, and he was eating his lunch when he discovered them. It was like a story from the trenches of a war. His grandfather had run with the matches like a live grenade, submerged them in a pool of sump water, and proceeded to mash them into a harmless chemical pulp.

If a couple of matches had sent his grandfather into such a panic, how could it be safe to drive into the same environment on this machine full of sparks and fire?

Brennan steered the rumbling tractor toward what could only be the portals of the mine, two doorways that angled sharply down into the ground. The pounding of Ziv's heart in his ears drowned out both the tractor and Brennan's voice as they descended. Without looking back to see if Ziv was listening, Brennan drove headlong down the shaft at what seemed to Ziv to be breakneck speed, pointing at this and that as they went along. Ziv heard the odd word: Quikrete, resin tubes, bulkhead, but he was swooning by the time the shaft levelled off and they'd reached what must have been a bottom, of sorts. Though he could see lights blazing around him, and the lamps on his and Brennan's helmets were lit, being underground to Ziv was like being submerged in murky water. The hum of his own blood began to mix with the hum of machinery. He clung to the rail of the platform at the back of the tractor and did not respond for a long time when the machine had finally stopped and Brennan, who had moved to the back, was motioning for him to come down.

Finally, Brennan looked good and hard at Ziv's face and said, "You're white as a fucking sheet, man. Are you sick?"

Brennan's voice came at him as though in a dream: faint and wavering, distorted into a series of endlessly drawn-out syllables. His mind held a sideways picture of Brennan's face for an instant, then he was aware of his cheek bouncing like a poorly inflated ball off the corner of the rail he'd been clinging to.

He was face-up on the floor of the shaft when he came to.

"Christ, man," Brennan was saying, slapping Ziv's cheeks to help bring him round. "What the hell is the matter with you?"

Ziv sat up for an instant and looked around at the mine shaft. Brennan was talking, but his voice buzzed meaninglessly in Ziv's head like a piece of far-off machinery. There was a dull ache in Ziv's face from his fall and he slumped over like a little boy where he sat. He felt stupid for coming down here in the first place. Facing his father was going to be the worst, telling him he'd quit after a single shift, quit the only job his father had ever understood or approved of, quit the only thing his father had ever said he was proud of him for.

He covered his face with his hands. "You'd better take me back to the surface," he said. He hoped Brennan was not able to hear the sob breaking his voice.

"We just got down here, man," Brennan replied. "Are you out of your Jesus mind?"

"I'm finished," Ziv said. "I'm done. You might as well take me back up."

## HEART BEATING FAST

One of the teachers at her college had told Meta that on Christmas most Japanese who were going to observe the day did so by buying a bucket of Kentucky Fried Chicken. Teenagers went out on a date and exchanged small gifts. That was Christmas. Desperate to make the holiday at least in some way familiar, Meta braced herself and shelled out fourteen dollars for an ounce-and-a-half of glass with sparkles glued to it. Fourteen dollars for a set of four glass balls to hang on a tree. As she paid for it, the cashier handed the box to a young woman at a table near the cash register. The young woman quickly and deftly executed a series of moves that resulted in the box's being wrapped artistically in pale-green and white paper. There was only a single short length of tape employed in the wrapping job, yet many fan-shaped folds creased the paper in interesting ways. On the white part of the paper a delicate texture rippled across the surface, giving the effect of a pond under a mild breeze.

The package was inside a plastic shopping bag, and when she emerged from the department store onto Shinjuku-dori, she peeked into the bag as if to make sure the tranquil pattern hadn't been obliterated by the chaos of Tokyo. After just three months in this city, she had not fully accustomed herself to the sight and sound and smell of the city streets.

Only a small proportion of the vehicles in the central city were private passenger cars. The rest were passenger buses, green-and-yellow taxis with rear doors that gaped open and slammed shut at the push of a button from the driver's seat, two-wheel, three-wheel, and four-wheel scooters, some with plastic bubble visors, some with roofs, used to deliver pizza, noodles, curry, coffee, developed photos, videos, groceries, alcohol, cooked rice in covered Styrofoam containers, uncooked rice in bulky plastic bags. Scaled-down cars that reminded her of Volkswagen Beetles with mumps, mini-garbage trucks, flatbed trailers, souped-up motorcycles ridden by messengers covered head to toe in red leather, chauffeur-driven sedans carrying government and company officials, limousines carrying gangsters with permed hair and tattoos, one-speed bicycles with rattly fenders and big parcel carriers fore and aft, carrying commuting business types from home to station and back.

Everyone dressed conservatively: blue or grey or brown business suits with white shirts and ties for men. Blue or grey or brown skirt suits with white blouses for women. Even on the weekends, the dress code was strict. Belted tan pants with a designer-logo sweatshirt and loafers for men, pleated slacks and loose-sleeved blouses for women.

Meta noticed that if she acted like a Canadian, said *sorry* when someone stepped on her toes, let others go ahead of her in line, she didn't stand a chance in Tokyo. No matter what day of the week it was, the prevailing pace in Tokyo was one of urgency. Everyone had to get where they were going quickly, as though all were perpetually terrified of tardiness.

Isetan sat directly atop Shinjuku Station, which someone at her college had told her was the busiest train station in the world. Meta could have descended to the underground without leaving the department store and taken a train to Yotsuya San-chome, not far from her apartment, but she'd been lost underground in Shinjuku Station already and she'd vowed never to go down there again. Having emerged from Isetan onto the street, she instinctively sought shelter from the mad-with-motion crowd. She rushed headlong down Shinjuku-dori in the direction of Shinjuku San-chome. When the crowd thinned a little after four or five long blocks, she ducked down a side street to where she remembered a Kohikan she visited a week before. Her legs were tired from walking, standing, waiting, and what she most wanted to do was go home. But at present, she couldn't face any of the means of getting there.

The Kohikan's gleaming shopfront of glass and polished chrome stood out in contrast to the block of sooty and dusty brick. She slipped through the door and made her way immediately to the booth at the back that was surrounded by a brass-plated railing. She liked this booth precisely because it felt so isolated. The light from the windows at the front of the shop didn't reach there, most customers didn't peer this far back into the shop. The smell of fresh, strong coffee being ground and brewed began to revive and console her. She took off her coat and hung it on a coatrack beside the booth and sat down.

A slim young waiter approached her tentatively, afraid, she

knew, that he'd face some unforeseen difficulty with this foreign client. He passed her a menu. Without looking at it, she said:

"Toki-meki kohi," *Heart-beating-fast coffee*. "Onegaishimasu." *Please*. He smiled with relief and bolted for the counter, where he would grind the beans, measure the grounds, boil the water, and filter her exactly one cup of coffee.

She took the wrapped box of ornaments from the Isetan bag, placed it carefully on the table and once again admired the beauty of its wrapping. The contents of the box were ornaments, but the box actually looked better than what was in it.

"I love you. I love you. I love you," someone in the restaurant said in North American English. "Why do they make this so complicated?"

Meta closed her eyes and shrank into her seat. She wished she could vaporize herself, disappear in a stream of particles and re-appear behind the locked door of her apartment. There were few enough foreigners in this city that it was relatively rare to find herself in a subway car or restaurant with another gaijin, but when she did, she was almost always mortified at how loudly other gaijin spoke in public. Hadn't they noticed how rude it sounded?

"Toki-meki kohi desu," the waiter said. She opened her eyes to acknowledge receipt of the coffee, and looked across the restaurant to the table directly in front of the shop window. There he was, the big obnoxious foreigner who gushed out loud about love in a public place. He was hunched over a piece of paper with a pen in his right hand, scratching. On the other side of the booth, two young women bantered back and forth in Japanese, now and then pointing to something on the paper the foreigner was filling out and explaining in broken English, so quietly Meta could barely hear what they were saying.

"What's the point in only having these forms in Japanese if they let you fill them out in English?" the man was saying to no one in particular. Neither of the women across from him was listening. "What's this part again?" He held the sheet up and pointed at a corner of it. Both women leaned in and looked carefully at the sheet.

The sugar on Meta's table was in the form of brown, rock-like crystals. She dissolved a few of these in the black coffee, then picked up the tiny white china creamer from the side of her saucer and emptied it into the cup. She stirred this mixture together with a small gold-coloured spoon and savoured the first sip of the bittersweet blend.

She took her green notebook from her handbag. HIGH GRADE NOTEBOOK was written in big black letters across the top. In smaller lettering beneath appeared the statement: *this notebook was made by automatic and excellentic machine.* Two months ago, when she'd seen this notebook on a shelf in a stationery store, it had delighted her. Since then, she had seen a pencil case with "The recycling strategy with a 100% increase in fascination" on it, a plastic ruler that said "Bastard!", and a T-shirt with a picture of a rooster on it that said "I am king of cock." She'd enjoyed having a chuckle at the slightly askew sentence on the notebook's cover before, and probably would again, but at present it only bewildered her.

*Dear Ziv:*

> *This is the first letter I'm sending to you since I've been in Japan, but it's not the first letter I've written. I've got the others back in my*

desk drawer (I'm writing this in a coffee shop, drinking a coffee that cost me three dollars and fifty cents), all of them in envelopes. Some of them even have stamps on them. I don't know why I didn't send them.

I can remember each one. I can remember what I said in it, what I was thinking about, how I was feeling. It's funny how you do things. You just end up doing them and you don't know why. Sometimes you don't even know that you are doing them until later when you look back. I keep writing "you" but it's not you I'm talking about at all. It's me.

The first letter I wrote you started off like this:

Dear Ziv:

I don't know what I was expecting when I came here. I guess I was expecting things to be completely different from Canada. But what I'm surprised at is how similar things are. The sky is still blue, people here walk on two legs, and if you drop something, gravity brings it to the ground. I guess the world is the same wherever you go.

One reason I didn't send that letter is that it didn't take long for me to realize how wrong I'd been. This place is so deceptive. Things look so familiar on the surface, but the interior of the place and the people is so completely alien to me. And the weird thing is, the longer I'm here, the less well I understand it.

"Excuse me."

Meta jumped back from what she'd been writing, and instinctively, without looking up, flipped the page so no one could read it. She glanced up to see the big foreigner she'd been watching fill out the form earlier. He stood over her with what he no doubt considered his best, most pleasant smile. His cotton dress shirt held big creases where the starch had given way. He wore a dark-blue tie and a navy suit that was slightly too large for his slim frame.

"Can you speak English?" he asked.

She leaned back from him a little and could not stop herself from quickly eyeing him up and down. His brown shoes were scuffed down to the undyed leather.

"Yes," she said quietly, cautiously.

"I'm sorry," he said, softening his face even more. "Was that a yes?"

Meta nodded.

"I need to ask a favour," the man said. His hair needed trimming, and his face was grey, as though he hadn't eaten properly in a while. Still, Meta realized now that he was younger than she was. He was twenty-one, twenty, maybe even nineteen. She did not respond, physically or verbally. She did not move a muscle to indicate that she'd even consented to listen.

"I'm going to marry that girl over there," he said. He pointed back to the table where he'd been sitting, where there were clearly *two* young women. He did not bother to acknowledge this, let alone differentiate his intended from his unintended. He paused now to regard Meta. His eyes focused on her forehead, then her lips, then quickly flitted down to glance at her breasts before returning to her eyes.

"I need . . ." he glanced over his shoulder and seemed slightly unnerved, much less sure of himself than he'd been a minute ago. "We need . . . another witness."

Meta bit her top lip as she thought a moment.

"What would I have to do?" she asked.

"Just sign this form."

"Just sign it. Nothing more?"

"Name and address is all this form asks for."

"I don't have to go to the ward office?"

"No."

"They're pretty trusting."

"One thing I really like about this country," the man said, "is it proves that if you treat people as though they deserve to be trusted, they will act trustworthy."

"I can't read this form, so I don't know what I'm signing," she said.

"I know it's asking for a lot in a way. It's just that we have to do this today because . . ."

"All right, I'll sign," Meta said. She interrupted him deliberately so she would not have to find out anything about him and his wife-to-be.

"This says *name* and this says *address*," the man said, pointing to the blanks on the page.

"Mathilde LeBlanc," Meta wrote in the square for name. Beside address, she furtively copied the address of the coffee shop off of the dessert menu posted on the napkin dispenser.

"Thanks so much," the man said as she handed him back the form. "We really appreciate this. Listen, can I buy you a cup of coffee or something?"

"No," Meta said, guilty that he was so appreciative of her lie.

When Meta got back to her own apartment, she was tired enough to sleep, though it was only mid-afternoon. There was a note taped to her door, a piece of pink paper, folded once in the middle.

*Please come to my place!* it said in the scrolly writing of someone to whom the Roman alphabet was straight and square and foreign. She left the note on the door in the hope that Yuka would think she hadn't returned yet. She almost had the door closed when a knock on the opposite side of it startled her. When she opened it, Yuka stood in the doorway in a faded floral smock. Her head was inclined forward in an attitude of supplication.

"Please come to my place!" Yuka said in a breathy voice.

Too tired to argue, Meta followed Yuka into her apartment and took off her shoes before stepping up onto the tatami.

Yuka and her son lived in an apartment only a little larger than the one Meta lived in by herself. Three of them had lived there for years, before her husband had died. Yuka herself had been here for at least nineteen years, since her wedding day in 1968, and it seemed to Meta that she had not had the heart yet to change much since the husband had passed on. Yuka's husband, whom she referred to as Mr. Tamaguchi, had been a highly placed salaryman in a Japanese pharmaceutical company. His salary had afforded them very nice furniture and appliances, but Yuka had explained that Mr. Tamaguchi's family, when he himself was scarcely old enough to remember, had been deeply affected by the hardships and scarcity of the war. Yuka's nice furnishings were crammed into the apartment alongside the older furnishings that no one would buy second-hand, but that Mr. Tamaguchi had not been able to bring himself to throw out. The apartment was overwhelmed with an accumulation of things. Their small living room contained two couches, two armchairs, two televisions, two stereos, a china closet so full that the contents seemed painted on the glass of the doors, a coffee table and four chairs, a portable sewing machine, a gas heater, a dehumidifier, and a partially covered stack of tightly folded clothing, for which there was no other storage space, that reached almost to the ceiling in one corner.

The cluttered room, along with the stale smell of years of smoking in this tiny place, pushed in on Meta's chest, making it difficult for her to breathe.

She sat at the dining table while Yuka poured coffee for them and took a seat opposite her. Her son, Kazuhiro, sat slumped, completely without expression or movement, into a corner of the newer couch. He did not speak any English, so Meta greeted him in Japanese. "Konichiwa." He did not respond. The newer television was turned on, but no one was watching it. On screen was a game show in which a group of shivering, frightened-looking young men were being forced to jump into a pool of ice water.

"What happened to your hand?" Meta asked, pointing at a circular mark at the V of Yuka's right thumb and forefinger. Yuka covered it quickly with her left hand. "I burn it at the cooker," she said. Meta stood up to get a better look at the wound. "My god, that looks really painful," she said, gently pulling away the concealing hand.

"Not so painful," Yuka said.

"Ouch!" Meta said in sympathy. She looked Yuka in the eye. "You burned this . . . at the cooker?"

Yuka blinked uncomfortably a moment, then looked away.

# PART FIVE

# 1989

# An Intellectual Ruffian

$E$ nnis attends the families' group meetings at the Plymouth Fire Hall, and unlike most others, he has never cried here with grief. He's never shouted, either, into a microphone or from his seat on the floor. He's never spoken, as a matter of fact, and except to raise his hand to vote for or against some motion, he has not participated at all in the proceedings. He feels emptied somehow of emotions, and comes to the meetings mostly out of a feeling of obligation to Arvel's memory, and the memory of the terrible thing that was done to him.

He sits today where he always sits: in the very last row at the back, in an aisle seat near the door so that he can get up and walk out quickly at any time he desires without being noticed or making a scene. Dunya has never come to one of these meetings, although he always asks her to go with him. She sits in her white room at the front of the house and quietly refuses. He feels this sitting is somehow something she must do now, and he himself has such mixed feelings about the meetings that he has no desire to try to convince her.

Ziv has also refused to join him here, and the two have fought recently, just last night, over whether there is any point in the families fighting for redress after their loved ones have died. Ziv accused him of living in the past, with his talk about justice and democracy, words that Ennis himself hardly felt he believed in any more.

"Going to those meetings is the least I can do for my son," Ennis had said.

"Well, I'm your son as well, and if you want to do something for me, don't ask me to go with you and watch people fight for what they won't get. It's too late to do something for Arvel. And why now? You never did a thing for him in life. You know, the only reason he took that job was to please you. If it wasn't for you, he would never have taken it."

At these words from his son, Ennis felt anger and hurt rise in him, but he merely lowered his head and walked away.

Despite the fact that the families were duped in this very building by Eastyard in the early days after the explosion, tricked under false pretenses into not speaking with the media while the whole world was still watching, family members seem to have grown attached to the Plymouth Fire Hall, the place where many of them had first met each other, first formed the idea of themselves as a group. They'd hoped here, they'd hugged here, they'd feared, they'd cried, they'd prayed, they'd mourned.

And so, with the disaster now months behind them, they gather here in the smell of motor oil and disinfectant, in the over-cleaned, underlit banquet room, still used most for wedding receptions. They plot and debate, searching for a way of rescuing some sense of justice out of such a terrible event. They want an investigation into what led to the deaths of their loved ones. They want financial compensation for survivors. Many of them want to see a criminal trial for former Eastyard managers, all of whom have fled the province.

From the podium today, all the talk is about money. On the floor is a demand for a forensic audit of Eastyard's books, partly to trace every dollar of taxpayers' money that got spent on the mine. The managers, the high-salary-drawers, are all still alive, and many family members want someone to track the government money and whose pockets it made its way into.

The whole idea of a forensic audit is a waste of time, as far as Ennis is concerned. None of the money is ever coming back to the government anyway, even if they do find out where it went. There are more important things they could be focusing on, things that might actually make a difference for the families who've lost loved ones. But he feels only half-present at the meeting as it is, and the prospect of standing up at the podium himself and speaking into the microphone seems impossible, unthinkable, like trying to breathe underwater. He would stand up and open his mouth to speak only to drown in his own despair.

The woman at the mike is Audrey Jenkins, the wife of Steve Jenkins, whose body was the first one recovered after the explosion, one of the eleven bodies actually brought back to the surface. In the first days after the explosion, she stood out as one of the strongest, patting others on the back in the fire hall, on her hands and knees with her own four children and the children of others, smearing poster paints over newsprint with the names of the missing in the vain hope that the miners would return. From the hospital, after he'd had his face broken,

Ennis saw her on the news, filmed from across a police barricade, breaking down on the way from her car to the fire hall, minutes after identifying her husband's charred body. She'd gone right to the ground, face-down and without movement, until her twin sisters each took an arm and dragged her through the door.

She is a small woman with wide shoulders under a brown T-shirt. "Is anybody adding all this up?" she is saying, her voice strong and firm, but just strained enough to suggest that it could crack at any moment. She waves a newspaper clipping over her head. According to what she has already said, the clipping dates from the planning stages of the Eastyard operation, and details the provincial government's promise of millions of dollars in loan guarantees for the company.

Ennis glances down into the coffee-stained khaki tote bag at his feet. On the outside there is a Co-op logo. Inside, brown manila folders are stuffed with his own collection of clippings.

"I can't make head or tail of these numbers," Audrey Jenkins is saying. There is a sudden rush of feedback and she pulls back from the microphone until it stops. "What's the difference between an operating grant, a tax break, and a loan guarantee?" The podium is a portable music stand. A single microphone plugged into a guitar amplifier is the only PA system. "We need an independent person who knows something about money. They've got to get into those locked cabinets over there." She points in the direction of the mine, although documents have been removed to RCMP headquarters. But mine officials had been given unimpeded access to company files for days following the disaster, and the chance of there being any incriminating documents among what the police have are nil.

Ennis puts a hand through the loops of his Co-op bag and rises to his feet. He's had enough already. The speaker looks at him accusingly. With hunched shoulders he excuses himself into his chest, inaudible to anyone but himself, and walks out through the main door.

It is a clear, windless winter day. The landscape is all white snow and grey trees. Here and there is the pale yellow of stubborn oak leaves, still clinging to their branches. Ennis's breath is pushing out now in crisp columns from his mouth as he contemplates the walk home, more than two miles. He sets the bag between his feet and it slouches heavily to one side while he zips his jacket.

"Ennis."

He turns at the sound of the voice, almost tripping over the canvas bag between his feet. Allie McInnis is coming through the double doors from the fire hall, the chemical smell of the interior coming with him.

Allie is part of the families group, although he is not closely related to anyone who died. His wife is a distant cousin of the Comber family, whose boy Nicholas is one of those still underground. Everyone in that family is still grieving too much to get involved with the group, so Allie stands in for them.

"Allie," Ennis says. "I didn't see you in there."

When Allie opens his mouth again to speak, Ennis notices that his lower dentures are missing a tooth, a black square in his smile. He wonders whether he is responsible for this.

"I was a way up front," Allie says. He looks down a moment at the bag at Ennis's feet. Manila folders are visible. Clippings of all sizes protrude at odd angles, "Ennis, can I talk to you for a minute?" Allie has already zipped up his heavy coat and is winding a long navy scarf about his neck. Long tubes of steam exit his nostrils as he exhales.

Ennis works his watch out of his sleeve and looks at it. "I have to walk home. It's getting dark."

"I've seen you walking a lot. You're looking real good. You look like you lost a lot of weight."

"Well," Ennis says. He shifts uncomfortably. "The face isn't looking so good."

"Swelling's come down a lot. I saw you up by the post office last month. I was just driving by."

Ennis looks at the ground and notices the pebbles of salt he is standing on. He scrapes a foot back and forth and listens to the gravelly crunch. "I guess the boys at the Tartan probably wonder what the hell happened to me."

"I haven't been back there much," Allie says. "Anyway . . . Look, Ennis. I'm not really a family member here, Ennis, or anything. I'm here for the Combers."

"I know that."

"Anyway, Ennis. More than one person has asked me to talk to you. I know others have asked you already. There's an executive committee you know, Ennis."

Ennis shakes his head. "I'm not interested," he says.

"We could use your help, Ennis."

"Things are going fine as far as I can see."

"Seems an awful waste, Ennis. A man with your experience."

"That young lawyer the executive hired. He knows more than I ever will."

"Anyway, Ennis. I don't want to be harassing you or anything like that. There's some people know I know you. They asked me to put a word in, is all."

Ennis looks out at the bare branches of trees in the valley. The sun is long down beyond the horizon and the clouds there are streaked deep red. Over in the east, the blue of the sky where it shows through clouds is deepening. Behind him, somewhere beneath the white and grey landscape he looks out on, lies the body of his son, soot-soaked and damp, rotting. Up over the little hill in front of him, the bridge that will take him across the river glistens.

"I'll see you later, Allie," Ennis says. He picks up the canvas bag and heads for the bridge.

<hr />

Ziv is slouched into the leatherette padding of the stand-up bar at Stumpy's, which is right across the parking lot from Zellers. He's come straight from work and is wearing his dress shirt, the tie and collar loosened now in the heat of the overcrowded room. The dance floor throbs with writhing bodies. He looks at it sideways, trying to make out individual people, but can only see darkness and anonymous shapes. He fumbles through a front pocket and extracts all the money he has left: two dollars and fourteen cents in quarters, nickels, and pennies. It's enough to cover one more beer.

He raises his head slowly and squints out along the periphery of the room, reorienting himself, then steers in the direction of the dark hallway that leads to the washrooms, shifting and elbowing his way there. Even the hallway is packed, and he stands at the end of it for a few moments before he realizes that the crowd here is not a lineup, but merely overflow from the dance floor. Some people are actually dancing in the hallway. The cigarette smoke is mixed with pot smoke. Ziv squeezes his way into the bathroom and empties his bladder into one of the urinals. He's at the sink, washing his hands, gawking drunkenly at his own drunken face, when a firm hand claps him on the shoulder.

"Hey, man," a voice says. "I haven't seen you in a long time."

As soon as Ziv turns around, he knows what is happening. "I don't know you," he says, and presses the button of the hand-dryer with an elbow.

"You don't remember me, do you?"

"You have me confused with someone else."

"Fuck! I can't believe it. PRVS. You were in electrical construction, I was doing welding."

"I'm telling you, you've got me mixed up with someone else."

"The hell I do. We used to go over the bank at the back at noon and smoke pot. You remember."

"Look," Ziv says. "You got me confused with my dead brother."

The man laughs. "Dead brother! You're still full of it. What was your name again? I remember it!"

Ziv turns away, heads out of the bathroom.

"Some queer name . . . Arbor . . . Anson . . . Anvil . . . Axel . . ."

Ziv orders a Keith's at the bar, dumps the change from his pocket onto the countertop, and heads toward the spot he'd been in before.

The space he left at the stand-up bar has been filled, so he steps back against the wall, guzzling down big mouthfuls of beer. These are the drinks he does not enjoy. He is already so drunk that he will be sick in the morning, and he knows himself and the limits to his capacity to drink well enough that the beginnings of tomorrow's hangover are already hammering the big muscles in his limbs, pushing inwards on the sides of his skull. The last drinks of any night are a compulsion, not a desire.

He feels angry at himself for being this drunk, when he has not had more than a beer or two in months. He feels angry for coming to Stumpy's, a place he swore off a long time ago. But he's come here tonight because he does not want to face his father.

He holds his beer bottle up to the strobe light on the dance floor and sees that it is three-quarters full. He curses himself. The money he spent on this could have got him a taxi at least part way to Albion Mines.

"Excuse me. Excuse me," Ziv says. He worms his way close to the bar and puts the beer bottle on it. He turns in the direction of the coat check at the entrance and begins pushing his way toward it.

"I remember now," a hand clamps his shoulder and pulls him back. "Arbel. It's Arbel. I remember because it rhymes with marble."

"Listen," Ziv turns around to face the man. "My brother's name was Arvel, not Arbel. You must have a brain the size of a fucking marble. I told you he's *dead*. He died in the Eastyard explosion. His dead fucking body is still a mile underground. Now leave me the fuck alone."

People quickly shrink back from the immediate vicinity of the two men, eager to stay away from trouble. Ziv pushes the man hard at the shoulders, sending him backward into the crowd. He comes back at Ziv, fists flailing. "You big prick!" he screams. "Think you can bully me!" He cuts loose with a heavy boot that misses Ziv's balls, catching him hard in the upper thigh. Ziv's skin begins to burn where he was kicked. He puts a hand down and feels the loose ends of the thready fabric where the boot shredded his pants. He grabs the little man around the throat with his left hand and squeezes until the man squawks. He lets loose with a right in a downward arc on the end of the nose and blood sprays out over his left arm. The man gives up struggling and Ziv lets him go. The next thing Ziv feels is the side of his face careening off the edge of a table on the way to the floor. He is drunk enough that he hears the sound of his head striking the tile floor, rather than feeling the pain of it. He is impressed with the pitch of the smack it makes. Someone is yanking his right wrist up the centre of his back. "Ow, ow! You cracked my fucking skull," he says over his shoulder to whoever has got him. His wrist and elbow scream with pain until his shoulder lets go with a *snap*, then all the pain zeroes in on the dislocated joint.

By the time the bouncer who tore out his shoulder is helping Ziv to his feet, the crowd is starting to go about its normal business of being drunk at Stumpy's bar. Some are still focused on the shrinking spot of bare floor where the fight was. Some are yelling throaty monosyllables that, over the deafening music, Ziv cannot hear.

The bouncer leads him behind the bar and through a door he's never noticed before. They go up a narrow, carpeted staircase and through another door to a modern, well-lit office. The place is clean and roomy and quiet, except for the muffled pounding of music that comes thumping up through the floor from the bar. There is a wall of black windows that look out on the night. The windows are striped across in white by several sets of venetian mini-blinds.

In a big, comfortable-looking chair sits a man with a broad, youngish face, salon-tanned unnaturally brown. His mid-length blond-brown hair is parted in the middle and brushed back at either side. As soon as he stands up, Ziv knows who he must be.

"Jesus Christ," he says. "It's Stumpy."

The man is no more than five feet three inches, but beneath a pair of tan Dockers and a light-blue shirt, his thick, muscular body makes him appear almost half as wide as his height. His black leather belt is cinched snugly at the waist of his trousers, revealing that not a pound of his bulk is fat.

"I never dreamed you were real. I thought you were just some catchy name."

"Guy was fighting," the bouncer says to Stumpy. "You want me to stay?" Stumpy shakes his head and the bouncer leaves.

"I'm no threat to you," Ziv says. "Your man ripped my arm off." He moves to hold his right arm up on display, but cries out in pain when it budges only slightly.

Stumpy opens a wood-panelled door at the side of the office and flicks a light, revealing a small bathroom. "Wash up," he says, and sits back down in his chair.

Ziv goes into the bathroom and closes and locks the door. He looks at himself in the mirror over the sink. He looks like Rocky Balboa in the last fight scene of the first movie. His face is swollen where his head hit the table, and then the floor. His eye is black and getting blacker. The swelling will close it soon. There is blood smeared on his face and on the side of his neck, but he feels around with his good hand for a cut and cannot find one. It must all be the other guy's blood. Where is that bastard? he wonders. Why isn't he getting an audience with Stumpy? He wets some paper towel and wipes his face and neck. He lets the water run ice-cold in the sink, stoppers the basin, and sticks the swollen part of his head into the coldness, keeping it under for as long as he can hold it. With his head upside down, he feels his equilibrium go. He lurches forward and knocks the back of his head on the tap.

Even washing with his other hand, there are involuntary movements in his right arm that cause shrill spasms of pain to shoot out from his shoulder. He carefully slips off his shirt and T-shirt and moves his left hand tenderly to the hurt shoulder. The joint has been dislocated before, and he knows there's not much to be done about it tonight. He pokes around at the joint, which doesn't hurt to be prodded, only to be moved. The ball has come right out of the socket but has snapped most of the way back in on its own. He pulls at the outside of the shoulder, trying to snug it up to the side of his body and bring the two halves of the joint back together completely, but he knows from experience that it will take a few days to slip back in on its own and a few weeks before it has completely returned to normal.

He uses the liquid soap from the dispenser to wash himself as best he can with only one hand. He holds his head under the cold-water tap and washes his hair. The harsh suds run down and burn his eyes. He rinses as much blood from his clothes as possible, then dries himself off, wrings himself out, and goes out into the office.

He half expects to find the New Glasgow Police in Stumpy's office, but Stumpy is still the only one in the room. "I've got this form here for you to sign," Stumpy says. He holds up a piece of paper, then puts it back on his desk. "It bars you from these premises for one year. Sign this and I don't call the police."

Ziv looks at the document. It is printed in blue ink, in small lettering that is cluttered with lettered and numbered sections and dotted and solid lines in which information can be filled.

"I'm too drunk to read this," Ziv says.

"Put your name and address here . . . your signature down here."

Ziv considers protesting signing something he can't read. He considers signing a false name. But he decides to follow the path of least resistance and puts the information where Stumpy asks him to put it.

"Now get the fuck out of here," Stumpy says. He opens a door to the outside. There is a metal railing and a set of stairs that leads to the parking lot. A gust of cold air whooshes into the office.

"I can't go out there," Ziv says.

"What are you talking about?"

"My coat is at the coat check downstairs."

Stumpy rolls his eyes and shuts the outside door. "Give me the ticket," he says.

Ziv checks his pockets. "I lost it."

Stumpy's eyes go for another roll.

"I'll go down and get it," Ziv says, making for the door to the bar.

"You're not going back down there until this time next year," Stumpy says, moving between Ziv and the door. "Describe the coat."

"It's a green down-filled parka. The bulky kind. In the front pocket there's a book called *Four Philosophical Ideas*."

Stumpy frowns in disbelief. "Are you kidding me?" he says. "What are you, some kind of intellectual ruffian?"

Ziv shrugs, then winces as his shoulder jolts with pain.

As Stumpy is headed down the stairs to the bar, Ziv calls after him. "Hey, can I ask you a favour?"

Stumpy stops and exhales in disgust. Without looking back up at Ziv, he says, "What?"

"Could you get me a cup of coffee? I feel pretty weak and I have to walk to Albion Mines."

Stumpy turns and looks up at him, half surprised, half curious. "You got fifty cents?" he asks.

"No," Ziv says. "That book's worth nine ninety-five." Stumpy is turned around again, almost at the doorway that closes off the bottom of the stairs. "That's less than two-fifty per philosophical idea!" Ziv shouts after him.

"Intellectual ruffian bum!" Stumpy says.

When he gets to his parents' back door, the coffee and the long walk have sobered him considerably. Both his mother and father would be asleep by now. Since the old man has been on the keg, he gets up every morning at five o'clock for some sort of physical exercise. Ziv walks right into the kitchen, where he gulps four of his mother's high-powered arthritis Aspirin and several big cups of tap water.

He looks at himself in the bathroom mirror. His swollen face is like a stranger's looking back at him. His one eye is now completely closed and the swelling has spread all the way to his jawline.

He climbs up the stairs, pulls back the folding door of his bedroom, shucks his clothes at his feet, and slithers into his bed, careful not to move or bump his sore arm.

Sleep is racked by frightening dreams that consist mostly of loud noises, just the other side of identifiable, flashes of faces contorted with pain. At least three times he awakes moaning, having rolled onto his dislocated shoulder. Each time it takes him a moment to realize how to get out of the painful position he is in without the use of the injured limb. Then the real dream begins.

One instant Ziv's grandfather is his grandfather. The next instant he is Arvel. They're standing outside the house on MacLean Street, the house where his mother grew up. His grandfather says something. Ziv says, Pardon? His grandfather repeats the same syllables, which are still incomprehensible. It's Ukrainian, Ziv realizes. Then instantly he knows he is dreaming. *I wonder if it's real Ukrainian or dream gibberish*, he thinks in his dream. He wishes he could write it down, knows he'll never remember it when awake. Over his grandfather's shoulder, he sees his grandmother through the window. She is standing at the pump by the sink, washing apples. He's only seen her in pictures; she died of TB long before he was ever thought of or born. He takes a good, long look at her, though it is difficult to see her clearly at this distance. He looks for anything recognizable, some small part of her that has survived in him.

His grandfather moves, shuffles his feet in the direction of the pit. Ziv moves with him and realizes they are both carrying lunch cans, the cylindrical ones he's seen at the miner's museum.

"Arvel! Arvel!" he shouts at the old man.

His grandfather looks at him, puzzled, says something in dream Ukrainian. As they round the turn, the ominous towers of the Allan Shaft come into view.

"Arvel," he says to his grandfather, he grabs the old man at the shoulders and shakes him. "Arvel, it is you! Arvel . . .!"

The old man becomes angry, shoves Ziv away, and begins running, awkwardly in heavy pit boots, in the direction of the mine.

When Ziv awakes in the darkness, his brother's name still on his lips, he realizes he's been shouting in his sleep. He waits a moment in the night silence, listens.

"Ziv," his father's voice is just beyond the folding door. Ziv pretends not to hear.

He opens his eyes and becomes aware that he has now crossed a boundary. It is more morning now than night. He is more hungover now than drunk. He notices a crack of light at the base of the bedroom door. He moans his way to a sitting position and swings his legs over the side of the bed. A knock sounds, his father tapping on the door frame from the hall.

The knock comes again and he stands unsteadily, kicks his discarded clothing away from his feet, and slides back the folding door in just his Jockey shorts. The face before him is familiar but distorted. Backlighting gives it a disembodied appearance. The eyes are clear in their sockets, but the features appear to have been dismantled, then put back together in approximately the position they belonged, nothing quite fitting.

"What the hell happened to you?" his father says, shaking his head in disgust. "Have you been to a doctor? You've got a fractured skull this time, you mark my words. I'd better drive you to the hospital. What's the matter with your arm, the way you're holding it?"

Ziv slides the door back across until the latch clicks, then limps back into bed and covers himself with blankets.

When he opens his eyes again, it is nine o'clock. He's not on until the four-to-ten shift tonight. He hauls himself straight on the mattress and lowers his feet to the floor. His head aches. His whole body, from the soles of his feet right up through his shoulders and neck and into the base of his skull, feels bruised and ready to snap. He looks down at his hands and opens and closes them. They are tight and achy. They feel as though they need to be soaked in hot water until they loosen. He puts the tips of his fingers gently against his injured eye. The swelling has already come down from last night. The eye is open enough that he can see out of it.

He goes downstairs and stops at the doorway to the front room. His mother sits like some Buddhist monk with her eyes closed in the middle of the empty room she'd had him paint white after the explosion.

"Good morning," he says it anyway, though he knows she won't answer. He has tried not speaking to her when she is in this state, but that is worse: too much silence. She'll talk, but she'll do it later, when she emerges from whatever reverie she is in.

The downstairs is bare and white since his mother threw almost everything they owned into the trash. The house looks so unfamiliar. He sometimes feels out of place here, alien, as though he's barged into someone else's place uninvited, but he likes the house empty. It has a refreshing feeling of possibility. On the kitchen table, the newspaper is separated into sections and folded. His father has read it already. On the front page must have been more news about the public inquiry. There are two big squares where articles used to be, a clear view to page 3, where his father clipped what he wanted from the front page. They are testifying now in one of the conference rooms at the new Miner's Museum in Albion Mines. In the remnants of one article, a little half-paragraph continuation on page 2, there is a list of the names of those who have already testified, along with who is about to. Ziv's eyes stop at Gavin Fraser's name. According to the article, he's on for late morning or early afternoon. Ennis never bothers cutting out pictures, and the photo of Gavin shows him clean-shaven with short hair, neatly parted in the middle. Gavin is a savvy customer, Ziv thinks. For four or five years he's shaved infrequently and worn his hair long. But he knows he'll be on national television, and that people are more apt to listen to someone who is clean-cut. According to the miners Ziv's talked to, Gavin is the star of the inquiry. He is smart enough to explain his points well. He has plenty of mining experience. But, mostly, it is that he quit, and he quit over safety concerns, which makes him a strong witness to the dangerous condition of the mine before the explosion.

Ziv pours himself a cup of lukewarm coffee from the pot his father must have made. He sits at the table and holds up the front page again to examine his father's scissor work. What must the old man be thinking as he carries out this task? Deep in the pit of his stomach, somehow mixed with the pain of his own idiocy and self-abuse from last night, he feels a pang of guilt. There was an earlier time when his father had been keeping news clippings and he'd used them to try to reach out to Ziv. And Ziv had made a complete mess of that affair. He wishes now that he knew how to ask his father what he is thinking about. What he is feeling. But both of his parents are closed off to him now. He and his father have hardly been able to hold a conversation about anything their whole lives, let alone how they felt. What can he expect either one of them to say to each other, after Arvel's death? His mother has gutted the house of furniture. She spent weeks sitting on the futon in the front room, quietly weeping. She seems lost in her own inner world as she sits every day and meditates, if that is what she is doing.

As Ziv turns the newspaper over, a square of newsprint falls to the floor. It is too small to have come from either of the holes on the front page. It must have slipped from his father's collection. "Lawyers Deny Pair in Hiding," is the headline. Ziv scans through the article. The story explains how two former Eastyard managers, who now live in Ontario, have so far refused to answer their subpoenas to appear at the inquiry.

As he showers, he tries to work the knots of tension from his limbs, but the more he pulls at and rubs his arms, the more they hurt. There is a dull ache in the shoulder that was dislocated last night.

Back in his bedroom he puts his clothes on, retrieves a tablet of letter-size writing paper from beneath his bed, and looks about the room for space to write. In the corner, there is the brown powder-box cabinet, one of the only things left in house after his mother's cleanup work after the explosion. He slaps the paper down on the waist-high shelf of the cabinet and opens to a fresh page. It's a little uncomfortable writing standing up, but he's keen on saying some things and the discomfort goes away quickly.

*Dear Meta*, he begins. They've exchanged several letters since her visit of last year. He cannot remember whose letter was last.

*Gavin Fraser is testifying at the inquiry today.*

He tears this sheet out immediately, drops it uncrumpled to the floor, and begins yet again.

*Dear Meta,*

*My parents are suffering tremendously since Arvel's death. I've never been able to talk to them anyway, regardless of what happened to Arvel. That's what was great about having you here. I had someone I could talk to.*

*I know you're making a lot of money over there and that it's great to have such a good job, but do you even think of coming home? For good, I mean? Permanently?*

*There was this show I saw on TV a while ago about people who get limbs amputated. They get something called a phantom limb, where they feel like their leg or arm is still there, even though it's not. That's what it's like with Arvel dead. I just cannot believe he's gone.*

*Arvel tried to kill me once. I've been remembering this in bits and pieces since his death. A fight we once had. To be fair, I tried to kill him, too. Whatever started the fight, I can't recall. But we were pounding on each other in earnest with our bare hands. In the middle of the living-room floor we smashed vases, slammed furniture around, screamed. At one point I remember biting him. I don't even recall what part of him I bit. I just remember finding my mouth a couple of centimetres from his body, reaching out with my teeth and clamping his flesh hard.*

*I know it must have hurt like hell. Under normal circumstances it would have, anyway. But we'd already been pounding on each other for a long time, when suddenly I bit him. I think we were both just numb. I know I was. Either he was too numb to cry out or I was too numb to hear him cry out. Later, we were both too exhausted to hit each other any more and, unable to lift our arms for another blow, we lay side by side on the floor, panting and out of breath. We started laughing. Just like that after an hour or more of pounding on each other and wishing the other dead, we had nothing left but laughter.*

*More than anything, though, it's that bite that stays with me. That I would have that in me: to bite someone. To bite my own brother. Not playfully, but viciously, with the intent to hurt him. I never saw the mark I made, but there must have been one. There must have been a mark, a purple circle on his skin, for a long time. There was probably a scar on him from that bite right up to the day he died. When they'd finally given up on finding him, I used to think of that mark on his dead body down there, metres and metres under the earth. I used to imagine it like a tattoo, dark in the middle, white around the edges. Maybe even the clear indentation of a tooth that I don't have any more. There is a part of me down there with him. Something only I am responsible for and only I know about. Something only he and I shared.*

*I feel afraid, but I don't even know what I'm afraid of.*

*I'll write again soon.*

Love,
Ziv

The weather has warmed and recooled recently, softening the snow cover, then locking the landscape in a skin of ice. When he emerges from the back door of the house, the cold catches in his lungs. He breathes in the air and feels it cool his whole body. In the centre of his chest, his fiery heart struggles to keep him warm. His feet slip over ice-slickened puddles and shatter shell ice as he makes his way to the end of the driveway. In his hand is the letter to Meta, sealed in a white business-size envelope and stamped with airmail postage. The sun breaks momentarily through the overcast, and the big, sick elm at the corner of Hudson Street shimmers under a crystal coating. He shields his eyes with the envelope and looks at the trees. Last week's warmth would have begun teasing up the sap from the roots. These late-winter freezes can crack a tree from the heart of its trunk.

At the corner of Foord Street he drops the letter in the red mailbox and pauses to look up at the statue on top of the miner's monument, the old-time miner with his safety lamp. There is no space left for names on the pedestal. Eastyard will require a whole monument unto itself. He turns left on Foord Street and heads for the new Miner's Museum, where the inquiry is being held.

# TELLING THE WORLD 19

Gavin Fraser grips the armrests of the witness chair and pushes the top of his back against the backrest. The afternoon session has just begun, and he knows this will be the hard part for him. He was called to the stand late in the morning and spent most of that time recounting his experience in the mining industry and telling the story of how he ended up at Eastyard. Now the important questions will be asked and he will have to answer them. He shifts in the seat, squirms until his fingers let go the armrests, tries to let his body loosen into a comfortable position.

Only one camera is allowed in the room, the official inquiry camera, but the inquiry releases hours of the procedures for broadcast every day on the channel that carries footage from parliament. News organizations broadcast snippets and sound bites on the nightly newscasts. The light necessary for the camera flushes the room white and stabs deep into Gavin's head. He squints against it, then when he remembers how awful people look when they squint on TV, he loosens his face blank, only to find himself squinting again just a few moments later. The technical crew with the camera is setting up for the afternoon, someone accidentally switches off a power plate and the television lights go black. As the public seating behind the lights colours into view, he makes out a single recognizable face. It is Ziv Burrows, Arvel Burrows's younger brother. He recognizes him because of how much the big forehead and wide cheeks resemble Arvel. His face is outlined in white light coming through behind him, making his face dark. All the same, his face appears swollen or bruised somehow.

There is a loud *conk*. Someone says *shit*. The lights blind him again.

"Continuing from this morning's testimony, Mr. Fraser, reference was made to your reasons for leaving Eastyard Coal."

He leans into the microphone and bumps his teeth on it. The sound echoes through the room. "I left because of safety concerns."

"Could you be more specific?"

"I did not think the underground operation met a basic standard of safety, from the viewpoint of the workers, and I quit when I realized that management had no intention of dealing with those safety problems."

"So in your opinion, the underground operation was not safe enough."

"That's right."

"Again, could I ask you to be more specific?"

"You mean tell you what specific things were not safe?"

"Yes."

"It's hard to know where to start." A faint, disgusted laughter sets up in the room.

"I can name several different types of safety problems, right off the top of my head."

The Inquiry Commissioner nods slowly. "Maybe you should do that, then."

"Well, right off the top of my head – I could probably do this better if I had a chance to write this down, make a list. But there were problems of tunnel construction, there were problems of maintenance and cleanup throughout the mine, and their were problems of worker training.

"Eastyard hired an outside company to design and plan the mine. That was Argon Engineering, a contracting company that specializes in tunnelling only. The big challenge of mining in this area is not simply getting the raw material out, it's building and maintaining a reliable system of tunnels to get men and machines to the mineral itself. To understand how tricky this is, you have to understand that the precise conditions of any given mine are unique. The thickness of the mineral seam, the stability of the strata surrounding it, whether there are faults in the seam, what sort of by-products tunnelling produces in a given area: water, for example, or dust, or gas." There is a stirring in the room somewhere and Gavin looks up briefly to see Ziv Burrows standing up noisily, scraping his chair along the floor. "Excuse me! Excuse me!" he says. He's moving his seat closer to the front.

The inquiry commissioner's face is a mask of neutrality, his gaze so blank he appears set to doze off. He glances briefly at the commotion in the room, then settles back to look at Gavin. But he keeps a pad of yellow paper in front of him, and though he never looks down at it, a cheap plastic pen in his left hand scratches non-stop across the paper, pausing only long enough to flip to a new page.

"So Eastyard hired Argon," Gavin continues. "And they surveyed the site and made their plans as to the best way to safely get at that coal. Part of their plan was the method of tunnel construction itself, considering that the Eastyard seam is surrounded by soft rock and is unstable and prone to rock falls. They recommended a system of arches and screens be set up, and that this be sprayed with Quikrete, a super-fast-drying concrete that would keep the tunnels from caving in. But as soon as Argon left the site, after Eastyard workers had been trained in this method of tunnelling, management ordered an end to the Quikreting of the tunnel roofs. It was too costly and time-consuming, they said, and they said it was unnecessary."

"Did you witness any rock falls yourself underground?"

"Regularly. Large and small rock falls were happening all the time."

"Did the rock falls occur in the areas that had been left without Quikrete?"

"Yes."

"Did you ever witness or know about a rock fall that took place in a tunnel where arches, screens, *and* Quikrete had been applied according to specifications?"

"No."

Silence. Gavin is conscious of the dramatic effect of this pause. He's giving people, perhaps across the entire country, time to process what he's said.

"Someone else could testify about shortcuts Eastyard made in the execution of the tunnel plan Argon laid out. I'm no expert there."

"What exactly do you mean by shortcuts?"

"I'm not a tunnel expert, and I don't know the specifics. But it was pretty common knowledge that changes had been made in the tunnelling company's original plans for the layout of the tunnels."

"What was the purpose behind these changes?"

"Well, Argon designed a system for getting the coal out safely. But the safest way of doing something is not always the quickest and the cheapest way of doing it."

"So the design of the tunnels was changed for the sake of saving money at the expense of safety?"

"There's no other reason for changing the tunnelling company's plan. They're the tunnel experts. They've done the complete assessment of the site to determine exactly how a safe modern mine could be built under local conditions. But as for exact details, you'll have to ask someone else."

Gavin becomes aware of the sounds around him. People breathe, they shift in their seats. They whisper and scratch on paper. The inquiry chairman is hunched over his notepad, scribbling something in point form.

"Now," the commissioner continues. "What about maintenance of the mine?"

"Maintenance."

"You identified that earlier as one of the areas where you thought there were safety concerns at Eastyard."

"The biggest maintenance problem was dust."

"Coal dust."

"Yes. It's explosive. It's a concern in any mining operation, but the coal we mined at Eastyard was especially bad for producing large quantities of dust."

"What exactly is the explosive hazard of dust?"

"From what I understand, and I've read a fair bit about this, now, but I've never conducted a scientific study, and, well, the fact I'm sitting here proves I've never seen coal dust ignite in any appreciable quantity. But I understand that coal dust on its own won't blow, but if there's a gas ignition, the presence of dust will turn a small rumble into a giant explosion. And because the dust can be present everywhere throughout the mine, it creates a domino effect. A gas explosion alone would normally be localized, especially with the kind of detectors and ventilation available now. If gas ignites, its not likely to be widespread. But dust can turn the whole system of shafts into a rifle barrel."

Someone in the room makes a guttural noise that sounds close to a deep cough. Gavin looks up at Ziv Burrows. Now that he's closer, it is obvious he's recently been in a fight. Aside from the bruise on his face, he's holding his body in a delicate, wounded manner. His face is framed by his hands. He is staring so intently at Gavin that the blue of his eyes appears almost aglow.

"If you saw pictures of the portal of the number-one deep at Eastyard, right after the explosion," Gavin continues. "Remember how the roof over the portal was all blown to bits, and there was debris scattered everywhere? *That's* what happens when dust ignites."

"What can be done to reduce this risk of dust ignition?"

"The coal dust can be removed, or it can be neutralized by mixing it with stone dust."

"This is what's called liming."

"That's right. The stone dust used is powdered limestone."

"Could you describe the liming process to us?"

"Well, like most procedures we carried out at Eastyard, I'm sure there are better ways to do it. But we just used to haul in fifty-pound bags of lime on a pallet, break open the bags with the nose of a shovel, and shovel the lime right onto the floor. A little bit like spreading salt on your driveway in the winter."

"So this procedure, liming the dust, it *was* performed at Eastyard."

"Well, I've seen it done. I did it myself a couple of times. Once I spent half a shift liming dust."

"Was this a regular procedure at Eastyard?"

"No."

A buzz in the hearing room. Gavin reaches for the glass of water on the table near him.

"To the best of your knowledge, how often was this procedure carried out at Eastyard."

"I know of two or three times that it took place in the nine months I worked there, but it might have been done more."

"In your estimation, how often *should* it have been carried out?"

"Liming dust should be an ongoing thing. There should be a little bit going on every day or every couple of days."

"When the liming took place that you were aware of, what were the circumstances of the liming?"

"On both occasions, it was on the day before a visit by the mine inspector."

More rumblings in the hearing room.

"Did you keep a diary, or another written record of these events?"

"A diary! Lord, no. My memory is all I've got in that regard. But I've been told it's a pretty good one."

"Part of the mine inspector's job is to meet with workers at the job site. To your knowledge, did these meetings take place?"

"Yes. The inspector visited people while they were working and spoke with them."

"To your knowledge, did anyone on these occasions express concerns to the inspector about workplace safety?"

"I doubt very much anyone did."

"Why is that?"

"Because the mine inspector was always accompanied by a member of Eastyard management."

"Eastyard management accompanied the department inspector?"

"Yes."

"Was there any time when the inspector was alone and could have spoken privately with an Eastyard worker?"

"Not at the job site," Gavin takes in a breath, lets it out. "But I met with him myself once, face-to-face, one-on-one."

The inquiry commissioner sits up straight. He cocks his head sideways and raises both eyebrows. The inquiry counsel has been sitting at her desk, rummaging back through some transcripts of previous testimony. She stops and looks up at the witness chair. No one at these hearings has so far mentioned a one-on-one meeting with the inspector. The inspector himself, testifying from the same stand, denied any complaints were ever made to him by an Eastyard worker.

The day of Gavin's meeting with the mine inspector came only a week or two after he'd quit his job at Eastyard. He knew from talking with the few guys from his old shift that Bill Reynolds, mine inspector for the province of Nova Scotia, would be in Albion Mines for a couple of days. He'd be meeting with management and looking at paperwork and plans on the Thursday, and on Friday he was scheduled to go underground to look at operations there. The men from Eastyard that he met and spoke with at Tim Horton's told Gavin they'd spent several shifts cleaning up and liming dust to put on a show for the inspector.

On Thursday night, Gavin walked through town to the Heather Motor Hotel. It was one of the first truly cold evenings of late fall, an overcast night when a few dry flakes of snow might waft before your eyes in the darkness and be gone so quickly that you'd wonder whether you'd actually seen them. Gavin stood on the orange carpet in the hallway and knocked on the door of Reynolds's room. The sound of the TV came blasting through the door, and Gavin pounded several more times before the latch clicked and the door opened to let him in.

Bill Reynolds's complexion was ghostly white and he walked back and back from Gavin as Gavin entered the room. He sat in a stuffed chair beside the blaring television and motioned to Gavin to sit in a straight-backed wooden chair positioned on the other side of the television. As Gavin took off his coat, he saw Reynolds scanning him carefully, looking him up and down, as though searching for the bulge of a concealed weapon.

When Gavin sat in the chair and edged it closer to Reynolds, Reynolds scraped his own chair backwards.

"I'm . . ." Gavin began to introduce himself.

"I know who you are," Reynolds said. He was speaking very softly. Gavin almost had to lip-read the words over the deafening television.

"I want to talk about . . ." Gavin began.

Reynolds leaned over and turned the television a notch louder. He scanned the room carefully, looked Gavin up and down. He walked to the bed, where Gavin had lain his parka, and picked it up. He dangled it from one hand and shook it over the bed. One of Gavin's gloves fell from a sleeve and Reynolds picked it up and turned it over in his hands. He went to the window and opened the curtains suddenly on the black night outside, thrust his face to the glass with his hands shading the sides of his eyes, peered out that way for a second or two, then pulled the curtains quickly back over the window.

He sat back in his chair, turned the volume on the TV a little louder still, then cupped his hands to the sides of his mouth as though about to scream. Instead, he began mouthing something wordlessly at Gavin, moving his lips in an exaggerated way.

Gavin gave him a puzzled look and he began again, this time more slowly.

*There – is – nothing – I – can – do*, Reynolds said without his voice. *There – is – nothing – I – can – do.*

Gavin finishes relating this story in front of the hot lights of the inquiry and there is a brief silence broken by a scuffling sound. He looks up, past the bright blind spot made by the lights, to see reporters scrambling out the door of the hearing room, some of them mumbling quietly into hand-held recorders, making their way to the lobby, where they can use their cellphones.

The inquiry commissioner seems stumped for a moment. The hum of the public address system swells to the fill the room.

"We've already spoken to Mr. Reynolds," the inquiry counsel says at length.

"I'm aware of that," Gavin replies. He is expecting a series of questions about the scene he's just related, but both the commissioner and counsel seem disoriented.

"And you had already quit by this time," the commissioner says.

"That's right."

"You'd already met with Fred Brennan, the underground manager."

"And with Don Barry, the general manager. They both told me the same thing: put up with conditions or quit."

The commissioner blinks against the television lights. He draws a folded handkerchief from inside the jacket of his suit and mops his brow with it. He looks down at his yellow pad and scrutinizes some of the notes he has made, then looks up at Gavin.

"This is a strange little incident you've just described, Mr. Fraser."

Gavin nods. "It certainly stands out in my mind," he says.

"Do you have any thoughts on Mr. Reynolds's behaviour? How do you explain what happened that day at the Heather?"

"Well, sir, you know that it's my job to tell you what happened and it's your job to figure out what it means."

The commissioner smiles and pours himself a glass of ice water.

"But just look at a timeline of events," Gavin continues. "Reynolds tells me there is nothing he can do. A few weeks later Eastyard explodes and kills twenty-six of my friends. A few months after that Bill Reynolds retires from the Department of Labour with a full pension."

"Do you believe Reynolds's hands were tied?"

"No I do not, sir. No I do not," Gavin's voice is rising for the first time in his testimony. "He was a mine inspector. Read the Coal Mines Regulation Act, sir. The inspector has power to enforce the act."

"Why would he say there was nothing he could do?"

"Well, I could make a few guesses. He was a provincial government employee. The province and the federal government were into the mine for millions. But if you want to know anything about Bill Reynolds, you'd better ask him, sir. I won't pretend to understand the actions of a man like that."

"And this meeting took place after you quit."

"As I said."

"You were no longer working at Eastyard when you went to see Bill Reynolds about safety underground."

"That's right."

"You had already made your decision about Eastyard. Why bother going to see the inspector when you were no longer working there?"

"Because," Gavin says calmly and slowly, "there were human lives at stake."

"If the dangers were so clear at Eastyard, why were you the only one to quit?"

"I wasn't. There were other guys who quit. They just hadn't kicked up as much fuss as I did. They quietly up and left."

"Why didn't more quit?"

"You'd have to ask them that."

"A lot of them are dead. What's your opinion? Why did people work under such conditions?"

"Money."

"They risked their lives for money?"

"What else? Money and a kind of blind faith that things had to get better. Progress. That's what we're all supposed to believe in. Everybody knew an explosion *could* happen. But they convinced themselves it *wouldn't*. Or that it might happen, but not to them."

The commissioner shuffles through some of the notes he's taken.

"Could I get someone to refill this water?" Gavin says. "Please."

A clerk comes by with a pitcher and fills his glass.

"We understand from previous testimony that, after you left the underground operation at Eastyard, there was a meeting between yourself and the rest of your former crew."

Gavin's stomach tightens. A pulse begins pushing in at his temples. "That's right." His eyes flit to the spot where Arvel Burrows's brother is sitting. The glimpse is so brief, he is unable to see an expression on the big man's face.

"Whose idea was it to have such a meeting?"

"I don't know, exactly. It wasn't mine. I don't know if one particular person on the shift asked for it, or if they all just agreed to it together."

"Why did they want to meet with you?"

"Well, it wasn't clear to me at first . . ."

"Where did the meeting take place?"

"At the Tartan Tavern." Laughter fills the hearing room.

"That's a local beverage room," the chairman says.

"It's walking distance from here, if you're looking for a place to get a steak for supper. Stay away from the fish and chips." More laughter.

"Why was the purpose of the meeting unclear to you?"

"Well, I didn't know if *they* had a clear idea of what they wanted to talk about right off. There was a lot of griping and complaining about safety, but that was nothing new to me. I told them if they all quit together, something would have to be done."

"Why would something have to be done?"

"Because a company with that much public money in it would come under real close scrutiny if a quarter of the workforce quit overnight. Quit or die, is how I explained it to them, more or less. They already knew that anyway."

"You told them they could quit or *die*?" The commissioner has a surprised look on his face. "What was their response?"

"Well, I could see they were thinking about what I'd said. But I didn't expect them to start writing out their letters of resignation on their napkins or anything."

"What did happen, then?"

"Well, I was getting ready to leave, I thought the conversation had reached an end when one of the guys, Arvel Burrows, a big guy, a guy who's dead now. One of the twenty-six. We worked together on the United Mine Workers drive."

Gavin stops in mid-thought and peers again into the gallery. He looks Ziv Burrows straight in the eye and feels himself tear up momentarily as the emotion of the memory overtakes him. "Arvel Burrows was a real good fellow," he says. He takes a drink of water, sets the glass back on the ring of condensation on the desk in front of him. "He told me they had a request to make of me," he continues.

"A request."

"Burrows said that if they died underground, would I make sure and tell the world what happened?"

"Tell the world what happened."

"That's right."

"And what did you say to that?"

"I told them I'd do what I could."

"Who, exactly, was at that meeting? Arvel Burrows. How many others?"

"It was A-shift. The shift that died. My old shift."

"It was the same twenty-six men who perished."

"Well, it would have been close to the same guys. Not everyone from the shift would have been there. But I'd say, of the twenty-six who died, there were, conservative estimate, fifteen or sixteen guys out of the twenty-six at the table that day in the Tartan Tavern."

"How do you feel about the request now? Do you feel burdened with a responsibility?"

"What responsibility?"

"Telling the world."

"I just did. *You're* the world," Gavin says to the commissioner. He points at the TV camera. "There's the world right there. The world knows what went on at Eastyard Coal. Now it's the world's decision what they want to do about it. You can't bring the dead back to life. I know that much for sure."

Gavin senses some movement in the gallery and looks over to see Ziv Burrows standing up, towering over the gallery and the whole proceedings before him. He has his mouth open as though he has just said something and is waiting for a reply. Gavin looks at Ziv's hands and notices how much they are trembling.

The commissioner looks nervously at Ziv and there is a momentary stirring among the security guards positioned in the corners of the room. The commissioner looks at Gavin, as though Gavin might know this massive man standing over them, trembling, his bruised face terrified or enraged.

"This man's brother, . . ." Gavin begins. But Ziv has turned around quickly and is halfway to the door before Gavin can finish his sentence.

# Movement

Meta crosses the square of bus gates behind the south exit of Shinjuku Station. For the only time ever, out of the hundreds of people visible, she is walking the fastest. The ground is dusted with enough snow not to have melted immediately, and the city has spun into confusion. Taxis have all been fitted with snow chains or belts of reinforced wire wrapped around the tires. These have turned the streets into a calamitous racket as the chains clank and squeal, the wire belts drum the roadway. Pedestrians are slipping and writhing about everywhere with no idea how to negotiate snow-covered ground. The more comical ones are motionless as if frozen, clinging helplessly to a light post or phone box, terror blanching their faces as they watch the people who have foolishly unmoored themselves from something solid sliding about in a completely uncontrolled manner.

Meta has never before thought of the ability to walk on snow-covered ground as a skill. When she got up this morning, she saw the snow and made sure she wore shoes that had a tread.

Once she was about and realized she was not experiencing the same troubles as others were, she noticed that she had adjusted her stride. She was taking smaller steps and focusing the thrust of each step upward rather than back. The other secret is to slide when the sidewalk dictates, skating on the soles of your shoes when conditions underfoot are especially slippery.

The cliché among the Japanese is that all Canadians ski. But as she walks toward her college, Meta forms a fresh stereotype: all Canadians can walk easily on slippery sidewalks.

She is the first to arrive in her section of the office, but she is just hanging her coat in the locker when Sue Shooltz, a teacher from Tennessee, arrives. She is wrapped in a down-filled parka. Half of her face is covered by a scarf. Thick lambskin mitts are pulled halfway up her forearms.

Meta bursts into laughter at the sight of her, so outrageously overdressed for such a mild cold. "Where's your Ski-Doo?" she says.

Sue pulls the tasselled wool hat from over her ears. "My what?" she says, her Southern accent drawing out the second word.

"You look like you came to work on a Ski-Doo," Meta says.

"A Ski-Doo? I'n't that one of those skimpy little bathing suits that men wear?"

"You're kidding me," Meta says. "A Ski-Doo! A Ski-Doo! You've never heard of a Ski-Doo!"

Sue looks blankly at her as she peels the heavy clothes off and tucks them into her locker.

"'Twenty-three skidoo,'" Sue says. "My granny used to say that. I have no idea what it means. It's freezing out there!"

"What a country!" Greg Ulesso says as he comes through the door. "Boiling hot in summer," he says. "Freezing cold in winter, typhoons, torrential rains. It's the worst of all possible worlds."

A tremor sets up in the building, the room begins shifting slowly from side to side. Everyone stands up straight and looks at each other with blank expressions. The Great Kanto quake flattened Tokyo in 1923, and the same tectonic plates and the faults between them are set to release a similar disaster at any time. Each time the floor begins to rock this way, Meta braces herself for the Next Big Shakeup. She closes her eyes briefly and thinks, *I wonder if I'll open my eyes to find this building destroyed around me. I wonder if I'll ever open my eyes again.*

She opens her eyes when the rocking gets worse. Someone in the room is screaming. The sound rises up against the rattling furniture, the growling of the walls and ceiling and floor. She grips the edge of the nearest desk and feels her stomach beginning to heave, her equilibrium lost. She goes down on one knee. Books and papers come down from shelves that are bolted to the walls. The coffeemaker skitters off its table in the corner and falls to the floor, the carafe disintegrating immediately, sending coffee up the wall beside it.

"Stand in a doorway!" someone in the room screeches, remembering an instruction from some safety pamphlet or other. But walking to a doorway is impossible. The floor has turned liquid, rising and falling in waves.

When the earth stops moving, the building keeps rocking a few moments longer, the walls reorienting themselves to the foundation.

Thank God, thinks Meta. Thank God. Thank God. This is not going to be it. She releases her grip on the edge of the desk, and when she looks at her hand, discovers that she was holding on tightly enough to make her fingers bleed. A few crimson pellets creep out from beneath the nails of the index and middle fingers of her left hand.

Sue Shooltz is flat on her back. Her hands cover her face, protecting it from whatever might have fallen on her but didn't.

"Hadja. Hadja-ja," Meta says to her. She is surprised to hear herself say this, since it does not mean anything, and what she was trying to say was, "Are you okay?"

She shakes her head. A mild aftershock rocks the building gently, sends the walls swaying in a manner that is almost soothing. She rights a seat that was sent over onto its side and sits on it. Greg Ulesso stands to his full height and smoothes the wrinkles from his clothing.

"Earthquakes!" he says. "I forgot earthquakes. What a bloody country!"

Meta tries hard to pull herself together after the quake. At her desk, she sits jittering and fluttering, drinking several cups of green tea from a pot someone had brewed just prior to the quake that had miraculously not been damaged or even spilled. Janitorial staff and a few teachers are moving noisily about the room, trying to put things back in order. They mop up coffee, stuff books back on shelves. Meta pulls all the materials together for her first class and tries to review them. She cannot hold a book still enough in her hand to read it. When she steadies the book by placing it flat on the desk, she finds it difficult to control her hand enough to turn a single page. With ten minutes remaining before the first class, she goes down the hallway from the teacher's room and through the door to Mr. Takeuchi's office.

He is a prim, excessively well-groomed man with soft features and big, round eyes.

"Nichols-san," he says when she enters his office. Unlike the staff room, which still looks like there has just been a strong earthquake, Takeuchi's office is as tidy and proper as ever. He must have been running around putting things back on shelves even as they were falling.

He does not mention the earthquake or ask her how she is. He merely sits with a scrubbed-looking face, his expression pleasant, his head cocked alertly to the side, waiting for her to say something.

"Mr. Takeuchi," she says. At least she's regained the ability to say that much.

He looks at her steadily.

She apologizes for such short notice, but tells Takeuchi she is not well enough to teach today. Except for the few weeks she was away last year, she has not missed a day of work. Takeuchi is not happy – though his permanently blissful expression will never show it. Meta surmises his unhappiness from the long silences that punctuate his speech, but he puts up no argument about her leaving.

She walks the whole way home. The temperature has risen enough to melt almost all the snow. Nothing anywhere speaks of the morning's earthquake. Businesses are all open. With the snow gone from underfoot, people rush headlong down sidewalks. Taxis and trucks and buses and scooters and buggies and bicycles and motorcycles choke the streets.

It takes almost an hour to walk from her college to her apartment. When she enters the hallway on her floor, she hears shrieking. High, desperate, wordless cries fill the hallway.

"Gai, gai, gai, gai!" The sound is so desperate and animal-like that it takes her a moment to recognize it as Yuka's voice. She knows that Yuka's boyfriend is a black belt in some martial art or other, so she quietly opens the door to her own apartment and rummages in the kitchen for a weapon. She finds a vase that has been drilled from a conical stone. She removes the dead flower from its centre and feels the weight of it steady her right fist.

She knocks on Yuka's door, but there is no answer. When she twists the knob, she finds the door is unlocked, and pushes it forward. The screams turn louder. "Gai! Gai! Gai!"

Meta imagines Yuka standing over a bloody body with a knife, stabbing, stabbing. There is a sound like a fist impacting flesh. She removes her shoes in the genkan, carefully steps up onto the tatami, and goes down the short hallway to the living room. The furniture is upset. Things are not where they should be. There are pieces of clothing spread about. The earthquake has strewn laundry and dishes and small appliances everywhere. A place has been cleared hastily in the middle of the floor. Yuka lies on her back with her eyes thrown wide open. The thick, hairy body of a naked man lies face-down on top of her. She is staring at the ceiling, screaming from between lips that stretch back to show her rear teeth. "Gai! Gai!" Her bare legs are bent at the knees and spread wide apart. The man's head is covered with curly black hair that is longer on top, but shorn close at the back of the neck. The shoulders, arms, back, buttocks, and legs of the man are swirled over with little black curls. The hairy buttocks pull up and thrust forward again. "Gai!" Yuka cries.

Meta is frozen in place, paralyzed as much by her fear of being suddenly discovered as by what she's seeing.

The man has his face buried in Yuka's neck. At first Meta thinks he might have his teeth clamped on Yuka's flesh, but he turns his head sideways to reveal his profile: pale white skin covered to just below the eyes with a thick black beard.

Yuka bends her neck up and looks at Meta. For less than a second, her face registers surprise. Then she lowers her head back to the floor, and her facial expression changes. As though to make clear to Meta exactly what is going on, she begins to speak in English: "Yes! Yes! Yes!" she cries.

Meta's heart is racing ahead of her, she gulps air to keep up. She goes inside her own apartment and is suddenly clobbered by exhaustion. She's been through too much today, and it is only mid-morning. She takes a bottle of apple juice from the refrigerator and sits at the table to drink it. Twice muffled, by her own door and then Meta's, Yuka's screaming is still audible. She switches on the radio to try to blot it out. The earthquake has thrown a few things out of place in her apartment. Some toiletries in the bathroom have been knocked off a shelf. Dishes that had been on the counter in the kitchen have fallen into the basin. She goes into the bedroom and slides the shoji closed. She takes off her clothes and crawls onto the futon, pulls the quilts over her head, but Yuka's voice still reaches her. She lies for what seems like hours with "Gai! Gai! Gai!" echoing in her head. It is such a low sound now that it could almost be her imagination, her memory of having stood in the living room over the naked couple. It seems she'll never be able to sleep, and then, suddenly, she wakes up.

Her doorbell is ringing.

She looks at the clock. It is two o'clock in the afternoon. She throws on some clothes and goes to the door, peers through the peephole, and sees Yuka, her body distorted, her head seemingly hundreds of metres above her feet.

Yuka comes in and sits at the table. Meta fills a pot with water and sparks the burner without saying anything.

"He's gone," Yuka says. Meta is sick of talking about this guy. Now that she's finally laid eyes on him, and in such ridiculous and yet somehow terrifying circumstances, she wants to talk about him even less.

They sit in silence for a while, the pot beginning to rumble on the stove. Yuka is obviously there to talk about something, and Meta does not want the conversation to begin. She's said enough about Yuka and her relationship to the man who beats her. She doesn't want to say any more. Yuka's very appearance now, in a flawlessly pressed pleated skirt and white blouse, seems a lie. It hides the fact that she'd spent the morning on her kitchen floor, howling like an animal.

"He went to Kyoto," Yuka says.

"Kyoto," Meta is surprised. She's known people to go to Kyoto on holiday, but it is usually at Obon or Golden Week, two popular holiday times.

"He gave me letter."

Meta takes a page of delicately patterned bone-coloured paper from Yuka's hand. It is of a quality meant for traditional calligraphy work.

*Dear Yuka,* it begins.

*I have tried to understand myself and failed. I don't know why I strike out at you. There is some rage in me that I cannot understand or control. I'm sorry for every terrible thing I've done to you. In the past I thought that being sorry would be enough, that if I could reach down to the farthest depth of sorrow, I would find a place there to begin again and rebuild a me I want to be. This is obviously not working.*

*I've tried therapy, I've tried immersing myself in ki. I've sat seiza in the temple at our dojo until I had no feeling in my body below the waist. I always return to do you harm.*

*I've talked to my sensei, and he knows a temple in Kyoto where the monks will welcome me and teach me to open to myself. There is something in me, hiding. Something that doesn't want me to see it. It is some first principle of myself that I have yet to know. I feel that if I can get a glimpse of this thing, maybe I can use it as the cornerstone of a new person I know I have to become.*

*I'll be gone for some time, maybe up to a couple of months. Maybe longer than that, if that's what it takes.*

*I'm not doing this for you. I'm doing this for me, because I love you.*

"He gave you this today?" Meta says.

Yuka nods.

"When does he leave?"

"He's gone now. Maybe he's on bullet train now."

"Did you know he was thinking about going to Kyoto?"

Yuka shakes her head.

"Are you surprised by this?"

Yuka leans forward for emphasis. "*Very* surprised," she says. "And about this letter." She takes back the paper and scans it quickly, finds the sentence she wants, near the top. She turns the paper so Meta can read and points at the place where she wants her to look. It is the sentence that says, *I don't know why I strike out at you.*

"What is this sentence mean?"

Meta glances back through the letter. She is so tired of the violence in Meta's life that she does not even want to explain what "strike out at" means, but she feels relieved at least that this bully is leaving for a while.

"I'm glad he's going away," she says. "You deserve a holiday from him."

# CANADA DAY, YEARS AGO

The apartment is in a four-storey walk-up behind a supermarket on Quinpool Road in Halifax. It is directly across the hall from Colleen's place, and looks out into the courtyard of the building, so that Jackie can let the girls outside to play and still keep an eye on them from the window.

It has been over a year since they've moved from Albion Mines, and almost a year that they've been in their own place. Kate is now settled in well to her new school, although the end of the last school year had been difficult. They'd moved in the middle of the year and the girls were still confused and angry over their father's death. The publicity surrounding the explosion had put Kate on display among her classmates. Melanie has made friends with a little boy from down the hall, and attends daycare when Jackie and Colleen's work schedules do not allow one or the other of them to take care of her. Colleen's predictions of great sales figures for Jackie at Gregor's have turned out to be optimistic, but Jackie likes the store's management, and she is able to make more money than she did in Pictou County.

It's eleven o'clock on a Friday. The girls have been asleep in their room for hours. Christmas is on the way. Jackie has the tree set up in a corner of the living room, where she's been watering it for days. But despite the girls' begging, she refuses to decorate so early.

Colleen sits across from her at the kitchen table. There is a box in front of them, its lid on the floor at their feet. She and Colleen are both tipsy, a word that just moments before had them giggling when Colleen had used it. They've had a couple of eggnogs each, the kind the dairies sell in milk boxes around this time of year. They've spiked it with Captain Morgan rum.

Colleen found the box in a closet in the bathroom and brought it out as a joke. "Look at this!" she shouted at the first thing she found inside. It was a school photo of Jackie from Grade 8 or 9. It showed her hair feathered away from her face in the style that was popular at the time.

They both laughed at the picture, but Jackie is uneasy about digging through the box. A lot of what is inside is Arvel's, and she is in no mood for tears at the moment. She has been focused on the present and the future since she's moved to Halifax. The past is a place she is in no hurry to revisit. She has made a plan to bring the girls to their grandparents' in Albion Mines right after Christmas Day and the commitment to make that trip has got her thinking she'll have had more than enough of the past by the time New Year's rolls around.

"Come on, let's put this away," she begs Colleen. She picks up the lid and makes a move to replace it over the box. When Colleen intercepts and puts the lid back on the floor, Jackie gives in and takes another sip of rum and eggnog. The mixture is rich and cloying. She can feel her system getting clogged with it.

Colleen is poking through the contents of the box with an almost scientific mixture of indifference and intrigue.

"Birth certificate, confirmation," she says. Her cheeks are flushed with the rum.

"Hmm . . . What's this?" She flattens a newspaper clipping against a bare section of the tabletop.

Jackie recognizes the photo of Arvel and Santa. "Oh, come on, Colleen," she says with some real frustration. "I don't feel like going through this stuff."

"Is this Arvel?"

Jackie sighs, slouches resignedly, nods. "It's Arvel," she says. "And take a look at Santa. I'm pretty sure that's his father."

Colleen looks intently at the photo.

"I don't even think Arvel knew that was his father in the photo. I wonder if his family has a copy of this."

"Unbelievable!" Colleen exclaims. She has already moved on to the next treasure. This one is a colour photo of Jackie on Melmerby Beach.

"Is this you?" Colleen asks. "You look amazing!"

Jackie snatches the photo away from Colleen. "You know damn well this is me! And don't sound so surprised that I look good!"

This was Arvel's photo, taken years ago. They must have been eighteen or nineteen at the time. They had gone to Melmerby Beach on Canada Day. She remembers Arvel taking the picture, and she remembers him almost gasping at it when it came back developed.

Like children, they had brought a bucket and shovels. Jackie remembers the two of them digging a big square hole in the sand. Arvel said, "This will be the foundation of our new house." She rested her cheek on the warm sand at the side of the hole and put a hand down into the moist coolness their digging had uncovered. "I want to live right here," she said. And she had meant it. She did want to live there. Right there on that exact spot on Melmerby Beach. There had been crowds of people around all day, on the sand and in the water. But after supper, the beach cleared off. They found themselves alone, back on a remote patch of sand with no one else around. Arvel folded the blanket over them and they snuggled up together, face-to-face, lying on their sides. He pressed his hips into hers and she felt her whole body as a flame. She reached down into his trunks and put her hand on his penis. She pushed the crotch of her swimsuit aside and brought him gently inside her. They lay there for what seemed like hours. Each propped on an elbow, facing the other, moving together so slowly and gently and magically.

The sun went lower in the sky. The sand and sea went the same colour of spilled gold. Arvel got up, and she sank back into the sand and drifted off to sleep. She woke up with his voice calling to her. The waves were dark and foamy and the sky above them had turned a dark and solid unstained blue.

Arvel called her name again, but she could not see him. When she sat up and looked around, over her shoulder, she found him behind her in the sand, near the edge of a swath of coarse grass, the sun behind him. All she could see was his silhouette. He'd gone to the car and got the camera. He was asking her to smile. She put a hand up against the light, to shade her squinting, and he snapped the shutter.

She does look beautiful in the picture. Beautiful in a way she is sure she has not looked since. It is the beauty of innocence that the photo has captured. She had been lying in the sand foundations of her dream house, and was now smiling not only for the camera, but for someone she loved.

Colleen must be able to tell from the expression on Jackie's face that she's in no mood for joking. She picks up the lid of the storage box and points at the word written there: *memories*.

"Let's go out on the balcony," Jackie says. She drops the picture back into the box and crosses to the sliding glass doors of the balcony.

They both stand coatless, sweaterless, in the cold air of winter. Below them, the building's courtyard is lit with a sprinkling of snow. Directly across, a woman has neglected to draw the curtains on her bedroom window. They watch her shamelessly as she slips out of her clothes, pulls a warm-looking nightgown over her head, and turns off her light.

Jackie puts a hand on the iron railing of the balcony and waits for the cold of this night to push away the memory of that warm day so long ago. Memory seems a rotten trick to her. It's unfair to be confronted now with these sweet thoughts when so much between her and Arvel had gone wrong since. What hurts most is knowing he went to his death unhappy, with their marriage a wreck. Though she knows it's a stupid notion, she feels as though it was she who condemned him, sending him out of his own house as she did, just before he died.

She scans the windows of the apartments opposite, but all the windows are black.

"It's freezing out here," Colleen says. She puts an arm around Jackie's shoulders and guides her back inside.

# A Moose

The bed is large without Dunya in it, but Ennis understands that Dunya is somehow doing what she needs to do. Whether he fully understands her actions, or whether she even understands herself, she needs time and space to herself. She sleeps on a futon in the front room downstairs and spends most days sitting quietly, gazing out the front window.

The extra room in the bed seems to have freed him up to dream. His whole life he has never remembered much about his dreams, but frequently now he awakes with a vivid image that has stayed with him. One night he dreams two full dreams and remembers them both. They both are more like memories than dreams.

One is short, little more than an image. It is the memory of a fight Ennis got into in Grade 7, and strangely, the dream is not from his point of view. He sees it through the eyes of the teacher who broke it up, Sister Catherine. After dragging Ennis to the office by the ear, she turns away from him, steps back into the hallway, and slams the principal's door behind her. The stiff folds of her starched habit crinkle and rustle in the silent hallway as she walks. When she has made her way to the staff room and shut the door behind her, she closes her eyes in frustration and exclaims, "That pig-headed little brat!" Overcome with disappointment in herself, she whispers into clasped hands, "Father, forgive me," and performs the sign of the cross.

The next dream is about something that happened when Arvel must have been only nine or ten years old, an incident Ennis has forgotten until now.

The family is having a picnic by the riverside at Iona Park, past Eureka. Arvel and Ziv are fighting over the last bottle of Pepsi from the old red Coleman cooler. After pulling the Pepsi bottle back and forth between them with the cap still on it, Arvel wrests the bottle from Ziv and pops the cap with an opener that is riveted to the side of the cooler. The shaken bottle explodes with foam, soaking the two boys, who both spring back from the spray. Arvel is first back at the bottle, now less than half-full. He grabs Ziv, who is already soaked, puts him in a headlock, and empties the rest of the Pepsi over his head. Ziv begins to cry and runs back toward the river.

Now Ennis sees himself as if watching out of Arvel's eyes. He appears like a dark cloud from behind the jet-black Chevy Bel-Air. Arvel runs headlong through the alders and scrub fir to a partial clearing. Cursing and panting, Ennis comes after him. Arvel, in a panic now, begins to cry, which slows his ability to run. He dives into some raspberry canes at the other side of the clearing, tearing his shirt and scratching his arms on the thorns. Ennis reaches into the canes and draws him out by the scruff of his neck, ripping the collar almost completely off of his T-shirt.

Ennis whacks Arvel hard over his left ear and walks wordlessly back to the car.

In the dream, Ennis's own ear burns like a hot coal on the side of his face.

First thing in the morning, Ennis faces himself in the bathroom mirror. He puts a hand on the ear that had been burning in the dream, but it feels normal now. He knows he does not look very good, and is reminded of the diagram in his wallet, a quick, gruesome portrait drawn up by the plastic surgeon who pieced his head back together. It shows a human skull: big, blank forehead, gigantic eye sockets, grisly nose holes. Black pen-ink squiggles spread out from the centre of the face to show the fracture lines, the places where his skull came apart against the impact of Dunya's pounding. Little squares, five in all, mark the plates, the pieces of metal the surgeon used to hold his face bones in place. The surgeon had told him that eventually the swelling in the damaged tissue would go down completely and no one would be able to tell he'd ever been injured. But the surgeon never saw what Ennis looked like before the injury, so Ennis has no confidence that he will ever be the same as he once was. He does not care. In fact, the less he looks like he did, the better, as far as he is concerned.

At first when he lay in bed in the hospital, his skull crumbled inside his head, he felt ready to die. He was not yet sixty, but he felt like an old man, a used-up old man who had been on a steady decline from age twenty-five. He had told his son he was happy to see him go into the pit. And his son had died there. He had driven his wife, a woman inherently gentle and forgiving, to a heinous act of violence. But he had no power to will himself to die. The spirit inside of him might curl up and wait to fade out, but his body kept pumping itself full of life.

Winter mornings are beautiful and clear. The cold wrings the moisture from the air, chiselling the outlines of things to a crisp sharpness. When there is snow, even the dark is light, the blanket of white like the thrown beam from a massive floodlight.

This morning, as always when he skis, Ennis wears a pair of work pants with red wool socks stretched up to the knees, a long-sleeved cotton turtleneck with a wool sweater pulled over it. He puts these things on in his bedroom and descends the stairs quietly. Dunya is asleep on her futon in the front room, and he pauses a moment to look at her, curled on her side beneath a thick comforter, the expression on her face peaceful.

In the porch, he covers the wool sweater with his parka while he gets ready to go. When he starts skiing, he'll take off the parka and leave it in the car.

He shuts off the coffeemaker and pours what is left in the pot into a plastic Thermos. He fills a water bottle at the tap and tucks it under the parka into a waist pouch that hangs from his belt. He takes the skis and poles from a corner of the porch, slips the blue wax, scraper, and smoother block into the waist pouch, and walks outside to the driveway. Slipping the *Chronicle-Herald* out of the box by the back door, he re-enters the porch a moment. With ski gear clutched under his right arm, he awkwardly unfolds the paper with his left hand and glances at the front page. Just a few months ago he would have gone through the whole paper and clipped out anything related to Eastyard. But he's given up on this clipping as pointless. He folds the paper and tosses it onto the porch floor.

It is still dark as night out, though the sky in the east is beginning to lighten. He straps the skis to the roof racks of the car, throws the poles into the passenger seat, and pulls out of the driveway.

The bulk of this snow is two days old now, but enough has fallen overnight to soften everything again with its fullness. He stops at a red light at the corner of Bridge Avenue and looks up the snow-blanketed surface of Foord Street to the south. The big red letters of the Tim Horton's gleam out of the crumbling darkness. Two or three cars are parked in front, and the fluorescent-lit interior beams out the big square windows onto the snow. Nothing moves anywhere. To his right, the new snow on Bridge Avenue where it comes down the hill is unbroken by tire tracks.

As he crosses the first bridge at Blue Acres, the still-lit silos of Eastyard Coal come into view on the right. If there were not fifteen bodies still underground, the government would have dynamited all surface reminders of the Eastyard fiasco the day after the explosion. Some in the families group are pushing to demolish this landmark, this testament to the province's rotten soul. He understands the desire to push the whole ugly incident into the past, but it is misguided. Getting rid of the silos would be playing into the hands of the government, who wish to erase the whole affair from history. But Ennis no longer attends meetings of the families' group. He'd never felt comfortable there to begin with, but as time went on he realized that he no longer had a fight left in him. His name is still on the members' list, and he still gets occasional reports in the mail, but he barely pays attention to what the group is doing any more.

The judicial inquiry into the explosion is still on, day after day of witnesses to the same crime. There is talk of a criminal trial for some managers. Ziv is going now most days. In the mornings he gets ready for his afternoon shift at Zellers and stops at the inquiry proceedings on the way. Ennis cannot bring himself to go. The inquiry is important and eventually some good may come out of its findings, some changes may be made to labour standards and how they are monitored and upheld. But none of this will bring Arvel back. No matter what the inquiry finds in their hearings, no matter whether a criminal trial takes place, and no matter the outcome if one does. His son is dead. Nothing is going to make his death right. Nothing can justify it, nothing can explain it, nothing can make it hurt less. His son is dead.

Ennis can do nothing about any of this. He can look at the silos, think these thoughts, then turn back to face the life he is living.

He drives to MacLellan's Brook and keeps going, taking the turn deeper into the woods every time the road forks. He passes old farms, some run by the same family for generations, some owned by greying hippies: American draft-dodgers and old back-to-the-landers who bought these properties abandoned and brought them back to life. Some of the houses out here are suburban-style bungalows and split-entries, constructed on building-sized lots and lived in by people who drive to town each day to work. Some of the dwellings are little more than shacks, covered over by tarpaper tacked on with laths or converted from camper-trailers and stuck up on railroad ties.

Ennis drives to the place where the snowplough stopped and turned back. He parks the car alongside the banked-up snow and pours himself some milky coffee into the red plastic cup from the top of his Thermos. The road continues before him, unploughed for miles, a perfect surface for skiing. The sun will not be up for some time yet, but enough light has crept into the overcast sky to set the snow atwinkle, each flake visible in the place where it has fallen. A fenced pasture slopes down on the left, rolls up into a knoll with four twisted apple trees on it, then drops steeply off into a little valley on the other side. When his coffee is finished, he steps out of the car. He frees the blue wax from the pouch and drops it into the snow to let it cool as he undoes the straps and brings the skis down from the roof racks.

He was here yesterday, and the trail he pressed into the snow is still clear and visible under the buff of the fresh fall. The two sets of circles his poles made, one from the trip in, the other from the return, show that no one else has skied here since. He keeps an eye out for other tracks as he skis, deer, moose, rabbit, anything that will show the landscape is still alive. When he was young and spent time hunting and fishing the woods, animals were plentiful. At dawn or dusk you'd almost always catch sight of a deer. If there was snow on the ground, you'd see moose and deer and rabbit tracks just about anywhere you went. The forest has changed in his lifetime. It doesn't seem so much like a forest any more. The wild has gone out of it, making it more like grown-over farm land: tame, fenced-off, predictable.

He waxes the skis, locks what he will not need in the car, steps over the bank, and drops the skis onto the grooves in the trail. Once his boots are clipped into place, he wraps his wrists with the straps from the poles and stands looking at the trail before him. The rising sun has suffused the overcast with light, illuminating the snow. In this state of partial light, the trees at the sides of the trail form almost solid walls of darkness at the edges of the luminous path. Big spruces and firs rise up to where their black silhouettes chafe at the purple-blue sky. Smaller, shrubby ever-greens and naked hawthorn and wild rose creep in low beneath them, filling in the lighter spaces between the trunks of the bigger trees. A plume of steam escapes Ennis's mouth at every breath.

The first movement is a push forward with both poles, setting the gliding in motion. There is a gentle incline downward for a kilometre or so until a steeper, banked turn curves in front of an empty farmhouse. He begins simply pushing one ski back, then the other, poling with the opposite arm until his legs and arms loosen. Blood moves quickly to all the places it is needed, and he feels himself get warmer, more relaxed. It will not be long and he'll be able to take his hat off. He pulls his heels up a little now at the back, bends each knee so the skis come up in an arc from the trail. When he reaches the curve in front of the old farmhouse he feels the evil of the world come chunking down directly onto his shoulders, like a cake of lodged ice from the lip of a roof. He breaks the rhythm of his poling and shakes his shoulders once. All the evil inside of him rises through his torso, quivers nervously in his chest a moment, then squeezes up onto his shoulders beside the evil of the world. The two evils fuse into one dark mass pressing down on Ennis's shoulders. He leans into a turn, poles and kicks and twists around it. He shakes his shoulders once more and the evil lump that's been weighing him down falls off. He hears it thump and curse him as it pitches headlong into the snow behind. He will not look back now. He can see where the upward incline begins, at the bottom of the curve. The sun cracks through a blue patch at the horizon and touches the tips of the bare trees overhead. He wants momentum for the uphill section, so he poles like hell for bottom.

The world is divided in two, and he enters at the edge of the dark dream half, lit by the eerie light of snow. As Ennis draws in breath, the landscape expands, the hills before him ripple out like the surface of a shaken blanket.

Double-pole, kick-kick. Double-pole, kick-kick. The back of a ski slaps the flattened snow behind him: a mistake. Fss, the tips plough through the white powder like dorsal fins. He begins poling with each kick, conscious of fully straightening each arm at the end of the push back, getting power from the full motion. The cotton turtleneck beneath the wool sweater begins to paste itself to his torso. His face flushes with warmth, and when his lungs take deeply from the cold air, bringing oxygen to refresh his blood, he feels his head tingle. Down low on the left, where some small dark fir trees push out from a wood grove to meet the road, a white rabbit flashes before the green, throws itself through a channel in the brush, and zags across the trail a small distance ahead of him.

Something inside of him is growing. He can feel it swelling like a sheltered flame. He feels lit from the inside, like a tent with a burning lantern at night, like an igloo he saw once in *National Geographic*, translucent and perfect, sending out rays to the snow beneath a dark purple clear Arctic sky.

There is a narrow little path that he has never taken before. It veers left through a ditch where some mountain ash berries, orange and wrinkled, still cling to their stems beneath tiny caps of snow. He decides to follow this little notch in the trees over the crest where the land falls away quickly. He finds himself in a place where a brook has cut a deep V through some shaley rock. The floor of this little valley is only as wide as the brook, which is mostly frozen over. He skis carefully down on snow-cushioned ice, watching for rocks in the brook bed that will scrape the bottom of his skis.

Where the walls of shale end there is a thick, low overhang of leafless willow branches that he must crouch almost to his knees to get under. He emerges on the other side and finds himself at the bottom of a shallow swampy basin. The country is pockmarked by holes like these, places where long-abandoned mine workings, far below the surface, have given way, collapsed. At the centre of the basin, up to its knees where the animal has gone through the ice, is the biggest bull moose Ennis has ever seen. The moose has already dug big holes in the snow with his snout. The giant rack of his antlers, jutting out from either side of his head like two half-sheets of plywood, are covered with dirty snow and mud from where he has rummaged for food.

Three steps and Ennis would practically be riding him. His heart thumps wildly in the cage of his chest. The moose turns to look straight at him, and beneath the pungent smell of the swamp where the moose has been digging, Ennis gets a hot whiff of the animal, the smell of fur and shit and musk. A single sweep of that massive head could break Ennis in two.

They stand there, man and beast, each looking curiously at the other. The moose chews slowly on some root it has pulled up from the cold mud. Black water drips placidly from the bell beneath its chin. Steam rises from its warm nostrils into the cold air. Ennis unclips his skis, gently shoves them to the other side of the willows, and crawls back through the way he's come.

On the other side of the thicket, he tries with trembling hands to reclip the skis to the boots. When his fingers prove unable to do this, he takes a step onto the snow with just his boots and finds himself up to his knees, as the moose had been, locked in place. He lies back on the snow and closes his eyes, waits for his breath to come back to him. He opens his eyes in the light of early morning and watches the steam rising up from his own nostrils.

When he arrives back at the house, Dunya is sitting alone on the floor of the front room. Her eyes are closed, her back is straight. A cup of clear tea steams on the floor beside her. Ennis peels off his outer clothes, right down to the long underwear, and goes into the room with her. She opens her eyes at the sound of him entering. Without looking, she picks up her teacup and drinks from it. She closes her eyes again. Ennis sits on the futon across from her. He feels himself trembling slightly, so slightly it would be invisible to Dunya, even if she had her eyes open.

"I saw a moose," he says.

She opens her eyes and regards him.

"A moose," says Ennis. "It was like . . ." He has no words for the experience. He places a hand flat on the centre of his chest until he feels the beating of his heart. He moves closer to his wife, sits on the floor in front of her, the closest he's been in months.

Looking at the soft features of her face, he remembers the petite, pretty girl she was growing up. She came from what then seemed the exotic north end of the Red Row, a place where the Poles, Ukrainians, Belgians, and other European immigrant families settled. She was always so gentle and shy. He walked past her house on the way to the tracks, taking the iron bridge to New Glasgow in the days before the highway. And there she'd be, bent over with her father in the garden at the front of the place, using her strong bare hands to pull weeds from the dahlia beds. They were no longer kids the first time he'd taken her out on a date. They had both been out of school and working for their keep for a long time. He remembers how tall and self-confident she looked in a short-sleeved floral dress on a summer night, standing at the far end of the plank-covered dirt walkway to her front door, waiting for him. When he reached the step, he smelled the late peonies against the fence. Through the screen on her front door, he heard her parents talking in the kitchen, speaking a language he did not understand. Ennis and Dunya walked the tracks down to the Roseland Theatre in New Glasgow, holding hands the whole way. On the iron bridge that crossed the East River, he thought he'd impress her by walking on the ties, which were not far enough apart to fall through, but were empty in between all the way down to the water. But she followed right behind him without saying a word. She'd done it a hundred times before.

Later, on the way back up the tracks in the dark, after the movie was over, he tried to slip his hand under the dress. She didn't say a word, but backed away quietly, and backed away again when he tried again.

Slowly, apprehensively, one hand still over his own heart, he reaches out and puts the other hand on Dunya's shoulder. She holds his gaze without saying anything. Her shoulder tenses at his touch, then relaxes again. She closes her eyes once more and he can hear her exhaling slowly.

# THE REST HOUSE

When their train pulled into the main station in Hakone, they transferred to a local that took them to a funicular station. They rode the funicular uphill about a kilometre to a pretty little subdivision on the side of a mountain. If the day were clearer, Meta doubtless would be able to see a great distance from the mountainside, but in Tokyo it is raining, and big, low pillowy clouds are banked against the mountainside, locking them in.

Yuka has a little map that is printed on the back of the glossy brochure for the rest house, and she peers into it for a few moments, orienting herself. A few times she peers up from the map and shifts her position slightly, lining up the map with the grid of streets before her.

Meta imagines the rest house will be a run-down concrete box of a building. She's learned that you get what you pay for in Japan, where she's been charged more than ten dollars for a simple cup of coffee. And she and Yuka are paying almost nothing for these accommodations, compared, that is, to what they'd pay for a hotel. Yuka has assured her that the price is low because it is subsidized by the municipal ward. "Rest house is beautiful," Yuka said when she'd first made the invitation for Meta to come along.

"Have you been there?" Meta asked.

Yuka shook her head. "I see a picture," she said.

"This way," Yuka says suddenly, crinkling the map into a pocket and picking up her Louis Vuitton bag. Meta struggles to keep up as Yuka heads off down a narrow street.

The rain that was teeming down when they left Tokyo is wafting slowly here in big flakes. The snow is on the wet side of firm, and the flakes are piling up quickly. The accumulation has been pushed back from the streets several times already. The banks beside Meta are almost waist-high. Still, the ground is covered with a thick white blanket, and though there are tire tracks on the streets and footprints on the sidewalks, the only movement in sight is the falling of snow.

Meta is pleasantly surprised at the sight of the rest house. At first glance, it appears to be less than five years old. Its steel and glass arches, though no more than three storeys tall, give the building an air of grandeur set against the snow-softened greenery that surrounds them. Inside the spacious lobby, walls of glass stretch all the way to the vaulted ceiling, letting daylight stream in. The hostess who shows them around takes them through the entrance and lobby into a vast games room that is carpeted and full of plush chairs and tables and cluttered with boxes of board games. On an elevated floor at the far end stand the ping-pong tables, two of them. Most of the guests, the hostess informs them, are getting ready for dinner, which will be served in twenty minutes.

"There is *very* nice onsen bath here," Yuka says. "I see a picture."

Meta plops down on the loveseat and feels herself sink into the plush. Their room is large, with windows at the far end that look out over a terraced balcony and a snow-covered garden of evergreen trees and shrubs. Just inside the windows there is a sitting area: a loveseat and chair with a coffee table between. Their room is so clean and new and spacious, the view outside the window so tranquil, that the effect is to immediately cleanse Meta of the crampedness, clutter, and grubbiness of Tokyo.

"This place is unbelievable," she says. She looks out over the garden, letting the peacefulness of the scene lull her. Yuka is scurrying about unpacking. Meta wishes her friend would slow down now that they are here in the mountains. Yuka made the reservation for the rest house long ago, before her boyfriend went to Kyoto. She'd even made arrangements for Kazuhiro to spend the weekend with a relative who lived near the seashore at Chiba, two hours south of the city. Meta knows she herself is an afterthought, second choice.

"Now is time for meal," Yuka says. She rushes to the door and holds it open, waiting for Meta to get up from where she's settled in.

The dining room is traditional, with tatami mats, low tables, and cushions to sit on, seating maybe 150 people or more. Everyone but Meta and Yuka is dressed in a yukata, a casual belted robe made from cotton. Most seem to be retirement-aged.

There are a lot of smiles in the room, which unnerves Meta somewhat. She is used to the stone-faced expressions people wear on the streets of Tokyo, but this is where people go to deliberately shed that disguise. People are actually laughing, calling out to each other.

A hostess shows them to the table that corresponds to their room number. The meal is already laid out for them, cooling.

Each place setting has several vessels, small and large, each containing a separate part of the meal. There is a bowl of miso soup with seaweed and tofu, a bowl of hot rice, a plate of grilled fish, a smaller plate with some fried tofu, several small dishes, each with a different sort of pickle, a tray for dipping sauces, a small plate of wasabi, some pickled ginger root, and a good portion of battered deep-fried vegetables.

Yuka raises a tiny glass of sake to her lips and takes a taste. "This is low-quality sake," she says. "But taste is not so bad."

Meta still feels cold and damp after being outside in the snow, and she drinks the miso before it cools. This does nothing to warm her, so she raises the sake to her lips and tips it back in a single swallow. She almost gags on the flavour, but the alcohol goes shooting through her, shaking her with a quick, invigorating shiver, then settling to a fiery ball in her stomach that begins slowly to spread through her.

They eat hungrily after their journey, with barely enough room between bites for conversation. Occasionally Yuka explains what some food item is, how it is prepared, or exactly how one is supposed to eat it.

At the end of the meal, Meta leans back and feels herself sink pleasantly into the cushion she sits on. The tightness in her begins to loosen. Beautiful scenery, some alcohol, a full stomach, these have worked a spell on her. Across the table, Yuka smiles at her, and two age lines bracket her mouth. It has been several weeks since her boyfriend's departure, and Meta thinks that part of Yuka's changed demeanour is probably due to a gradual loss of physical pain. She isn't pounded on regularly, and this may be the first time since Meta has known her that Yuka is not nursing a fresh injury.

They return to their room when the meal is over. There is light coming in from the windows on the courtyard, but the sun has set and the light shines down from the still-lit clouds and reflects up from the snow. The maids have come through and laid out their futons, taking them from the big closets in the walls. Giant, thick quilts cover both beds, and Meta throws herself onto one, wiggling down into its softness. Face in the bedding, she opens her eyes just wide enough to see the pure, clean light that suffuses the room.

"Don't fall asleep yet," Yuka says.

Meta opens her eyes fully and rolls onto her back to see Yuka standing naked over her. Her clothes are folded neatly on the chair beside her, and the yukata, supplied with the room, is draped over a forearm. Meta startles at this sudden vision of flesh. On the only occasions Meta had seen Yuka's skin, it has been burned or bruised or bandaged or swelling over a broken bone. Now in the magical light of Hakone, her dark, wheat-coloured skin glows with the same wavelength of light as the room. Her two small, round breasts curve up slightly to peak into large, dark nipples. Yuka slips the robe over her shoulders and cinches it at the waist.

"Now we will go onsen," Yuka says.

Meta lies back on the futon. She does not want to move. Everything inside her is leaning toward sleep. "I don't want to go anywhere," she says.

"You *must* come onsen," Yuka says. Her tone expresses an absolute lack of choice. "But first is small surprise."

She bends down to her suitcase and pushes through some clothes until she pulls out a brown paper bag with black kanji on the side. Meta recognizes the symbol for alcohol. On top of the clothes in the suitcase, there is a package of SomeTime cigarettes.

"This is top-quality sake," Yuka says, sliding the traditional 1.8 litre bottle from the sack. She unscrews the cap from the bottle and fills two small glasses. "This should be much warmer, but . . ." She sets the two glasses on a dressing table. Meta reaches for a glass, but Yuka puts a hand on her wrist.

"When you are in your yukata and ready to go onsen, then you may take sake."

"All right, all right," Meta says, conceding to the desire for sake. She slips out of her clothes, and keeping her eyes down, pulls the yukata quickly around her.

The two women stand with their small glasses of sake. "Good sake is drink very slowly," Yuka says. She brings her glass to her lips. A pink tip of tongue moves out to meet the lip of the glass as it nears her mouth. She takes a microscopic taste. Meta watches her carefully and repeats her exact motions. The sake is delicious. It is absolutely tasty. For the first time she understands why someone might want to drink sake. The flavour is so delicate, crystalline. At the taste, the blood begins to move quickly inside her. She feels her face flush.

At the far end of the onsen room is a one-and-a-half-storey wall of glass. On the other side of the glass: a pond, some large rocks, greenery, snow. The onsen room itself is huge, luxurious, what the Japanese would describe with the English word *gorgeous*. The floor and walls are laid with thick, earthy, contoured tiles. The stools and basins are made from a lightweight, delicately grained wood. A few small groups of older women sit at the low shower heads, basins lathered full of soapy water. They intermittently lean their heads toward one another and laugh, sit back on their stools diligently soaping, scrubbing, and rinsing their bodies.

The large, steaming basin of the onsen bath itself is dotted here and there with the greying heads of women joyously clucking to one another. Meta and Yuka find two adjoining shower heads, sit down, and begin silently lathering.

Meta loves the ritual of a Japanese bathhouse. She sits down to her task of washing in order to give it her full attention. She takes her hand towel, lathers it up till it's dropping thick gobs of soap, and scrubs her face, her neck, her arms as though she wants the skin to come off. Then she fills her basin with clear water from the spout and rinses off the lather. She soaps her hand towel and scrubs herself again.

When she is finished washing, she sits fidgeting with her basin, trying to seem purposeful, waiting for a signal from Yuka to move toward the tub. Yuka stretches, then stands up, and Meta follows her to where the tiled floor gives way to the pool of volcanically warmed water.

The greenish water is unbelievably hot. There is an invigorating mineral snap to its odour, and she can feel it soaking through her to the bone. The tight muscles in her hands are first to begin to loosen, then her forearms and up to the shoulders. When she gets too warm, she rests at the side. Yuka does not come out of the water once, and Meta begins to wonder how she does it.

"I'm Japanese," Yuka says when Meta comments. Yuka believes this explains everything.

The water, the tiles, the steam, the heat, these give their voices a shivery, other-worldly quality. With her hair slicked back and her skin aglow from the heat and the scrubbing, the bones of Yuka's face stand forward, giving her a tranquil, noble aspect. Outside, the big flakes of snow continue to fall in the dark. The garden on the other side of the windows is dark now, but a faint glow from some light source nearby illumines enough so that the flakes of snow and what they fall on remain visible.

When they arrive back in their room, Meta sits on a cushion on the tatami. Her body is electrified. She has scrubbed every square inch of her skin almost raw, and now she feels all of herself, feels the good thick cotton of the yukata rubbing against her. Yuka goes directly to the sink, where she had placed a small decanter of sake in warm water. She pours two small glasses full and hands one to Meta. Meta brings the sake before her nose and smells it. Then she sniffs the warm skin at the back of her wrist. Everything in this country is so achingly well-suited to every other thing, Meta thinks. How can the manufacturers of this sake, somewhere, God-knows-where, in the Kansai maybe, know that the smell of their product is exquisite alongside the exact combination of minerals present naturally in this particular onsen in the mountains of Hakone?

Yuka puts the decanter on the nearby tatami and sits on a cushion next to Meta.

A sad, subdued expression comes over her face, and Meta wonders if she is thinking about the boyfriend in Kyoto.

"Today is special day," Yuka says.

Meta nods in general agreement, then realizes that Yuka means something more specific.

"Today I am forty years old," Yuka says.

"This is your birthday! Yuka! I'm angry with you! You didn't tell me that! I don't have a present for you!"

"Don't need present," Yuka says. "Trip is present."

"Well," says Meta. "Let's have a toast." She raises her cup. "To forty years," she says.

"Kampai," says Yuka, and brings her cup forward. They drink. They sit in silence for a time, their bodies and minds quieted by their soak.

"You know what they say about turning forty. The best is yet to come."

Yuka begins slowly shaking her head. "No good," she says. "No good." She averts her eyes as they fill with tears, then reaches for the decanter and tops up the two glasses. Meta puts out a hand to take the decanter from her. Her fingertips rest on the warm back of Yuka's hand. Yuka relinquishes the decanter, and Meta puts it far on the opposite side of her, out of Yuka's reach.

They settle back onto their cushions. One of Yuka's legs comes free of the yukata and is suddenly bare almost to the hip. Her hair is drying in layers against the side of her cheek. She puts her drink on the mat, picks it up, puts it down again. Her face appears to droop with fatigue.

"When I am married, I am nineteen," Yuka says. "Mr. Tama is twenty-five. I am university student and he is young salaryman with his company. This is not arranged marriage. I love him. He is so handsome man! He is so kind man! This is sixties. University student protest American Army bases. Police arrest a lot of people. Everyone say new Japan is coming. I tell Mr. Tama I want to make new Japan. I'm not typical Japanese housewife." She stops and finishes her sake. She looks out the window at the falling snow. "Now is over my happy life," she says.

Meta leaves a long silence, waiting until she is sure she's not cutting Yuka off. "Have you heard from . . . Kyoto?"

Yuka shakes her head.

"What will you do? When he comes back?"

Yuka leaves the cushion she's been sitting on and crawls on all fours, deep into the shadows of the room. From her futon she says, "I love him," and begins crying quietly.

Yuka is obviously drunk and tired and overwhelmed with emotions. Meta is not exactly sure whom she's saying she loves, the boyfriend or the late husband.

Meta sits in silence a while, noticing the stillness that seems to penetrate the room so completely. The smell of fresh tatami mats calms her further. Before long, Yuka is asleep. Meta can hear her deep breaths rising and falling evenly in the darkness. Meta fumbles around on the floor for the sake decanter and pours herself one last small cupful. Halfway across the world, Ziv is up and starting a new day. He would already have received her last letter. He may have already replied to it. She imagines him a moment, sitting in his bedroom with a pen in his hand, crouching over a stack of writing paper. In a moment this image of Ziv shimmers halfway between imagination and dream as she drifts off to sleep.

When Meta awakes, it is not yet morning. She pulls the quilt from her head. Except for the dim light given off by the snow outside, the room is dark. A low sound hovers at the corner of her attention. At first she thinks it is water moving slowly through plumbing in the walls, or maybe a draft seeping in at the window. Then she recognizes it as a quiet sob. Yuka is crying, her face buried in bedclothes, muffling the sound.

"Yuka!" Meta whispers. She doesn't know if her friend is asleep or awake. If asleep, she does not want to wake her.

There is no answer.

"Yuka," she says again. She sits up in bed. In the dim room, she cannot make out where one massive futon ends and the other begins. Thick quilted blankets are billowed and pushed up, casting shadows on themselves. She looks for a shape she can recognize. "Yuka," she says. She crawls out from under her quilt, the half-open yukata letting in the cold. There is a slight movement ahead in the sheets, but it could be the shadow of a tree from outside. She reaches what she thinks might be the head of the other futon and pulls back the quilt there. A splash of black hair gleams out from the sheets. "Yuka," she whispers. No reply. She puts her face right down into the hair. The sobs are much more audible at this distance, but she still cannot tell whether Yuka is crying or dreaming of crying. Her hair smells like the onsen. Meta's nose tingles at the familiarity and association of the scent. She feels the cold creeping into her and pulls back a corner of the quilt to slip beneath it. A knee touches bare skin – the small of a back? a buttock? – she wiggles in behind Yuka and sidles up to her. Yuka is curled away in a fetal position. Her bare buttocks nestled in Meta's lap. Meta slips back the side of her Yukata and puts the skin of her belly on the small of Yuka's back.

Yuka's sobs have quieted, but not ceased. Meta reaches a hand over Yuka's slim waist, letting her fingers come to rest on Yuka's small, taut navel.

Meta closes her eyes. But she will be content to sleep now, to go back to sleep holding and comforting her friend. Encircled by Meta's larger body, draped over by a consoling arm, Yuka ceases crying. Meta opens her eyes and looks over the back of Yuka's head to the window. It is still dark. She cannot tell whether it is snowing. She closes her eyes again.

❈❈❈

Meta arrives back in Tokyo relaxed, yet somehow uneasy. The atmosphere at the Hakone rest house, the food, the sake, the onsen, these have brought her to the deepest sense of contentment and belonging she has felt in all her time in Japan. The noise of Tokyo is what she notices first. The sound of cars on the streets, the hum of trains whizzing past overhead. But the peace of Hakone has taken up residence inside of her, and the commotion of the city seems distant and incapable of affecting her. She feels sure of herself now in her relationship to Yuka. She crawled into bed with her for no other reason than to comfort a friend. But Yuka is a volatile and sometimes confused person. How is she interpreting what took place?

In the hallway outside their apartment doors, Yuka and Meta hug briefly before keying their own locks. Meta is careful not to draw Yuka too close in the hug and to turn her head far to the side to receive Yuka's kiss on her cheek.

So many ideas and emotions are coursing through her when

she gets inside her apartment that she takes out a notebook, sits at the kitchen table and begins writing.

*Dear Ziv,*

*I spent two days outside of Tokyo in a place called Hakone. There was snow there, and the whole experience of quiet and cold reminded me so much of Canada.*

*Did I ever tell you about my neighbour Yuka? What this woman has been through since I've known her I could not even begin to describe for you. I seem to be her only friend.*

Meta pauses to choose her next words.

*Sometimes I'd like to walk away, but somehow she always manages to pull me back. But can I be responsible for this person's well-being?*

Meta is interrupted in her writing by a knocking at the door. She turns the notebook face down on the table, crosses the kitchen floor, and opens the door. Yuka is standing in the hallway with something in her hand.

"This is in my mail slot," she holds up a postcard with a reproduction wood-block print on one side. On the other side is a very short note written with thick strokes in black pencil. "Please don't be angry when you find out what I have done. I am doing it because I love you." And then his name.

Meta's stomach drops. Her hands holding the card begin to tremble.

Yuka looks at her in bewilderment. Meta can see that, although Yuka understands the words, she has not decoded the empty finality beneath them.

"This is postmarked Tokyo," Meta says.

"He is in Kyoto," Yuka says.

Yuka dials his number from Meta's place and leaves a message on the answering machine. When she hangs up the phone, she begins to look worried. "What is card's mean?" she says.

Meta hesitates. "I can't say for sure. It's not clear. Do you have a key to his apartment?"

"Yes," Yuka says.

"I think we'd better go there." She sets the powder-blue envelope from Ziv on the centre of the table and locks the door on the way out.

The rain that had been falling when they left Tokyo for Hakone has cleared up. The streets still glisten with humidity. To Meta's surprise, the boyfriend's apartment is walking distance from where she and Yuka live. They make their way down the exhaust-clogged corridor of Gaen-Higashi dori. The sun has moved far into the western sky and steam rises from the cracks around sewer caps. The door of a Korean restaurant is open, and the smell of kimchee and barbecuing meat bursts hot onto the cold street. They turn right onto Yasukuni dori, then hook right again, up one of the side streets in the direction of Fuji Television. Yuka leads the way to a seven- or eight-storey apartment building. She peeks into one of the mailboxes inside the door, slides the mailbox open, and brings out a handful of envelopes and pizza flyers. She tucks them under her arm and fishes through her purse for the keys. They climb the stairs in unison, Meta two steps back from Yuka. The building is relatively new, but something of the dull gun-metal paint that had been used on the stairwell makes it seem old and dingy. They stop outside apartment 3B. Bare bulbs in the hallway give just enough light to make walking into the wall unlikely. There is brighter light coming from the crack under the apartment door. A blunt metallic smell hangs in the air.

Yuka raps the steel door with her fist.

Nothing happens. They stand looking at the door. Yuka holds the key in her right hand, but does not make a move. Meta is looking at Yuka, waiting to make eye contact with her. She wants to cut the suspense and move forward, quit hesitating. She feels like taking the key from Yuka's hand and opening the door herself. She feels like stealing the key, leaving with it, taking Yuka by the hand and leading her away from that place, telling her to forget she'd ever known the idiot who lives in that apartment and to start a new life, better than the one she is leading, one with self-respect and some independence.

Yuka slides the key into the lock, turns it, and pushes back the door. The metallic smell that was just detectable with the door closed now billows out into the hallway. Meta swoons. Yuka puts her hand on the switch for the kitchen light but Meta stops her with a touch, and they walk into the apartment. They take their shoes off in the genkan and step up onto the softwood parquet. The wall opposite the door contains a big row of windows. The curtains are pulled back on the western sky. The sun, blazing through the clouds, casts the apartment in a white suffusing light. Yuka steps over something bulky in the middle of the floor and slides back two panels on the windows, opening them to the air from outside. She steps over the bundle again and goes back to the door, props it open with her shoes. Meta shivers as the cold outside air blows through the room, but her light-headedness subsides almost immediately. Yuka bends to where the gas nozzle emerges from the baseboard near the bedroom door and shuts off the valve. The blue hose that comes from the nozzle snakes to the middle of the kitchen floor, where it sticks into a plastic-wrapped object there. Meta notices that the cherry-red gas heater, a small blue protrusion of hose coming out of its side where it was cut free, lies upside-down against a wall.

Yuka sits on the couch with her back to the two open windows and looks down at the body. The gas hose has been pushed through a hole in the end of a green garbage bag and the hose and the bag have been secured in place with heavy plastic packing tape. He lies on his side, curled in a fetal position. His bare feet are blue, the tops of the toes tufted with long black hairs. He is dressed in new blue jeans and a green T-shirt of thick, high-quality cotton. His head is obscured by the garbage bag except for where a small hole reveals a tip of purply flesh. His arms and shoulders are massive, his fists, clenched in the grip of death, as big as blocks of stone.

Meta slides back the door to the bedroom. In the middle of the floor is a suitcase. She walks across the tatami to the futon closet. She opens the first door, but it is full of hangers and clothing. Behind the next door are the futon and quilts. She pulls out a folded sheet, brings it into the kitchen, and drapes it over the body, so that only the blue hose, still attached to the nozzle in the wall, is visible. Most of the gas has dispersed. She moves the shoes from before the door to the hallway and lets the heavy spring draw the door shut with a clunk. She steps over the body and sits next to Yuka on the couch, puts an arm around her shoulders. The first notion that fills her is relief. Yuka is free of this monster. Meta herself is free of worries for Yuka, that she'll be killed, that she'll experience more senseless pain and humiliation.

The overwhelming emotion she begins to feel is that of anger at the dead man. By implicating her in his suicide note he continues to punish Yuka, even after his death. He claimed he performed this act for love, to cleanse the world of himself. What an act of courage and compassion!

Whatever his motivation, cowardice or love, he can no longer harm Yuka. Meta realizes she herself is free now. She feels released, as though she can breathe for the first time in a long while.

# UNDER THE WEIGHT OF SNOW

A week before Christmas, Ennis is surprised to see the letter in the mailbox is from Jackie. It does not look or feel like a Christmas card, but the envelope is somewhat bulky. His and Dunya's names are written above the address, but Dunya is gone now, gone to visit some distant cousin in Halifax for the holidays. She said that she'd only be away a few days, she'd return right after the New Year, but Ennis sometimes fears she might never come back, or if she does, it might be a long time from now. He stands in the Albion Mines post office and turns the envelope over quickly, glancing at the blank side before stuffing it into a big pocket on the front of his coat.

Jackie and the kids are supposed to drive down from Halifax on Boxing Day. They'll stay over at the Heather Motel a night or two, visit with him and Ziv during the days. Staying at a hotel seems like a big expense to Ennis, and he said so to Jackie the last time she'd called, but she said she could afford it. He hasn't seen

Jackie or the girls in almost a year, but she sounds happy any time he speaks to her.

The strange thing about the letter is, if it isn't a Christmas card, what is it, just a short while before Jackie will be here herself?

It is still early in the morning when he enters the house through the back door. The Eastyard inquiry has not yet adjourned for the holidays, which means Ziv will be down at the new Miner's Museum, attending the hearings.

He drops the envelope on the table, bends over, and unlaces his boots. He sits at the table and rips the letter open with his thumbnail. A photograph of his grand-daughters falls out, a studio shot in front of a painted backdrop.

*Dear Ennis and Dunya, . . .*

Ennis cringes when he realizes that he hasn't even told Jackie that Dunya has left. How will he explain when she and the girls arrive?

*Here is the latest picture of the girls. We've got more pictures, of course, and we'll bring them with us in a few days when we come to visit. The other picture here is one I thought Ennis might want to have in time for Christmas. Arvel saved it. He never said how important it was to him. I don't think he ever fully understood.*

Ennis reaches into the envelope for whatever he's missed and pulls out a newspaper clipping. At first glance, he thinks the photo is of one of his grandchildren, sitting on Santa's knee. But the image is too dark to be recent, the paper too yellowed with age.

He hasn't seen the picture in years, probably since the day it originally appeared in the *Evening News* all those years ago. He sits down and smooths the clipping flat against the tabletop.

It was the only time he ever dressed up as Santa. The man who'd done it for years was in the hospital with chest pains. Ennis could not remember his name. The Steelworkers Christmas party was coming up and there were presents for the kids. They always had a Santa. Somehow, it got decided he'd do it.

He'd put on the red suit in the bathroom and felt like the biggest fool in the world. They gave him a jar of clear glue to put the beard on and it burned his face until it dried. He looked at himself in the mirror and thought he'd better have a drink of rum. He got Scrub Forrester, who was the bartender at the Steelworkers' Hall at the time, to let him into the cabinet where they kept the liquor under lock and key. Ennis was screwing the top off the bottle when he changed his mind. No, he thought, I can't do this. I can't let these kids smell booze on Santa's breath.

There was a big chair set up at the far end of the hall, on risers and decorated with streamers. The kids lined up across the front and had to climb up a few steps to sit on Santa's knee. Three or four kids had already had their turn, some of them trying to pull the beard off, some of them screaming, terrified. Then he remembered that Arvel would be sitting on Santa's knee. Dunya was there with both kids, but Ziv was just a baby then, not even walking. He looked at the lineup and saw Arvel, three or four children along, dressed in a little red jacket with a bow tie. He looked scared and lost, but so did every kid in the line.

Then finally it was Arvel's turn, and Ennis became agitated. Here was his own son. But he had never held him this way before, taken him up on his knee, put his arm around him. Ennis cannot now remember what Arvel said, cannot recall what he asked for for Christmas. But he can still see the light brown hair, the bangs cut straight across his brow. "Hi, Santa," Arvel said. He had no idea it was his own father.

Ennis sits quietly for a long time, holding the photo flat against the kitchen table with his fingertips. He thinks for a moment about Jackie, and how considerate it was of her to send the photo to him. There is no way she could have known just how strong a feeling the memory would spark. Of all the people he might show the photo to, only Dunya would understand what it really means to him. He raises his head and looks out the kitchen window to where the light of winter morning is brightening into the broad day.

※※※※※

The small room in the Miner's Museum where the inquiry carries out its hearings has become familiar to Ziv. Its nondescript white walls and cheap grey carpet were probably meant for some administrative office for the staff of the museum, but the room has been taken over by collapsible tables and folding chairs, installed here on what was supposed to be a temporary basis over a year ago. The room seats about fifty people, but today there are fewer than twenty here. It tends to be only the high-profile political testimony that draws the big numbers of media and the family members, crowding into the room.

There are a few people Ziv does not know, but has come to recognize as relatives of someone who died in the explosion. Yesterday Jeff Willis was here. His brother is one of the fifteen still underground. Ziv saw him on TV a few weeks ago. He is fighting, against the wishes of most of the other members of the families' group, to have the Eastyard silos declared a memorial site. The idea has taken root in Ziv's mind and he's sorry now he did not approach Willis about it when he was here.

Ziv is seated next to the aisle that leads from the door at the rear of the room to the commissioner's table and witness stand at the front, and he can see where footsteps of spectators and witnesses have permanently darkened the carpet. Allie McInnis, a friend of his father's, is here today, as he almost always is, on behalf of one of the bereaved families. There is a line of tape on the floor near the back of the room beyond which the news media are not permitted to take their cameras and recording equipment. The wall behind this line is scuffed with black marks, where machinery and boot heels have scraped past.

In the months since Gavin's testimony, something has compelled Ziv to return to the hearing every day. Gavin was a man who'd known and worked with Arvel, a man for whom Arvel had told Ziv he'd had great regard. This man had sat before the world, staring that TV camera in the eye, and told the truth. Ziv had felt the power of that, the power of bearing witness. There is a freedom or promise in that word: witness. But the straightforward truth of Gavin's words, words that had seemed everything to him that day, had changed nothing. Twenty-six men are dead, fifteen of them are still lying where they died. What more needs to be known?

But for reasons he cannot understand, day after day, Ziv sits listening, absorbing information. Maybe it is because he feels he owes this much to Arvel, that someone be here for him, on his behalf.

During the testimony of a seemingly endless roster of mining experts, Eastyard employees, rescue workers, and government officials, memory has clashed with memory and fact has piled upon fact in such a relentless way that Ziv feels as though his head might explode from the pressure of it all. Each witness, each new point of view, each new word, seems to do nothing more than undermine those words that have come before.

Today has been another day of technical testimony. This time, the commission has flown in an expert, all the way from Pennsylvania, who has been going on and on about the hazards of explosive dust. Yet another expert about yet another esoteric subject. These experts, Ziv is beginning to realize, would continue speaking their gibberish in this room for months. This one has been talking about physical barriers, oxygen starvation, and chemical suppressants. He's talked about things that have seemed like nothing more than common sense, how to put out fires by starving them, cutting off their air. But there have been parts of his testimony that have been so specialized that Ziv is hard-pressed to imagine how it could possibly be understood, much less shed any further light on the explosion and what led to it.

His legs have gone to sleep on him, and as he moves his heels up and down as noiselessly as he can to bring back the feeling, he becomes aware that others in the room have succumbed to boredom. Almost everyone is slumped over in their seat. Someone right up front is reading a magazine.

Glancing down at his watch, Ziv notices that it is now just after three. He folds shut the small notebook he carries and puts the pen in his shirt pocket. He is already dressed for work and, if he leaves now, he'll just have time to walk comfortably to Zellers.

He is just inside the front doors of the Miner's Museum building, zipping his parka and looking out at the large, sparse flakes of wafting snow, when a serious-looking man with blond hair and a full beard comes in.

"Hello, Ziv," the man says. Ziv recognizes the eyes, but the beard is disguising the face. He puts out a hand and says, "Hello."

"It's Ken Morrison," the man says. "Alec Morrison's brother."

"Jesus, Ken! I didn't recognize you behind that beard."

Ken rubs a hand back and forth across his chin. "Someone told me I'd find you down here. I thought it might be your father that was taking such an interest in something like this."

"The old man? No, he wouldn't be caught dead at one of these hearings." Ziv notices a change come over Ken's face and he realizes he should not have spoken of his father that way. "You came here looking for me?" he says, hoping to steer the conversation back in Ken's direction.

"I'm only home for a few days," Ken says. "I'm in law school now in Ontario."

"Good for you, man. Jesus! Good for you!"

"Anyway, I'm not able to take a holiday over Christmas, like most normal people. I have to go back tomorrow to try to catch up on some school work and I thought if I could see you for just a few minutes, I would."

"I haven't seen you in years," Ziv says. He feels awkward that Ken has come seeking him out. "You look good. That beard makes you look some old, though."

"I tried to get in touch with you right after the explosion, you know. I was in Toronto. I did call, but couldn't get through."

"Oh well," Ziv says and looks down at his shoes.

"I guess I should have kept trying," Ken goes on. "Anyway, I just wanted to explain something. I wanted to say that I know what it's like to lose a brother." He pauses a moment and takes a breath.

"Here," Ziv says. He motions toward a padded bench against a far wall. "Let's sit down for a minute." They walk over and sit side by side on the bench.

"I don't want to take your time," Ken says.

"I'm just off to work," says Ziv, "but I've got a minute or two."

Ken is white and a little shakey, as though he is standing on a stage before an audience with a speech he's been trying to commit to memory. "There is something else I've been wanting to say to you. Ever since Alec died."

"That's a long time ago, now," Ziv says. "How are your parents doing?"

"I felt guilty for years about Alec's death. I still feel it. But what I've been wanting to say to you is, if the rest of us in my family treated Alec as well as you did, he'd probably still be alive."

"Nobody knows why Alec killed himself. For a long time I asked myself why I couldn't have done something to stop him. But in the end, Alec killed himself and that's all you can say." Ziv observes Ken's face for a reaction to what he's just said. He meant the comment to reassure Ken that he did not blame Alec's family for his suicide, but he realizes now that the statement may have sounded harsh or unkind.

Ken carries on. "You were a better brother to Alec than I ever was. Arvel was lucky to have you."

"I'm sure that's not true," Ziv says and stands up. "Ken, listen, I have to go now."

"I mean it," Ken says. "I just wanted to tell you." He gets to his feet. "Well, nice seeing you, Ziv."

"You too, Ken. Good luck with the law-school business, eh? I guess the next time I see you you'll be wearing pinstripes, no doubt." Ziv gives a friendly laugh.

"Ya, thanks. Take care."

They step outside the door and turn in opposite directions as Ken heads into the parking lot and Arvel makes for Foord Street.

Ziv stops at the top of the drive. The Miner's Museum sign points to where he's just come from. There is a space between houses here and he can see down across a field to a place where two branches of the river meet. Beyond this, the silos of Eastyard Coal stand silent and brooding, as though facing each other defiantly against the shifting pattern of grey and blue sky behind them.

In a magazine article he saw some time ago, there was a cutaway drawing of the Eastyard mine. The picture showed approximate depths and equivalent surface distances. There was a red dot to mark the place where most of the recovered bodies were found and another to show where company records, "shockingly inadequate," according to the article, indicated the remaining fifteen bodies might be located. It would take someone who knew a lot more about maps to locate that spot on the surface of the ground. But as Ziv looks out across the landscape, he strains to see the tunnels as they would be now, black and burnt and airless, Arvel's body decomposing on the floor. The body that in life seemed so hulking and large, crushed and puny beneath countless tons of earth.

Ziv remembers a geometrical figure he studied in Grade 12 math. It is called a hyperbola. It consists of two curves that never intersect, that move endlessly away from each other. As a student, it took him several days to grasp the idea that these two curves that never touch are not two objects, but that they form one shape, a shape that can be expressed in a single formula. This is what brothers are: non-intersecting curves that form a single entity. With Arvel gone, Ziv is half of something whose wholeness has ceased to exist.

The next morning Ziv gets up at nine to find a letter from Meta sitting on the kitchen table. His father has obviously been to the post office already. Today's *Chronicle-Herald* is folded up near the letter. As he moves the paper out of the way, he notices a small article at the bottom of page 1. The headline reads "Brother of Killed Miner Battles Government, Families Group for Memorial." He scans the first two paragraphs quickly. The Eastyard families' group has apparently issued a news release taking Jeff Willis to task. To many in the group, the silos are an unnecessarily painful reminder of an event they will in any case never forget. Passing through Pictou County on the Trans-Canada, they are unignorable, one of the most visible landmarks in the province. They are a symbol of all that's wrong with Nova Scotia's political and economic life.

Willis is sensitive to those family members who want the silos removed. But according to the article, he's critical of the Nova Scotia government for the way it is pushing through its plans. "They're trying to sweep the history of this event under the rug. And the death of my brother along with it," the paper quotes Willis as saying. "My brother is buried at Eastyard Coal. Until his body is recovered, those silos are his gravestones. To tear them down would be as disrespectful as the desecration of any cemetery."

Ziv gets up and goes to the window. The sun is up now, and Bundy Burgess stands squinting in his backyard, shielding his eyes with his hand. He's got the shaft of an old hockey stick in the other hand and he's knocking big icicles off the eaves of his house with it. Ziv turns back to the room and pours himself the half-cup of lukewarm coffee his father left in the machine. When he settles back down at the table he opens Meta's letter.

*Dear Ziv,*

*I spent two days outside of Tokyo in a place called Hakone. There was snow there, and the whole experience of quiet and cold reminded me so much of Canada.*

*Did I ever tell you about my neighbour Yuka? What this woman has been through since I've known her, I could not even begin to describe for you. I seem to be her only friend.*

*Sometimes I'd like to walk away, but somehow she always manages to pull me back. But can I be responsible for this person's well-being?*

*I started writing this letter yesterday and I got interrupted. What has happened in the meantime has been so horrible. Now, suddenly, everything has changed, and it has changed in such a radical way I can't really put it into words. I'm not sure I understand it myself.*

*I won't write any more right now. I just want to let you know I'm thinking about you, and thinking about home.*

Ziv folds the letter up and puts it back inside the envelope. He examines the outside of the envelope, looking for something else from it, something that might help him comprehend not just the words of the letter, but a feeling he can sense beneath the words. He's not sure what he's looking for, perhaps some further sign of Meta's state of mind when she was sending it, maybe even some last-minute postscript she wrote on the way to the mailbox. But there is nothing but a Japanese stamp and the coloured markings of an airmail envelope.

He resolves to write to her. He wants to tell her he misses her. He wants to tell her to come home, that this is where she belongs.

"Somebody told me the Morrison boy was around."

Ziv startles at the sound of his father's voice. Ennis has entered the kitchen without Ziv's having heard him.

"Ken Morrison," Ziv says. He turns to his father, who is busying himself with something in the cupboards. "He said he was surprised you weren't attending the inquiry hearings."

There is no reply from his father for an instant, then he says, "What? Who?" as though he's just been roused from a dream and has no idea where he is.

"Ken Morrison said he was surprised you weren't attending the inquiry hearings."

"The commissioner's going to reach the same conclusion whether or not I attend the goddamn hearing." Ennis has fixed himself a bowl of something. He begins making his way into the living room with it.

"Don't you think . . . " Ziv stops in mid-sentence. Ennis has walked right past him and out of the kitchen. Ziv feels like calling after his father. He feels like giving him hell for his apathy about everything since Arvel died. He feels like chasing the old man into the front room and shaking him until his false teeth fall out.

He picks up the *Chronicle-Herald* from the table and follows his father into the living room. "Look at this!" he says. He dangles the paper from one hand so the full front page is in view. His father looks up at him with a peculiar, puzzled look.

"A few months ago this paper would already be torn up with holes. There's a bag of clippings up in your bedroom, stuffed full of information. Turning newspapers into confetti is next to useless, but you've given even that up now."

"What do you want me to do? What the *hell* can I do? Can I bring my son back from the dead? Tell me that, eh?"

"Look at this Willis guy, here," Ziv points at the article on the front page of the paper. "He's *doing* something. He's fighting to get the mine silos declared a memorial. We can't bring Arvel back, but we can make sure nobody is allowed to forget what happened to him. Go on outside and take a look at those silos. They'll make the biggest memorial to workers killed on the job in the country."

Ennis shakes his head. "Those silos are coming down in the spring. Haven't you even read that article? The government has already made the decision. It's a foregone conclusion. It's over."

"I can't believe I'm hearing this from you." Ziv throws the newspaper on the floor and walks into the front room, where he stands in front of Ennis's plaques hanging again on the wall. "According to this stuff, these so-called plaques of recognition," he turns to look back at his father, "you actually had some guts at one point in your life. But you're a coward now. Your whole life has come apart, your son is dead, your wife is gone, she pasted your face to the back of your fucking skull for you before she left. And *you* don't have the guts to try to put it all back together.

Look at this." Ziv takes the picture of Ennis and Tommy Douglas off its hook on the wall.

"Take a look at this!" he says, walking up to his father, "You with your arm around one of the greatest men this country ever produced. You don't deserve to be in the same room with him now. You should be ashamed."

Ennis's arms are twitching at his sides. "Give me that picture," he says.

Ziv recognizes the fury in his father's eyes and backs away from it.

"I said give me that Jesus picture or I'll snap you in two."

Ziv holds out the framed photo, and Ennis grabs it from him.

"Don't you tell me how I should feel," Ennis says. "You haven't lived my goddamned life. You don't have to tell me I'm not the man Douglas was. Maybe I've made mistakes with my life and maybe I've got regrets, but you have to do something before you can make a mistake. And you haven't done a fucking thing. Take a look at yourself, man, if you can stand to do it. What have *you* ever done that's changed anything?"

His father glares at Ziv an instant, picks up the bowl of cereal from the floor, and brushes quickly past Ziv to the kitchen. He sets the bowl he has not yet eaten from on the table and goes into the porch where he begins putting on his boots and coat to go outside.

"Go ahead," Ziv says after him. He feels sick in the pit of his stomach, as though he's been kicked. "Run away. What difference will it make? Bury your damn head in the sand."

His father slams the door on his way out and Ziv goes to the window. He watches him walk between the banks of snow shovelled up on either side of the driveway, past his own car, and into the street.

"To hell with you," Ziv says aloud. He picks Meta's letter from the kitchen table and storms back through the house and up the stairs to his bedroom.

His father's words have stung him. He lies down heavily on top of his bed. His thoughts are reeling. When he was a boy he always looked up to his father. His father was the one, he thought, who would protect what was right, the one who would fix whatever might be broken. Then it all changed, and for as long as he could remember after that, there was anger spilling into everything between them, as if when they looked at each other, they saw themselves.

A short time later, he gets up to go downstairs, but stops in front of his father's bedroom door. The canvas bag of news clippings is on the floor at the foot of the father's bed. Ziv puts off going out to mail Meta's letter a moment and steps into the room. With the slightest twinge of guilt, he plucks up the bag by the carry handles and takes it into his bedroom. He palms the bedspread flat on the top of his bed, then carefully spills the contents of the entire bag onto the spread. His father has organized everything carefully into labelled file folders. *Testimony*, *Political Promises*, *Company Claims*, *Legal Action* are the first of the labels he reads. He pulls out a folder at random from the stack. *Families' Group* is written on the tab. He opens the folder, and clippings slide out onto his lap. Suddenly, he feels a wave of sadness. All this care his father has taken. All this care that has come to nothing.

Ziv wonders if it has taken Arvel's dying for him to see that maybe his father is right – what has he done to change anything?

Ziv wakes suddenly when he hears a loud noise from downstairs. It's Christmas morning, not yet light out.

He goes downstairs and sees his father sitting at the kitchen table, dressed in a flannel shirt and thick wool socks. There's a pot of coffee on, and Ziv pours himself a cup without even looking at his father, who is finishing up a piece of toast. They have exchanged only a bare minimum of words and have mostly managed to avoid each other since their fight several days back. He puts bread into the toaster and takes the jam out of the fridge.

"Look," Ennis says abruptly. "There's only the two of us here so we might as well act like we have something to say to each other. Why don't you take those skis I got you last winter and come with me."

"Skiing!" Ziv is surprised. He's never skied in his life.

"I've got everything we need." Ennis picks up an orange nylon backpack from the floor near the door. "You'd better put on some warm clothes."

Ziv looks at the serious expression on his father's face. "Fine. Fine, I'll go, if it's so important," he mumbles awkwardly.

"Go on, get yourself ready."

"I have to eat something. That is, if you don't mind," Ziv says, throwing his toast on a plate and taking it with him upstairs.

When he comes down a few minutes later he puts on his parka and boots. His father is already outside, clearing snow from the car with a broom. Ziv sees two sets of cross-country skis and poles strapped to the roof rack of Ennis's car.

Snow has softened the backyard. His father has swept the step, but the driveway is unshovelled. A plough has gone by, but that could have been hours ago, and snow has fallen since, though now that it has stopped, there are clear patches of sky overhead, a dusting of stars over purple-black that will turn blue before long.

Ennis throws the backpack into the trunk and sits down in the driver's seat. Ziv settles in beside him.

"So where are we going?" Ziv says.

"Out past MacLellan's Brook," Ennis says. "I saw a moose out there not long ago."

Ennis pulls the car out of the driveway and turns down Foster Avenue, steering between high banks of snow on either side. They pass the miner's monument, towering over them like a figure from Greek mythology. The heater motor in the car hums noisily as they drive south and east.

When they get to a section of Bridge Avenue where the Eastyard site is visible, Ziv is almost surprised at the sight of the silos. The two pale columns of featureless concrete could not look more like a memorial if they were originally designed that way. Lit with floodlights, they are visible far above the roofs of houses.

Ziv is convinced the silos must be saved, preserved, made part of a larger display that memorializes the whole ugly history of coal mining in the county. The people in the families' group who want the silos removed will come to see what a powerful symbol they've got, right there on the landscape.

He will call Willis and offer to help in the fight to preserve the site.

"The Eastyard Memorial," he finds himself saying aloud.

"What?" Ennis says. He turns the car off Bridge Avenue and up the hill in Blue Acres, headed for MacLellan's Brook, leaving Albion Mines behind them. Snow has clung in blankets to houses and cars, trees are heavy with it. The temperature has dropped overnight so that the earlier layers of snow, which were moist and sticky, have frozen into ice on the road, and the more recent layers, lighter and more powdery, have dusted the surface of the ice, making it even more slippery.

Ennis tells Ziv he has been skiing recently at the place where the plough stops and turns around, but heavy snowfall has erased any traces of his visits. They pull up next to a snowbank and park the car. They untie their skis and stand them in the bank. Ennis throws the stick of blue wax into the snow next to them and opens the backpack. He takes out the Thermos and pours coffee into a small cup. He offers a larger cup to Ziv.

"My father took me out here when I was a kid," Ennis says. "It's so long ago now that I don't even recall if we came here just once or if it was more than that. We were hunting. I'm pretty sure this is just about exactly the spot. I remember the way the road curves. He had his brother's truck and we parked it over here." He indicates a place in the woods to the left of the car. "This was all a field at the time, and there was an abandoned farmhouse right behind the field. I remember we took the old Winchester out of the box of the truck. I was too young to carry it. I couldn't have been more than six or seven. And we walked over to a spot about here where the tops of those two hills almost line up."

Ennis nods to the right. There is so little light yet that Ziv can just make out the two hills his father is indicating.

Ziv takes a drink of his coffee, which is rapidly cooling in the cup. He and his father are standing almost shoulder to shoulder. The snow squeaks under their ski boots as they shuffle their feet a little to stay warm.

Below them, to the east, there is a shallow valley that undulates under a thick blanket of snow.

The sky above the horizon is beginning to streak purple and red. Then an orange-yellow spire appears above the trees, pointing upward from the place where the sun will soon rise. Then an odd shape begins to form under the spire.

After a moment, a flat wedge of bright orange begins to lift out of the trees in the distance. It's such an odd sight, Ziv finds himself holding his breath, as though waiting for something else momentous to accompany it. But the wedge rises, broad end first until it takes on the shape of a long flag or banner. Then, even more quickly than it arose, it sinks into the horizon again and immediately the sun itself begins creeping above the horizon, exactly the colour of the wedge that preceded it.

"What the hell was that?" Ziv says. "I've never seen anything like it."

"When the conditions are right, you can get this," Ennis says. "False sunrise, my father used to call it. He showed it to me once a very long time ago. He died when I was eight. I've only seen it a couple of times since."

In the half-light, with his back to the dark sky in the west, his father's face is unreadable.

"Let's go," Ennis says, and they turn back to the car.

They look west now, out over the trees and down the first hundred metres of the trail they're going to ski. It's still dark enough that the snow acts as a light source, illuminating the ground beneath trees. The snow covers the trees thickly, but in the places where patches of evergreen needles are visible, they appear black in contrast to the snow.

Ziv notices some emotion on his father's face. His eyes are glistening and Ziv wonders if he is about to cry. With a mittened hand, his father digs the blue wax out of the snow and begins rubbing his skis with it.

When the skis are waxed and ready, they clip the toes of their boots to the bindings.

Ziv hangs back and lets his father lead. He follows, nestling his skis into the grooves his father has made. It will take a few moments to adjust to the exact grip the wax has on the snow. His kicks are unsteady and off-balance. He is unable to pick up his heels. He looks ahead at his father in disbelief. His big shoulders are squared out, the arms working the poles like pistons. He looks frail somehow, despite his competence.

As light creeps into the sky, Ziv becomes more aware of the snow-laden trees around him. A few branches have cracked under their burdens, but most are arched gracefully in unaccustomed directions. Big spruces and firs stand over him, on either side of the trail. Under the weight of snow they bend toward the ground. Two white spruces, squared off on opposite sides of the trail, appear to be bowing to each other. The tips of their branches reach out across a lifetime's distance toward the other, ready to shake hands or embrace. Even evergreens are dormant in the winter, Ziv knows, not dead but the next thing to it. After the coldness of a dark season, one that seems to go on forever, they manage somehow to rekindle, within themselves, a life.

# ACKNOWLEDGEMENTS

For first-hand details about underground mining, I leaned heavily on Shaun Comish's incredible *The Westray Tragedy: A Miner's Story* (Fernwood Publishing, Halifax, 1993. ISBN 1-895686-26-1), which I recommend every Canadian read.

For salient wisdom from the point of view of miners themselves, Judith Hoegg Ryan's *Coal In Our Blood: 200 years of coal mining in Nova Scotia's Pictou County* (Formac Publishing Company, Halifax, 1992. ISBN 0-88780-215-X) was indispensable.

For political and economic insight into the Westray case, *Calculated Risk: Greed, Politics, and the Westray Tragedy* by Dean Jobb (Nimbus Publishing, Halifax, 1994. ISBN 1-55109-070-8) was a valuable source.

For general background information on mining in Pictou County, *The Pictonian Colliers* by James M. Cameron (The Nova Scotia Museum, Halifax, 1974) is the old standby.

Finally, *The Westray Story: A Predicable Path to Disaster: Report of the Westray Mine Public Inquiry*, Justice K. Peter Richard, Commissioner (Province of Nova Scotia, 1997. ISBN 0-88871-465-3), is a lucid, accessible, heart-rending account of the whole fiasco.

***

I wish to thank the following:

Ellen Seligman, my editor, for pushing me and this book to be the most we could be. Denise Bukowski, my agent, for getting excited and doing something about it. Kathy, Joel, Mairi, and Laura, for letting me disappear into the red room. Mum and Pop, for a warm bed, some peace and quiet, and high-calorie meals. Friends, colleagues, and family members, for providing encouragement, writing space, coffee, babysitting, whatever. Students, past and present, for keeping me honest and reacquainting me with the beginner's eye. Dale Saunders, for accounting acumen and patience.